I0822424

Lost to the Moon

K. Loraine
USA Today bestselling authors
Meg Anne

This book is a work of fiction. The names, characters, places, and incidents are products of the author's imagination or have been used fictitiously and are not to be construed as real. Any resemblance to persons, living or dead, actual events, locales, or organizations is entirely coincidental.

ISBN:

978-1-951738-55-6 (Paperback Edition)

978-1-951738-56-3 (Hardback Edition)

Edited by Mo Sytsma of Comma Sutra Editorial

Cover Design by CReya-tive Book Design

Photographer: Wander Aguilar

Model: Sam Myerson

This one's for the puffins, please always remain crisis free.

If Asher's rubbed one off on you, uh...rubbed off on you, and you'd like to support the pufflings, please check out Savepuffins.org.

And yes, we've already adopted a puffin and named him Toderick.

"Love makes your soul crawl out from its hiding place."

— ZORA NEALE HURSTON

LOST
TO THE
MOON

AUTHORS' NOTE

Lost to the Moon contains mature and graphic content that is not suitable for all audiences. Such content includes dubious consent, degradation, impact and blood play, bondage, and more. **Reader discretion is advised.**

As always, a detailed list of content and trigger warnings is available on our website.

CHAPTER ONE

ROSIE

"Where the fuck is that bloody demon?"

Gavin's words pierced the sleepy fog I'd been floating in. Ben's blood still lingered on my tongue, his firm body warming me as he dozed with me in his arms. The single moment of happiness I'd found in this tempest of chaos dashed with my husband's harsh question.

I sat up, rousing Ben as I spoke. "What? He's chained up and secured. As he should be." I said the words on pure instinct; it wasn't like I actually knew. I hadn't been allowed back in the room with him after the failed exorcism. My other mates deemed it too unsafe. I wasn't one to blindly take orders from a bunch of overprotective alpha males—just ask Noah—but I didn't want to rock the boat any more than necessary after what we'd all been through.

Pan and I would have our reckoning. Just as soon as Remi got back.

Gavin's posture was rigid—shoulders tight, jaw clenched, brow furrowed so deep I worried it would stick that way. This wasn't the man I'd grown accustomed to. The one who observed everything with feline grace, an air of disinterest shrouding him at all times. "He was. He . . . broke free."

"How?" The lone word was snarled, Ben's wolf responding to the perceived threat.

"I assume he used brute strength, Bentley. Unless he gnawed through the chains with his teeth. I wasn't there, or I'd have stopped him."

Gavin's deadpan delivery dripped with disdain. My surly wolf and broody vampire were hardly friends, begrudging allies more like, but this was the first time in a long time it felt like they were back at square one with each other.

"S-so there's a p-pissed off d-demon running around and w-we c-can't find h-him? Just g-great."

"I'm sure he won't get far. A hulking purple brute is sure to garner some attention," I offered, not feeling particularly comforted by the thought of Pan strolling down Main Street.

Gavin turned his gaze on me. "Perhaps, before the hellmouth opened and demons began to run rampant through the town," he said dryly.

"Good point," I said, chewing on my bottom lip. Dread sat heavy in my belly as I pondered what sort of damage Pan could do with his demonic form unleashed.

"I n-need to t-tell Remi. F-for all we kn-know, he c-could be Pan's t-target." Ben stood but swayed as soon as he was upright, one hand shooting out to brace himself on the headboard. "F-fuck, sugar. You t-took more than usual."

I didn't. In fact, I'd fed lightly this time because I was worried about overtaxing him. Snagging his phone out of the pocket of his discarded jeans, Ben sat down on the mattress and grunted, thumb and index finger rubbing at his temples.

"Are you all right?" I asked, running my palm across his broad shoulders in soothing circles.

"H-headache."

I frowned. Maybe I took more than I thought. Ailments of any kind were rare for supernaturals, and it wasn't like he was hungover. Even if the affliction was possible for shifters, Ben hadn't had a drop to drink.

I got to my feet and covered my body with the hoodie Remi had left for me to snuggle in when it wasn't his night to donate blood. It smelled of him, which usually calmed the anxious energy that pulsed from my mate bond when we were separated. Not this time. If anything, his scent triggered unease.

"Gavin," I whispered. "We need to find Pan."

"You don't say."

"Kn-knock it off," Ben snapped. "W-we're all on edge. D-don't take it ou-out on her."

"Forgive me, petal," Gavin said, surprising me by coming over and taking my hand in his and then feathering his lips over my knuckles.

"Oh my God, it *is* the end days." I stared at my husband, mouth agape, as I let his apology sink in. "I never thought I'd live to see the day you apologized for anything."

"Come now, that's not fair. I've—"

"No."

"At least once or twi—"

"No."

"C-come on, Remi," Ben grumbled, pulling us out of our playful fight.

"He's still not answering?"

"N-no. I h-haven't heard a d-damn thing since he l-left last n-night."

That had been nearly twenty-four hours ago. It wasn't like Remi to go radio silent. My phone was always filled with flirty texts or silly, suggestive GIFs throughout the day.

Apprehension burned even brighter, knotting beneath my ribs and making it hard to draw a full breath. Between our demon problem and my missing mate, it felt as though I was slowly being tortured.

"If Pan did anything to him, I'm going to have his horns." Except, of course, a demon's horns were the source of their power, so that would mean his death, which would only create a bigger problem for me since he was my mate.

"You could try, *ma petite monstre*. Now, tell me, what did I do and to whom? I do love to keep track of my misdeeds." The demon in question strolled into the bedroom, naked as the day he was born . . . hatched? The details were fuzzy on demon procreation. One could assume he slithered out of the bowels of hell like a snake.

His sudden appearance caught all of us off guard. Ben growled, and Gavin blurred to Pan, shoving him up against the wall.

"Demon," he snarled.

"Vampire," Pan mocked.

"Where have you been?" I demanded.

He slowly looked at the towel he was still using on his damp hair, entirely unfazed by Gavin's rough treatment. "Do you really require an explanation?"

"With you? Yes. Always. If I've learned anything from our dealings, it's to never trust a demon."

Pan shrugged out of Gavin's hold, a huff of annoyance leaving him as he muttered, "Do you mind?" Then he locked eyes with me. "If you must know, I took a shower. I simply couldn't lie there with the stink of priest and holy sacrament all over me any longer." He looked from Gavin to Ben and back to me. "What's with all the suspicious looks? You lot should be thanking me. I could have simply shat the bed and then where would we all be? Yes, I slipped free from your puny chains. Boo hoo. I did you a favor. Get over it."

"Get out of Asher's body," I countered.

"No. And technically, this is *my* body. Did you see my tail?" He practically preened as the aforementioned appendage wriggled behind him. "I happen to recall you're quite fond of it. Moreso than me, even."

"For fork's sake, Pan, read the bloody room. You waltz in here as if you are a welcome guest. Do you not realize we are furious with you? You've proven time and time again that you cannot be trusted. You hurt and took advantage of the people I love. How can you ever expect us to accept you as one of the group? You stole Asher's body—"

"Not my fault."

"—lied to me, repeatedly. And are working with the literal enemy to end the world. I can never trust you. And I certainly can't let you fanny about like there's no risk to my mates with you being here. What do I have to do to keep them safe? Shackle myself to you for all eternity?"

"Sugar." Ben stiffened, a low growl of warning filling the room.

Pan chuckled, but there was a flash of something across his face. It was gone before I could register the emotion, but I would have sworn it looked like remorse. Except I knew he was incapable of the emotion, so it must have been wishful thinking on my part. Like it or not, he was my mate. I was predisposed to seeking out redemption where there wasn't any.

"Already done, remember? Though I suppose I could abscond with you and make you my demon bride. That would be a scandal, wouldn't it?"

"Pan! Stop fucking around."

My use of the curse seemed to do the trick. His smirk vanished. "You really are cross with me. For the life of me, I don't see why."

"I just gave you a great bloody list of reasons. Weren't you listening?"

"I'm still here, aren't I? I could have left if I truly wished to. Gotten up to Lucifer knows what three times over by now. But I didn't. I'm here, with you, right where I belong."

Something flickered in his eyes, and I wondered if he was lying. Or was he truly worried about my feelings toward him? *No. Don't get waylaid by a few pretty words, Roslyn. He is a silver-tongued devil, and he means to destroy you.*

"Why didn't you?" Gavin asked, coming up beside me and placing a possessive palm at the small of my back.

Pan simply shrugged. "I didn't want to. Rosie here is my toy. I can't play with her if I'm gone, now can I?"

That got my back up, and I was about to retort, but Ben spoke before I could.

"She's n-not a t-toy."

Ignoring Pan's smug smirk, I leveled my gaze on him with all the authority of a fed-up school teacher. "I suppose there's no use in locking you up again, is there?"

"Not unless you want to take me for a ride. I know how whips and chains excite you. I wonder if you'd enjoy them as much if you were the one wielding them."

Gavin snorted. "She wouldn't."

"Are you certain, Duke? She's enjoyed many a scenario with me. Did you tell him about the piercing, *mon ange?*"

"You mean the one I rid her of?"

"Pan, Gavin, stop. We have enough problems without adding petty nonsense to the list." I lifted my eyes back to Pan's lavender gaze. "We won't try to restrain you, but you have to behave."

"No promises."

"Then get out." It was a bluff, but instinct told me he wouldn't call me on it and actually try to walk out the door. We could never set him loose without some sort of insurance that he wouldn't go on a murderous rampage. Again.

His eyes widened a fraction before he smirked. "But then how will you get what you need from me? You'll crave me sooner rather than later. You and I both know it. Just like you thirst for each of them. Face it, Rosie, you. Need. Me."

"I don't have to like it."

"You don't have to, but you do."

We weren't getting anywhere with this conversation. Pan didn't deserve any more attention from me, especially since it was exactly what he wanted. I turned away from the demon, giving him my back as I set about fluffing pillows and straightening the duvet. But then that curl of panic pulsed in my heart again, this time stronger than before. What was causing it? Not Pan. Not now that I knew he was here and no one was in immediate danger.

“I n-need to talk t-to Remi. H-he n-needs to know wh-what’s happening.” Ben pulled on his jeans and bent down to snag his t-shirt from the floor, but a pained groan left him, and he fell to his knees. “Fuck. S-something’s w-wrong. My head.”

“It wasn’t me!” Pan said as Gavin lunged toward him again.

“Why should we believe you?”

I ignored them both and rushed to Ben’s side, taking his face between my hands. “Ben, what is it? What’s wrong?”

“It’s n-not him. I think . . . sh-shit. It’s Remi.”

CHAPTER TWO

BEN

What was wrong with me? I've never felt like this. Ever.

Every single part of my body ached. My neck. My head. My teeth. My fucking scalp. Sometime between falling asleep with Rosie in my arms and waking, I went from perfectly healthy to at death's door. It felt like my head had been replaced by a two-ton brick, and a boulder now sat on my chest, making each breath labored.

Remi and I had been through a lot in our lives, our twin bond so generously sharing a glimmer of what the other experienced, but this was something else entirely. One time when we were still kids, he'd fallen from a tree and broken his leg, and I'd started walking with a limp. It had been the palest imitation of his injury, but more than enough to let me know he needed me. I'd gone on alert and found him before long. My instinct guided me to him. Just like it would now.

If a limp was all I got for a broken leg, I could only imagine the state he was in to make me feel like *this.* My brother needed help, and he needed it now.

"I h-have to go," I croaked through a tight throat as I finally got to my feet. My belly cramped as nausea threatened to bring the meager contents of my stomach up right here and now.

"Go where? We don't even know where Remington is." Gavin's polished accent couldn't hide the incredulity in his words. Although, I didn't think the vampire was even trying. He probably thought Remi was as good as dead.

They may not know. But I did. There was only one place my brother would go. He wasn't like me. He wouldn't seek solitude in the forest. He'd want a crowd to distract him from his thoughts. "He's at th-the bar."

"How do you know?" Rosie asked.

"Twin th-thing."

"Let me go with you," she pleaded, her voice thin and worried.

"Roslyn, he's—"

"Oh, let her go," Pan interrupted. "She may like your domineering ways in the bedroom, but my little slut isn't one to be told what to do. Trust me. She's practically allergic to an order. Besides, she won't be as much fun if she's pouting."

"Who the bloody hell asked you?" Gavin sneered.

"You didn't have to. You get the benefit of my expertise for free." Gavin rolled his eyes, but Pan kept talking. "Don't act so high and mighty. You're no better than me, Duke. I'm part of this little sex club now too. Because whether you want to accept the fact or not, I'm her mate, every bit as much as you are."

"Don't remind me."

"Seems to me you could do with the reminder."

"You stay out of this," Rosie shot back. "You're in my world now, Pan. I don't need you interjecting on my behalf."

"Oh, I like you with some fire. It gets me hard."

"Everything gets you hard."

"True. Perhaps now's a good time to help you recall how much you enjoy my *interjecting?*"

The demon stood there, dick at full mast as he toyed with Rosie. I hated it. I wanted him gone for so many reasons. For what he did to

Rosie, how he ruined Asher and Remi's relationship, and now, for how he stole Asher from all of us. And there wasn't a single thing I or any of the rest of us could do about it. The mate bond between him and Rosie ensured it. Like it or not, we were stuck with the purple prick.

Rosie and Gavin seemed to have come to the same conclusion, because they both stood there staring at Pan and silently fuming. I might not be able to cut her ties to the bastard, but I could at least get her away from him for a while.

"Get s-some clothes on, sugar. L-let's go." Another spike drove itself between my eyes, the pain making me grimace. "W-we need to f-find him."

Rosie threaded our fingers as soon as we were both fully dressed. "I'll be back. Don't"—her uncertain gaze bounced from demon to vampire—"don't kill each other while I'm gone. I'll be very cross with both of you."

"No promises," Pan said, repeating his earlier words.

"I'll only maim him a little."

Gavin's quip had a smile twitching at the corner of her mouth. "As long as it's only a little. Asher's still in there, and we're going to get him back."

"I beg your pardon?"

The vampire grinned by way of an answer.

"They don't call him the Duke of Tears for nothing," Rosie said, her smile stretching.

"I don't cry. Ever."

"We'll see about that," Gavin crooned with the eager anticipation of a man looking forward to a challenge. Turning his attention on Rosie, he added, "If you need me, petal, call down our bond. I'll come for you."

I tightened my hold on her, my eyes locking with his. "I w-won't let anything h-happen to her."

"See that you don't."

I didn't respond. I couldn't add anything else to the already ominous warning. Instead, we headed out into the night, uncertain and apprehensive of what we would find. The optimistic part of me hoped I was misreading things and Remi was just fine. That we'd get to The Tip and find him sleeping it off upstairs after drowning his sorrows about Asher. That my world wasn't coming crashing down around me. That the voice in the back of my mind screaming at me something was terribly wrong with my brother was all a lie.

Even though, deep down, I knew it wasn't.

REMI

I DID up the buttons on my black shirt, staring at myself in the mirror and smirking. I couldn't wait for Rosie to get here for her confession. I was like a kid in a candy store. This was going to be the best anniversary, hands down.

Taking off my wedding band, I carefully placed it on the dresser before I adjusted the white collar at my throat, winking at myself in the mirror as I did. "Just call me Father Ledger."

Hmm, maybe I should use an Irish accent too? Rosie had definitely enjoyed Caleb's. Fuck, so had I.

"Come here to me and unburden yourself, my child," I said to the empty room, an Irish lilt coloring my words.

It sounded good, but I wasn't sure I could keep it up once we really got going. That took a lot of brain power, and I was pretty sure once the blood started rushing south, I'd be struggling to string together a coherent sentence in my normal accent.

A soft knock on my door had me giddy with anticipation.

"Remi? Are you in there?" Rosie's sweet voice was temptation itself. How fitting.

"Come in, Mrs. Mercer," I said.

She opened the door, laughing as she said, "Mrs. Mercer. So formal this morning, Re–oh, my—I mean, Father . . ."

My lips twitched. "Ledger."

"Of course. My apologies, Father Ledger. I wasn't expecting to see you."

"Neither was I. We don't have an appointment, my child."

"I wasn't aware I needed one. You've always accommodated me before." I could see the twinkle of laughter in her eyes at our game, but she was an expert at staying in scene these days. Gavin had seen to that.

"You simply assume I'm at your beck and call? How presumptuous of you. I'm a very busy man. Confessions to take, absolution to give, rites to perform."

"Punishments to dole out?"

My grin was sin itself. "Oh yes." My cock twitched before I let my next words free. "Do you need to be punished, lamb?"

She bit her lower lip, and heat flooded her cheeks in the form of a blush. "Yes."

"How does your husband feel about what we do in my office?"

"Which one?"

"Such a sinner."

"I just can't seem to help myself."

"Perhaps you should get on your knees for me, then." Fuck, now I understood what hot under the collar meant. I was sweating. Kind of uncomfortably, if I was being honest.

She sank to her knees, raised her face to look into my eyes, and moaned.

"Are you feeling all right, Remington? You look a little flushed." Rosie's mouth was moving, but the voice that came from her was all wrong as the dream faded into darkness. "My, my, I fear you may have taken a turn for the worse."

CHAPTER THREE

BEN

Rosie's hand was tight around mine as I pushed open the bar's apartment door. He was here. We could both feel him. What was worse . . . I could smell the sickness in the air.

I couldn't force his name from my throat. The one word lodged itself there like a stone.

"Remi?" Rosie spoke for me, taking the lead and earning a wave of my gratitude I knew she could feel through our connection. She called out his name a second time, louder and more confidently, but there was no answer.

We shuffled inside, both on high alert. My heart raced with every step, fear of the unknown heavy in my stomach. Even without the bond, I would have known it was the same for her. She gripped my fingers like a vise, her breath sawing out of her in shallow pants as she shadowed my steps.

A deep rattling cough broke the silence, sending my heart lurching and my protective instincts roaring to life.

"R-R-Remington. A-answer m-m-me."

Rosie locked eyes with me, and I knew what she was going to say before she opened her mouth. "Shifters don't get sick. Pestilence has to be behind this."

"If Pan d-d-did this t-to him, I'll f-finally be g-guilty of m-murder."

Logically, I knew I couldn't lay a hand on him. Fucking mate bond. But the sentiment stood. There was nothing stopping me from employing a little light torture. Maybe I could take the sexy out of Asher's dungeon and just make it a prison. Or a Dexter-style murder room.

"You won't have to. I'll do it myself," she promised.

As much as I loved her for volunteering, we were both all talk. If Pan died, Asher died, and so did Rosie. Surviving one broken bond was hard enough, but two? I doubted she would make it an hour without them.

I hated the bastard for a multitude of reasons, but his connection to my mate was top on my list.

That awful cough filtered into the living room again. Fuck.

"H-he's in the bedroom. S-stay behind me, sugar. I d-don't want y-you to g-get sick."

"That's not how germs work, Ben."

"Th-that's exactly h-how they w-work." Though, come to think of it, walking in front of her like a wolfy mask didn't really seem all that effective.

"If it's airborne, I'm already infected—and so are you."

I growled low in my throat at her logic, hating that I had blindly put us both at risk.

"We're here now. Remi needs us. He's worth dying for."

God, I loved the way she loved us. This was why she was a Queen. I could feel it even if I didn't understand a damn thing about the lore surrounding vampirekind's chosen saviors.

My gut churned as soon as I pushed open the bedroom door and caught sight of my twin, shivering, covered in sweat, his skin a sickly gray. Despite my fear, the moment I saw him the terrible discomfort I'd been dealing with eased, the echoes of his illness fading now that I knew he was within reach and help was on the way.

Rosie's panicked cry rang out as she shoved me aside and raced to him. "Remi!"

"D-don't t-touch h-h-him."

She glared at me and immediately reached out, brushing the damp hair off his forehead.

Remi whimpered the instant her skin touched his. At the same time, she jerked her hand back and shot a worried glance at me. "He's burning up. We have to get his fever down."

"Benny, is that you?"

My twin's voice was barely more than a pained rasp. His eyes were still shut, but he weakly lifted his hand as if searching for me.

"Mmm, smells like cookies. Did you bring me cookies? Can you get me Junie? I need Junie."

His brow was furrowed as he slurred his delirious requests, but my chest squeezed at the innocence in his tone.

"Who's Junie?" Rosie asked, her topaz eyes bright with concern.

"J-Junie Johnson. His stuffed m-moose. He u-used to take her everywhere w-with h-him." I closed the distance and knelt at his bedside, taking his hand. Fuck, Rosie was right; he was blazing. "W-we boxed h-her up y-years ago, Remi. With N-Nanner, r-remember?" For Rosie's benefit, I added, "M-my b-bigfoot."

"You named your bigfoot Nanner?"

"L-long story."

Remi's frown deepened, and he shifted restlessly, drawing our attention back to him. "I need her."

"I'll g-get h-her for you."

Just the promise seemed enough to soothe him. His expression evened out as he breathed, "Thanks, Benny."

"Get him up, Ben. We need to cool him off before he ends up with brain damage. I know shifters run hot, but this is dangerous." Rosie had shrugged off the fear she'd been radiating since we arrived and was all focused determination and in caregiver mode.

She darted into the bathroom so fast I only saw a blur of motion before I heard the shower cut on.

"C-come on, b-big guy. Y-you heard h-her."

Remi groaned and tried to shove me away when I grabbed him by the armpits and hauled him upright. I knew I was probably only making him feel worse, but I didn't have time to fuck around.

Rosie watched as I got him settled under the cold spray, my twin so out of it he didn't even flinch from the water as I sat in the tub with him. I swear to God, steam came off his back as the droplets hit his skin. If it hadn't been for her, I wouldn't have known what to do.

"H-how did y-you know we sh-should do th-this?"

She offered a sad smile. "We had human staff at home. Some of them had children. My mum used to be a human as well. She taught me to care for them. He needs hydration and a doctor once we get this fever down."

Remi shivered so hard his teeth chattered, but at least he was sitting up on his own now. I stood and took the towel Rosie offered as I got out of the tub, unease eating away at me with every passing second. I couldn't lose him.

"Why so sad, baby girl?"

Remi's voice was still rough, but he'd managed to crack his eyes open and offer our mate a lopsided grin.

She released a watery laugh. "I'm not sad. I'm scared. You were talking nonsense, and you didn't call us for help. How can I take care of my mate if you won't tell me you need me?"

Remi wrinkled his nose. "That's redundant."

"What?"

"Always need you."

Even though he was lucid, every word seemed taxing. His lungs were fighting him. I could hear it in his wheezed inhalations, in the rattle deep down, and in the gravel of his voice. He was trying for charming wolf, but I saw right through him.

"R-Remi. Wh-what happened? Wh-when did y-you f-first get s-sick?"

His eyes were slow to shift from Rosie to me. Once they landed on my face, the rest of his head followed. With his black t-shirt and wet hair, he reminded me of a barely recovered Dread Pirate Roberts resting against the castle wall.

"It started at the bar. Just a cough. Then my head hurt so bad. I came upstairs after closing so I could take a nap. Thought it was stress. Then . . ." He gestured to himself before closing his eyes and leaning heavier on the tile behind him.

Fuck, was he asleep again?

"Remington," I said, no hint of stutter in the name.

He blinked his eyes open, his irises so bright with fever they were nearly the neon of his wolf. "Ben. Shhh. Use your inside voice. I'm sleepy."

"You n-need to s-stay awake."

"Rude."

I would have laughed if I wasn't still so fucking scared. Nothing about this was normal, and I couldn't shake the panic that this might be the last time I heard my brother's voice. What if he fell asleep and didn't wake up?

"Just until your fever comes down, darling. I promise we'll let you sleep soon," Rosie soothed, kneeling beside him and running a hand over his brow.

He grinned. "Daaaaaah-ling. I like that." Then he nuzzled into her. "I like you more. Is it time for sexy nurse? We already played priest."

"Did we?"

"Aye, lamb. We did." He said this with a lazy Irish accent. "You've been naughty. So much to confess."

"I'm sorry I missed it. We'll have to arrange a do-over once you're feeling better."

He clumsily ran a hand down her back to cup her ass. "Anytime you want, baby girl. Siri, add a white collar to my shopping list."

When he didn't get a response, he frowned.

"Siri! Hey, Siri!"

Nothing.

"Stupid cockblocking robot." Then he chuckled to himself. "Frock-blocker."

Rosie shot me a look over Remi's head. "He's delirious."

"Y-you think?"

"We should probably get some fluids in him."

"I'll put some fluids in you. Hey-oh!"

Through the open door, I heard the faint sound of Siri responding. "I'm sorry, Sexy Beast. I didn't quite get that."

"She did hear me!"

"I'll take care of it, Remi. One priest collar coming up. I'll add it to my list for Christmas shopping." Rosie offered him a soft smile and pressed her palm to his forehead. "He feels cooler now."

"I'll t-take him back t-to bed. You g-get the juice."

Rosie nodded and stood while Remi glared at me. "I don't want *you* taking me to bed."

"Buddy, even if Rosie was t-taking you to bed, you w-wouldn't b-be any use to her."

"I dunno. Let's fuck around and see what happens. No, that's not right. How's it go? Find out? Yeah, that one. We can fuck around and find out."

I groaned, somewhat relieved he was up to his usual bullshit. It couldn't be that bad if he was still a walking dick joke, right?

After helping him change out of his wet clothes and getting him back into bed, I made a cool compress for his forehead and draped it over his eyes. Rosie came in with a drink for him and a pinched expression on her face.

"I still have that feeling. The one that tells me he's in danger, Ben."

"Me t-too." Glancing down at him, I heaved a sigh. "What n-now?"

"I think we need to call a doctor. Neither of us is prepared to deal with this on our own."

I didn't have the heart to tell her a doctor wasn't any more prepared than we were. Not a supernatural one, anyway. Shifters didn't get sick; it's not like they'd seen anything like this before.

"Maybe there's a tonic or something we could give him?"

"I have n-no idea w-what to do. B-but I'm n-not leaving here until h-he's b-better."

"Neither am I."

Considering we could very well be infected with whatever he had, that was probably the responsible move anyway. But I didn't mention that either. Especially since sooner or later, Rosie was going to need to feed, and that would require her other mates. I barely had my head wrapped around our current problem. That one could wait its goddamned turn.

Remi let out a little laugh. "It's a party. Pants optional."

Rosie sat on the side of the bed and ran her fingers through his hair, ignoring his statement. "Call the doctor, Ben. I'll stay here with him."

CHAPTER FOUR

GAVIN

This was going to be a right bitch to pull off, but Pan couldn't be allowed to walk free.

No matter what promises he made, I'd have to be a bloody idiot to believe him. And I was many things, but an idiot was far from one of them. Demons were notoriously tricky. They were bound to their deals, but they always left enough loopholes for you to hang yourself. I couldn't let my petal get entangled in his games again.

I hated that he'd used her innocence against her twice already. Especially since the first time had been to get away from me. I'd always resent him for the part he played in her disappearance. But not as much as I'd hate him for burrowing his way into her soul via a stolen mate bond.

The audacity.

She didn't even realize he was there when she'd given him her mark. If he were a vampire, I'd drag him before the Council myself and . . . and . . . have him impaled on a silver spike for all eternity.

God, if only we could kill him and be done with it.

I sighed, shifting my hand to ensure the canister of salt was still safely tucked in my sleeve, my fingers pressed against the holes that would allow it to pour free.

"Come on in, cuckold. I know you want to." Pan's voice grated on my nerves through the partially open door, but I wouldn't let him get a rise out of me.

I shoved inside, expecting to see him up to no good and instead finding him right where I wanted him. The demon was draped on the ostentatious four-poster bed that sat in the middle of the room, clearly the centerpiece of the suite. This wasn't a place for relaxation. This was where dark deeds were done in the night. Originally, I'd planned to use it for my own purposes, but no longer now that he'd sullied the atmosphere.

"Well, are you just going to stand there and gaze at me or come in and say whatever it is that's so clearly on your mind?" He didn't bother looking up as he taunted me. Instead he lazily used his tail to flip the page of the—I squinted, double-checking that I hadn't misread the gold etching on the cover. I hadn't. The hellspawn was reading the bleeding Bible. "Mmm, what a riveting piece of fiction this is. Imagine a boat that could hold all the animals in the world!"

"Only two of each," I muttered.

"Even so."

"Seems like they got parts of it right, I mean . . . that is why *you're* here, isn't it?" I was careful to keep my voice bored and edged with disdain as I slowly prowled inside, ensuring his eyes were still glued to the pages as I peeled my fingers away from their prize. The white grains poured free, and I continued my slow pace, moving carefully about the bed.

"A broken clock is still right twice a day. What's your point?" Pan turned another page and snorted, then brought a glass to his lips using his free hand. Drinking down a long gulp of amber liquid, a smoky scotch by the scent of it, he closed his eyes and sighed. "What. Do. You. Want? I'm having some *me* time, if you haven't noticed."

Knowing the narcissistic arse would love nothing more than to talk about himself, I gave him a bit of truth. "I'm trying to figure you out. Why are you here, Pan? What is it you want with my Roslyn?"

"*Your* Roslyn?" He cocked one brow before smirking wickedly. "I believe I claimed her first."

"Just because you fucked her before any of us doesn't mean you claimed her. I didn't steal her mark from her. You had to resort to trickery." I continued strolling around the enormous bed—who needed a bed this large?—and kept up my digs. "If you want to split hairs, we were already married before you ever laid eyes on her. Speaking of, she's mine in the eyes of—"

"Ugh, if you say God, I may vomit. Demons are known for their projectile aim, you know. How do you think the author of *The Exorcist* came up with that one?"

"According to you, there isn't much demons aren't responsible for. Next, you're going to claim that demonkind is also responsible for that god-awful song in *Titanic*."

He winked but then shook his head. "Can't claim that one, but I'll let you in on a secret. We're the reason the dinosaurs died. One of our better moments, next to the Black Death, of course."

"A personal victory for you?" I inquired drolly, nearly done with my circuit.

"Well . . . my mother's, but that's *really* splitting hairs, don't you think? Seeing as I was the demon on the ground."

"Ah, I see. You're her minion, a pathetic foot soldier. Not even a general. How sad for you."

He sat up, a growl rumbling from his chest. "I am a demon of the first order!"

Trap set, I stopped and gave him a genuine grin. "Bully for you. Although, I don't think that's really gotten you anywhere. I mean . . . look at you."

Pan glanced down his robe-clad form. "What about me? Besides the fact that I'm perfection personified. Have you seen the size of my—"

"Ego?"

Pan's smirk was slow. "When you're as blessed as I am, can you really blame me?"

Christ, this guy . . . and I'd thought Remington was deluded.

"And yet she forgot all about you." He bared his teeth, but I kept going, baiting my trap. "She begs for my cock. Presents for Bentley, whimpers for Remington, and has shed sweet, perfect tears for Asher. But you know who has been missing from her thoughts? You. It's almost like she was relieved to be free of you. And I can see why. Roslyn deserves more than a weak . . . desperate . . . pawn. You're just a mummy's boy. And that's all you'll ever be."

Pan lunged, his Bible and scotch falling forgotten on the duvet as he flew toward me.

Only to be brought up short by an invisible barrier.

"What. Did. You. Do?" he snarled, eyes practically glowing with anger as his chest heaved.

"I do hope you're comfortable in there. Enjoy your reading material. It's all you'll have until this place rots to the ground around you. It's not a silver spike, but it'll do."

Pan growled, but with him safely locked away in the salt circle, it was easy to ignore the threat.

My phone buzzed in my pocket as I stood there grinning.

"Oh, look, there she is. My *wife*."

I answered, putting her on speaker so Pan could hear.

"Hello, petal."

"Gavin, is Pan there with you?"

The fucking demon smirked. "Apparently I'm never leaving."

"Good," she said. "Tell me what you did to Remi?"

"What? I have no idea what you mean. As much as I'd love to take responsibility for any misfortune that befell him, I can't."

"He's . . . I think he's dying. He's so sick."

Pan grinned. "I can see why you'd think it was me. That's certainly my type of parting gift, but as you well know, I've been here with you. Being exorcised. So while I clearly have the means and motive, I am sadly lacking in opportunity."

"Then who did this?" she asked, her voice wobbling.

Pan mimed zipping his lips.

"I'll get it out of him, petal. You have my word."

He tutted. "Look at you, making promises you can't keep."

I ended the call, then stared him down. "Oh, I'm going to keep it. There's no doubt about that."

"How do you intend to do that? I'm not a human. You can't pluck the answers from my head."

"I don't need to. You're going to tell me willingly."

Pan raised a brow. "Is that so?"

"Yes, because Remington is going to die and take Roslyn with him due to their bond. Which means *you* are going to die. So you'd better tell me everything you know."

A frown furrowed the demon's purple brow, his eyes going hazy before he let out a pained grunt and confusion flitted across his face.

I lifted my arms on instinct to shield myself from the potential projectile vomit he'd warned me about, but instead I watched in fascination as his form morphed before my eyes. In moments, the man sitting on the bed was no longer a hulking purple demon.

"Well . . . that was unexpected."

Asher blinked sea-blue eyes as he shook his head and glanced down his body. "What the fuck am I wearing?"

CHAPTER FIVE

ASHER

"Where's Remi?" I asked, tying the stupid silk robe that fucking demon had put on tighter around my waist. That dick thought he was the demon equivalent of Hugh Hefner. Pan would probably pay for companions too. No. He'd lock them in deals they could never get out of so they'd have to pretend to want him.

I grimaced as I realized he wouldn't do that either. I hated that I now knew my hitchhiker well enough to have insight into what he would or wouldn't do. Pan might be a narcissistic asshole, but he had a surprisingly strong moral code when it came to consent. He would never make a deal along those lines unless he knew for a fact the person involved truly wanted him. Rosie was proof of that.

Don't get me wrong, I'm not saying he's *good* by any means. But he's not all bad either.

Fuck. Am I siding with a demon? Am I *understanding* him? How the fuck had that happened?

Because he's your brother, and you are *a demon, numbnuts. Unless that creepy ass voice in my head was all a dream.*

But frankly, I wasn't that creative. And the icy dread I'd felt when she spoke to me, along with my newly reclaimed memories, only confirmed it was all true.

I was a bona fide freak.

And not in an 'in the sheets' kind of way. Okay, maybe I was, but that's not the point.

Focus, Asher.

"Asher. Is that really you?" Gavin stared me down, his shrewd gaze trained on me. He was suspicious. Good. He should be.

"Yeah, it's me. How long was I out? That exorcism was brutal."

"We didn't think you were ever coming back. Pan has been here since Father Gallagher's visit."

"Pan was *here*? You mean like"—I made a pair of horns with my index fingers, scrunched up my face, and hissed as I stuck my tongue out in my best demon impression—"that kind of here?"

"I don't know what the bloody hell that was supposed to be, unless you were just in the midst of a seizure. But if you're asking whether he was present in his demonic form. Yes. That's what I meant."

"The robe makes so much more sense now."

"Why?"

"I may not know exactly what he looks like, but he's a demon. No human clothes are going to fit him."

"He is rather . . . large."

"Yes. Yes, I am. Good to see the duke recognizes his betters."

I flinched at the sound of Pan's voice in my mind. It scratched at my consciousness like nails on a chalkboard.

Oh, goodie, I guess whatever barriers keeping us separated were gone now. Apparently that meant we got to talk to each other all the time. That was going to be fun. Not.

"My question is, how did you turn back into yourself? Are you some kind of shifter now?" Gavin settled on the ridiculous fainting couch across from the bed, both arms draped over the back, collar open, hair tousled. I could see why Rosie liked him. The expression dashing rake came to mind when I looked at him. Or maybe billionaire playboy, though I supposed those were basically the same thing.

"You said Remi was sick, and I just . . . charged forward."

He made a soft humming sound, and his gaze shifted away as he rubbed at his jaw. "Interesting."

I blew out an annoyed breath. "I'm glad you think so. Somehow I doubt you'd feel the same if you were the one who suddenly discovered you had to spend the rest of your life playing Dr. Demon and Mr. Jackass."

"Hey now, is that any way to talk about yourself?"

"You are *Mr. Jackass."*

"No, I'm Captain Aubergine. Ask Rosie."

"More like a shy courgette."

"There's nothing shy about me."

"Get out of my head. I'm having a conversation."

"With me."

"Not willingly."

"Asher?" Gavin sat forward, intent gaze on me.

Returning my focus to the vampire in front of me, I ran a hand over the back of my neck, uneasy and restless. I swung my feet over the side of the massive bed and stood, needing to stretch and move, maybe get my hands on a computer so I could do my own research about exorcising this fucking freeloader.

"You're stuck with me, little brother.*"*

"So you knew? Thanks for the heads up, dickstain."

"Actually, I didn't. Not until you thought it. I wondered why my mother was so invested in you. Now it all makes sense. She just couldn't keep it in her pants. Like mother like son, I guess."

"I guess that makes her the Lady Aubergine, then."

"What?"

"Nevermind. I was trying to do something there. I don't think it worked."

"Clearly. Leave the moniker creation to me. I've a talent for these

things. Maybe you should have a drink . . . or perhaps a shower. The steam is brilliant."

"While it's fascinating to watch you stare into space, Asher, I should warn you I've got the demon trapped. You—"

As Gavin's words landed, I stepped forward, over the circle of salt so I could take Pan up on his suggestion. Instead of a hot shower and drink, I was blasted back by a jolt of magic. I landed on the mattress with an *oof.*

Pan's laughter floated through my mind. *"Welcome to the dark side, little brother."*

Ignoring him, I reached out and tested the barrier again, this time feeling the buzz of the spell containing me but not getting the zap of a lifetime. Panic shot through me at the implication of my newly discovered heritage.

"Gavin, let me out."

He shook his head. "I'm afraid I can't do that."

"Yeah, you can. Break the circle and let me free. I can't protect Rosie from in here."

"And *he* can't hurt her from in there either. You see my predicament."

"But . . . how am I supposed to take a piss?"

"I'll get you a bucket."

I was not pissing in a bucket. "This isn't going to work."

"We'll figure it out. For now, you're a liability. Pan is likely to take over any minute. I will not risk her for the sake of your comfort."

I sighed. It was hard to be upset at the dude when he had a valid excuse. Of course Rosie's safety needed to be the priority.

Suddenly inspired, I blurted, "But what about when she needs to feed?"

His expression darkened. "I haven't gotten that far."

I stayed silent, trying to figure out a solution to this problem. I wanted freedom, but not at the cost of letting this jackwagon run loose.

"Don't forget me. You aren't the only one whose blood she'll crave. Ma petite monstre *will require access to* all *of her mates."*

"Fuck off," I muttered, forgetting to send it telepathically. Gavin cocked a brow. "Not you. No, actually, you know what, yes you. All of you can fuck off."

Falling back into the pile of pillows, I stared up at the gathered canopy of deep purple velvet over my head. I was glad to be back in my body, but what good was it if I couldn't help anyone I loved? Maybe I could convince Remi to sneak me my laptop.

"You still haven't told me where Remi is. Rosie said he's sick. Shifters don't get sick. What's going on?"

Gavin stood, strolling to the desk at the other end of the room and snatching a subpar computer before returning to his seat. That thing was only good for a Google search and some basic as shit incognito browsing. If I got out of here, I'd get him set up with something solid. Something with a firewall and VPN. That way the guy could at least look at porn without risk.

"All I know is what she told me. He's very sick. She's beside herself, hasn't left his side since she and Bentley found him."

"But he'll get better, right?" I couldn't keep the fear out of my voice.

"No."

"Fuck you. Did you do this?"

"No. I can't be sure, but I imagine Mummy Dearest took this into her own hands."

"How do we fix him?"

"We? Who is this we *you speak of?"*

"Pan. I need him."

"Aw, you're so cute when you beg. You're like an excited little puppy. The runt of the litter. The true little *brother in every sense of the word."*

"Pan!"

"What? I don't know how to fix him. I haven't seen the extent of the damage. Even if I had, that's not exactly what I do. In case you've already forgotten, we're Pestilence *demons. We infect. We don't heal."*

But . . .

"This is getting old. Do you two want to be alone?" Gavin rolled his eyes as he opened the computer.

"Yes. I already asked you to fuck off."

Ignoring me, he focused on whatever he was doing on the laptop. I was itching to do something helpful. To prove I could be trusted. But part of me also agreed with Gavin. If I could take over, Pan could too. Who knew what the trigger might be for him, if he even had one. Or needed it.

Minutes passed, maybe hours. I couldn't tell because apparently no one in this goddamned house believed in clocks, and Gavin's frown grew deeper and deeper as he typed and clicked and scrolled. Over and fucking over. God save me.

"What are you looking at? It's driving me crazy watching you fight with your browser. That's what you're doing, right? Trying to search for weird shit and coming up with nothing?"

Gavin straightened and shot me a baleful glare over his shoulder. "Yes, I'm researching, if you must know."

"That's not how it's done. You should let me help. I'm sort of an expert."

Gavin looked between me and his antiquated laptop.

"What's the worst that can happen? It's not like you'd know if I was up to no good, given the way you're currently typing with two fingers like a newb."

"I'm not a . . . newb."

"Says the newb." I scooted myself to the foot of the bed and reached out one hand. "C'mon. Hand it over. Tell me what we're looking for."

Pursing his lips, Gavin glanced at the laptop, then at me. "Fine." He stood and walked toward the circle, hesitantly handing the computer to me.

I wasn't exactly an expert in all things witchcraft, but I knew the basics of a circle. The salt kept demonic entities *in*, but at the end of the day, it was still a ring of salt. So there was no issue with Gavin passing an object to me. Out of curiosity, I grabbed a pillow and lobbed it across the room.

"What was that for?"

"Just testing a theory," I murmured, taking hold of the laptop, pleased to know that other objects, say a pretty vampire, might be able to move freely into and out of my prison. Maybe I wasn't going to be so alone after all.

The coating of the containment spell lingered on the device, but it was bearable as I brought it to my lap.

"All right." I cracked my knuckles before opening the computer and waiting for it to wake back up. "Jesus, man. This thing is a fucking dinosaur."

Gavin shrugged. "Don't look at me. It came with the house."

"Old people," I muttered.

His search history finally populated as Google appeared on the screen. I gave him a dubious look. "Queen? That's what you typed in? Are you a Freddie Mercury fan or something? Seems like an odd choice. Or is this some sort of Royalty kink I'm not aware of?"

"She's a vampire Queen. The first in ages. I need to know more about them."

"Who's a queen?"

"Who the bloody hell do you think? Roslyn, you twat."

Something twisted in my gut. Pan's too. I could sense his unease as though it was my own.

"What do you know?"

"Nothing I'm comfortable sharing."

"That's not how this works."

"Isn't it?"

I growled in frustration.

"What is it?" Gavin asked.

"Pan knows something. As soon as you mentioned Rosie being a Queen he got all . . . itchy."

"No one likes a tattletale."

"Yeah, well, you should have thought about that before you started keeping secrets."

"What can I say? I learned from the best."

"Who, me?"

"No, you fucking numpty, our mother."

"Oh. Yeah, I guess that makes more sense."

"You want to know about Queens? Use your brain. Where would you find information even vampires don't want their brethren knowing?"

Was Pan . . . helping me? Why?

Either I'd telegraphed the question, or Pan was attuned to my every thought, because his sigh was beleaguered as he replied, *"I don't know. Maybe I feel sorry for you. Or perhaps I'm simply livid Mum kept you a secret from me. Take your pick, but I don't suggest looking a gift horse in the mouth. It's liable to kick you."*

"That's not how that saying goes."

"Have I mentioned yet that I despise you?"

"Right back atcha, big bro."

"Oh dear Lucifer, save me."

I couldn't ignore the suggestion he'd offered, though. The Vampire Council archives had to be the only place he could mean. It would be hard, but if anyone could get past their firewall and into that database, it'd be me. Assuming, of course, the living corpses had joined the rest of us in the twenty-first century. Hell . . . even the twentieth would be impressive. It was run by a bunch of millennia-old dusty windbags. For all I knew, they might still be using—shudder—paper and ink.

"There you go. You're not just a pretty face. You really do have some brains in there."

"If I can hack into their archives, I can find everything I need."

"We've established this, yes."

"Why does her being a Queen make you so uncomfortable?"

"It . . . changes things."

"What kinds of things?"

"Let's just say Mum won't like it. Not at all."

"This is hell. I'm in hell." Gavin groaned and pinched the bridge of his nose, reminding me that I'd all but ignored his existence for the last handful of minutes. I was going to need to work on that. Nothing sexier than a guy who'd randomly stare off into space mid-conversation so he could argue with the voice in his head.

"How did I get stuck babysitting the demonic version of Tweedle Dee and Tweedle Dum?"

"We're brothers, not twins," I blurted, correcting him on sheer reflex.

His eyes snapped open, rage burning in their depths. "What did you just say?"

"Well done, brother. Now you've stepped in it."

CHAPTER SIX

ROSIE

"Sugar, go l-lay down. Y-you're dead on y-your feet." Ben's palm slid over the small of my back as I stared out the window, listening to the rattling breaths Remi dragged in far too infrequently.

"I could say the same for you."

My voice was hollow. Exhausted. These last couple of days by Remi's bedside had done a number on me. I hadn't slept, let alone showered, and was hardly feeding, which didn't help matters, but it felt *wrong* to worry about those kinds of mundane things while one of my mates was literally dying beside me, and I couldn't do a forking thing to stop it.

"H-he'll come th-through this."

I spun on my heels and found blue eyes focused on mine. But they weren't filled with determination and his usual steady strength. They were red-rimmed, tired, and defeated. He was simply going through the motions, repeating words he thought he needed to say even if he didn't believe them.

How could he when he could feel echoes of what Remi was going through? Ben looked nearly as bad as his twin, and he wasn't even the one infected. Reaching up, I stroked his cheek before threading my fingers through his hair. He released a weary sigh and dipped his head, pressing his brow to mine.

I hated that he was in pain. That we all were.

"I'm sorry," I whispered.

"It's n-not your f-fault."

"You don't know that."

He wrapped his arms around me and held me tight. "I kn-know. Y-you didn't d-do this."

"Maybe not personally, but come on. We both know none of this would have happened if Remi hadn't been connected to me. I'm the one that brought Pan into our lives, and with him, the attention of his mother. And suddenly, Remi is sick? How am I *not* responsible for this? At least in part?"

"S-stop, sugar. No m-more blaming yourself." He stroked my cheek with his thumb before brushing my lips with his.

"I love you, Ben," I murmured against his mouth before it feathered over mine a second time. His kiss was about comfort, but my fangs still tingled with the need to turn it into something more.

"Always hugging good ol' Benny Boo Boo. A guy might get jealous." Remi's voice was a welcome interruption, but he sounded just as fatigued as ever.

We broke apart, both of us rushing to his bedside. "Remi, I . . ." Tears clogged my throat. He'd been out far longer this time. I honestly worried he wouldn't wake again.

"Missed me?"

"So much."

His smile, while strained, was filled with his usual swagger. "'Course you did. I'm the sexy twin. Come here and give me some sugar, baby girl." The offer might have been more tempting if it wasn't immediately followed by a phlegm-filled cough.

"I d-don't think that's a g-good idea."

Ignoring Ben's warning, I sat on the edge of the bed and ran my fingers through Remi's dark hair. He hummed in appreciation and closed his eyes, leaning into the touch. I leaned down and pressed my lips to his forehead, which was still far too warm.

"You're so fucking pretty, Rosie. The prettiest." His words were a soft murmur, and when he opened his eyes, I saw the truth behind the veil of cocky confidence. He was in agony, but smiling through it for our benefit.

I desperately wanted to tell him he didn't have to pretend, but I knew it would only hurt his feelings if I called him out on faking. He was trying so hard. The least I could do was play along.

"I'm going to tell Asher you said that."

His jaw tightened. "I'll probably see him before any of you. That demon likely killed him by now."

Oh, my heart. I smiled gently, thankful I could give him some good news. "No. He's here. Whole and unharmed."

"It worked?" The hope in his voice twisted me up inside.

"K-kind of."

"What do you mean?" he wheezed before being overtaken by a fit of coughing.

Ben and I exchanged worried looks before I did my best to explain what Gavin had texted us. "They're sharing a body. But Asher is fully himself when he's in control. The same for Pan. No more body snatching."

When Remi frowned, Ben helped me clarify. "Asher l-looks like himself. Pan appears as a d-demon."

"Fuck. Asher's gonna hate that. He's not good at sharing."

"Except with me," I offered, smirking.

"Well, that's fun, baby girl. Speaking of our hacker, if he's back in the driver's seat, why isn't he here holding vigil with you two?"

I glanced down at my hands, not wanting to share this next part, but knowing I had to so he wouldn't hold Asher's absence against him. "In order to keep Pan contained, Gavin had to trap him in a circle."

"Which means Asher has to be there too." Panic flashed in his eyes, and he began breathing fast, his face paling. "I'm . . . never going to see . . . him again."

I threaded our fingers and squeezed tight. "You will. I swear it."

"Don't make promises . . ." His voice trailed off into deep, wracking coughs.

"Remi, listen to me. You are not going to die here. I won't allow it. I only just found you, and I refuse to let you leave me. We are going to find a cure, because I simply will not accept any other alternative. In fact, I'm going to call my brother and have him send my Aunt Callie. She's a genius. If anyone can help us figure this out, it's her. She cured sun sickness after all. Well, sort of." I was spiraling, bargaining however I could because denial was all I had.

Ben's strong fingers slipped around my nape just as Remi lifted his to my lips to stop me.

"Your heart is racing. Take a breath, baby. It's okay."

"I love you, Rosie. And I'm not leaving unless I have no choice." For the first time since he woke, he dropped the façade, and the full weight of his pain hit me. "But . . . it's not looking so good."

"R-Remi, s-stop."

"No. She needs to hear this. You too. If anything—"

This time I was the one who cut him off. I pressed my hand over his mouth and shook my head, tears spilling from my eyes. I could not handle the 'if anything happens to me' speech. It would sound too much like the end, and I simply could not bear it.

"Don't give up yet, Remi. Please. I need you to keep fighting."

A soft rapping on the front door pulled my attention from the terrible grief welling up inside me. Grief that was only emphasized by the weight of what my two shifter mates were feeling.

"I g-got it." Ben's voice was rougher than usual as he squeezed my neck before leaving.

Remi's eyes were fever-bright when they met and held mine. He took my hand from his mouth, his thumb brushing gently over my knuckles. "Will you tell him I love him?"

He didn't have to say which *he* he was referring to. Ben already knew, which only left Asher.

"You're going to tell him yourself."

"God, we're a cliché, aren't we?"

"I don't give a damn."

His brows lifted. "She curses now?"

"When the occasion calls for it."

His smile turned wicked, his voice a low, sexy whisper. "Go on, give me a good hard fuck, baby girl."

"I wouldn't recommend that in your state, Remi," the doctor said from the open bedroom door. "You need to conserve your energy, son."

Remi and I turned our heads toward the door, my mate's lips dipping into a frown as he looked over the older gentleman with his red sweater and thick white beard. "Give a dying man his last wish. Jeez. Cockblocked by Santa Claus. Jolly Old St. Nick, my ass."

"R-Rosie, this is D-Doctor Hatchet."

"So, not Father Christmas, then?" I asked, amusement in my question.

"I did ride a reindeer once." He leaned in and whispered conspiratorially, "They're not as nice as they're made out to be."

"Hatchet? Has anyone ever told you you should consider a name change? Bad branding. You might as well call yourself Doc Bundy or Lecter. You're not hiding an icepick in that black bag of yours, are you?" Remi tried to sit up, but couldn't manage more than an inch or two before he gave up and fell back onto the pillows.

"I left that in my other bag, I'm afraid."

"*You're* afraid?" Remi muttered, giving him a serious side-eye. "I'm the one in the bed, buddy."

"Th-that's enough s-small talk. Wh-what took you s-so long, D-Doc?" Ben asked, interrupting our lighthearted banter. "I c-called you t-two days ago."

Dr. Hatchet frowned apologetically. "I am sorry about that.

Believe it or not, your brother isn't the only one who's taken ill. As the only doctor in a hundred-mile radius, I've been quite busy."

"Ben," I softly chastised, shaking my head. I was just as frustrated as him, but there was no need to pile on the poor man who was simply trying to do his job.

"More p-people are sick?"

"Yes. From what I can tell, it's not airborne and looks like a slow spread, but I can't pinpoint the strain of virus. It seems flu-like in nature but isn't as bad as what's affecting your brother. I can see that from where I stand." He came closer and sat his bag on the end of the bed before opening it and pulling out a stethoscope. "Can you sit up?"

Ben was there instantly, helping his brother. "I've g-got you."

"Lift your shirt for me?"

Remi tossed him a weak smirk. "I bet you say that to all the boys."

"Only the sick ones who need their vitals checked, Mr. Mercer. My husband wouldn't be very happy if I flirted with my patients."

"So there's a Mister Claus. Why wasn't that in the books I read as a kid? Please tell me his name is Rudolph. Wait, it's Prancer, isn't it? I always knew that guy was a shifter. And you did say you rode a reindeer . . ."

No one said a darn thing in response, though Remi's patented irreverence had us all wearing small smiles. Instead, we watched as Doctor Hatchet checked Remi's vitals, his expression growing graver by the second. He swabbed Remi's cheek and nose, took a few vials of blood, and when he was finished, after packing away all his supplies, he turned serious eyes to us.

"Walk me out?" he asked.

Ben and I nodded, while Remi gave a tired grin. "I think I'll just stay here and have a little nap."

"Good idea. Rest is always the best medicine."

I brushed a kiss on Remi's forehead and stood, following Ben and the doctor out of the room. He kept his voice low, giving us care instructions as we moved through the apartment.

"Keep him hydrated. I'm leaving you some fever reducer, but I don't know how much good it'll do. Try to keep him comfortable." He sighed. "If I can isolate the virus causing this, I'll be able to do more for him."

"Thanks for coming all the way out here, Doctor," I said when we reached the door.

"Is h-he gonna come through th-this?"

Dr. Hatchet looked back toward the bedroom and then leveled us with a serious but compassionate stare. "Listen, I don't make it a habit to give my patients false hope, and I'm not going to start now. I'll do everything I can, but you should prepare yourself for the worst. If there's other family, call them. Make the most of the time you have together. And"—those compassionate eyes locked on mine, but they did nothing to soften the blow—"say your goodbyes . . . just in case."

Ben silently took my hand, his grip tight as his body trembled. This was for his support as much as my own.

"I'll be back in a few days. Call me if his condition changes."

I nodded, and Ben gave him a soft grunt of assent. I knew if he tried to speak right now, nothing would come out.

As the door closed behind the doctor, I turned to face my mate, my throat tight with emotion. "Ben?"

He pulled me into his chest and held on for dear life as our world began to burn down around us. "I-I know."

CHAPTER SEVEN

ASHER

"Hey, your lordship! I'm wasting away up here. You can bring my dinner any time! Humans have to eat, you know." I sighed as my stomach growled again. "Fucking vampires. Not everyone can exist on a liquid diet."

Gavin appeared in the doorway, a scowl curling his lips as per usual. "Technically, it's Your Grace."

"What'd you say?" I asked, eyes locked on the ham and cheese sandwich on his plate, alongside a lone red apple. Wonder Bread never looked so good. It was far from my sandwich of choice—hello, Remi and Rosie—but it could have been Fancy Feast and I would have been just as excited about it.

"Never mind. Back up." He waited at the edge of the circle for me to do as he commanded, then, as soon as he was sure I wouldn't do something to break the spell, he slid the plate onto the mattress.

I lunged, grabbing the plate and pulling it toward me. The sandwich was in my mouth before I'd had a chance to settle myself. "Thanks, Lurch," I said through a mouthful. " Though you could've at least sprung for some mustard."

His expression darkened, then he reached past the barrier and snatched the apple. "Just for that, no dessert."

"An apple isn't dessert. It's a lure. Curses, spells, trickery. You name it. Never trust an apple."

Gavin rolled his eyes. "An apple is hardly a lure."

"I wouldn't be so sure about that. Remember Adam and Eve?" I asked around another bite.

"I'm not sure what I expected to find, but you two debating the finer parts of the book of Genesis definitely didn't make the list." Rosie appeared in the doorway, looking beautiful despite the fatigue and grief clinging to her.

"Now *that's* dessert."

Gavin ignored me, turning his attention to Rosie with a hunger in his eyes that I was sure mirrored mine. Except he could have her, and I was stuck here watching. Lucky motherfucker.

She took a few steps closer, her toes likely right up against the salt barrier, if Gavin's reaction was any indication.

"Petal, you shouldn't stand so close. It's dangerous."

"I'll take my chances." She held up a hand, and I mirrored her position, scooting closer on my knees and holding mine as close to the barrier as I could without touching it. I could fucking *feel* her heat.

"How is he?" I blurted, worry for Remi overpowering all other thoughts.

Sadness flitted across her face, and I knew. It was bad. "We're taking it one moment at a time."

"Is Ben with him? He's not alone, right?" The thought of him being sick and alone hurt my soul. If I wasn't stuck here, a risk to everyone, I'd be at his side. But I couldn't leave, and it killed me.

"Yeah, he stayed. It was the only way I'd agree to come home to . . ." Her gaze trailed from my eyes to my throat. I hated that I couldn't help Remi, but I absolutely could do something for her.

"Hungry, princess?" There was no missing my offer.

She licked her lips, leaning forward a hair before Gavin snarled and pulled her back.

"No. He's off the menu."

"He can't be. I need him."

"Ha! She's got you there, Bridgerton. Crawl on up, Rosie. The water's fine."

Her lips twitched, but Gavin gripped her chin and jerked her face back to his. "Well, you aren't going to get his blood by traditional means if I have anything to say about it."

Rosie gave him a stern look. "We tried that once before with Ben."

"And you survived."

"I need my mates, Gavin. All of them."

"Hear that, brother dearest? Looks like I'm on deck."

"Fuck off, purple people eater. No one wants you here."

"That's not what it sounds like to me."

"If you go to him, what's to stop him from tearing you apart when he changes back to that demon filth?"

I cocked a brow, answering the question even though it hadn't been aimed at me. "Ever heard of a mate bond? I'm pretty sure you have, since you yourself gave her one. Pan can't hurt her."

"Aw, look at that. You're defending my honor."

"You have no honor."

"What's he doing?" Rosie whispered to the vampire.

"Talking to himself."

"Hey, I'm not talking to myself. I'm talking to Pan, thankyou-verymuch."

Gavin gave a long-suffering sigh. "He's talking to himself. The only difference is the voice in his head has a name."

"And a British accent."

"Oh yes, we can't forget that. Mention my massive cock too. And my tail. Ma petite monstre *loves my tail."*

"Oh, go stuff yourself."

"I'd rather stuff her."

"Sorry, that's my job."

Gavin's groan pulled me out of my conversation with Pan. "See what I mean? It's par for the course with him these days. Rude as well. He has a tendency to zone off in the middle of a conversation."

I laughed because I couldn't help myself. "It makes me happy to know I get under your skin even when you have me locked up."

"It's your brother who gets under my skin."

Rosie's eyes widened. "I beg your pardon?"

"Now who's keeping secrets?" I didn't even try to keep the teasing note out of my voice. Was Pan influencing me? Or was I always like this? Yeah, I'd always been like this.

She whipped her gaze to Gavin. "Explain."

"I was going to wait to tell you in person. Apparently your hacker is Pan's half brother."

Her eyes shot to me. "Is that true?"

I shrugged, equal parts uncomfortable and defensive. "That's the word on the street. Or in my head." I frowned. "I might need to talk to somebody about that. There's a surprising number of voices that aren't mine in there these days."

"Sounds crowded."

"I might have to raise the rent."

A small smile turned up her mouth. "Perhaps." Then her brows drew together. "How long have you known? Surely not all this time. You wouldn't keep that from me."

Fuck, I hated the idea of her not trusting me.

"No, not the whole time. Only since I woke up. Caleb's demon eviction seemed to have unlocked something in my brain. Not only did I get a bunch of fun memories back, and by fun, I definitely mean *not remotely fun*, but it also allowed my mom to chat me up."

"Wait, Pestilence is your mother? You didn't think to lead with that?"

I winced. "I was trying to ease you in."

"It's not a cock, Asher. You don't need to warm me up first."

I couldn't help but laugh at her comparison. "Careful, that was close to cursing."

"Sod off."

"British cursing still counts, princess."

A little growl rumbled in her throat, and my dick gave a happy jerk. God, I've missed her. I've missed them both. Her and Remi. Not her and Gavin. That stuffed shirt could be literally anywhere but here.

I positioned myself so she had a good look at what I was offering. "But hey, it's not all bad news. Even if I am part demon, at least I'm not cursed anymore."

"I don't know how to feel about that, because it means you're trapped in there, and I can't get to you."

Gavin made a considering sound. "You know, now that you mention your curse, I wonder if our little friend Pan had anything to do with that."

"Little? Who does he think he's calling little? I tower *over you all. And the expression 'monster cock' came from somewhere. It certainly wasn't vampires."*

"Did you have anything to do with my curse?"

"You mean the binding marks you used to have? I'd take credit if I had been the one to send that witch to you. That was all Mum's doing. Sort of a lock-and-key situation connecting me to my true vessel. Everything changed when she threw me into your body permanently. Now, there's no need for the marks. We are soulbound."

"Lucky me," I muttered aloud, causing Rosie and Gavin to cock their heads. "Sorry. Pan just gave me another reason to hold on to my mommy issues."

"Care to enlighten us?" Gavin asked, lifting a brow.

"Apparently he and I are soulbound, and my curse was how The Incubator—"

"Incubator?" Rosie asked.

I sighed, pausing to elaborate. "Pestilence. It feels weird thinking of her as my mom. Mothers are supposed to be . . . maternal. She's the antithesis of that. Incubator felt more accurate. Sort of the female version of a sperm donor, but more than an egg donor since she grew me or whatever." I shuddered at the mental imagery. "Anyway, *she* was responsible for the curse and soulbinding, but I don't think that's really new information considering Pan's current living arrangement. Namely, me."

"In case I wasn't clear before, you *are* my *vessel. Made specifically for me to use as needed."*

"I don't see how that changes what I just said."

"No, I don't suppose you would appreciate the nuance. Perhaps this is a good time to mention that I've been taking joyrides in your body since the moment you arrived here."

Memories flooded my mind. Me stumbling out of my truck, barely aware of how I got to Aurora Springs, my arm freshly marked with what I'd called a curse still burning from the magic etched into my skin. Of waking up in random places with no recollection of how I'd gotten there. Entire gaps in time, days and nights just gone as if they'd never existed at all. I wasn't sure if I was relieved or horrified to learn he'd been responsible for all of it.

Dots began to connect now that the mystery had been solved. The morning I met Toderick flashed into my mind . . . the same night Rosie met Pan for the first time to strike her deal.

"You sonofabitch."

"Right back at you. It is an accurate sentiment, all things considered."

I'd been used as her pawn since the day I was born. So had Pan, even if he didn't realize it yet. I sighed again, my shoulders slumping in defeat. "I'm not going to die from the curse, but I can't ever leave this circle either."

"We'll find a way out of this, Asher. It's going to be okay."

I'd never been very good at hiding my feelings from Rosie. She always managed to see straight through me. And there was definitely no hiding from her now that we were bonded, so it shouldn't have surprised me that she caught on to my disappointment and immediately softened her voice.

"You're right. Your curse being gone *is* good news. You no longer have an expiration date." She reached out like she was going to try and touch me, but Gavin stopped her, and she balled her hand into a fist instead. "We have time now. Time to figure this out." Her expression changed, eyes hardening slightly. "Can you . . . can you two trade places at will?"

I thought so. We hadn't done it yet, but I was pretty sure Pan and I had equal footing now.

"Why?" I asked, worried that she didn't want to spend time with me now that she knew about my parentage. Another part of me knew that was stupid; Rosie had never cared about shit like that, but still. She'd gone from wanting to feast on my blood to asking about the other guy.

"This prison isn't for you. It's for him. To keep him from wreaking havoc and ruining lives, correct?"

"Yes," Gavin answered, but her eyes never left mine. They begged me to understand.

"Then I need to speak to him."

"One demon of the first order, coming right up."

"Wait—"

But it was too late. I was pushed back and Pan took over, my body changing and my consciousness no longer in the driver's seat. His voice echoed as he stretched out on the bed like a jungle cat.

"Ah, *ma petite monstre*, how I've missed you."

CHAPTER
EIGHT
PAN

My little mate tried so hard to hide her reaction to me. She failed. Oh, how she failed.

"Miss me, darling?"

"No."

"Liar."

"Takes one to know one."

She squared her shoulders, her eyes dark with denied thirst, and if she thought I was going to let her get away from me without doing something about it, she was wrong. Incredibly so.

I stretched, my body on full display for her. Silk did wonders for my physique. Every bulge was beautifully accented by the royal purple-hued material. And I do mean *every*.

The flare of her pupils proved it. As did that sweet fleck of drool right at the corner of her delectable mouth.

"You've got something . . . just there." I pointed to her lips.

Her eyes narrowed, and she growled.

"Hangry?"

"Where did you learn that phrase?"

"My little brother's mind is filled with all sorts of interesting tidbits."

"Ah, I see. You've been snooping around in things that don't belong to you."

"One could argue, *ma petite*, that possession is nine-tenths of the law." I grinned in smug satisfaction as the play on words landed.

My cock thickened as the tension between us grew. I did so love our repartee. She may not like me, but there was no denying she wanted me as badly as I did her.

And who needed to be liked anyway? Hate fucking was so much fun.

"Only a thief and a miscreant would think so."

"And yet, your knickers are practically dripping at the thought of all the wicked things this *miscreant* can do to you."

"No, they're not."

I arched one brow and then took a long, indulgent inhale. "That's not what your cunt says. Aren't I right, vampire?"

"Leave me out of this."

"And here I thought you liked games, duke. How disappointing." I untied the robe and let it fall open, not bothering to hide my erection from either of them. Then with one long claw, I dragged a line up my inner thigh, cutting deep enough that blood welled to the surface. "If you're not going to play with us, you should leave."

"I wasn't aware there was an actual invitation."

"There wasn't. I was just trying on politeness for size. It didn't fit. Unlike my cock, which is a perfect fit. Every. Single. Time."

We all knew the words were for Roslyn. My filthy little slut was practically panting as she eye fucked my swollen shaft. Her irises flashed molten amber, and her body vibrated from the effort it took to hold herself back.

"Petal," Gavin warned.

"I need him."

"Whatever you do, don't break the circle. Do you understand?"

"Yes . . . *petal*," I taunted. "Do you?"

She bared her fangs at me. "Don't think I don't know what you're doing, Pan."

"Is it working?"

"Yes, damn you," she snarled, leaping forward.

"Roslyn, wait!"

But there was no stopping her. Before Gavin even opened his mouth, she'd already landed on the bed, her fangs grazing my throat.

Good to know Asher's theory about the circle was true.

"Was there ever any doubt?" Asher's voice put a slight damper on my moment of victory, but I'd done the same to him. Turnabout *was* fair play.

"Oh no, you had your fun. Kindly fuck off. I don't need you ruining this for me."

"I'm sure you'll take care of that all on your own."

She distracted me from my inner retort by wrapping her legs around my hips and pinning me to the mattress, her strength adding a thrilling danger to our situation. I liked her rough.

"Yes, there's my shameless whore. Take what you want. Then I'll get mine."

"Don't think this means anything. I still despise you and the dreadful things you've done."

"Yes, yes. Keep telling yourself that as you scream my name like the dirty cum-guzzling slut you are."

I could feel the heat of her cunt through the fabric of her shapeless sweatpants. No, no, no. That wouldn't do. I needed her bare, riding me, making me hers.

Wait. Hers?

No. She was *mine*.

"Is she? She doesn't have your mark anymore. Or your cute little piercing."

"She's about to have my cum filling her to the brim."

"She's about to take it from you. Not the other way around. I'd say you *are* hers. *Just like the rest of us."*

Closing my eyes, I focused on the pussy I was about to impale. I would deal with the rest of this clusterfuck once my balls were drained and I was dripping out of her.

Rosie, completely oblivious to the direction of my thoughts, ran her nose along the cord of muscle in my neck, breathing heavily as her body shook with barely leashed desire.

"Stop playing with your meal, petal."

"No, don't stop. Play all you like."

She shoved my shoulders down as I moved to sit up. "I'm . . . I can't control my need. I want him."

My little monster ground her cunt against my shaft as she said the words. She wanted my body and my blood. This was working out just fine for me.

"It's all right. He's your . . . mate." Gavin spit the last word like it left a bad taste in his mouth. "It's natural to feed like this. Just like you do with the rest of us."

"He doesn't deserve me or my body," she said, her eyes locked on mine as she rolled her hips once more.

"No, he doesn't. But you shouldn't deny yourself to spite him. Take what you need, Roslyn. A Queen does not go without."

I smirked, my tail working its way around her waist, searching for an opportunity to flip this situation so I could drive inside her. But she stopped me with a sharp look.

"No. I'm the one with the reins tonight, Pan. Not you. Don't make me gag you."

"That's it, petal. If you're worried about him turning the tables and taking more than you're willing to give, then don't cede control to him. He's not your lord or your daddy. You do not owe him your submission. In fact, I think you should demand *his*."

"Hmm, I like the sound of that," she purred, her gaze molten.

Truth be told, so did I. I think. It was hard to know what I was feeling. I'd never allowed anyone to top me before. Come to think of it, I don't think anyone dared try.

Rosie's small hand went around my throat, the tight squeeze of her fingers cutting off my air supply and sending a thrill through me.

Well, fuck me.

That was . . . hot.

"Yes, *mon coeur*. Fuck."

"Do you want my body, Pan?" she asked, her voice a breathy thing filled with pent-up arousal.

"Yes . . . Mistress."

She shuddered, her head thrown back, fangs extended. "First you're going to give me your blood."

"Take it. It's yours."

I'm yours.

Fuck, where'd *that* come from? These pesky intrusive thoughts had to go.

"Told you."

I couldn't even respond to Asher; I was too focused on my sweet monster as she licked her lips and leaned over me, her other hand still pressed to my throat, though she no longer squeezed.

"Maybe this time I won't let you come."

I growled. She could fucking try, but I would blast inside her like a freight train before this was through. Fuck, I'd punch a hole straight through those ugly sweats if she kept taunting me.

"Love to see you try. You want me just as badly. Your cunt is hot and wet for me."

"Shut up."

"Put something in my mouth, and I will."

She leaned even closer before pressing her lips to mine, filling my mouth with her tongue and her taste and . . . Lucifer's tits, I wondered if this was what love felt like.

I'm sorry. What the fuck was wrong with my brain? Love?

"Aw, that's cute. The big bad demon just found out his heart is three sizes too big."

"No, I didn't."

"Okay, buddy. Whatever you say."

My hands went to her hair, tangling in the silky strands, clutching her and keeping this for as long as I possibly could. I let her drugging kisses distract me from thoughts of love and forever and a white picket fence with a view of our very own hellscape while our little demonlings ran around . . . oh, angel feathers.

"Oh wow. Epiphanies are way more fun this way. All rollercoaster and no consequences."

"Fuck off, Asher."

"No. Shan't. This is great. Pan and Rosie, sitting in a tree. K-I-S-S-I-N-G."

"I think you mean F-U-C-K-I-N-G."

Rosie rolled that hot cunt along my shaft again. But this time, it was slick and bare and when had she taken off her clothes? How had I missed it?

"Do you mind not distracting me while she's about to rail me?"

"Oh, she's not going to rail you. She's railed me. This is not railing."

A picture of Rosie bent over Asher while she took him had me snarling with jealousy. And then my thoughts took a decided turn, my mind suddenly filled with my filthy girl taking my ass while I confessed my undying love and devotion. My balls drew up at the idea. What in Satan's unholy name was going on? I was broken. I had to be.

"You've tainted me with your . . . feelings*."*

"No way, my dude, those are all you. Shockingly, I might add. I didn't know you had it in you."

"Me either."

"It's kinda cute."

"Shut up. Any more of your insufferable rambling and I'm liable to lose my erection."

"There's a pill for that."

I was about to shoot back a pithy zinger, but her fangs pierced my skin, and I had to focus every ounce of my energy on not blowing my load all over myself. I needed that to happen inside her. How else could I get my very own little family?

No.

Motherfucker.

No.

Never family.

You made sure of that, remember?

But as she continued to pull from my vein and send me spiraling higher, my erstwhile thoughts continued down a forbidden path. *You could undo it.*

That little thought was all mine, but the next one wasn't.

"Or maybe you could enter a deal with Lilith, and you *could be the one to bear the children."*

"Stop. Too far," I scolded my brother, and his amused chuckle echoed in my head.

"Tell that to the entire genre of romance novels based around the concept. Women love the idea of men getting knocked up and having to deal with all the consequences. It's called fantasy for a reason."

I couldn't even respond to that. Every moment that passed with Rosie latched onto my throat, I fell further into her web.

Satan's balls, she'd punted me straight down Domestic Avenue without a map. Now I wasn't even thinking logically. This mate bond was destroying me. I didn't even recognize the wholesome fucking fantasies pelting my brain. Me wearing an apron and baking cookies while little purple-haired brats bit my ankles. Me dusting the fan while Rosie lounged naked—round with another of my spawn, of course—in bed, cracking a whip.

Okay, so maybe they weren't completely wholesome. Maybe there was still hope.

"Rosie," I panted. "I need more. You're killing me."

She moaned and didn't even lift her head from where she suckled my neck as I palmed her arse.

"I want you. I'm fucking desperate."

With one hand, she reached between us and gripped my length, lining the crown of my cock up with her soaked entrance. Then she sank down on me to the hilt, and I cried out in relief. Oh, sweet mystery of Rosie's cunt, at last I've found you.

"Good grief."

"Don't like it? Get the fuck out."

"I'm usually a fan of watching, but this is starting to feel more like a bad threesome. I think I need my porn with a little more separation. Maybe we should institute a rule about Rosie time. Make it sacred."

"Like you stay on your side of the curtain, and I on mine?"

"Exactly."

"Sounds great. Let's start now. Unless you want to feel me pump her full to bursting."

"No thanks, you're liable to start imagining gardening when you bust."

"Gardening?"

"I don't know, man. Your mind is fucking weird."

"I'm. A. Demon."

"Who gets his rocks off thinking about chores."

"Rosie rule. Right bloody now."

"Pan, God, yes," Rosie cried, bringing me back to the here and now. What was I doing, letting Asher distract me from her? I knew that had to have been his intention. Payback for what I'd done to him. I couldn't even summon the proper amount of outrage. I was too busy trying not to come.

I watched her as she moved above me, her tits bouncing, a flush creeping across her chest, a drop of my blood clinging to the side of her mouth.

"Take me, love. Make me yours, just as you claimed the rest of them."

Her eyes fluttered open, and she stared at me in shock, her movements halting. "What?"

"Don't spoil it. Just accept the moment for what it is, *ma petite*."

With uncharacteristic tenderness, I reached up and swiped my thumb across her lips, collecting the droplet of blood. Then I slid the digit into her mouth, and I swear, when she sucked on my thumb, I felt it all the way to my tail.

Shivers broke out along my skin. I was so attuned to every swipe of her tongue and graze of her teeth. If asked, I'd say our hearts were even beating in time.

"Please, Roslyn. I need to be yours. Make me yours."

Her eyes flashed, the hand still clutched around my throat tightening to the point her nails pierced my skin. "You're already mine."

I came so hard my eyes lost focus as I bucked up into her, trying to plant my seed as deep as possible inside her.

"Pan," she moaned, her walls clenching around me, and all I wanted was for her to never let me go.

She'd done it.

Ma petite monstre absolutely ruined me.

CHAPTER NINE

ROSIE

I'd done it. I'd absolutely ruined Pan.

And I wanted to do it all over again.

From the domination to the eavesdropping on his surprising fantasies to making him come so hard he nearly blacked out, I craved his subjugation. Just like he craved mine.

I also sort of hated myself for it. How could this have happened? After everything he'd done to me? To Remi? To Asher? To the people of this town? How could I want anything other than his immediate demise?

"Yes, *ma petite*. Fuuuck. I need to be inside you all the damn time. It's been too long since I got to have you in my true form."

"Wearing a costume not all it's cracked up to be?" I asked as I moved to shift off him, but he held me fast.

"Not yet. I'm not ready to be parted."

If I hadn't already heard a similar litany of thoughts running through his head, Pan's tender declaration would have caught me off guard. Well, to be fair, it still did. I just knew better than to trust anything that came out of his gorgeous mouth.

Okay. Okay. My brain knew. My body, however, was still a work in progress.

Holding me firm with one clawed hand, he raked the tips of the other down my spine, making me break out in goosebumps.

"If I didn't know better, I'd say you were getting attached."

"Currently, we are as attached as two creatures can be."

"Thankfully that's a temporary affliction."

"Not as temporary as you might think, *mate*."

That one word made my heart lurch, reminding me this was far more complicated than I'd bargained for. In fact, I hadn't bargained at all. I'd marked Pan without knowing he'd taken over Asher's form. I'd been duped.

Bargain or not, you still want him, you jezebel.

My conscience was a real twat sometimes. Even if she was right.

Before I could be swept away by the truth of my feelings for Pan, which were as unwanted as they were real, I latched onto something else.

Bargain.

Maybe there was a way to use this unintended bond to my advantage. He might be my mate, but he would always be, first and foremost, a demon. And what was more irresistible to a demon than a deal?

"What is going through that mind of yours, my little slut?"

I laid down across his chest, his palm splaying between my shoulder blades and gently running across my skin in what could be considered a caress. But Pan didn't touch me with tenderness. Ever. I was a possession to him. Not a treasure.

"What are you doing, petal? You got what you needed. Get out."

I'd grown accustomed to my mates' thoughts floating through my head, so thankfully I didn't react. *"I have an idea. Give us a second?"*

"Leave you alone with him? Absolutely not."

"Please, Gavin. You don't have to go far. I just need the illusion of privacy. It's the only way to get him to trust me."

His frustrated growl reverberated down our bond. *"Fine. I'll be right outside, but I won't close this door."*

I had to bite back a smile. *"Thank you, my lord."*

"Don't try to play obedient now. You will *be paying for this impertinence, petal."*

"Can't wait."

As soon as Gavin left the room, I rested my cheek on Pan's broad chest, fingers playing across the firm slab of muscle that was his pec. He sighed and stroked my hair. The scary hulking demon was *stroking* my hair.

"What happened to make you so . . . different?" I asked, not missing it when his body tensed.

"What do you mean?"

"You're being . . . sweet."

"No, I'm not." His denial was vehement, but he made no move to shove me away. If anything, he clung to me tighter. "Don't get used to it. It's probably this blasted bond. Although, it could also be lingering contamination from Asher. Do you have any idea how bloody exhausting *feelings* are?"

"As a matter of fact, I do."

"Hmm . . . yes, I suppose you would."

"It's okay to feel, you know? It's just another way we can recognize we're alive."

"Don't give me that bullshit. I'm far from living at this point. Caged in this bed, no way to escape. You might as well call me your captive and let your daddy know you've followed in his footsteps. Blackthorne vampires do love to keep their pets."

And as he spoke, I realized this was my opening. I turned my face to look up at him. "Perhaps I could help with that."

"With what? Being a zoo animal?"

"Yes, actually."

It was his turn to give me a dubious lift of his brow. "You can try, *mon coeur*, but I doubt the others will be on board."

"I have more sway than you give me credit for."

"That's where you're wrong, love. I give you more credit than you'll ever know."

If he only knew how the tables had turned and that I was now the one with inside access to his mind while mine was safely locked away behind my mental barriers. I'd seen it all. His truth. He wanted so much more than to be a pawn in Pestilence's game. He wanted a real future. A real life.

With me.

"Help us, Pan."

"I beg your pardon?"

"You and Asher are sharing an existence, correct?"

A low rumble of laughter escaped him. "Yes. You could say that."

"Don't you want to exist outside of this prison?"

"Of course I do."

"Then it would seem we've come full circle. I made a deal with you. Now it's your turn to make a deal with me."

Gavin's warning pulsed through me, not in words, but in emotions. He didn't like this, but he was trying to trust that I knew what I was doing.

"Go on . . ."

I began to doodle on his pec with my fingernail, drawing a hiss from him as I let the sharp tip pierce his flesh and draw blood. "I need to feed from you—"

"That's not all you need from me, my beautiful whore." He rocked his hips against mine, drawing a groan from me.

"True. But I also need Asher in all the same ways."

This time his hiss was annoyance rather than pleasure. That wouldn't do. Pushing up slightly, I dragged my tongue along the beads of liquid dotting his skin. God, the taste of him was rich and heady. Different than it had been when he and Asher were fighting each other for control of the same body. This was all Pan. Power. Magic. Danger. That hint of brimstone I'd tasted when I'd thought he was my hacker was now strong and smoky.

That wasn't all I was feeling. For the first time since I'd turned, I felt settled. Calm. Fully in control of myself. I'd have to be an idiot not to realize it was because I'd finally had this moment with my fifth and final mate. When he'd been hiding in Asher, I'd gotten hints of both of them, but not the real thing. That endless hunger, the ache that was never truly sated, had been because Pan was missing. As much as I hated it, I needed him. But not in the same way I used to. Pan was no longer the one in control here. I was the Queen, and as I'd learned early on, she was the most powerful player in the game. It was about forking time I acted like it.

All the pieces were lined up exactly as they should be. I had them. My men. The board was loaded and ready for me to make my move.

"What are you proposing?"

"An alliance. A promise, if you will."

The beautiful bastard smiled and tangled his fingers in my hair, tugging so hard I moaned. "I'm listening."

"I let you out of this circle, but you promise not to harm any of my mates or the people in this town." He opened his mouth to accept, I was sure, but I stopped him with the press of my index finger to his lips. "And you let Asher have his time in the proverbial driver's seat. For every minute you are in control, he gets two."

He nipped my finger, the flicker of pain pulsing right in my clit. "That hardly seems fair."

"You want to talk about fair, Pan? How about the part where you possessed his body and lied to me and everyone else for weeks? Or what about the part where you stole my blood for your mother and all the other nefarious deeds you've committed since you arrived in town?"

He rolled his eyes. "Demon."

"Arsehole."

"Yes, but I'm your arsehole, darling."

Gavin groaned from his place in the hall.

"Do we have a deal?" I asked, all business even though I was bare-arsed and leaking his cum as I laid astride him.

"How often do I have to give up my body?"

"Every twenty-four hours."

"What? That's . . . what if I'm in the middle of bringing you to a screaming orgasm?"

I shrugged. "Asher can finish the job."

"Rude."

"Take it or leave it, Pan. It's the only way you'll ever see anything beyond these four walls again."

His eyes narrowed, and he tilted his head on the pillow. "I doubt that. Someone will fuck up sooner or later."

"Do you really want to take that chance? I'm immortal now. Forever is a long time."

He grumbled something about mate bonds and being pussy whipped but eventually heaved a sigh. "Fine. Agreed."

"How shall we seal the deal?" I asked, knowing exactly how I wanted to do it.

"Traditionally, these things are finalized by an exchange of something precious. You might recall our initial agreement was quite . . . intimate in nature."

"I see."

A thrill ran through me at the thickening of his length. He was still inside me, though he'd softened throughout our conversation. Not any more. He was hard and filled me all over again.

"Let me fuck you until you forget your name, *ma petite monstre*. Then our deal will be sealed."

CHAPTER TEN

ASHER

"You promised, Pan. It's his turn. You successfully made me forget my name, and I'm spent after that last round, so be a good demon and give me back my hacker."

Rosie's voice floated to me, pulling me out of my self-induced retreat. Apparently the 'Rosie Rule' was no longer in effect, and I was being allowed to come back out and play. Pan must've really enjoyed his time with her.

"Firstly, there is no such thing as a 'good' demon, unless by good you mean evil and conniving, but I don't seem to be that anymore either. Secondly, of course you're spent. You just came so hard your pretty cunt almost amputated my cock. Although I must admit, I'm quite pleased you'll be too tired to do anything fun with any of them."

She giggled, and I could almost feel her in my arms as Pan held her. Almost.

"Are you jealous? Does someone have FOMO?"

"I do not have . . . FOMO. I simply don't want them sullying your memory of me between your thighs so soon."

"Okay, that's enough. It's my turn, Pan. She said it. You agreed." Did I sound like a grumpy old man? Yep. I didn't care.

I felt his resigned sigh before I was suddenly in my body, naked on the bed, with Rosie wrapped in my embrace. "I'd say we have to stop meeting like this, but . . . I'm kind of here for it. You have one of the nicest asses I've ever eaten."

"Top two at least," she teased.

Remi's ass filled my mind, and I let out a soft hum of agreement. "Definitely top two."

"It's good to have you back, Asher," she whispered as she rolled on her other side to face me.

Her fingers trailed across my jaw, then over my brow as though she was trying to make sure I was all there. As I adjusted to being me again, Pan's memories from their time together flitted through my mind—or was it *our* mind now?—and filled in the gaps.

I stiffened, and not in a sexy way.

"Why did you do it, princess?"

She frowned, that cute little wrinkle appearing between her eyebrows. "He's my mate. Just as you are. I don't need to justify being with him."

I wasn't going to touch that with a ten-foot pole. Her reasons for being with Pan weren't anything I wanted to talk about. "No. Not that. Why did you make that deal? Free him."

"Oh. I . . . You don't deserve to be locked up, and he is part of you. There was no way around it aside from this. At least with the deal, he's bound to the terms and we know he can't do anything to hurt us." She chewed on her bottom lip. "Well, more than he already has."

Dread twisted my gut. "I'm less worried about him and more worried about me."

"What do you mean? He can't hurt you."

"No . . . not that. I meant maybe I'm the problem."

Rosie laughed and ran her fingers through my hair, the feel of her nails on my scalp sending tingles down my back. "How on earth could you be the problem? Asher, you're—"

"Part demon. Pestilence's son. Tied to all of this just like he is."

"You're good. You'd never hurt me or any of us."

Fuck, I wanted to believe she was right, but now that I knew who my mom was, I couldn't be so sure. And Pan himself just confirmed it. There's no such thing as a 'good' demon.

"You don't know what she made me . . ." I trailed off, the rest of my thoughts lodging themselves in my throat.

Rosie sat up, genuine concern etched on her features now. "Tell me."

How could I tell her I'd given the horsewoman of the Apocalypse, my mother, carte blanche in order to save myself? I couldn't even remember the details of what I'd agreed to. I was a goddamned coward. No better than my shitty half brother.

"Ouch."

"Not right now, Pan. I'm in the middle of a breakdown."

"I know. It's wonderful. Do carry on."

"I agreed to—" But the words wouldn't come. They were stuck on my tongue, and for the first time, I understood what it must feel like for Ben when he worked so hard to get something out.

"Asher, you're scaring me."

"I'm scaring myself." I hadn't realized I'd spoken aloud until Rosie's eyes narrowed on my face.

Huh. How come that came out so easily?

"Mummy is such a sneaky bitch, isn't she?"

My stomach sank.

"Ah, there it is. I see you're starting to understand your predicament, as well as her depravity. There's no way you can speak the words aloud. Sorry, not sorry."

I squeezed my eyes shut as he confirmed my worst nightmare. *Sonofamotherfuckingwhore.*

"You mean Pestilence. But again, you really aren't far off."

"Asher?" Rosie squeezed my knee and pulled my attention back to her. "You know you can tell me anything, right? I mean, you know all my secrets."

She looked so earnest, those big amber eyes blinking up at me. I'd never hated myself more than I did in that moment.

"I . . . I can't say it."

"Is it that terrible?"

Yes? I thought.

"Yes . . . you naughty boy. She's never going to forgive you once you go through with it. Whatever Mum has roped you into is going to ruin everything you have with Rosie."

He wasn't wrong. The worst part was I had no idea what Pestilence was going to make me do.

"You shouldn't have freed me. I'm too big of a risk. I'm a fucking demon, Rosie, just as bad as Pan. Maybe worse."

"I beg your pardon. Now you're just talking nonsense. Frankly, I find that offensive. I have centuries of experience on you. Entire plagues under my belt. What have you done? A few lies of omission? Oh, do get over yourself." He scoffed, mocking my voice in a surprisingly good, albeit petulant, imitation. "'As bad as Pan. Maybe worse.' *Ha! In your dreams."*

Rosie got out of bed and stared hard at me, defiance shining in her eyes as she dragged her foot through the circle of salt and broke the containment spell. "You would never hurt me."

"How can you possibly know that? We only just found out what I really am. None of us know what I'm capable of."

She held my gaze and shrugged. "You're my mate."

I stood, stepping over the ruined circle and striding naked toward the wardrobe. I couldn't look at her as I pulled out the first things I could find. Did the man who owned this house have anything other than weird robes and military sweats?

"Asher," she murmured, coming up behind me and wrapping her arms around my waist. The way she pressed her cheek into my back and held me felt so fucking good. I'd missed her. But apprehension circulated through my veins with each beat of my heart. This was worse than my curse. At least then, I was the only one who was going to get hurt. Now? Who the fuck knew what I was going to be forced to do.

I was a goddamn Trojan horse, and even if I had known the details, I couldn't warn them about what was coming. Pestilence had seen to that.

Fuck my fucking life.

"I didn't only let you out for my own purposes," she whispered. "You need to see Remi. The doctor said it's bad, that we should prepare for the worst and say our goodbyes."

"What?" I tried to spin around, but she held me fast, my muscles no match for her vampiric strength.

"He's been quarantined and . . . I don't know what's going to happen. Ben said he's been in and out of lucidity, asking for you. I knew you'd never forgive yourself if you missed your chance to see him."

One last time.

She didn't say the words, but she may as well have for as heavy as they hung between us.

The sting of tears pricked the corners of my eyes, and I had to swallow against the sob that bubbled up.

"Are . . . fuck. Are you serious? Are we losing him?"

"I don't know. But it seems we've been in the market for miracles a lot lately, and I'm afraid they're in short supply."

"Where is he?"

"Why don't we shower and get dressed and I'll take you to him?"

Part of me wanted to say fuck the shower, but I'd basically been living in my own filth besides a few half-hearted sponge baths, so a shower was definitely in order.

She released me and threaded our fingers, giving me a tug as she led us to the attached bathroom. I stared at it unseeing for a moment, my head swimming with the possibility of losing Remi again so soon. Why was it that one or all of us was always under the threat of imminent death? Couldn't we just enjoy each other for one fucking second before the rug was pulled from beneath us?

What did a half-demon hacker have to do to get a happily ever after around here?

"Asher?"

"Hmm?"

"Shower."

"Right . . . shower, and then . . ."

She shoved me gently into the steam-filled stall. "And then you go see Remi."

Something about the way she said it had me looking back at her through the spray of warm water. "What will you be doing?"

Translation: what could possibly be more important than being by his side?

"I'm going to keep searching for that miracle."

CHAPTER ELEVEN

ROSIE

Asher's knuckles were white as he gripped the steering wheel and drove us into town. It hurt my heart to see him so tense and twisted up inside. But I felt the same. We were losing Remi, and so far, we hadn't been able to do a forking thing about it.

Not so long ago, it had been Remi and I desperate to save Asher, and now, here we were, tables turned. Would we ever get a chance to simply be happy? Not if Pestilence had anything to say about it.

Then I guess we have to ensure that bitch doesn't get a chance to open her fat mouth.

"You're looking mighty fierce over there, princess. Wanna share with the class?"

I blushed. "Just giving myself a little pep talk."

His lips twitched, but that did nothing to ease the storm clouds in his eyes. "Okay. Let me know when you're ready to fill me in. That looked like a lot more than a pep talk."

He took my hand, the firm squeeze doing wonders for my nerves, but then thoughts of losing them all hit me hard and fast. First, it had been me running from Gavin, then Ben accused of murder, followed by Asher and his curse-turned-possession, and now Remi wasting away. Not to mention, I forking died and came back just in time for Pestilence to kick off the Apocalypse.

It was constantly one thing after another with no time for us to breathe, let alone wrap our brains around any of these catastrophes. I was walking a tightrope, and if I lost my balance, I'd lose them.

My chest grew painfully tight, and I could barely draw a full breath.

"Princess?"

"I love you, Asher. I hope you know that."

"Rosie, what's going through your head? Is there something you aren't telling me? I thought it was Remi we needed to say goodbye to, so why does it sound like you're trying to do the same with me?"

"It feels like ages since I've been able to tell you. If Pan hadn't agreed to give you back, I might never have seen you again, and I don't want us to waste any more time by keeping our feelings close to the vest. The state Remi's in . . . It's clear to me none of us knows how this is going to end, especially with the game Pestilence has begun and the part we all seem to be unwillingly playing in it. I just . . . I need you to understand how deep my feelings are. In case . . . in case . . ."

"I know. I always knew, even when Pan had me locked away. We'll fix it. We'll stop her."

"How?"

He shook his head. "We'll find a way. Your brother and his motley crew stopped it once. We can too."

I let out a hysterical laugh. "Sunday stopped it by having a baby. That's not exactly in the cards for me." Then I sobered, my voice small when I asked, "Asher, is this all my fault?"

"What? Why would you say that?"

I chewed my bottom lip as I searched for the right words. "War came for Noah, Sunday, and her other mates. Is Pestilence here for me? Does this have something to do with the Blackthorne line? With my blood? It always comes back to the blood of the sun. Pan was collecting it. I thought it was because he was a demon and they liked their trophies. But he's her son."

Asher looked like he desperately wanted to say something, his mouth opening and closing like a fish.

A little thought niggled in the back of my mind. Earlier, Asher said he couldn't tell me what was worrying him, not that he didn't *want* to. Perhaps he was being manipulated somehow, prevented from speaking directly about his mother or her plans. It certainly seemed in keeping with what I'd learned about demons and the horsewomen. And I'd seen a spell like this in action before when it came to the secret fight nights my shifter twins were required to attend.

"Asher, are you trying to tell me something but unable to?"

He nodded. "Try asking me that another way," he said, frustration giving his voice an edge as he parked at The Tip and shut off the engine.

"Um . . . blink once for yes and twice for no?"

"Go ahead."

A thought I'd long tried to suppress swam to the forefront of my mind. It was my secret fear. The one thing I hadn't allowed myself to consider because it was too horrible a possibility. But the time for denial was over.

Taking a deep breath, I asked, "Is Pestilence using my blood to end the world?"

He stared hard at me, then blinked once. I waited, hoping his lids would lower a second time. They didn't.

"Brilliant. Just bloody brilliant."

"Pun intended?"

It took a second for the joke to register, and when it did, it had the intended effect. I let out a huff of misery-laced laughter, my eyes misting with tears. "I can't be the reason good people die, Asher. I just can't. I don't want to hurt anybody."

"It's not you doing this."

"It may as well be."

"From the sound of things, this goes way beyond me and you and the other guys. I mean, think about it. Pestilence had this in motion the day she got knocked up by my dad. That was at least a few years before you were even born, so how could it possibly be your fault? You're a means to an end."

"Thanks."

"No, I just mean, if it wasn't you, it would have been somebody else. Honestly, if anyone's to blame, it's probably me. I'm the one you came to for help, right? That can't be a coincidence."

"It's not your fault."

Gentle blue irises trained on me, he reached out and tucked a stray lock of hair behind my ear. "It's no one's fault but hers. And maybe Pan's."

Heaving a long sigh, he opened his door and got out before walking around to mine. As soon as he opened my door, I asked, "How do we stop her?"

"Good fucking question. I really wish I had the answer."

Frowning, I let myself finally accept what I needed to do. What I'd been hoping to avoid doing since the people who just might have the answer had already more than done their part. "I think it's time for me to have a little chat with my brother and his wife. Maybe Noah can give me some insight into dealing with a devious monster-in-law."

"You Blackthornes sure know how to pick them."

Taking his hand in mine, I squeezed it. "Technically it's fate who picks for us, but I wouldn't have it any other way."

"Me neither."

He released my hand and instead slipped his arm around my waist, pulling me against his side as we used my spare set of keys and made our way through the empty bar and up the stairs to the apartment.

I was eager to see Ben, to wrap myself in his scent and make sure he was okay. Every time I called to check in, I could hear the turmoil in his voice. The stress of this situation had brought his stammer to the forefront, a sure sign he was struggling. And Remi . . . Part of me didn't want to see him this way; the other wanted to cling to him for dear life.

No, Rosie. It's better to know. No more burying your head in the sand. Remi needs you. They all need you. You have to be strong for them. And if that means bearing witness to Remi's pain and Ben and Asher's grief, then that is what you are going to do.

Not so long ago, I would have had a very different reaction to the day's revelations about the part my blood played in this awful plague. I would have run in a misguided attempt to save the men I loved rather than stay and fight. But no more. My days of running were over.

If Pestilence wanted to try and take my mates—or anyone else I cared about, for that matter—she was going to have to go through me. Because I wasn't letting them go. Not for her or anything.

I stopped just outside the apartment door, pulling myself out of Asher's hold and facing him as he reached for the knob.

"Aren't you coming in?"

"Not yet. Tell Ben I'll be there soon. I have to make a phone call."

"Come on, Noah," I grumbled, pacing in the quiet of the empty bar as I waited for him to answer the video call.

When the screen finally opened and Sunday appeared instead of my brother, I had to choke down a frustrated sigh.

"Rosie? Wow, it's good to see your face. Noah and Caleb filled me in on what's been going on with you. I'm so glad you're okay."

"Okay might be a bit of a stretch."

Her pretty face went from pleased to concerned in a matter of seconds. "What's wrong?"

"So, remember how you found yourself in the middle of a showdown with War?"

"Uh, yeah, I'd consider that a pretty memorable experience."

"It seems I've found myself in a similar situation."

Sunday visibly paled, the pulse in her neck thrumming wildly. Before I could blink, there were four figures behind her, stoic and silent as she swallowed. "She's back?"

"Not War. Pestilence."

Noah joined her on the couch, and the other three stood together, Kingston surprisingly silent. I suppose after what they'd been through, none of them took the threat of a repeat occurrence lightly.

"What are you talking about, Rosie?" my brother asked, his expression drawn.

"Pestilence is here, and it's clear to me now that I've been her target. I need to stop her."

Caleb heaved a weary sigh before raking a hand through his hair and stalking away, grumbling something in Irish under his breath.

Noah turned back toward the other two men. "Go after him. See if you can help. He's been a wreck since returning, and now I see why."

"I'm so sorry for bringing him and the rest of you into this. We had no idea what we were dealing with, I swear to you."

Sunday took a deep breath. "Don't you dare apologize. This isn't your fault. I'd hoped we would have more time before one of the other three tried their hand at ending the world. I guess that was too much to ask for. And none of us imagined it would be someone close to us at the heart of the next round." Her voice wavered on the last.

A baby's cry filtered through the phone, causing Noah and Sunday to tense. He leaned close to his wife and pressed a kiss to her temple. "Go on, dove. You take care of Edie, and I'll help my sister. It's going to be all right. I promise."

As soon as Sunday left the room, I knew things were even worse than he'd let on.

"Noah?"

"What's been happening? How do you know for certain it's Pestilence?"

"I can't believe Caleb didn't tell you."

"If he made a promise he wouldn't, he'd have taken your secret to the grave."

I filled him in on everything: the deal with Pan and how he'd stolen samples of my blood, Asher's possession and surprise parentage, Remi's illness, along with the other supernaturals in town. My eyes brimmed with tears after I finished bringing him up to speed. "I don't know what to do."

"The first thing you need to do is talk to Aunt Callie. She may be a spirit, but she will be able to help you research this plague. Without her, sun sickness would still be ravaging our kind."

I nodded, hands trembling as I fought the urge to fall apart. I'd already considered the same. It was heartening that he also thought she might be able to assist me.

"And the next?"

"Find Pestilence and kill the bitch."

My laugh was filled with derision. "Great, sounds easy. Why hadn't I thought of that?"

"I mean it, Rosie. This won't end until you take her out. It's not going to be easy. Fate brought you your mates for a reason. It will likely take all of you together to defeat her."

I couldn't help but be a little disappointed my brother didn't have anything more enlightening to share with me. "Any other pearls of wisdom for me?"

"Don't trust anyone. She could be wearing the face of your dearest friend at this point. If we learned anything from War, it's that the horsewomen love to hide in plain sight."

"I guess that means Pan comes by it honestly, then," I muttered.

"What was that?"

"Nothing."

He heaved a sigh. "You have to stop her."

"And what if I fail?"

"You can't. Don't make me break my promise to Sunday. Everything depends on you now."

"Great. No bloody pressure."

"You can do this, Winnie. You were chosen for a reason."

My heart turned over at the nickname, even though my voice was wooden as I replied, "For my blood, you mean."

"No. That could have been any of us, but you and your mates were the ones selected. That means *you* are the only ones who can stop it."

"I didn't sign up for this, Noah. All I wanted was a simple, happy life."

"Well, that was your first mistake. You're a Blackthorne. When was simple ever part of the equation?"

My gaze flicked to the stairs, and I must not have done a good job of hiding my emotions because Noah offered me a pitying glance. "Go. He needs you. I'll contact Callie and let her know to get in touch."

"I love you, Noah."

"And I you."

The phone went black as he ended the call, and I stood there, shaking, terrified, and filled with resolve.

This bitch was going down.

CHAPTER
TWELVE
REMI

The soft creak of my bedroom door as it opened had me forcing myself to sit up as much as possible. I didn't want to worry my brother by showing him just how bad things were, but I wasn't sure how much longer I could hang on. Every breath hurt. My entire body was one persistent ache. And I could no longer distinguish between being hot or cold. I was constantly sweating *and* shivering, but no amount of cold showers or fuzzy blankets seemed to make a difference.

"I'm fine, Ben. I just need to sleep," I said through a fit of coughing. Fuck, was that blood? Was I coughing up blood? How would I hide *that* from him?

"It's me, Remi."

My belly did that stupid swooping thing when I heard Asher's voice. I wanted to believe it was him, but my mind had tricked me before. More than once. Ben didn't know about that either.

The hallucinations, I mean. He knew about Pan's deception . . . obviously.

I tried to push myself up farther, but my arms shook and I fell back on my pillows in a cloud of feathers and coughs. "You . . . should probably . . . stay back."

"And I'll tell you the same thing I told Ben when he tried to get me to wear a mask. I'll be fine."

"You don't . . . know that. I'm . . . contagious." Christ, I was as bad as Ben with these coughing fits. Every sentence was a nightmare.

"I'm not afraid. My mom is literally Pestilence. I feel like that means I come with superimmunity or something."

I'd gotten used to the bitterness in his voice a long time ago, but it still made my chest ache a little to hear it now. We'd come so far since Rosie fell into my lap.

"Yeah, I heard. So . . . you're a demon now. Have any sexy new appendages we can play with?"

"You must not be that sick if you're making jokes."

I wish. "I'll be good as new soon."

Asher pulled the chair from the corner of the room closer to the bed and settled himself next to me, reaching for my hand.

I pulled away slowly because it fucking hurt to move. Thankfully my lungs seemed to have stopped drowning in sputum long enough for me to deliver a halfway decent comeback. "Please don't tell me you came to say goodbye. I'm really not here for all of that melodramatic lovey-dovey shit."

He snorted. "Are you kidding me? You live for that shit."

"True, but not when it revolves around me."

He cocked a brow.

"Okay, okay. *Fine.* I love when things revolve around me. But not like this. Not when you're sitting there looking like I killed your puppy."

"Deal with it, Mercer."

I sighed. "You know, the last time we were in this position, I seem to remember a lot more fun. I thought I was never going to see you again, and I still made you come. Talk about a happy ending. What the fuck kind of Faulkner bullshit is this?"

"Huh?"

"You know, *As I Lay Dying*? It's an American classic."

"Haven't heard of it. Besides, I doubt you could even get it up right now."

I attempted to wiggle my brows, fighting a wince at the throb in my head. "Is that a challenge?"

"No. Dammit, Remi, be serious for a minute. I—"

His voice was wavering, and fear shimmered in his eyes. He knew this was bad. I wasn't coming back from this, no matter how much I pretended otherwise. If I was going to get better, I would have started by now, but every day—honestly, every minute—only got worse.

"You're Pestilence's kid. Why don't you ask her to fix me?"

A weird expression crossed his face before he cleared his throat. "I can't. It's not like we have a . . . relationship. I've never even met the broad." He dragged his fingers across his jaw, then leveled a serious look on me. "We need to figure out what this is that's making you sick so we can fix it."

"Doc Krueger is already on it."

"Your doctor is named Krueger?"

"Might as well be."

"Talk about a missed opportunity."

"I know, right? That's what I said."

We shared a smile, but mine was more of a grimace, and his didn't reach his eyes. I sobered, finally taking his hand like he'd originally intended.

"This sucks."

"Yeah. It really does."

I couldn't hold back the terror anymore. Seeing him so heartbroken over me, knowing my nights with him tangled in the sheets while we . . . Oh God, I'd never be able to see his dick again. I loved his dick. It was perfect. Not as perfect as mine, but I was a tough act to follow. Only one person in the world came close, and I'd bet my last fucking dollar Bentley couldn't dick someone down as good as me.

"I'd offer you a farewell handy, but I don't have the stamina."

Asher's shocked laugh was a welcome distraction from the anxiety. "Meh, I really like your mouth better anyway. Softer. Warmer. Wetter."

"I think you've confused my mouth with Rosie's cunt."

We both let out soft moans of appreciation.

"Maybe I am. I guess you'll have to get better and remind me."

"I'm going to miss this." I'd like to say my voice remained steady, but it was practically filled with gravel.

"Me too."

"Fighting with you was always my favorite form of foreplay."

He swallowed convulsively. "Was?"

"Yeah." That damn cough took hold again.

Asher grabbed my hand and held tight, his panic evident in the way he said my name. "Remi."

"I'm not . . . leaving you yet."

His laugh was uneven as he tried to smile. "You had me worried there for a second. So why *was* that your favorite? You have a new one?"

"Yeah. When we gang up on her and"—I sucked in a wheezing breath before I could finish my sentence—"make her blush."

Asher gave me a lopsided grin. "That is pretty great."

"She's great. She gave me you." Asher tried to deny it, but I squeezed his hand. "We both know this"—I gestured weakly between us—"never would have been more than hate sex without her. Where is she, by the way?"

"Trying to figure out how to save your ass. She's calling in reinforcements."

My eyelids felt like they had ten-pound weights attached to them. Every time I blinked, it took me longer and longer to open them again.

"You look tired, Remi."

“Gee, thanks. That’s just my fucking face, Asher.”

He cupped my cheek and brushed his lips over my forehead. “Nah, your face is fucking gorgeous, and you know it, Mercer. It’s your eyes that are exhausted. You should get some sleep. I’ll go check in with Ben.”

He made to stand, but I used every last bit of strength I had to hold him in place. “Stay. Please. I don’t want to be alone anymore. My dreams . . . they’re awful.”

“S-stay? Are you sure?”

“Yeah. Would you hold me? Just for a little while. I need to feel your arms around me. I missed you.” I dipped as the bed did, and Asher slipped in next to me, tucking my body against his. “Mmm . . . you smell good. I’m just gonna close my eyes for a minute, okay?”

“Okay,” he whispered, his voice tight with emotion.

“Promise you won’t leave.”

“Not until you’re asleep.”

“Asher?”

“Yeah?”

“If I die . . .”

“I’ll bring you back from the dead and make you answer for leaving me.”

I snuggled back against him, trying to get as close as I could. “I’m serious. If I die, I need you to know how much I—” This goddamned cough was ruining my swoony moment.

He held me tighter, his palm pressed to my chest, right over my heart. When I was done, my gasps uneven and labored, he drew his own ragged breath, body shuddering. “I know, Remi. I love you too.”

“And they say demons don’t have hearts,” I mumbled, my mind already drifting off and my voice slow and thick with sleep.

“According to Pan, they don’t.”

“Hmm . . . guess you’re defective.”

“Guess so.”

“Lucky me.”

He pressed his lips to my nape and whispered, "Go to sleep, Remington. I'll make sure only the good dreams get in, okay?"

"My hero."

His strained laugh was the last thing I heard before darkness claimed me.

CHAPTER THIRTEEN

ASHER

I waited until the door snicked shut behind me before falling the fuck apart. I couldn't keep the sobs at bay, no matter how hard I tried. Everything I'd held back just came to the surface in a rush. God, was my chest caving in? It sure felt like it.

"All right, all right. That's quite enough of that. It's bad enough feeling my feelings. I don't need to wallow in yours as well. Look at the bright side—he's a dreadful bore anyway. No big loss, right? You'll get over it."

"If that's your way of consoling me, you are garbage at it."

"Well, can you blame me? It was my first time. I thought I did rather well, all things considered."

I tried to shove Pan away and into some mind prison like he always did to me, but it didn't work. The fucking nuisance was still there, eavesdropping on my heartache. So, instead, I slammed the back of my head against the door, using the pain to distract me from the tears I couldn't seem to stop.

"Asher, h-hey. D-don't hurt yourself." Ben's voice pulled me out of my wallowing.

I sucked in a breath and opened my eyes, but the second they landed on him, I burst into a fresh round of sobs. Who the fuck thought identical twins were a good idea anyway?

"Sh-shit." Ben's arms were around me, the shifter reeling me into his large frame that was so much like Remi's, but also completely different. "It's o-okay, m-man. It's o-okay."

"No, it's fucking not. He's dying, and I'm losing him. How can you say it's okay?"

"I-if I don't, I'll f-fall apart t-too."

"Do me a favor and stop lying to us both. Just join the damn club."

A tremor worked its way through him as his breath hitched. We held on to each other, each of us mourning the man in the bedroom behind me, even though we hadn't lost him yet. With the way things were going, it was only a matter of time.

He gave me a firm squeeze and released me before clapping me on the shoulder with a harsh sniff. His cheeks were wet with tear tracks, but I didn't say anything as he rubbed the back of his hand across one. "C-come on. E-everyone's meeting d-downstairs."

"Everyone?"

"Y-yeah. R-Rosie made some c-calls."

I wiped at my eyes, taking a shuddering breath or two before I finally pulled it together enough to face them all. I never wanted to do this again. This was what happened when you loved someone. When you made yourself vulnerable. They up and died. When you thought about it, falling in love was just an inevitable journey to abandonment. It was terrible. As Remi would say, zero out of ten stars. Would not recommend.

My mind was still churning as I followed Ben downstairs into the closed bar, where everyone was indeed waiting. Gavin stood like a vulture in the corner while Rosie spun toward us immediately. One look at my face and she was moving, blurring over and cocooning me in her warmth. Fuck, I was going to cry again. But as I sank into her embrace, her compassion and need to comfort me flowed through our bond, making it hard to care.

Okay . . . maybe this love thing wasn't all bad.

"I'm so sorry, Asher."

Fuck, I felt like such an asshole. Rosie was losing him too, and I was over here acting like the only one whose heart was breaking. Clinging to her tighter, I tried to offer her the same strength she was giving me. "Me too."

A light filled the room, making me tense and pull Rosie behind me as an uninvited visitor stepped through what I now realized was a portal that had opened in the middle of The Tip.

Oh fuck, what now? I couldn't deal with another crisis. I was wrung the hell out.

But as Moira Belladonna shook out her bone-white locks and leveled her stare on us, something in me relaxed. "Okay bitches, I've never had Alaska on my to-do list, yet I've been here twice now. Tell me there's some kind of loyalty stamp card. Five trips and the sixth is free. Or at least I get to go home with a beaver or something."

"You help us get through this and we'll erect a statue in your honor," Rosie promised with a laugh as she peeked around my shoulder, her arms wrapped around my waist.

"Oh, well, you should have done that after the first visit, babycakes. Get on it."

With a squeeze, Rosie let me go and moved to where Moira stood. "Thank you for coming."

"Yeah, Moira. Thanks for coming, but why the fuck are you here?" I asked, my tone only just on this side of friendly.

She quirked a brow, not impressed with me in the slightest. "Because your woman called, and I couldn't possibly miss the end of the world . . . again."

"Why'd you call Moira? I thought you were going to call your brother?"

"I did, and then I called Moira."

"But . . . why?"

"Why wouldn't she call me for help? I'm a pretty big deal, Asher.

As you already know, seeing as how you yourself called me for help not that long ago."

"Oh, sorry, are you suddenly a healer? Because last I checked, you were a witch who barely graduated and was on the verge of being kicked out of your coven."

"Ouch. And to be fair, it was a miracle any of us graduated. You know, since the school was all but destroyed by a legion of rogue demons." She pursed her lips and tapped her chin thoughtfully. "Do you think your brother was there? Were you? I hear you're slumming it with their kind now. Do you like it when Rosie calls you a bad boy? Does she make you wear horns while she spanks you? At least now there's an aura of authenticity when you play demon and angel with her."

"Enough of your jokes, Belladonna," Gavin grumbled. "This is hardly the time."

"Oh please, you're just upset anyone besides you gets to do the spanking these days." She rolled her eyes, sighing heavily. "It's called a bright side, Donoghue. But I guess you wouldn't know anything about that, would you? You just sit there in your stuffy suit and brood. 'I'm a dark and stormy vampire, and I only have one expression. RBF. Resting brood face.'"

Rosie, Ben, and I exchanged looks, our thoughts clearly all running along the lines of 'she's not wrong' if the smiles and unexpected laughs we were all trying to suppress were any clue.

Gavin opened his mouth to retort, but she held up a hand, her eyes flashing dangerously. "I'm not here for you. Mind your manners." Moira turned her attention back to Rosie. "Now. You mentioned something about a spell we need to break?"

"Well, like I said, it's Asher. He can't talk about anything that involves Pestilence's plan. I think she has him spelled."

Pan's voice infiltrated my mind as soon as our mother was mentioned. *"She's adorably earnest, isn't she? Poor lamb. She wants to save you so badly, but she won't be able to. Nothing can get those words from your mouth. This witch doesn't hold a candle to Mummy's power."*

Moira's eyes landed on me, and she made a musing sound as she gave me a slow once-over. "Wouldn't be the first time. What better way is there to ensure secrecy? But I hate to disappoint you, sweetie. If Pesty is behind the silencing spell, I'm no use to you. I might be a badass witch, but not even I'm strong enough to take down a horsewoman on my own."

"See. Told you so."

I fought a sigh. *"You don't have to be so smug about it."*

"Yes, I really do. I must say, I'm enjoying your discomfort so much. You're bursting to share everything you know, so eager to help. But even if you could, you've only heard a fraction of it."

This asshole. He knew so much more than he was letting on. He'd literally been part of her plot until I don't fucking know when.

I knew exactly how to get to him. Attack his pride. *"And they say I got the brains in the family."*

"Who says that? No one."

"People. People say it."

"You wish."

"Okay, prove it, dungeon master. Show me you know more than I do. Because I think you're bluffing."

"Nice try. I am in your brain, you bellend. I know what you're trying to do."

"They're doing it again," Gavin groused. "It's like watching a silent film. All strange expressions and no volume."

"Pan knows more than any of us."

"Brilliant. Let's get him out here, and we can make him talk. I'll get the chains." Gavin's excitement was a little unsettling.

Rosie's shoulders drooped. "He can't. Per the terms of our deal, Asher is in control for at least another . . . day, give or take a couple hours."

Gavin glowered, but it was Ben who jumped in. "Wh-what deal? H-haven't you l-learned your l-lesson?"

She tossed him a defiant look. "Give me a little credit. This one benefits us. Pan can't do anything to hurt us, and for every minute he's in control, Asher gets *two*."

Gavin huffed. "Well, it certainly doesn't benefit us now."

"Oh goody, I love sowing seeds of discord without even trying."

Rosie wilted a bit at Gavin's observation, and Ben curled her into his side, comforting her as he shot Gavin a chastising glare. "N-no need to m-make her feel worse."

"I'm a sadist," Gavin said, but he was quick to take Rosie from him and press a kiss to her forehead, murmuring, "Apologies, petal."

"It's okay. You weren't wrong."

He tucked a finger under her chin and lifted her face to his. "I rarely am, but that's no excuse for being an arse." Then he kissed her like the rest of us weren't standing around watching.

"Well, they just love passing you around, don't they?" Moira said with a knowing smirk.

Rosie blushed as she pulled away from her duke. "Only when I'm lucky."

Moira made a honking sound and put a finger in each ear. "Nope. Don't want to hear about it. Save the kinky stuff for girls' night."

Then the witch strode toward me, only stopping when her face was practically in my chest. She reached up and placed both hands on my jaw, tilting my head down.

"Can I help you?" I asked.

"No, but I may be able to help you." She stared into my eyes, a strange trance-like quality to her focus. "He really is in there, isn't he?"

"I already told you that." Gavin's retort was a sharply thrown barb.

"Excuse me for wanting to check your sources."

"I like this one. She's a spitfire."

"I'll remind you that you said so when you're the one she's coming after." Then I shifted my focus back to the witch and her question. "Yeah, he's in there. Think you can do something about it?"

"Well, not permanently. But I know a way to help him come out and play for a while without affecting the terms of your deal."

"Are you sure the girl isn't part demon? We do love a loophole."

"How c-can you h-help?"

Moira turned to Ben. "Well, he's sharing a body with this . . . parasite."

"Oi. I am far more complex than a parasite."

I nodded, confirming her assertion while ignoring Pan's complaint.

"Perfect." She clapped her hands like that was the greatest thing she'd ever heard.

"How can you possibly think that's good news?" Gavin asked.

"Well, I may not be able to do anything about the spell, but a demon I can handle. And I happen to be an expert at astral projection."

"A-astral what?"

"Pro-ject-tion." She gave Rosie a concerned look. "Are you sure this one's your mate? He's cute, but he doesn't seem too bright. Maybe it's a shifter thing? All sausage, no stuffing." Ben growled, and Moira rolled her eyes. "Oh, calm down, Fido. I was teasing. It's my love language."

"Forgive me i-if I'm n-not in the m-mood to be teased. M-my brother's upst-stairs dying and w-we're wasting t-time with j-jokes."

If anyone would approve of ill-timed jokes, it would be Remi, but I wasn't about to mention it. Ben had a point.

"How do we do it?" I asked.

"You don't. I do."

Rosie's brow furrowed. "Do we need supplies for that? I'm not sure Asher can force Pan's soul out for a walkabout."

"It would be fun to see you try."

"Shut up, Pan."

"I thought the whole point of this was that you wanted to hear me talk."

"Not to me."

"You really need to make up your mind."

"I hate you. There, mind made up."

"Tell me something I don't know, brother dear."

"Guess Pan had feelings about that," Gavin said, proving just how closely he was monitoring me. I got the sense he didn't much trust me, but instead of making me defensive, it was actually a relief. If I was some sort of secret sleeper agent for my mother, Gavin would be right there to make sure Rosie was safe.

"Pan has feelings about everything," I grumbled.

"Ugh, don't remind me."

Rosie and Moira must have continued their conversation while Pan distracted me, because the witch was pulling a little satchel from a backpack I hadn't noticed.

"What's that?" I asked.

"My astral projection kit, obviously."

"Th-that's something you c-carry around?"

"What, like most witches don't?"

"N-none I've m-met."

"Hmm, their loss. You never know when you'll need to wander, and I can't always rely on Ash to make my soul leave my body at the drop of a hat." She wiggled her brows, and I knew she wasn't talking about her wife's magic skills.

"Are you sure that's safe?" I asked. "Letting him roam free?"

"He won't have a real body. But he can still talk, and this way we can all hear what he has to say without playing the supernatural equivalent of telephone."

Rosie stepped forward. "So what are we waiting for? Let's do this."

With a smirk, Moira dropped the velvet satchel onto the bartop. "Okay, but just remember, you might not like everything you hear."

"It's Pan. I don't expect to."

CHAPTER FOURTEEN

GAVIN

I didn't like this. Not one bit. Pan was a wily sort, and even though she promised he couldn't walk free, I didn't trust him.

Stalking around the bar, I began rooting through the supplies stored beneath the polished wood. What kind of establishment was this? Nothing was where common sense would dictate it to be.

"Wh-what the f-fuck are y-you d-doing?"

"I'm trying to find some pissing salt, but apparently you lot don't think it's an important ingredient to keep stored in a sensible location."

"S-salt?"

"For the circle."

"C-circle?"

I rolled my eyes and sighed. "To keep the demon contained, obviously. Keep up, Bentley."

His brow wrinkled in confusion. "But h-he's not r-really going to b-be here. Just his s-spirit. Can y-you contain a s-spirit?"

"I don't know, Bentley. Care to risk it?"

"You guys, we don't need a circle." Moira crossed her arms over her chest, then huffed and looked to Roslyn. "Are they always like this?"

Roslyn simply shrugged. Clever girl, opting to keep her answer to herself.

"It's a good thing I decided to stay and supervise. This could easily turn into a disaster."

"I don't want him getting loose, Belladonna. He's caused enough of a ruckus as is." My gaze shot to Asher, who'd sat himself on a barstool and waited patiently.

I'd spent enough time supervising him recently not to mistake his calm exterior for a lack of attention or interest. The cogs were spinning, his mind a flurry of activity as he processed everything going on around him. The man was surprisingly astute. He'd made a series of rather enlightening observations while we'd been researching together to pass the hours of his captivity. I found myself curious to know what he made of the situation we'd found ourselves in. Would it be a relief to be free of Pan's ramblings? Or another kind of torture, knowing it was only a temporary reprieve?

"We don't need a circle. And I don't want to keep Asher trapped because of your paranoia."

Asher raised a hand. "I also would like to not be trapped. Not that anyone asked me."

Roslyn sidled up to him and wrapped her arms around his waist. "We aren't going to trap you, I promise. Especially when I worked so hard to free you. Besides, if Moira deems it unnecessary, it's unnecessary. Full stop." She shot me a look.

"Fine. Let's get on with this, then. I'd like some time with my mate. I have certain needs only she can see to."

"D-don't we all?"

"How can you think about sex while Remi is upstairs dying?" Asher asked, his expression dark.

"I was referring to my need to feed, not fuck."

"Isn't that the same thing for you bloodsuckers?"

"Hey," Rosie protested.

Asher frowned and raked a hand through his hair. "Shit, sorry. I'm just . . . overwhelmed."

"It's okay. I get it."

"Wouldn't it be great if one of these days we could just be regular whelmed? But noooo, Apocalypse drama everywhere we turn." Moira cracked her knuckles and unrolled the velvet package with a flourish, revealing an honest-to-God witchy emergency kit. She pulled free what looked like a hunk of smoky-looking white stone with crystals jutting out every which way.

"Asher, you hold this."

He took the rock from her and gave it a dubious glance. "Oookay."

"All you need to do is focus on Pan."

Given the way his expression twisted, Pan had some sort of comeback for that. I could practically hear his purred, *"Oh yes, focus on and adore me. Worship me and my glorious tail. We deserve it."*

I groaned and rolled my eyes, not checking the impulse to pantomime a wank.

Moira caught me, one of her brows raised. "Uh . . . you need a moment?"

I actually blushed as I smoothed my already pristine shirt. "No. My thoughts wandered."

"Clearly."

"Guys. Wh-what's that?" Bentley asked, pointing at Asher.

"Um, something's happening," Roslyn said, pulling both of us from our sidebar conversation.

Something certainly was. Pan's form appeared next to Asher, a cocksure grin on his lips. "You rang?"

Moira turned her face toward Roslyn, though her eyes never left the fully formed purple demon. "I get it now."

"Really, but he's not even your type . . ."

"I mean, I could do without the penis. But the combination of danger and narcissism? That's totally my bag. And he's purple to boot."

"D-don't encourage him." Bentley's hands were balled into fists as he crept closer to Roslyn. I didn't blame him. We were all protective of our little mate.

"Oh, please, do continue. I could remove the trousers if you really want a good look."

Moira wrinkled her nose. "Ugh, you ruined it."

"He usually does," Asher muttered with a sigh.

"I have a hard limit when it comes to toxic masculinity. Okay, demon. Tell us everything you know." Give the witch an interrogation room and a harsh spotlight, and she could be a cop in a bad police procedural.

"Well, in the beginning there was nothing . . ."

"We d-don't have fucking t-time for this sh-shit," Bentley grumbled.

"Yes, demon, we've all heard that story. Fast forward to the relevant bits, would you?" I drawled, impatient to get this over with.

"What do you want to know, and why should I tell you?"

Asher scoffed. "Always what's in it for you, huh?"

"Of course. What other reason is there?"

"Un-fucking-believable," Asher groaned.

"What?" Pan asked, looking genuinely confused.

"Just t-tell us everything," Bentley said, arms crossed over his chest as he leaned against the bar.

"I need you to be a little more specific. I already tried to start from the beginning, but you didn't like that."

The shifter growled. "W-why Rosie?"

Pan sighed, inspected his nails, then flicked his gaze to her, raking down her form with unmasked hunger. "Aside from the obvious?"

"I don't think it's so obvious," Roslyn said, moving until she stood just in front of Bentley. Almost as if she was trying to protect him. The shifter placed a large palm on the nape of her neck, fingers running gently over the mark he'd given her.

"Pity for you, then. If I had my body right now, I'd take you into the back room and show you."

"Pan," Asher warned.

"Asher," he sniped back, but when his gaze landed on Roslyn, his amused expression dropped. "Oh, all right. Her blood, of course. Magic blood, specifically blood like hers, is hard to come by. It's a perfect storm of timing, magic, and genetics."

"What do you mean by that?" I narrowed my eyes as I waited for him to answer me.

"She's a descendant of the Blackthorne bloodline, but more than that, she has the blood of the sun. That makes her part witch. Two supernatural species for the price of one. It didn't hurt that she was part human, too. It allowed my mother to craft her virus well. Maximum damage to supernatural DNA."

"Of c-course."

My gut clenched. Roslyn had a reputation from birth, along with her brothers. They'd saved our kind from sun sickness with their blood. "You're using our cure against us?" I whispered.

"And the penny drops. Poetic, isn't it? One of her better ideas, if I do say so myself."

"That's not all she's using," Asher said.

Pan blinked at him. "Was that supposed to be some sort of scathing announcement? You might need to work on that. It wasn't even humorous."

Asher lifted one shoulder. "Oh, I don't know. I find it pretty *humorous* that you're so quick to point out how Pestilence got one over on us, but you seem to have completely missed that she's done the same to *you.* She's using you, Pan. You're her number-one fall guy. The stooge who does her dirty work. You think of yourself as this massive part of her scheme, and yet she left you here as a way to get rid of you. You mean nothing to her. You are a means to an end."

His purple brows pulled together. "I . . . she trusted me to—"

"To be her fucking gopher. You collected the blood, gave it to her, and got dumped in Aurora Springs with the rest of the outcasts once she had what she needed. Where's your power? Your reward? You're trapped here, and if it weren't for the exorcism we tried, you wouldn't even have your own body."

Oh, this was delicious. Every thought was telegraphed in his expression as Asher's hard truths hit their mark. The rest of us just let the hacker keep going.

"How do you know she's not going to keep you imprisoned after she gets what she wants?"

Pan opened and closed his mouth, looking conflicted.

"That's what I thought," Asher said. "You blindly offer her your loyalty, and for what? Clearly, it's not a seat at her side, because she couldn't drop you fast enough. Maybe it's time you look around and smell the horse shit, big brother. You've been used. You want to get back at her? It's not too late to teach her a lesson. Ally yourself with her enemies. Hit her where it hurts."

"No. It's Rosie's fault. All of this is. I was supposed to get her blood and then keep her for myself as a prize when this was over. But you lot let her get killed, and then I got sent here to do my fucking job. I was nearly done, but she woke up and mated me. She marked me, made me hers, bound what constitutes my soul to her own, and now here I am. Ruined. Tainted by emotions a demon should never possess. Don't you see? She did this to me. This is all her fault. I wasn't ever meant to fall in love with her!"

Everyone in the room gaped at him. Bentley was the first to break the silence.

"Are y-you fucking k-kidding?"

"Holy shitballs," Moira whispered. "I thought Kingston was a disaster, but you're a whole disasterpiece."

No one laughed; they were too busy staring at Pan. Roslyn looked stricken, and the demon was no better. He seemed just as dumbfounded by his confession as the rest of us. Well, except for Asher. The hacker seemed pleased. Like he'd been in the midst of a chess game and had just called checkmate.

"Pan?" Roslyn said, moving closer.

The demon clamped his lips together and shook his head.

"Oh, come on," Asher groaned. "Stop dancing around it. You said it yourself. She's your mate. You love her. You aren't going to do anything to hurt her. So stop pretending like you are still Team Pestilence. You have to choose a side, Pan. And it seems to me you already have."

"Unless it's not real. What if it's all because she's . . ." Pan clammed up, but Asher kept pushing.

"A Queen? Bullshit. You're just as willing as the rest of us. But that brings up a good point. You reacted to her being a Queen earlier but wouldn't talk about it. Why does that mean so much to you?"

I leaned forward, my interest piqued. Asher and I had discovered quite a bit about the legendary vampiric beings through his illegal access to the Council's archives. But nothing that would explain why Pan or his horsewoman mother would care one way or the other. Could this be the piece of the puzzle I'd been looking for?

He shifted from foot to foot, his tail flicking.

"F-fucking tell us, P-Pan. Sh-she deserves to know." Bentley had threaded his fingers with Roslyn's. An attempt to stop her from going to the demon, one I would have used myself.

"The last time Mummy Dearest tried to kick off her Apocalypse was 1918."

"The Spanish Influenza," Asher murmured.

Pan shot him a withering glare. "Yes. Of course. Glad to see you're able to keep up."

"Obviously, she failed," Roslyn offered.

"Obviously. But here's the part you don't know. The answer to your question. There's a reason she's nursed her wounds this long before her next grand attempt. She nearly died herself in the process. Trust me, if she'd known what our Rosie would turn into . . . well. Let's just say there's not a chance in hell she would have been left alive."

"You're s-saying a lot w-without saying a d-damn thing."

But we didn't need him to elaborate. Given the topic at hand, I'd already pieced together what he'd merely hinted at. Casting a serious glance at each man in the room before stopping on Roslyn, I brought them up to speed.

"It was a Queen who stopped her."

~

Pan

This whole thing was bloody ridiculous. I'd been ambushed. Bamboozled, if you will. They dangled freedom in front of me like a carrot and then beat me with it. What was worse, I'd said the words aloud in front of all of them.

I love her.

If I could, I'd punch myself right in the face.

"Well, you got what you wanted. Send me back, witch."

The Belladonna heir blinked her long-lashed eyes at me, her hair transforming from bone white to an angry orange. "Watch your tone when you speak to me, demon."

"What are you going to do to me? I'm not even really here."

She smirked. "You'd be surprised what I can do with that little crystal there."

I wanted to be a cocky arsehole and taunt her, but I didn't have it in me. I was knackered. All my energy was drained by being forced to manifest my form through that stupid rock. "Let me be."

"Aw, is the wittle demon tired?"

Rosie crossed the room and put her palm on the witch's shoulder. "Moira, let him go. Today's been a lot for all of us."

I'd barely allowed myself to look at her since my impromptu confession. I could feel my little monster through our bond. Her questions, her surprise. But I wasn't ready to deal with any of it. Especially not in front of these knobheads.

"Fine. You're no fun."

Moira took the crystal from Asher, and with zero pomp and circumstance, I was back in his head, no longer on display.

My relief was instantaneous. I'd never felt so vulnerable or raw in my life. Usually, wearing my form came with a sense of power and invincibility, but in one conversation, they'd stripped me bare. Cutting me off at the knees and proving just what a fallacy that was.

Who knew I, Pan, would ever seek solace by hiding behind a mortal's face? Though I suppose there was no way to hide from the man himself. A theory he proved almost immediately.

"I need to fucking talk to you." Asher's incessant voice just wouldn't quit.

"I don't fucking care."

"We can do this in front of everyone, with me sharing all your thoughts with the class, or I can take this upstairs so you and I can have some privacy. It's your call, but it's happening."

Who did he think he was? I was the strong one. I was in control. Except they'd just proven that wasn't the case at all. I'd never been powerful. I'd been a pawn. A fool. And my mother had used me from day one.

Everything I've ever known was upside down. A lie.

What was I supposed to do with that?

I'd gained a mate and lost a mother. But had I ever really had a mother to begin with?

Rosie had been mine since the moment she summoned me. And I'd never felt so drawn to any creature in my existence. Had Mum inadvertently thrown me headlong into my future, or was it damnation?

"You mean her *damnation. You're on our side now, remember?"*

Was I?

I suppose I had betrayed my mother with the truths I'd revealed. But she deserved it. She started it by leaving me a hostage in this stupid vessel. Turnabout was fair play, wasn't it?

Why was I giving any more of my time to my mother's cause

when she tossed me in the bin like so much rubbish? Why, when I could have Rosie, roam free, and create my own perfect chaos?

In for a penny . . .

"All right. Let's go upstairs and have a chat then."

CHAPTER FIFTEEN

ASHER

The apartment was exactly as we'd left it, a sickroom for the man I loved, the place I'd first realized how important Rosie was to me, and now the location where I'd have a heart-to-black-twisted-heart with my brother.

"Purple."

"What?"

"My heart, it's purple. Just like the rest of me."

"Jesus Christ, do you ever stop?"

"No. Ask Rosie."

The rough, rattling sound of Remi's labored breaths was a strange sort of comfort to me. I should be torn up to hear them, but each and every one meant he was still here. I hadn't lost him yet.

"So, we're alone now. What was so important that we had to discuss it right the bloody fuck now?"

"You and I have to come to some kind of truce if we're going to love the same woman and share a damn body."

"I thought we already took care of that with the Rosie Rule."

"Not good enough. I need to know you're not going to fuck this up for

me with her. I've never had a family before, Pan. I'm so close to having one now. I can't let you ruin this."

I could feel his surprise rippling through me. If I had to guess, I'd say it was the first time anyone had approached Pan from a place of such vulnerable honesty. I was practically on my knees, begging him to let me have my life back. No, to let me finally *start* my life. I'd been cast aside as a child and then on the run for longer than I can remember. I was so fucking tired of it. I wanted roots. I wanted Rosie. And dammit, I wanted Remi too. I wasn't ready to let go of any of it after finally getting a taste of what life together could be like.

"It's too quiet in here, Asher."

My heart fucking stopped as I tuned in to the absolute stillness of the apartment. "Remi, fuck. No."

I ran. No, I bolted with everything in me to the bedroom.

"Remi!"

There was no answer as I crashed through the door to his room. Remi was deathly still, his skin pallid, drops of blood dotting his chin, dark circles ringing his closed eyes.

"Jesus, Remi. Come on. Don't do this. Don't fucking leave me."

I held his hand. God, it was still warm. I'd been in the apartment, fighting with fucking Pan about my own selfish needs while Remi lay here dying. Alone.

"Asher. Asher. ASHER!"

"WHAT?" I shouted, not bothering to speak in my head.

"He's not gone . . . yet. I'd recognize a death rattle anywhere. You've got a handful of breaths left at best."

For once, Pan's words made me feel marginally better. At least I'd be here in his final moments.

"Good fucking Lucifer. Are you really that stupid?"

"Excuse me for not having a goddamned medical degree. I don't know what to do. He's not breathing, and I think mouth-to-mouth is out of the question."

But then I saw it, a strident breath lifting Remi's chest. Too weak.

Too difficult. And much further apart from his last than it should have been.

"Tick tock, brother."

"You. Are. Not. Helping."

"Aren't I? Why is it you are missing the most obvious thing? A bloody child would have put it together by now."

Before I could argue, a vision of Cupid the cat hit me hard. But I watched the memory as though from above as little Asher brought that fucking cat back from the brink of death. I had never realized what truly happened that day. But now it all made sense.

"How do I do it? I don't know what to do. Help me."

"How the fuck am I supposed to know? I make people sick, not better."

"Fucking guess, you asshole. Before I stab you with a Q-Tip."

He sighed. *"I don't know, just think about it. Touch him and heal him. You did it as a child. It can't be that hard."*

A hysterical sob left me. If Remi were awake right now, he'd have made a joke about that.

"Then wake him up, Asher. This is your last chance. I'm trying to help you. Satan knows why."

I didn't close my eyes. Instead, I stared at the man I loved with everything I had and let instinct guide me. Palm flat on his chest, I leaned over him and pressed my forehead to his. Tears I hadn't been able to hold back fell onto his cheeks as I whispered, "Don't you fucking die on me, Remington Mercer. I'm not done loving you yet."

"Gag."

"Stay the fuck out of this."

"I literally can't."

I tuned out the demon on my shoulder and focused on my shifter. "I need you, Remi. Rosie needs you. Please."

I replayed the memory of Cupid, of everything leading up to the cat coming back to life in my arms. Focusing hard on what I was feeling . . . what I was thinking . . . but all that I could really recall was the desperation.

"Not enough. Dig deeper."

I wanted to punch him and thank him all at the same time. What was that one thing I needed that I couldn't tap into?

"Oh your fucking God, Asher. YOUR LOVE. It was your love for that stupid fucking cat that saved him. Satan, save me from this idiot."

I was an idiot. It was my love. Had I never read a book in my life? Love was always the answer to every riddle.

"I love you, Remi. Love is hard for me. You know that, and you're fucking with me by testing me right now. I don't know how else I can say it." I straddled his hips and grabbed him by the shoulders, getting angry as my desperation ratcheted higher and higher. Shaking him, I continued hurling my love at him like it was a damn grenade just hoping it would hit the mark. "Wake the fuck up, you undeserving fucking llama."

"Uh . . . not exactly what I meant."

But I couldn't give a single fuck about the demon in my head because beneath me, Remi's eyes opened.

"I'm a wolf . . . you ass pastry."

My breath caught in my throat as I stared at the man under me. His eyes were clear and bright, color returning to his cheeks and lips. Fuck . . . he was alive. Not just alive, healed. His fever was gone. Not a single cough racked his big frame.

I'd done it.

I'd saved him.

I hiccuped a laugh as I pulled Remi up off the bed, clutching him to me. "I'll take that as a compliment so long as you never try to die on me again."

"Deal."

"I'm just gonna go ahead and add a Remi Rule. Do me a favor and don't need me again until you two finish up."

It was on the tip of my tongue to tell him I never needed him, but . . . Pan had proved me wrong. If not for him, I would never have pieced things together in time.

"Pan . . ."

"Oh hell, you're already disregarding orders."

"Thank you."

"Oh. Uh, you're welcome, I guess."

"Asher?" Remi asked, his palms gripping my thighs.

"Yeah?"

"What the fuck just happened?"

"I healed you."

"How?"

I was just as shocked as him. "Um, with the power of love, apparently."

Remi snickered. "Okay, Celine Dion."

"I think that was Huey Lewis and the News."

"Agree to disagree."

"How do you feel?" I asked, sobering slightly despite the giddy relief flowing through my veins.

"Stiff."

"Remi, come on. Be serious."

"If you would have given me a second to finish my sentence, you would have realized I *was* being serious. I didn't mean that kind of stiff. But if you give me a minute . . ." I groaned as he winked. "Stiff like I haven't moved in days."

"You haven't."

"How long was I . . ."

"Too long," I said, my voice cracking.

"That's oddly vague."

"To be honest, I missed a lot of it."

"Pan," he growled, trying to sit up.

I shoved him back down. "Not so fast. Pan is . . ." *God, how to explain this?* "Well, he's not so bad, I guess."

"What? He literally stole your body and took it for a joy ride."

"Well, yeah. But there were extenuating circumstances."

"Is it possible to get Stockholm in your own body?"

"I'll get you all caught up, I promise. We might need Rosie to fill in some blanks, but for now, all you need to know is that you were out of it for a while. But you're back now."

Remi grimaced. "I am. And I really need a fucking shower. Can we continue this conversation after I don't smell like five-day-old garbage?"

"You smell great to me."

"You're a terrible liar."

I pressed a kiss to his cheek because, honestly, I *was* lying, but I was just so damn happy he was awake and talking. I really didn't care that he had dried blood on his chin. But having just gone through my own bout of five-day funk, I could appreciate the desire to get clean. So I got off him and stood next to the bed, holding out a hand. "Come on. A shower sounds perfect."

"Is this going to be a group sport?"

"Definitely not."

Remi pouted. "Why the hell not? I just made a glorious comeback. If ever there was a time."

"You were knocking on heaven's door and about to step over the threshold, Remi. We aren't fucking in the shower until you prove you can handle a set of stairs without keeling over."

Considering the way he swayed when he tried to stand, I knew that was the right approach. He might be healed, but his body had still been through the wringer. He needed to take it easy, at least for an hour or two.

"Okay, but . . . could you just come with me? I don't want to be alone." The way Remi's question gripped me by the heart and squeezed would have scared the shit out of me if I hadn't already admitted my feelings.

I started the shower, letting the bathroom fill with steam as I pulled my shirt over my head and dropped it to the floor. Then I let myself look at the man standing next to me. Well, he was leaning heavily on the vanity, his eyes raking my bare torso.

"Arms up, Mercer," I ordered.

Remi offered the ghost of a smirk but obeyed. Once I got him naked, I shoved my jeans down my hips and did the same.

"We've gotta stop meeting like this," he quipped, but I could see the fatigue lining his features. Not to mention his less-than-aroused dick.

"Your heart's not even in it, Remi. Get in the shower."

"My heart is, but my downstairs parts aren't listening right now." His eyes went wide. "Asher . . . what if my humper is broken?"

"Your humper?"

"Yeah. Like, what if it's some side effect from being plagued? Oh God. Will you still love me if I can't dick you down?"

I could see he was genuinely worried, so I rested my palms on his shoulders and looked him straight in the eye. "First of all, I'm the one who dicks you down. Second of all, I just brought you back from the verge of death because of how much I love you. I feel like you already have the answer to that question."

"So, yes?"

I rolled my eyes. "Yes, Remington. I'll love you for the rest of my life. No matter what parts of you stop working."

"Asher Henry, you swoony motherfucker." His eyes roamed down my body, his lips curling up in a familiar smirk. "Well, would you look at that. Parts of *you* are working."

I groaned and gave him a gentle shove. "I said no, Remi."

He sulked but didn't push the issue, which told me more than anything he could have said out loud. I followed him into the shower, a rag and soap in hand. I kept waiting for an 'oops, I dropped the soap' joke, but it never came. My poor shifter really was out of it.

I disguised my inspection of his body as helping him wash himself. I'm not sure he bought the excuse, but he didn't complain either, instead making contented noises as I ran the cloth over his soapy skin. Once I was sure he was both fully healed and clean, I shut off the water and grabbed a towel.

"I can do it myself, Asher."

"I know. I just like taking care of you. It's kinda my kink, remember?"

He grinned. "I thought that was mine and Rosie's kink?"

"Well, now it's mine too."

"I'm not complaining," he said around a mouthful of toothpaste as he brushed his teeth for the second time. Once he rinsed his mouth, he grabbed me by the back of my neck and reeled me in close, stealing my breath with his stupid sexy smirk. "I forgot something."

"Oh yeah?"

"Yeah, this."

He leaned down and kissed me, tasting like mint and hope and everything good in my life. Fuck, I'd missed him so much. My throat tightened, and motherfucking tears burned the backs of my eyes. I would *not* let this man see my cry over him again. I was already trash for him. He didn't need more reason to use his mouth and hands and big heart against me.

Just as his hand started to make its way down my torso, a very loud, very insistent gurgle made us both freeze.

"What the fuck was that?"

Remi blushed. "I think it was me. My stomach, I mean. Not sure I've really eaten anything recently."

I laughed. "Come on, let's get dressed. I know of a place with a pretty decent kitchen and a couple of people that are going to lose their shit when they see you."

"Does one of them happen to be a pretty brunette?"

"I wouldn't call Ben pretty. Ruggedly handsome, hot as fuck, grumpy sex on legs?"

Remi pressed a hand to his chest. "You did *not* just say my brother was hot."

I laughed again, happiness bubbling up inside me as I wrapped my arms around him, kissing him before pulling away and saying, "Relax, you're the only Mercer for me."

"Damn right. No Mercer sandwich for you."

"Shoot, there go those fantasies."

"Asher. Henry."

"Kidding!"

CHAPTER

SIXTEEN

ROSIE

"It's o-okay, sugar. It'll all b-be okay." Ben's lips were at my ear, his voice low and soothing as he stroked my hair and snuggled me on his lap. Moira had already returned home, and after Asher's departure, it was just me and my other two mates left to wait for whatever fate saw fit to throw at us next.

"Here, petal, drink this."

It was times like these I really missed grilled cheese and tomato soup. Was there anything more comforting in the entire world? Perhaps Ben's arms around me, but I don't know. It was pretty close. Tomato soup was top drawer. My mum always used to make it on a cold day.

I accepted Gavin's offering of mulled wine, noting the marks on both his and Ben's wrists. "You hurt yourselves."

"We're f-fine."

"We couldn't agree on which one of us got to be the one to add the blood to your wine, so we both did it." Gavin's tenderness made my heart swell. He'd changed so much, yet he remained dominant over me in so many ways. I didn't think I'd ever stop being surprised by his casual displays of care or affection. Nor did I want to. I loved it when my duke surprised me.

"Thank you. Both of you." I glanced at each of my Doms in turn, then brought the mug to my lips.

"Y-you know we'll always t-take care of you."

Without warning, my gut churned, nausea clutching at my throat. Something was very off with my mates upstairs. I broke out into a cold sweat as Ben's entire body tensed in time with mine.

"Something's w-wrong." His voice was low and filled with trepidation.

Nodding, I closed my eyes and tapped into my mate bond with Asher. He'd be my first line to an accurate understanding of what was happening. Remi was too out of it to make any sense of his thoughts and feelings.

I was hit with his panic first. If I was anxious, Asher was in a full-blown meltdown. That didn't bode well. But along with his panic was a thread of calm certainty. *Pan*. They were working together. I'd bet my fangs on it.

Everything was a chaotic swirl of emotion, but it was easy enough to gather that Remi had taken a turn. I itched to go to him, but almost as soon as the urge swelled within me, I was met with overwhelming relief. Followed quickly by love and gratefulness.

"Sugar? Wh-what's happening?" Ben's fingers dug into my thighs.

"He's okay. Remi. Asher . . . healed him."

"Wh-what? How?"

Ben tried to stand, bringing me with him, but as soon as my feet were on the floor, I stopped him with both palms pressed against his broad chest. "No. Let them have a moment together. They'll come down when they're ready. They need this."

He looked uncertain, and I got it. I truly did, but after everything they'd just been through together, they needed a minute to come back down from the emotional high and regroup before being faced with the rest of us.

"I promise you, he's right as rain."

Searching eyes met mine. "You sw-swear it?"

"Cross my heart."

He brought his finger up to my chest and made the x for me. "I trust y-you."

"As you should," Gavin grumbled. "She's your fucking Queen."

"Yeah. Sh-she is."

I blushed under the intensity of their gazes, my heart loads lighter than it had been even a quarter hour prior. Remi was okay. Whatever had happened had saved him, and I wasn't going to have to say goodbye to the cocky shifter I loved.

My relief was as intense as theirs, happiness making me nearly buoyant. I wasn't sure if I wanted to laugh or cry or spin around in a merry circle until I fell down and could do little more than pant and catch my breath. It was torture to wait them out as minutes passed until it had been over an hour of waiting, pretending I wasn't on pins and needles to see them. Gavin and Ben kept me as distracted as they could, though we all fell into an anxious silence after a while. Finally the door upstairs creaked as it opened, then closed, the sound filtering down to us and calling all of our attention to the mouth of the stairs. They were coming.

The second Remi came into view, Ben and I were up and running. His eyes were locked on mine in an instant, as if he'd known even before setting foot in the room exactly where I'd be. After an hour of waiting, I thought I'd been prepared for this moment, but as soon as his beautiful blue eyes found mine, I absolutely lost it.

My breath hitched, and I let out a slight whimper. "Remi."

"Come here, baby girl." His own voice was tight with emotion as he held out his arms for me.

"G-go on, sugar," Ben echoed, answering a question I hadn't realized I even had. I knew he was as desperate to go to his twin as I was, but knowing he was willing to wait so I could have my moment meant the world to me.

Asher was right behind Remi, a sort of exhausted satisfaction painted on his face. He gave me a smile and nod as if to say, 'He's fine. It's okay.' I threw myself into my shifter's body, wrapping myself around him like an octopus.

"Never leave me again, Remington Mercer. Do you hear me?"

Remi's chuckle rumbled in my ear as he held me tight. "I never wanted to in the first place. But it's real good to know you missed me so much."

"Missed you? I was ready to call in every favor the Blackthornes had ever acquired to save you. I wasn't about to give up, Remi. Not ever."

He cupped my face, leaning back so he could look at me. "I'd expect nothing less since I'd do the exact same for you. We all would," he added. "Now stop telling me what you were going to do and fucking kiss me, baby girl."

I raised onto my tiptoes, not needing any more encouragement to do the very thing I'd been dreaming about.

He let out a low, needy groan the second our mouths met. "God, I've missed your lips."

"Did it get hot in here, or is it just me?" Asher asked, causing me to open my eyes as Remi pulled away.

"Jealous, hacker?" I teased.

"A little."

"You shouldn't be. I can smell you all over him," Gavin said in his usual bored drawl. "Seems like you already got a taste."

It was Asher's turn to blush. "Well, I mean, I did save him."

"No w-wonder they t-took an hour," Ben said.

"Hey, I resent that. It would have taken a lot longer, but Asher kept me honest."

"Technically, that was your stomach."

"True, I'd murder a fucking sandwich."

"On it," I offered, but he curled a finger in my belt loop and held me fast.

"Uh, thanks, but no thanks, baby girl. I only just recovered."

"I'll do it," Asher said with a laugh as he strode to the bar's kitchen. "We don't want you dying all over again."

"I beg your pardon," I protested, but Ben tugged me away, his lips at my ear.

"L-leave it. H-he has a p-point."

I huffed and appealed to my husband. "Gavin, are you really going to let them all gang up on me?"

"Come here, love." He held out his arms for me, his lips twitching with amusement.

"Oh, stuff it, Donoghue," Remi said. "You've never tried a Rosie special. You'd be singing a different tune if you were the one she nearly poisoned."

"I quite enjoy her cookie," he murmured, wrapping his arms around me and surprising me by joining in on the joke. "So moist and delicious."

Remi snickered, but his laughter stopped when he finally locked eyes with his twin. Ben was all tense muscle and clenched jaw, the need to go to his brother vibrating from within him.

"Miss me?" Remi asked, his voice cracking a little.

"D-don't t-t-try it a-a-again."

"I didn't try anything the first—" Remi started, but Ben crushed him in a huge hug, the anxiety bleeding out of him as though pumped through a severed artery.

"I c-can't l-l-lose y-you too, Remi."

The brothers stayed in their embrace as Gavin and I watched, my heart whole again after too long. They didn't break apart until Asher returned with what I assumed was about a half dozen BLTs.

"Oh, fuck yes. I am going to demolish you," Remi grunted as he snagged one in each hand.

"Is that a promise?" Asher and I both asked at the same time.

Remi was mid-bite when he grinned and nodded. "Mmm...great idea. Dinner, then dessert."

"More like dinner and a show," Gavin murmured in my ear.

A shiver raced down my spine, and my knees buckled, and Gavin caught me in his arms.

"Are you all right, darling?"

I gave him a slight pulse of positive energy through our bond as he led me to a chair. I was just drained from all the emotions of the last few days. It seemed like this night was never-ending. One crisis after another, my mates always at risk. Because of me and this Apocalypse.

As I sat at the table, my limbs began to tremble, the release of adrenaline strong and uncontrollable. I was suddenly weak, needing every bit of my strength just to keep myself in my chair. My skin felt so tight I could feel my pulse pounding in every cell, and my senses were on overdrive. It was all too much.

"Turn down the lights. And the music, please," I whispered, my eyes squeezed shut, my hands lifting to cover my ears.

Ben must have been the next to notice something wasn't quite right with me because his voice came out in a snarled demand. "What's wrong with her?"

Even with my eyes closed, I could feel the second Remi and Asher's attention turned to me.

"Jesus fuck. This is the worst game of musical chairs I've ever played," Remi groaned. "First Ben imprisoned, then Rosie dies and Asher's possessed, then I'm plagued. Now Rosie again. When are we getting off this ride? Also, Gavin, why hasn't anything happened to you?"

Gavin let out an offended huff. "Technically, I thought I was a widower long before this all started." I heard a rustle of cloth and metal, the sound not making sense until he spoke again. "And then I was all but neutered, so believe me, I have not remained unscathed by recent events."

He was referring to our amulets. Since we primarily fed off each other, they hadn't been more than a passing nuisance—if one didn't count the incubus encounter. We really were on one insidious ride.

The light clicked off, the sound of heavy footfalls coming near a welcome balm. Ben's scent hit me a second before he grabbed my nape and began massaging the tight muscles there.

"She's depleted. Her energy stores were completely drained by the combination of her, as well as her mates', emotional upheaval," Gavin explained.

"Understandably," Asher said. "These last couple of weeks have been intense for all of us. It couldn't have been easy carrying the weight of all those feelings."

"Is th-there anything w-we can d-do to help?"

"She needs to feast." Gavin's voice was closer now, and when his fingers trailed across my cheek before he cupped my jaw, I sighed into his touch, finally able to reopen my eyes.

"Do you want one of my sandwiches, baby girl?" Remi crouched in front of me, resting one large palm on my knee.

"I can make her something else," Asher offered, taking both my hands in his.

"She needs our b-blood," Ben said, his hands on me as if ready to catch me the second it seemed I might keel over. He had moved from my neck to my shoulders, strong fingers kneading the tight muscles under my shoulder blades.

As soon as all four of them were touching me, my chest loosened enough to draw a full breath. I wondered idly how much better I'd feel if Pan were here too. If I had all five of my mates touching me at the same time.

"How much does she need?" Asher asked Gavin, looking worried. "She fed from both Pan and me before we came over."

"A whole hell of a lot. And since the two of you have shared a form since the bond, it would stand to reason she has never truly fed from you, Asher."

My head lifted from where I'd dropped it into my hands. Something about what Gavin had said sent a little shiver of knowing down my spine. "You said feast. Not feed. Why?"

"Yes, I did." Gavin slid his gaze to Remi. "Eat up, Mercer. You're going to need your strength."

Remi took a big bite, polishing off the second of his sandwiches.

"You d-didn't answer her question, Gavin. How is a f-feast different from a r-regular feeding?"

A flash of desire flickered in his eyes. "When a Queen must replenish her not insignificant stores, she feasts from her mates. It's one of the primary reasons she has more than one to serve her. Consider it something like a blood orgy."

"Kinky," Remi offered.

"Fuck, that's hot," Asher whispered.

Ben stopped rubbing my shoulders and left the bar, heading upstairs without a word.

"I guess he's out," Remi grumbled, standing and taking his brother's place behind me.

But almost as soon as he left, Ben returned, arms laden with fluffy blankets and a couple of pillows. He flicked his gaze at me before placing everything at my feet.

"What's that?" I asked, fighting a smile.

"Sounds a lot l-like h-heat. We'll n-need a nest if w-we're going to serve our m-mate properly."

"Fuck yes, we are." The excitement in Remi's voice couldn't have been disguised if he tried. He dropped to his knees and started rolling out the blankets in the middle of the floor, which was thankfully already cleared since most of the tables and chairs hadn't been returned to their usual spaces.

Gavin hummed in approval. "Didn't know you had it in you, Mercer."

Ben simply growled and began working open the collar of his flannel shirt. "When it c-comes to my m-mate, I'll d-do anything."

Sex and blood had been the furthest thing from my mind, but as soon as Gavin explained what was happening to me and I caught the combined scent of my mates' arousal, I became a slave to my basest urges. Not exactly feral, like I'd been upon turning, but damned close. Immediate slickness pooled between my thighs, and my fangs tingled in my gums as my throat burned, desperate for relief. Only they could quench this thirst. Just like only they could fill me the way I needed.

My clothes were too much against my oversensitized skin, so I stood and peeled off my jumper and jeans. Their reactions to my nudity were painfully loud to my enhanced hearing. Ben's tight swallow. Remi's soft groan. Asher's pulse picking up. Gavin's hiss of approval. They sent slick flooding between my thighs, readying me to take them.

All of them.

As a forking Queen should.

"You're all mine." One by one, I met each of their eyes, my voice little more than a growl. "Now serve me."

CHAPTER SEVENTEEN

GAVIN

In all my research over the past few weeks, I'd learned a great deal about Queens, but the one thing I'd looked forward to the most was this.

The feasts.

My petal would be insatiable as she fed from us, fucked us, took everything we could give her, and then demanded more. I couldn't wait. I'd already devised a plan of the most pleasurable ways the four of us—yes, four, because who the fuck would have guessed Pan would be mate number five—could see her through it.

Roslyn's lips twitched, her voice floating through my mind. *"I can tell you're eager, husband. Your thoughts are quite loud."*

"Why wouldn't they be? I have nothing to hide from you. When I realized this was an inevitability for us, I took the steps necessary to ensure it would be everything you needed. As I always do."

"In that case, my lord, moonlight."

That one word set me on fire. She started the scene and gave me control of her pleasure and pain. I couldn't fucking wait to make use of my power.

"Remington, strip and lie in the nest, on your back," I commanded.

Roslyn licked her lips as my order landed and Remington moved toward the pile of blankets.

"D-doesn't she n-need to feed first?"

"Ben, don't you dare ruin this for me. I've been mostly dead all day. Week, even. I've earned this," Remington said, already stripping and claiming his place in the center of the largest gray blanket.

"This isn't a-about you."

"If my dick is involved, it's about me."

All too familiar with how conversations could devolve when Remington was involved, I took the reins once more, knowing this was what my Queen needed, what she'd requested I do when she ceded her control to me. "She will feed, Bentley. Frequently and with abandon. She'll take everything we have, and to do that, she needs our bodies. If you're not willing—"

"I n-never s-said I w-wasn't w-willing. I'll g-give her the h-heart out of m-my chest if sh-she w-wants it."

Roslyn made a soft hum that almost sounded like a purr. It seemed to do something to the shifters, who both visibly reacted. I wasn't immune either, and from Asher's soft grunt, neither was he.

"Good. It's a marathon, not a sprint. And for the first course . . ."

"Please have her sit on my face. Please have her sit on my face," Remington chanted, stealing my thunder.

I sighed, already weary. "Petal, let our erstwhile pirate taste your sweet cunt."

"Fuck yes."

My wife was less loquacious, but no less enthusiastic as she claimed her place and then sank to her knees like the fucking goddess she was, one leg planted on either side of his head.

Remington reached up, cupping her arse and tugging her down that last inch. "He said sit, baby girl, not hover."

Asher and Roslyn moaned in unison, the hacker's hand sliding into his pants to adjust his noticeable bulge.

"Make her scream, Remi. Fuck, you both look so hot like this."

I shot a glare Asher's way. "I'm in charge here, not you. Now if you're going to stand there with your dick in your hand, at least put it to use."

He grinned. "With pleasure. What should I do with it?"

A flash of the two of them together came from Roslyn's thoughts. *Oh, she liked that.* Seeing them tangled in each other, sharing herself with them while they enjoyed one another. I could give her that.

"Get between Remington's thighs and tease him until he cries for you."

I didn't have to tell him twice. He was on his knees and spreading Remington open as he shoved his joggers down his hips. Those clothes would be torn to ribbons before we were finished, but that was his call. I didn't care one way or another if he ended up needing to buy more horrible trousers.

"Wh-where do you w-want m-me?" Bentley asked, his voice rough and tight.

"I want you to watch until you can't stand it anymore."

The thrill Roslyn experienced at that shot through our connection, making my cock ache with the need to be touched.

"And wh-what will you b-be doing?"

"What I do best. Directing the rest of you and fucking her face, of course."

Bentley's eyes flashed with the neon blue of his wolf. Neither of them appreciated being benched, but I knew how much Roslyn loved it when he watched, and this was all about her pleasure. Not his. Bentley could wait his turn. It would come soon enough. And I'd be lying if I said I didn't sort of love the idea of his misery. The thought made my cock twitch. I might be a mated man, but I was still a sexual sadist.

"Remington, our mate is a little too quiet under your attentions. Do I need to rearrange you?"

The shifter reached up, grabbing her by the hips and seating her more firmly on his mouth. Roslyn shuddered and fell forward, her palms landing on the blankets. She cried out and writhed, her hips undulating in search of that perfect friction. Then her mouth lowered to Remington's straining erection, the glistening tip and swollen length betraying how close he was to release already. Amateur.

"Not so fast, petal," I crooned, blurring to her side and snagging her hair in my fist as I tugged her upright. "Your mouth belongs to me."

Roslyn's hungry whimper was nearly drowned out by Remington's moaned protest. And Asher cursed in appreciation while Bentley's attention never wavered from the woman we all served. His hands were clenching and unclenching on his knees, veins pulsing in his forearms, beads of sweat dotting his brow. We'd only just gotten started, but I knew he was struggling to remain in his seat.

"Please, my lord."

Everything was going according to plan, and I couldn't deny her anything. Especially not when it involved her lips around my dick.

I straddled Remington's waist, one foot on either side of him as I stood over both of them. "If it's a cock you're in search of, mine is ready to choke you."

"Fucking hell," Asher whispered.

She blinked up at me, her cheeks flushed and eyes bright with pleasure as the shifter under her continued to eat her. "I can't get to it, my lord. It's covered."

Tearing open my fly, I pulled out my cock and let the crown kiss her lips as I shoved my trousers and pants down to my thighs.

"Asher, Remington could use a little attention, don't you think?" I asked.

See, I could be kind when the occasion called for it.

"I need some lube. I'm not just gonna shove inside him with no prep."

I sighed. "Grab his cock and give him a stroke. He'll go off like a fountain in two pumps. I guarantee it. You'll have plenty to work with then."

Remington's strangled moan proved just how right I was.

"That's it, Remi. Come for me so I can fuck you the way you were begging me to earlier."

A pulse of desire raced through me at the sordid words. I couldn't tell if it came from me or through the mate bond I shared with Roslyn. But when she wrapped her lips around my crown, I didn't give a single fuck. All I wanted was her sucking me down, draining me dry, and sending me into oblivion.

She hummed around my cock as she worked me. Asher and Remington both grunted and moaned together as they moved in rhythmic thrusts and rolls of their hips. At some point, the hacker had done exactly as I'd suggested, and he was fucking Remington in earnest.

God, I needed Roslyn to find her release as well. Inspired by her reaction to Asher's growled command, I glanced back over my shoulder.

"Asher, while you're back there, do me a favor and give my balls a tug."

His eyes snapped open, and he blinked at me in surprise. "What?"

"I want you to reach forward, wrap your hand around my balls, and tug. Hard."

"Oh fuck, I'm gonna come," Remington moaned against Roslyn's cunt. She was right there with him, her climax surging through our bond and lighting me up from the inside out.

"Come, petal. Now." My order was a garbled sound, torn from my throat as Asher followed instructions and grabbed my sac just hard enough that when she swallowed around my length, I spilled into her mouth.

My fucking knees nearly gave out as she drank me down. Asher released me, panting but holding onto my thighs for support as he chased his climax. I felt more than heard it happen, his fingers digging into my skin, tremors working their way from his body to mine.

As if that's what she'd been waiting for, Roslyn swallowed the gift I'd given her and released my cock. Then she feathered a kiss over my inner thigh before she rolled her eyes up to meet my own.

What a good girl, asking for permission.

I caressed her cheek, dragging my knuckles from her temple to her jaw. "Go ahead, petal. Take what you need."

Her fangs flashed as she gave me an impish grin. "Oh, I intend to."

"You little—" But my chastisement was lost on a groan of pure pleasure as she bit down and drew deep.

We all felt her reaction to my blood hitting her tongue, our moans loud and heartfelt.

"Fuck, I can't st-stand this any m-more."

I locked gazes with Bentley as my cock hardened all over again and another wave of arousal flooded us all from Roslyn's mate bond.

"Then get over here and do something about it, Mercer."

CHAPTER EIGHTEEN

BEN

Rosie's scent filled the space, begging me to join in. I wanted to be where Remi was, rubbing my face in her slick, coating my tongue with her. Feasting on her every bit as much as she was on us.

My wolf thrashed in my chest, desperate to claim his mate. We could feel everything she was experiencing, her mental barriers completely lowered, sensations rushing through us all and making things . . . hard. At least for me. My dick was a shaft of granite, but Gavin had given me a challenge, and I refused to back down.

Even if it killed me.

Which it might. Fuck. I was lightheaded from all the blood in my body rushing south. Rosie might need to feed from my cock before she tried any other veins.

I was struck by the image of her on her knees, taking me down her throat, my cum and blood mingling in a carnal cocktail . . .

Fuuuck.

I couldn't tell if that scene came from me or her, but I was *this-close* to coming in my fucking pants. Then all of them found their releases at almost the same time, and I thought I was going to burst at the seams. I couldn't stand it anymore, but had I missed my chance? They were done, and I'd been so stubborn I just sat here and watched like a goddamn idiot.

I could practically hear Remi shouting at me, "You never sit out of an orgy, Ben. Are you fucking new here?"

But then Rosie leaned forward, lifting her glistening cunt from Remi's face and presenting for me as she sank her fangs into Gavin's inner thigh. I didn't care what she did with the vampire. All I needed were the two words she sent through our bond.

"Please, Daddy."

"Fuck, I can't st-stand this any m-more."

Gavin's eyes were closed as he groaned, "Then get over here and do something about it, Mercer."

I hadn't exactly been asking for permission, but I'd let the duke continue thinking he was the one running the show. I shucked my jeans and stalked toward the tangle of bodies. I waited just long enough for Rosie to pull away and lick her lips before I took her hair in my hand and tugged her head back.

"You think you can grind that dripping pussy of yours all over Remi, show me that perfect peach of an ass, and get away without taking every fucking inch of me, mate?" My wolf was all growl and dominance as I let him speak through me.

"No," she breathed, her eyes glassy with her arousal.

"Damn straight." I dropped to one knee, my mouth at her ear. "I told you I w-was going to take your ass, baby. Buckle up."

"Fuck, Ben. I can see her fluttering. Whatever you're saying, she likes it," Remi groaned.

"Of course she d-does. She's my good girl, aren't you, sugar?"

"Please, Ben. Don't make me wait."

I liked her begging me, but I wasn't going to last much longer, and she hadn't even touched me.

"Did y-you get her nice and ready f-for me, Remi?"

"You know I did."

Reaching between her thighs, I sank two fingers inside her slick pussy and coated them in her arousal, bringing them to my lips for a taste before the main event. Goddamn, she was soaked. But it wouldn't be enough. She needed to be prepared to take me in that tight little hole. I tilted my head down and parted her ass with both hands before spitting right where we'd need it most. Then I slid my cock through her wet lips, back and forth, coating myself in her cum and brushing her clit with each pass. My thumb pressed into the ring of muscle at her ass, testing and teasing all at the same time. I spit on her again, loving the way she whimpered in response.

"You like that, sugar? When I s-spit on you?"

"Yes."

I was vaguely aware of Gavin standing to our left, lazily stroking himself while Remi put his hands behind his head and hummed in approval.

"Best fucking seat in the house."

"You c-can participate if you w-want," I told him.

"No, I can't. Your dick is in the way."

"Not f-for long."

At some point, Asher must have gotten up from the floor because Remi called, "Where do you think you're going?"

"Don't worry, I'll be right back."

I slid out of her wet heat, notching myself at her ass while Remi rolled onto his knees in front of her. As I pressed into her, I reached around with my free hand and curled my fingers over her throat, gripping just hard enough to make her gasp before I pulled her up so that her back was flat against my chest.

"I've g-got you, baby. Let g-go."

Remi's eyes met mine as he slipped his hand down between them, and while I couldn't see what he was doing, I knew it the instant his fingers sank inside her. I felt it through both the thin wall that separated us and my bond with Rosie.

"Fuck, she's tight like this," Remi groaned.

"T-tell me about it."

"Harder, Ben," Rosie gritted out. "Choke me."

My gut reaction was the same as always. I hated the idea of hurting her.

"You can't hurt me. Please, Daddy. I need it."

Cock straining, I thrust deep as my fingers clamped down around the delicate skin of her neck. She'd wear my bruises when this was over. I shouldn't have liked the thought, but fuck, I did. Any mark of mine on her skin had me nearly howling with pride.

Gavin came closer, reaching down to adjust my grip. "Like this, wolf. Keep the pressure focused on these two spots. She doesn't technically need to breathe, so these pressure points will slow the blood flow and give her the same sensation."

If I were a weaker man, I'd have been threatened by him coming to give me pointers while I was balls deep in her ass. But then again, Gavin could have easily kept his expertise to himself, ensuring he was the only one who could give her this. Instead, we were both more focused on serving the woman we loved. There was no room for pettiness or pride in the wake of that.

And the way she clenched down on me as I followed his instructions pushed any inkling of uncertainty out of my head.

"That's it, baby girl. Let Daddy Ben make you come so hard you see stars." Remi dipped his head and bit down on her nipple as I drove into her.

She cried out, the sound a faint gasp because of my hand around her throat, and as she reached her climax, so did I. I pulsed long and hard inside her, filling her ass with my cum and never wanting it to end.

Loosening my grip on her, I tilted her face toward me as I leaned forward and offered my neck. Even if she hadn't needed to feast, I wanted it. I never thought I'd have these feelings, the desire to be bitten by a vampire, to feed her, but that didn't change the fact that my cock was already stiffening inside her again at just the promise of her lips on me.

"You take such good care of me, Daddy," she whispered, her lips ghosting over the sensitive skin before her fangs found purchase.

Remi's voice rang out loud enough that it broke through my pleasure-filled daze.

"Jesus, fuck, how can I be hard again?"

Gavin's low chuckle was the only appropriate response. "I warned you it was a marathon, Remington. What part of feast did you not understand?"

CHAPTER NINETEEN

REMI

"Oh, I understand a feast. I was just down there having my very own Rosie-catered Thanksgiving dinner, in case you missed it." I swayed a little, my limbs not really ready for so much activity. While Asher had healed the sickness riddling my body, there wasn't much anyone could do for the muscle loss caused by the extensive bed rest.

Thankfully, my shifter DNA would take care of that in a couple days, and in the meantime . . . Well, suffice it to say my humper was not, in fact, broken. My dick was working just fine, as my three explosive orgasms proved. I would just have to ride out this orgy on my back and save the athletic stuff for the rest of them. What a hardship.

"Where do you want me, baby girl? I need you to direct this scene for me."

She writhed in Ben's hold, her eyes darkening and a drop of my twin's blood glistening on her lower lip. "I need someone inside me."

"I am i-inside you, sugar."

"Not only there."

"S-someone give her wh-what she n-needs."

I grinned, fisting my length and giving it a slow stroke as I laid back down. "You need to go for a ride, don't you? That can be arranged."

"I want inside her as well," Gavin said, his eyes hungry as he watched Ben pull out of her.

"Sharing is caring. There's room for two."

Rosie moaned, a flood of slick slipping down her thighs at my words. I could fucking see it.

"Looks like I'm just in time for round three." Asher's voice sent a curl of desire through me as he strode into the room again, nude and hot as fuck. I could just make out the crisp scent of our soap over the more earthy musk of sex, telling me exactly what he'd been up to.

Intent on taking me up on my offer, Rosie crawled over me but stared hard at him. "You are."

His answering grin was pure sex. "Then I guess all I need to know is where I fit in this complicated pretzel."

"I've got dibs on her pussy this ti—" My words cut off on a guttural moan as she sank down on my cock in one delicious slide.

She let out a cry of her own as soon as I was fully seated inside her. "I want Asher in my mouth. And Gavin . . ."

"Arch your back, petal."

He must've pushed into her tight ass, already well lubed by Ben, because her eyes flared wide and she shifted her chest closer to change the angle, bringing her full round tits to my face. I barely resisted the urge to motorboat her, but there was no stopping me from greeting my two best girls.

"Mary-Kate, Ashley, how I've missed you," I murmured in appreciation, taking them both in my hands so I could say hello to them properly.

She giggled, but it cut off on a whimper as I sucked one nipple into my mouth.

"My turn, princess. You said you wanted me in your mouth, and I got all cleaned up just for you." Asher stood over me, his legs spread, giving me a full view of his thick length and already tight balls. Fuck, *this* was the best seat in the house.

"Yes," I whispered desperately, even though he wasn't talking to me. I really wanted to watch him give her what she asked for.

Asher had to kneel in order for her to reach him, but I didn't mind. I was an excellent multitasker. Look at me, shattering stereotypes left and right. His thighs surrounded my head, balls right there in sucking distance. But not yet. I'd save that ace up my sleeve until just the right moment.

Rosie rocked her hips in time with Gavin's slow thrusts, whining in pleasure as she opened her mouth to take Asher's cock.

I wasn't sure which of us groaned louder. Asher, me, or Gavin. I didn't hear my twin, but I wouldn't be surprised if he was using this reprieve to clean up and prepare for round four.

"Fuck, Rosie. You suck me so good." Asher's words were tight, and from that tone alone, I could tell he was close.

I think we all were, to be honest. It was a tight fit with Gavin working her ass, and she was squeezing me like I was an orange and she needed every last drop of that vitamin D. *Yes, I know it's C, but come on . . . that was too good. Although C works just as well. Because cock. God, I'm funny. See, multitasking.*

"I'm close," Asher gritted out, bringing me back to the moment. "God, I'm really fucking close."

Just wait until I get my mouth on you.

This was it. My moment to shine and earn myself an orgy gold star. I lifted my head and sucked on his balls, making him jerk and cry out. Then, with one hand, I traced the line of his taint, and that was it for Asher Henry. He went off like a rocket.

Rosie hummed as she drank him down, a pearly drop escaping the seal of her lips.

Couldn't let that go to waste.

Using my index finger, I reached up and gathered Asher's cum before putting it in my mouth. "Mmm . . . finger-lickin' good."

Asher chuckled, a deep husky rasp that had my stomach clenching, but then Rosie was clamping down around my cock and bringing me to an orgasm I hadn't seen coming. I'd been too focused on them.

Before I could register what was happening, Gavin yanked Rosie by the hair and pulled her off Asher's dick, his lips at her ear. "Feed, petal. Take Remi's wrist and drink from your mate while I empty my balls into your pert arse."

"Yes, my lord," she whispered, but it was no submissive whisper. It was a feral promise.

Hell yes. I'd give her everything she required of me, no questions asked. I was already lifting my arm so she could take me. The pressure of her bite had my eyes rolling back in my head, the burst of pleasure she sent through our mate bond triggering a second orgasm as she drank me down.

Christ, I would need to invest in Gatorade if this kept up much longer. *Maybe I should set up an IV hydration station in the back office.*

She released my wrist and stared down at me, her eyes glowing amber from the feeding, breaths coming in harsh pants, skin dewy with sweat.

"More," Rosie growled, her eyes ravenous as she peered up at Asher.

For the first time probably ever, I was genuinely relieved there was someone else to take the reins. The heart was willing, but fuck, I needed a breather.

I'd never planned on a marathon sex feast with all of us together. To be fair, I didn't even know that was on the table, but as I served her alongside her other mates, I thanked my lucky stars I'd lived to experience this. And I couldn't wait to do it again . . . after I hydrated.

CHAPTER TWENTY

ASHER

"If you need a break, now's the time, boys." I backed away from the tangle of bodies, my gaze never leaving Rosie's. "I've got her."

Half of me expected some sort of protest, but none came. Not even from Remi, which might have been concerning if not for the blissed-out smile curling his lips.

"Are you sure you're up for it?" Rosie asked, rising and using the pad of her thumb to wipe her lips.

I slowly and purposefully lowered my gaze to the erection that hadn't flagged once since we'd started and then back up to her. "You tell me, princess."

The rest of the guys staggered to their feet, even Gavin looking spent. This was my time to shine. The others had all had their chance to fuck her; now it was my turn at bat. And I wasn't much for sports-ball, but I was for sure about to score a basket.

Tenderness flickered across her face as she approached me, her fingers trailing up my bare arm, sending electricity along my over-sensitive flesh. Fuck, I had goosebumps. It was like we hadn't just all blown our collective loads minutes ago.

Multiple times.

Thanks to the research I'd been working on with Gavin, I knew this was her doing. Part of her vampire Queen pheromones that helped her ensure we would all be ready and able to serve at her pleasure. And it wouldn't stop until she'd gotten everything she needed from us.

Distantly, I knew that meant *all* of us, and while I didn't mind an audience—I'd have to be an absolute fucking hypocrite to want privacy right now—I wasn't about to share this moment with *him*. Pan could wait his goddamn turn. It served him right to miss the orgy. Sorry, feast. We must be accurate about these things.

"Are you three ready to watch what a human can do?" I asked, smirking at them as they all sat in chairs, still breathing heavily.

"I'm intimately aware of what you can do," Remi said, his voice —and the shock of hearing him not just healthy but flirty—lighting me up inside. "But also, you're not human, numbnuts, so I'm pretty sure you've been cheating."

"I'm part human."

"Yeah, but which part? Seems like a monster cock to me."

Rosie reached between us and cupped my dick. "I have to agree. I'm well-versed on the subject."

I fucking knew Pan would have something to say about that. I could practically hear him crooning in my ear. *"He fucking wishes. Does it change size? Vibrate? Have special ridges for your pleasure? Can it* do any *of the things mine can do? No? Then clearly he cannot claim to compare."*

Wait. He was *actually* crooning in my ear.

"Pan, what's the rule?"

"I'm sorry. The barrier is thinner than normal. I'm trying to keep out, but she keeps pulling me back in."

"Whatever, just stay quiet. I'm busy."

A tickling in my mind was his only response. He wanted to retort but *was* holding back. I wasn't sure what surprised me more—that he was able to resist her lure, or that he was genuinely attempting to behave. Both seemed out of character for him. Was the big, bad demon going soft?

Another tickle, this time more of an angry buzz, yet he still kept his thoughts to himself.

"Asher? Are you talking to Pan?" Rosie ran her palm up my chest and tilted her head as she stared into my eyes.

"I was. Sorry. I can't control it. Our consciousnesses sort of bleed together sometimes."

"Don't apologize, but tell him he can wait his turn. Right now, you are the one I need. I'm desperate for you."

If I was a peacock, I would have been fucking preening.

I was *never* the one anybody needed. Well, I mean hacking-wise, sure, but not for shit that mattered. I may have joked about being 'the human,' but the truth was I still thought of myself as the weak link in this mate chain. The disposable one. The tag-along. Everyone's least favorite Girl Scout cookie.

But Rosie didn't think that. I could feel the truth of her assertion through our bond. She did need me. Just me.

Asher Henry.

Demon castoff and human nobody.

Pestilence's trojaniest of horses.

The foster kid from the wrong side of the tracks who was such an unwanted handful, not even nuns liked him. Though . . . that might have something to do with the demon bit, come to think of it. Surely they had some sort of evil sixth sense.

I see demon people.

"Asher," she whispered, sadness and longing mixing in her eyes. "You're not nobody."

Well, fuck. Apparently, I'd been telegraphing those thoughts through our bond.

"You're a vital part of me. Just as they are."

My chest swelled with pride and love and fucking gratefulness. I had to do something before I let down my walls and started sobbing like a sap. So I wrapped my palm around her nape and pulled her against me, kissing her long and deep. My tongue danced with hers as she moaned into my mouth. I could taste the coppery tang of Remi's blood, the salt of my release, and the flavor that was distinctly Rosie.

The frenetic need was still there, dancing along our bond, but it was a slower burn this time, more tease than demand. I had no way of knowing if that was because her immediate needs had been met or if it was because she wanted to show me that she cherished me. Either way, I didn't care. Just because this was a feast didn't mean we couldn't make love too.

The lyrics to my favorite Tenacious D song flashed through my mind, and I grinned against her lips.

"Hump you sweetly? Really, Asher?"

"*Fuck off, Pan.*"

"Don't make me put you in timeout, Pan," Rosie muttered, which only made me laugh. Clearly she was getting the hang of dealing with my Bruce Banner and Purple Hulk lifestyle.

I took her face between both hands and kissed her again, backing her up until her ass hit a table. Instead of stopping, I kept kissing her as I cupped her ass and lifted her up, spreading her thighs wide open for me.

A moan burst from me as I slid just the tip inside her slick heat. Chest heaving, I pressed my forehead to hers.

Her eyes fluttered open, finding me. "I love you."

My heart simultaneously exploded and melted. Did she know how much power her words had? "I love you more."

She grinned. "Doubtful."

Then she wriggled her hips, attempting to take more of me, but I stopped her. "Not yet. Slow, princess. I need this to last, and you already have me worked up."

She made a soft sound of protest, but she was nothing if not obedient. Gavin had certainly seen to that. I rewarded her with another inch, and it was torture to keep from sinking all the way inside, but I was going to draw this out as long as I could. Who knew when I'd have her all to myself again? Even our audience was respecting her request that this was about the two of us. I could still feel them there, their eyes on us, hear their low grunts as they took care of their own needs. But it was as close to alone as we may ever get.

"Asher, please," she begged. "I can't stand it."

"You want me all the way inside you, Rosie? You want my cock buried as deep as I can get?"

"Yes."

I wrapped my hand around her throat, not squeezing, just collaring, knowing she enjoyed the possessive move as much as I did from the way her pulse jumped as my thumb slid down the side of her neck.

"Asher," she moaned as I continued my slow thrust.

"Roslyn."

"Please," she whined.

"No."

"I'm begging you."

"I know. I like it."

I wondered if she realized how hard this was for me. My legs trembled from the restraint it took not to slam home. Then the minx squeezed my cock with her inner muscles, milking me before I was ready.

"Rosie, stop."

"Stop what?" She tightened around me again.

"I'm serious."

"So am I."

"I'll come if you keep doing that."

"So stop teasing me and give me what I want. I need to feel you filling me until you can't go any farther."

There was only so long a man could deny himself. And that throaty demand, along with my own raging need, sent me driving the last few inches home. Almost immediately, I drew out and slammed back inside, hitting her cervix hard enough that she cried out. Her nails raked down my back as she hissed in pleasure. I didn't stop to ask if she was okay. I knew she was. She liked the pain, craved it, and I'd give her everything she wanted.

There was a slight sting as sweat dripped down my back. The delicate flare of her nostrils and the dilation of her pupils told me she'd drawn blood.

"Do you need to feed now?" I asked between ragged breaths as I fought off the climax building at the base of my spine.

"May I?"

"Do you even have to ask? Whatever you need, it's yours. I'm yours."

"I just know it will . . . bring you off."

"I'm seconds away anyway. Do it, Rosie."

She licked her lips, her fangs glistening and making my cock throb with anticipation as her warm mouth pressed to my throat. Jesus, it felt like I was already tipping over the edge. She bit down, and it was like every cell in my body attempted to flow out of me and into her. I wasn't just coming; I was . . . fuck, it felt like I was being unmade.

A strange sort of tingling sensation filled my mouth. It reminded me of when my foot would fall asleep after I sat funny. Pins and needles, concentrated in my upper gums.

Was I having a stroke?

Just my luck. I get the girl, save my guy, and then croak.

Rosie continued to feed, and the tingling spread. Now it was my lower *and* upper gums. And my forehead? What the hell was wrong with me?

So not the time for a crisis, Asher.

"Uh . . . guys, are you seeing what I'm seeing?" Remi whispered harshly.

"Y-y-yeah."

"So I'm not imagining the two tiny white horns that just sprouted out of his head?"

"Definitely not," Gavin confirmed.

"Should we be worried?"

"Sh-she doesn't s-seem to be."

Rosie released me, her legs wrapped around my waist and keeping us joined as she inspected me. She reached up and ran a gentle fingertip over the spots on my forehead where the tingling had been most intense, and my fucking knees nearly gave out from the pleasure.

"Oh God, do that again."

Remi chuckled. "Does she make you horny, baby?"

"J-Jesus, Remi."

"What? Someone *had* to say it. It was right there. Low-hanging fruit. I couldn't not."

Gavin sighed. "I'm starting to believe that's actually true."

She rubbed at them again, and my cock jerked inside her, making both of us moan.

"Asher," she gasped as I threw my head back, a growl of pleasure rumbling beneath my ribs.

"Yeah?"

"You have fangs."

My heart tumbled. "Fangs? Like . . . you fangs?"

She shook her head, her eyes wide, but not with fear. She looked . . . curious.

"Two sets," she murmured, her finger gently prodding my teeth and sending another shiver of need through me. "Like Pan."

I ran my tongue over my teeth, and sure enough, there they were. How was I going to hide this?

"You look hot. It's really sexy." She dragged her nails over my chest and flicked my nipple.

"Do I have a . . . you know . . . tail?" I asked.

"No, your ass is perfect, as always," Remi called.

I wasn't sure if I was relieved or disappointed. Pan was always going on about the uses he found for his tail. And Rosie sure seemed to like it. Unbidden, an image of the two of us tying her down with our tails while Gavin teased her filled my mind.

Oh God, where had *that* come from?

Rosie bit her lower lip and ground against me. “Asher, I need more. Can’t you feel it?”

I could. Every cell in my body needed to own her in a way I had never done before. It was a magnetic pull between us. I wanted to bite her, to taste her blood and leave my mark on her skin just like the others had.

I wanted to make her *mine*.

I must have been telegraphing my thoughts again because she was nearly incoherent as she nodded and gripped my neck, urging me forward.

“Do it, Asher. I need it too.”

I pushed her back until she was splayed out on the table for me, then I leaned over her, fucking her deep as my lips wrapped around her nipple. The moment my teeth found purchase with the full, soft globe of perfect flesh, I knew without a doubt this was what I’d been waiting for.

She was mine in every way possible.

My mate, every bit as much as I was hers.

I hadn’t known demons mated the same way other supernaturals did. And maybe they didn’t. Maybe I’d just marked her. Either way, she would wear my mark now, right alongside theirs. I wasn’t disposable. This was permanent. For-fucking-ever.

The joy of that thought burst through me, sending me catapulting into another orgasm and bringing her with me.

“Fuck, Asher. Oh my God.” She gripped me tight, her inner walls holding on to me as tightly as the fist in my hair and the nails digging into my tail-less ass.

One last possessive thought flitted through me before I released her breast.

Mine.

"Yours," she agreed, her voice content and sleepy in my head.

I felt it the instant Pan's patience snapped. He pushed forward, his voice strong. *"Yes. Yes. Good for you, little brother. I wasn't certain you had it in you. But you've had your fun. Stand aside and let a real demon show you how it's done."*

I could practically feel his grin.

"That's right . . . It's my turn now."

CHAPTER TWENTY-ONE

PAN

Patience was a bloody virtue, they said. Then I should be the most—*gag*—virtuous of this lot. Satan's balls, how can I be this hard and this disgusted at the same time? It was the angel porn all over again. I couldn't help it; their wings are so decadent. And sensitive too, though you didn't hear it from me. Demons had their horns and angels, well, you get the picture.

Technically due to our deal, I shouldn't be able to manifest, but Rosie's Queen powers must be overriding the terms, ensuring her needs would be met. Lucifer knew I wasn't about to complain.

She whimpered as I took control and shifted forms from Asher to the glory that was her Pan. She could thank me later. But the moment I had the reins, sensations flooded me fast and hard as her warm, slick channel stretched to accommodate the gift that was my cock.

Now that, my friends, was a monster cock.

"Pan."

"Surprise, *ma petite monstre*."

Two deep growls filled the room, and I grinned. I did so love to stir jealousy in the wolves. It had become a favorite pastime.

"Get him away from her," Ben snarled as he jumped to his feet, all wolf, no lumbersnack. "He can't be trusted."

I didn't have to spare them a look to know her three other mates charged forward, intent on removing me.

Rosie stopped them with a soft plea. "Don't. Please. I know there's . . . friction between you, but I need him, same as the rest of you."

"If it's friction you want . . ." I nudged deeper into her as I sent her the thought, drawing out another sweet moan.

Gavin sighed, fists clenched as he grumbled, "She's right. During a feast, a Queen needs all of her mates. Including this one, unfortunately."

"Then let her feed and be done with him so we can send him back." Remi's voice was stricken. Oh, how I loved it.

"Run along, lads. It's my private time with this dirty little—"

Rosie covered my mouth with her hand, stopping me from finishing that sentence. What a brazenly naughty thing to do. It made my tail twitch.

"W-we're not g-going anywhere." Ben reclaimed his seat, palms on his knees, gaze hard on me.

I was literally balls deep in my woman, and I could not resist the urge to look over at the shifter. Flashing him my most charming smirk, I raised a brow and asked, "Why? Do you need to take notes?"

His growl permeated the space. "I know exactly h-how to f-fuck my m-mate."

"I know how to fuck your mate too. Doesn't that make you angry, wolf? Perhaps you should go for a run and cool off. But be careful. You might be charged with murder again. We wouldn't want that, would we?"

"I'm n-not fucking l-leaving." Ben's eyes flashed neon blue, and he made to stand, but Remi pushed him back down with a hand on his shoulder. "If anyone gets to kill the fucker, it's me."

"Still upset about my little deception, *Remington*?" Did I let on that being trapped in Asher's body wasn't technically my choice? No. This was too entertaining. I loved winding them all up.

"You h-have to sleep s-sometime, asshole. I'd be m-more careful about ch-choosing the w-words that come out of y-your mouth if you p-plan on waking up again."

"Ah, but then your twin wouldn't get Asher back, so we both know these are nothing more than empty threats." And all of us knew we couldn't *actually* harm each other anyway. Not without hurting Rosie in the process. But I understood the desire to pretend otherwise. It allowed us to maintain some illusion of control. Which is probably why Rosie felt the need to issue her own warning.

"There will be no killing." She wriggled her hips, trying to get free of me, perhaps. All that served to do was send my eyes rolling back in my head.

"Leave us," I snarled. "You've had your turns, and I didn't interfere. The least you can do is show me the same respect."

"Respect, he says." Remi's lip curled back in a snarl. "The demon wants a little respect. Quick, someone play the tiny violin clip."

"Fine, you won't leave, so be it." I pulled out of Rosie, flipped her on her front, and grabbed her by the hair, making her cry out as I drove into her from behind. The sound of her arse meeting my hips was music to my ears, as was her garbled, half-sobbed utterance of my name.

I folded myself over her so my lips were at her ear. "Let's show them just what a perfect slut you are, hmm?"

"Yes, please. Oh God, I need more."

I didn't give her the option of that *more* being one of the others. This was all about Pan. Besides, I had a tail, and I knew exactly how to use it.

"If it's more you want, it's more you'll have."

My tail slid up her spine before wrapping around her throat and collaring her. She was fully at my mercy, and if the fluttering of her cunt around me was any indication, she loved it.

"Mmm, dirty slut indeed." I cast my gaze back toward the three men who watched us. "You should feel her. Fucking gagging for it."

Their expressions were priceless. The vampire's face was blank, but interest burned in his dark gaze. I knew we were the most similar in our predilections, but not even he could give her what I could. That pesky morality of his got in the way of going the final mile for her. I may have caught—*bleck*—feelings, but I was still blissfully free of *that*.

As for the wolves . . . Ben still looked murderous, but that was really par for the course. And Remi . . . well, if that flagpole was any indication, he was enjoying the show.

"Hold on to the table, *ma petite*."

She reached forward, grasping the edge of the table and subtly arching her spine to take more of me as she did. I didn't hold back my moans as I pistoned my hips, fucking her so hard the legs of the table scraped across the floor with each thrust. She'd have bruises on her thighs from the tabletop, and no matter who was in control, me or Asher, they'd all look at her skin and think of me.

"Jesus, he's going to hurt her," Remi whispered.

"She wants it, Remington. Don't you know her at all?" The vampire understood her better than I would have liked.

"W-we'll take c-care of her . . . a-after."

I could hear the strain in his voice. He was struggling to remain seated, and not because he wanted to join in. I'd bet his protective nature was repulsed by my treatment of her, and if not for her clear enjoyment, he'd have already put a stop to it.

Well, he would have tried.

The showman in me wanted to drive the point home. Rosie needed me. As much as them. I *belonged* here. She found freedom in my debasement. Relished my rough treatment. Sometimes their darling girl just needed to be a whore. *My* whore.

My little monster.

And who could blame her?

I was her first introduction to pleasure. She could never go back to anything resembling vanilla after me. They'd never be enough for her. Tender Ben would make sweet love to her. Hell, he probably wept when he came. Remi would let her top him, which would be a momentary thrill. And Gavin would come as close to me as he could, but he couldn't degrade and debase her like she needed. Then there was Asher, my opposite in every way. Though he was good at the dirty talk. He probably got that from me. Our sole familial resemblance.

I bit down on her shoulder, drawing a soft scream from her, which cut off as I tightened my tail's hold on her. Then I licked it better, the two halves of my forked tongue dancing along her skin as I moved back to her ear. "What do you say, Rosie? Shall we give them a proper show?"

She nodded, her lips forming a silent agreement as she sent one word through my mind. "*Moonlight.*"

"Out loud, *mon doudonette.*" I didn't want the others to try and butt in again when I took things further.

I loosened my tail's hold on her enough that she could rasp out, "Moonlight."

Gavin stiffened, his eyes narrowing. I fought a smug smile. *That's right, vampire. You aren't the only one who can control her.*

I'd show them exactly why she could never truly leave me. Even when she tried. In one smooth move, I pulled out of her cunt's tight grip and brought her to standing with me, then I spun her around to face me, the hunger in her eyes unmatched. My little Queen was ravenous. For me.

Of bloody course she was. She belonged to me.

Does she? an intrusive voice asked. I couldn't even blame it on Asher. This time it was all me. My own insecurity reared its ugly head as my eyes raked down her body, noting each and every one of her mates' marks. Teeth clenched, I counted them. Four in total. Two on either side of her neck. One on each of her perfect breasts. One for each of her mates.

Except for me.

Lifting her up to sit on the table, I shoved her thighs wide and knelt between her legs. Fingers trailing over the soft flesh of her inner thigh, I hummed before looking right at her mates. "Such pretty unblemished skin. I think it's time I change that and ensure you all realize exactly who owns her."

She grabbed me by the horns, making me moan as she pulled me closer.

"Yes, Pan. Do it."

I could feel the other men's surprise. Or maybe that was my own. Perhaps deep down I thought she might resist my reclaiming. Not wanting to give her a chance to change her mind, I bit down, giving her the final mark she needed. Sealing the last of her bonds. Ensuring we were wholly joined.

As soon as it was done, I pulled back, rising to my full height and bringing her with me.

"On your knees for me. That's how I like you best."

She sank down gracefully, the slight tremor of her fingers and the roll of slick down her thighs giving away how desperate she was to see what I was going to do to her.

Everything, Roslyn. I am going to do every fucking thing so you never forget you are mine. I claimed you first. And last. There was something poetic about that, though I didn't care to dwell on it at the moment.

I loosened my tail's hold on her, using the end against her chin to forcefully tip her head back.

"Open wide."

She opened her mouth.

"Wider."

A pulse of arousal hit me through the bond. She was loving this.

My gaze raked her form, flushed skin, bright eyes, nipples furled and begging to be slapped and pinched. Her lips were swollen from the way she'd been biting them to try and stifle her moans.

I leaned down, gripped her cheeks in one hand, and spit in her mouth.

Her eyes widened, and then she moaned, surprised, but not repulsed, by the act.

"You're welcome. The first of my gifts was free, but you'll have to beg me for the rest of them."

Her eyes darted from my face to my straining length, then back up. "Please, Pan?"

"Please, what?"

"Let me have it."

"Have what?"

Her throat bobbed. This was always the hardest part for her.

"Your cock," she whispered.

"I didn't catch that."

"I want your cock," she tried again, a slight wobble in her demand.

I moved my tail like a whip and slapped her between the thighs, my tail angled just right so that the tip caught her greedy clit.

"Then suck it. Open your mouth and swallow me down until you can't take any more."

The way she rocked her hips in search of more friction from my tail had me chuckling, but then I grabbed her hair harshly, tugging and controlling her head as she worked her lips around my crown.

I briefly considered adjusting my girth for her, as I had in the past, and then decided against it. She was a vampire now. There was very little I could do to actually harm her. Besides, my beautiful slut loved it most when it hurt. Already crystalline drops beaded the corner of her eyes. My balls tightened. I wasn't a sadist, per se, but I could appreciate my mate's tears.

My tail flicked her clit once more before sliding down until I pressed inside her, giving her what she truly craved. See? Not a sadist.

I shoved forward, sinking as far into her mouth as I could, then continuing my way down her throat as she gagged around me.

"You suck me so good," I groaned. "Does she suck you like this, wolf?"

Ben and Remi both made warning growls deep in their throats, which made sense considering I hadn't specified which wolf I'd been speaking to. I guess they didn't appreciate the reminder I had her right where *they* wanted her. And here I was, trying to extend an olive branch.

"Pity for you then. What about you, vampire?"

"My duchess knows exactly how to serve me. She's well trained."

"Of course she is. I broke her in for you."

"Keep telling yourself that, demon, if it helps you sleep at night."

I grinned, my fist tightening in the silky strands of her hair. "I don't sleep at night. I fuck."

Rosie surprised me by swallowing, the ripples of her throat causing me to jerk my hips forward and sink my tail deeper inside her. Tears streamed down her cheeks as she looked up at me, her thighs quivering, both hands reaching up to hold the base of my dick and work me where she couldn't take me.

A bright burst of pain shot through my length, the shocked gasp I let out unable to be contained.

"Sh-she's b-bleeding. S-stop him." Ben was on his feet, coming to her defense, but Gavin stopped him with an arm across the shifter's chest.

"That's not her blood."

"Fuck," Remi breathed.

I groaned, my fingers flexing convulsively in her hair. "She's feeding. It feels so fucking good. I always wanted a piercing."

"Is that safe?" Remi asked. He sounded almost jealous.

"Quite," Gavin assured him, though he too sounded jealous. Perfect.

Rosie sucked harder, taking a small amount of my blood from the place her fangs nicked me. I couldn't hold back anymore. I fucked her with my tail and let her use my cock like it was the only thing she ever wanted. When I felt her climb toward her crest, I let myself go too, both of us coming together in wave after wave of pure euphoria.

I'd never admit it, but I'd never felt this whole. This complete. Oh fuck. Rosie completed me. I was a nineties rom-com cliche.

If my mother knew, she'd never forgive me. It was a worse offense than the angel porn.

I slid free of her mouth, releasing her hair so my hand could cup her cheek. "You were perfect. As always."

She beamed under my praise, blinking up at me slowly. She looked as contented as I felt, if not a bit sleepy, as she nuzzled into my hand and let her eyes fall closed.

"I think it's finally over," Remi said. "My dick's soft again. Pretty sure that means she's full."

Of my cum. This time I couldn't contain my smirk.

"C-come on, sugar." Ben stalked over to us, scooped her into his arms, and shot me a warning glare before taking her upstairs.

"Is he always like this?" I asked, manifesting a pair of leather trousers. I'd already humiliated them enough, might as well do them a kindness and put the beast back in his cage.

"He's a caregiver. Your scene was intense. Ben will make sure she has the aftercare she deserves." The vampire said it so matter-of-factly, like this was something I should know about.

Apparently it was my turn to be jealous. Confusion tangled with the unwanted emotion in my belly.

I wasn't her Dom. She wasn't my submissive. She was my little slut. *Ma petite monstre.* Aftercare didn't exist in my world.

But perhaps it should?

CHAPTER TWENTY-TWO

BEN

"I've g-got you, sugar." I nuzzled her neck and pressed a soft kiss to her skin as I carried her upstairs.

Her breaths were slow and easy, not heavy like they would be if she were dreaming. She may not be asleep, but she wasn't exactly aware of her surroundings either. It was almost as if whatever energy surge had fueled her during the feast vanished as quickly as it had come on, leaving her thoroughly worn out.

She'd need rest as she came down from such a powerful experience. And it had been powerful. The feast, as Gavin called it, might have started off as an exchange of blood and sex, but there was magic involved too. I'd felt it. Not just through our bond, but in the air. I wouldn't pretend to know what that meant for any of us, but I had a feeling we were going to find out. Sooner rather than later.

Rosie sighed and wrapped her arms tighter around the back of my neck as I cradled her. We were sweaty and sticky, the aftermath of it all visible on both of us. I'd help her get clean, then hold her until she fell asleep, safe, warm, and loved.

"B-bath or sh-shower?" I asked.

"Bath. I don't think I can stand," she murmured against my shoulder.

"Whatever you n-need. I'll w-wash you."

She hummed in approval. "It's a good job you put in a tub big enough for two."

"Th-that was all Remi. He l-likes to s-soak."

"I can see that. With bubbles and a rubber duckie."

"It's a-actually a r-rubber unicorn, but d-don't tell him I t-told you."

Her giggle was so fucking sweet. I held her a little tighter, brushing my lips over the crown of her head.

I kicked open the apartment door and strode inside, my chest tightening at the memory of the last time we were here. What a fucking rollercoaster. Remi had been on his deathbed. I'd been beside myself. But now, the scent of sickness was gone, replaced by fresh, clean air and laundry detergent. When had Asher found time to change the sheets and clean?

I was already dreading letting her out of my arms, but I knew I'd have to eventually so I could start the water. Or . . . maybe not.

When I walked into the bathroom, I found the tub already filled, the air thick with steam and the scent of orchids and jasmine. Most of the available surfaces were covered with purple pillar candles, all gently flickering.

Rosie gasped.

"Wh-who did this?" Given the awed state of her face, I really wished it had been me. Caring for her was my job.

"Pan."

My hackles rose. "Wh-what?"

"He got the place ready for us. He just told me." She tapped her temple, indicating their bond.

"Boo."

I fucking flinched at the sound of the demon in my mind. What the fuck? I wasn't bonded to him in any way.

Rosie reacted to the tension in my body instantly. "What is it? What's wrong?"

"N-nothing." And then I silently added, *"Get out of my head, Pan."*

"I believe 'thank you' is the phrase you're looking for, you ungrateful wanker."

I couldn't stop the tightening of my shoulders as that smoky voice infiltrated my thoughts. But then he was gone, slinking back to whatever hole he crawled out of. If he could talk to me now, did that mean I could do the same with the others?

Not sure what I was doing, I sent out a test thought. *"Is this thing on?"*

Remi's response was immediate. *"Holy fucking shitballs. Give a guy some warning. Jesus. Wait, is something wrong? I'm on my way."*

"No, stay put. We're fine. But apparently telepathy is a thing we can do now."

"Hold on . . . you're not stuttering. You sound great, buddy. Also, we have superpowers! Awesome."

"Do you two mind? I didn't sign up for a group chat." Asher's voice held pure annoyance, and I grinned.

"You know you like having a front row seat to my dirty thoughts."

"Remington, please. No one enjoys that." Gavin was less than thrilled we were in his head as well.

"Count Dooku over here is such a stick-in-the-mud," Remi continued, entirely unfazed. *"This is great. Now I don't even have to text you. I can just think it all. We can stay up late swapping stories."*

"No," we all said at the same time.

"Someone teach him the finer points of selective mutism, please. Before I muzzle him myself." Pan popped back into my head, making me snarl. I *really* didn't like that guy.

But my dislike was quickly overshadowed by a new revelation. All of us were connected now. I wondered if this was the only new trick the feast had unlocked or if I could expect more surprises in the days to come. Given our track record, I was counting on the latter.

"You five are very loud," Rosie whispered, her brow furrowed and smile strained. "Charming, but loud."

"S-sorry, sugar."

I sent one last thing down the line to the guys. *"Everyone hang up, or whatever. No more mental group chats until we figure out how to control it, okay?"*

I was half expecting Remi to come back with a 'you started it,' but no one answered, which I took as their agreement. The last thing any of us wanted to do was hurt Rosie.

My lips brushed her temple before I helped her into the heated bath, making sure she was comfortable and able to relax.

"How's th-that f-feel? W-warm enough?"

"It's perfect." She sighed and wrapped her arms around her drawn-up legs, resting her cheek on her knees as she watched me kneel beside the tub. "You're not getting in with me?"

I shook my head. "C-can't wash y-you properly if I'm in th-there too." I grabbed the washcloth and dipped it into the scented water before lifting it and squeezing, trailing drops down her curved spine.

With a sweet smile, she closed her eyes, relaxing under the combined effects of my touch and the heat. I worked slowly, repeating my initial steps as I dunked the rag and dragged it gently across her skin. She moved without needing to be told, revealing new spots for me to clean. Her throat, where the silvery scars from mine and Remi's marks were, down to her breasts, where Gavin had claimed her, then my gaze landed on the still healing wound where Asher had bitten her tonight. As I watched, the imprint of his fangs faded and was replaced by a tattoo of a constellation curving across the swell of her full tit.

"Holy sh-shit," I breathed.

"What?" She sat up, and I gestured to the silvery stars. With a tentative touch, she traced them. "It's like the curse he had."

"D-did he c-curse you?"

She shook her head, the wet tips of her hair causing ripples in the water. "No. But I think it was part of him so long it sort of became his, you know? A symbol that represents him instead of the curse."

I didn't, but as long as she was safe, I wasn't going to press the issue. I continued washing her clean, frowning at the strange scar on her inner thigh where Pan had staked his claim as well. His was some kind of rune. Angular and sharp. Foreboding, like the demon himself.

"Tilt y-your head back. L-let me wash y-your hair."

She did as I asked, my cupped hands wetting the strands over and over until I could massage sweet-smelling shampoo and then conditioner into her scalp. I loved doing this for her. Seeing to her needs. Being the mate I was supposed to be. A true Alpha who gave his fated everything she deserved and more. I could so clearly see a thousand more nights like this one, and I wanted each and every one of them. Fiercely.

But we'll be lucky to get a handful of these moments if we don't stop Pestilence.

That niggling inner thought broke through as I rinsed her hair. It made my stomach churn. Pulling the plug on the drain, I helped Rosie out of the tub and dried her off, then snagged one of my spare shirts from the closet in the bedroom for her and a pair of sweats for me. We didn't need to be naked for what I had planned. This wasn't about sex. It was her and me. Together. Taking comfort in our companionship. Loving each other with no expectations for more.

Once I got us both settled under the blankets and turned off the light, she snuggled deeper into me.

"I heard your thoughts in there, Ben. You're right. We have to stop her." Rosie's whisper broke through the silence of the darkened room as we lay together on the bed.

I tightened my arms around her. We'd deal with the rest, but not right now. Not when I had her here with me like this. I was going to cling to this one perfect moment as long as I could. Call me selfish, but we'd been through hell and back these last few weeks. I needed a slice of heaven before we ran headlong back toward the chaos. We both did.

I knew Rosie well enough by now to know she wasn't going to be happy taking time for herself to regroup. But she needed it. She'd run herself ragged trying to take care of the rest of us. It was my responsibility to take care of her. All of her.

Which is why I kissed her forehead and whispered back, "Shh, baby. W-we will. In the m-morning. I promise."

CHAPTER

TWENTY-THREE

ROSIE

"Mmm, that feels nice," I murmured, my eyelids fluttering closed as Ben's fingers softly stroked my hair.

With my head pillowed in his lap, I could only just make out the satisfied curve of his lips above me. But I had no trouble hearing his whispered words. "You keep m-making noises l-like that, sugar, and we're g-going to m-miss the end of this episode."

Gavin's strong hands stilled on my foot, the pad of his thumbs pressing against the arch. "She's not going anywhere, Mercer."

"I d-didn't say she w-was. I can f-fuck her right h-here."

"This is cuddle time. Not sexy time, Benny-bear. You know the rules. Sunday is for snuggles." Remi dropped his head back so he was touching my thigh.

Asher chuckled from beside him, their fingers interlaced on Remi's lap. "I mean . . . I'm always down for fucking. Isn't that basically just sexy snuggles?"

"Hush. I need to know if the angel and the rugged one ever act on their obvious lust for one another."

I giggled and reached out, playing with Pan's horns, tipping his head back so I could peer into his lavender irises. "I thought you said this show was a nuisance."

"It *is* a bloody nuisance. Fifteen seasons and no one ever really dies. What a waste. Also, my brethren have been sadly misrepresented. No one would be able to have that many fuck ups and still be allowed to walk on the surface. Ludicrous."

"Look at him, fact-checking the writers," Remi snickered.

"They should bring me on as an accuracy reader. I mean, someone needs to hold them accountable for their blasphemy."

"It's fiction, Pan. It's not supposed to be real," Asher told him.

Pan huffed. "Just wait. A few more years with your extended family, and you'll change your tune. Details matter. Isn't that what you said last night?"

"Well, when we're talking about the number of orgasms I gave our girl, yes, details matter. Especially since *I* won the bet," Asher shot back, tossing me a wink.

"Technically I won. I gave her two extras before we all started," Gavin murmured, his grip on my ankle tightening.

"Mmm. Should w-we tell them about wh-what we were up to earlier?" Ben's fingers slid down between my shoulder blades and lower until he was running his hand up and down my spine, making me shiver with longing as we continued to watch the show. With his lips pressed against my ear he whispered, "God, your s-skin is s-so soft, baby. I w-wish we were n-naked right n-now."

"See! Blatant sexual tension between them." Pan threw his hands up and scoffed. "Not you two. *Those* two." He motioned to the telly.

"Someone has been hitting the fanfiction sites," Remi muttered.

"Those who live in glass houses shouldn't cast stones. Exhibit A: ghost porn."

"Do we need to talk about your browser history, Pan?" Asher asked, his voice teasing.

Pan actually blushed, his cheeks turning a deeper purple.

"Also, literature isn't porn. It's smut," Remi corrected. "Besides, Ruby Spector knows what's up. A whole group of rock star ghosts?

Come on. It's us, but dead. I just ordered a signed hardback copy for my library."

"You have a library?" Asher asked. "And we haven't played sexy librarian yet?"

Mouth still at my ear, Ben murmured, "But w-we have. Should we t-tell him?"

I squirmed and pressed my thighs together at the reminder as Remi shot Asher a wicked smirk. "Easily remedied. And I can be a way better library patron than Ben."

"I w-wasn't the patron. Miss Blackthorne w-was very n-noisy in the s-stacks."

"Did you show her your ruler?"

"All t-twelve inches."

"Nine," Asher corrected. "I should know."

"Uhh it's at least ten," Remi protested.

Gavin sighed. "Shall we drop our trousers right here and end the debate once and for all."

Hands already at his belt, Remi said, "I need a second before I whip it out. I'm a grower."

"Are w-we really asking Rosie to m-measure us?"

"Count me in," I said, earning a couple of smirks of my own. "But I'm quite interested in the rock star thing. Can we add that to the list as well?"

"For the last time, we aren't rock stars." Gavin's huffed response had me giggling again. This was hardly a new debate for them. Ever since Asher and I introduced Remi to *Rebel & The Haunts,* he'd gone on and on about this very thing. And every time, Gavin protested. I wasn't certain why my husband hated the comparison, but I had a feeling it had something to do with that movie about a vampire named Lestat. Whatever the reason, it got his dander up without fail.

"*You* might not be, but ask Asher or Rosie, and they'll tell you something different about me."

"Just b-because you d-dress like one, Remi . . ."

"In that case, he's also a pirate," I quipped.

"Arrr, did you want me to plunder yer booty again?" Remi glanced up at me and waggled his brows.

"Of course I do, but Pan called dibs on the next time." I turned my face toward Pan, but he wasn't in front of me any longer. "Where's Pan?"

"Who?" Asher asked.

"Pan. Tall, purple, horns?" I sat up, legs on either side of Remi as I looked around the living room.

There was no trace of him. Not even the lingering scent that was inherently Pan.

"I don't know what you're talking about, baby girl, but I really like this new seating arrangement." Remi tipped his head back again, and I pushed aside the lingering unease at Pan's disappearance.

Raking my fingers across Remi's scalp, I smiled as he practically purred in pleasure. "I love the way you touch me," he whispered.

"I love touching you. All of you."

I reached out for Ben, needing both of my Mercer men, but found nothing in the space where he'd been sitting.

"Ben?" I called, worry worming its way through me. "Where did you go? This isn't funny!"

Remi nipped my inner thigh. "What isn't funny is you calling out another man's name. You know the rules, baby girl. Only if we're roleplaying."

"Not even then," Gavin said.

I turned back toward my mates, my eyebrows furrowed. "What are you talking about? I'm looking for Ben. He was just here."

Asher and Remi exchanged confused looks before shaking their heads. "Uh, we don't know anyone named Ben, princess."

"Of course you do! He's your bloody twin, Remi."

"I'm an only child, baby. You know that." Remi laughed. "But I can totally understand why you'd want more than one of me."

"One Mercer is more than enough," Gavin drawled.

I thought for sure Asher would back Remi up, but when I sought out my black-hatted knight, he wasn't there.

"Okay, you lot think you're a bunch of comedians, don't you? Are we playing hide and seek?"

Remi turned around and knelt before me, his smirk distracting me from my unease. "We could play hide the salami."

"I'm serious, Remi. Asher was right next to you, and now he's gone."

He trailed his hands up my thighs. "So?"

"Gavin, tell him—"

But just like the others, Gavin was gone. Vanished as if he'd never been there at all.

"Remi . . ." My voice quavered, betraying my fear. "Where is everybody? What is going on?"

This time instead of denying my claims, he rose to his feet, his expression shifting from playful to grim. I had to blink, thinking it was a trick of the light, but no. Remi was . . . fading.

Right before my eyes.

"We were never yours to keep," he intoned, just as he winked out completely.

"No!"

I sat up, reaching out into the dimly lit room, breaths coming in rapid gasps as my heart hammered. The scent of leather and vanilla filled my nose, mixed with the warm aroma of melting beeswax. Candles? As I got my bearings, my surroundings made everything clear. It was a nightmare. I was in a bed, but not the one I'd fallen asleep in.

"Gavin?" I ventured, slipping out of the nest of blankets and padding toward the light at the far end of the room.

My husband strolled in, shirtsleeves rolled up to display his forearms, collar open, hair disheveled as though he'd been raking his fingers through the strands.

"Ah, you're awake. Feeling better, petal?"

I had to consider his question for a moment, surprise making my lips curve upward as I realized I did. The best I'd felt in weeks. For once, everything was right in my world. Well, mostly right. Asher and Pan were still sharing a body, but at least I had a way to connect with each of my mates and a deal that kept Pan on a figurative leash.

Hmm . . . maybe he needs a literal one.

"It'll be you on the end of my leash, ma petite. *Don't test me."*

A little shiver ran down my spine, but Gavin snagged me by the chin and forced my stare to meet his as he brought his face a breath from mine.

"The only collar you'll wear is mine."

His softly growled declaration set off another wave of shivers. "Promise?"

Gavin's eyes darkened, and I could feel how much he liked my breathy question.

"I swear on our bond. In fact, I have something for you. I've been holding on to it since before our wedding." He pulled open the wardrobe and revealed a safe the previous owners had hidden there. I didn't even question how he'd figured out the combination. With quick movements, the door was unlocked, and he brought out a velvet-wrapped bundle.

"You've really carried this around with you all this time?"

"Well, there hasn't been a good time to give it to you. First I thought you dead, and then when I found you, you weren't exactly happy to see me."

"What about after we mated?"

"Well, if I recall, we went straight from that to dealing with your bargain, and then seeing to Bentley and the Council. Oh and we mustn't forget the duel with your brother . . ." Gavin let out an aggrieved sigh. "And then, of course, there was Asher's curse and Remington's illness, not to mention the Apocalypse looming and you turning."

The corners of my lips tipped up as his frustration built, and my strong, stoic duke began to crack. "But now seems like the right time?"

"Yes. Before that fucking demon beats me to it. Again."

He unwrapped the parcel and revealed a choker encrusted with one of the rarest gems I'd ever heard of. Fire opals forged from actual dragon's breath. Each perfect stone contained a fragment of flame.

I swallowed, my jaw dropping open. "Gavin . . . how did you get dragon's breath?"

The pride was unmistakable in the set of his jaw as he ran his fingertips over the stones, the flame trapped within each one flaring brilliantly.

"It wasn't easy. I saw them come up for auction at The District, but not even I could get away with attending one of those black market events. So I had to enlist the help of a warlock to bid on my behalf. It cost more than you want to know, but I wanted my bride to understand she was worth everything I had."

"You did all that before you knew for sure I was your mate?"

"I did."

There was a rare flicker of vulnerability in his dark eyes.

"Why?" My question was little more than a whisper, but instinct told me I needed to hear this secret as much as he needed to admit to it.

"Because from the second I saw you on your knees before me, I knew you were meant to be mine. That the Seer was wrong when she said I didn't have a mate. She had to be. But even if you didn't truly want me, I was resolved to win you over. To make you feel so treasured you'd accept me eventually."

I wasn't sure why that surprised me so much, but it did. I hadn't thought my duke the sort of man to care about such things. At least not back then, before I really knew him. Now I understood it was never a lack of emotion, but perhaps an abundance of them. He'd spent so many years repressing everything. Crafting a mask of indifference and superiority to hide behind to avoid being deemed weak. But that's all it was. A façade. I'd wager that priceless bit of jewelry he was holding that no matter how much he'd protest otherwise, Gavin Anthony Donoghue felt things more deeply than us all.

Reaching up, I gathered my hair and lifted it off my neck. The mayor's amulet sat heavily between my breasts, reminding me of the very short leashes Gavin and I were already on. Speaking of the mayor, we were due for an inspection soon. But now that the hell-mouth was open and all manner of creatures roamed the streets, was it really necessary? We might be vampires, but we were hardly the most fearsome beasts around. Leashed or otherwise.

Hmm . . . I wonder what Pan would say if he knew that woman had achieved his goal before anyone else?

"I'd say we should drop a house on the witch and be done with this nonsense."

Ignoring Pan, I focused on Gavin.

"Would you do the honors, my lord?"

"Gladly."

He placed the collar around my throat and secured the lock with the key that accompanied the jewelry.

"Mine," he murmured.

"Yours."

Just like a wedding band, I could remove this easily—my vampiric strength saw to that—but it was the symbolism of the piece that mattered. It was a claiming. More than that, a vow. The sentimentality of the piece far outweighed its considerable value. So I'd wait until my husband unlocked the collar every time I wore it.

His fingertips dragged along the stones, lightly brushing my throat as they went, and a wash of arousal hit me, causing his eyes to darken in response. I sent him a mental picture of exactly how he could claim me if he wanted, and he chuckled in return.

"Not yet. But I'll have you soon while you're wearing this and nothing else."

"Why not yet?" I asked, resting my hand over the steady beat of his heart.

"I'd happily spend eternity buried inside you, my love, but you need more time to recover after a feast. All my research points to it."

There was that word again. Research. My stuffy duke was a secret nerd.

"What research have you been doing? How do you know so much about what I need as a Queen?"

The way his eyes sparkled with glee, you'd think I just told him Father Christmas was coming. "Come, darling. Better to show you. There's . . . quite a lot."

My brows lifted as he dragged me with him into a walk-in-closet he'd converted into his . . . murder board? Were murder boards supposed to take up an entire room?

"Gavin, what is all this?" I observed the space, every bit of wall covered in clippings and photos, red string connecting notable details to each other, along with scribbles in his masculine scrawl to keep track of his suspicions.

I reached for the nearest Post-it Note, about to pluck it off, but he stopped me with a hand on my wrist.

"Please don't touch anything. I've only just fixed it after Asher tried to *help* me last."

"Asher helped you with this?"

Gavin gave me a distracted nod, his eyes scanning the wall. "It's how we passed the time when he was . . . sequestered."

"I see. So you two have grown close, then?"

"I tolerate him."

My lips twitched. "And what conclusions have you drawn so far?"

"Nothing much aside from what you already know. You're stronger with us nearby. You have to feed from us. The powers you naturally have as a vampire are enhanced to a level that frightens the Council, which is why Queens are secreted away and there are only a couple on record."

"I haven't experienced any extra powers."

"Not yet. But I'm certain you will."

"And . . ."

Discomfort thrummed through our bond, the sensation reminding me of the time my youngest brother plucked at the wires inside our piano, eerie and unsettling.

"Gavin, what aren't you telling me?" He looked away from me, not favoring me with an answer, which only made me more insistent. "I'm trying to respect your mental barriers, but I need you to be honest with me."

Brows pulling together, he linked our hands and locked eyes with me. "The last time Pestilence was thwarted, it was by a Queen."

"We already knew that."

"Yes, but we didn't know how it was done until I put it together just a few hours ago."

Apprehension built in my belly. "Stop dragging it out. How did the Queen stop the Apocalypse, Gavin?"

"She died."

CHAPTER TWENTY-FOUR

GAVIN

"I beg your pardon? She . . . died? As in, permanently? I don't know if you realized this, but that is a rather important detail you forgot to mention, Gavin."

The dread that had coiled in my belly at the reminder of my discovery turned swiftly to anger. "You little fool," I snapped, grasping her chin between my thumb and forefinger. "Do you really think I'd keep something like this from you?" I could see the protest building behind her lips, waiting to be unleashed on me, but I didn't give her a chance to backtrack. "I'd only just discovered this a couple of hours ago while you were asleep. I've been looking for further details ever since. I can't come to you with a fucking grenade of this magnitude and not offer you any sort of answers or protection or . . . I don't know, some sort of metaphorical bomb shelter."

The emotion in my voice was uncharacteristically fervent, leaving me shaking. I released her chin in favor of crushing her tight against my chest as I worked to pull myself together. I'd lost her twice already. I couldn't . . . no, I *wouldn't* go through it again.

"I'm not a fool," she murmured.

"Yes, you are. But apparently you make me one too, so I suppose we're even."

She chuckled and wrapped her arms around my waist before falling silent and whispering into my shirt. "I know we need to stop her, but . . . I don't want to die, Gavin."

My heart ached at the vulnerability in her words. "I won't let you."

"So . . ." She took a shuddering breath, her fingers clutching tight to me. "How did the Queen die?"

I broke away from my wife, even though it pained me to stop touching her. "I don't know. I'm still working out the particulars." Gaze raking the wall of clues I'd amassed, I verbally retraced the path my research had led me down, pointing to various notes I'd tacked onto the wall as I did. "As I've explained, every Queen has made herself known during a time of extreme risk to vampirekind. But what we didn't understand until now was that the trigger wasn't simply danger to our species, but a truly biblical event."

She quirked a brow. "You mean an apocalyptic event."

"Precisely. Which is why sun sickness didn't trigger a Queen. That was something your parents fought, but it wasn't caused by Pestilence herself."

"No, it was magic. A spell."

"But"—I gestured to an article about the Spanish Influenza pandemic—"in 1918, the world was dying, nearly resulting in the starvation of vampires. Then a Queen rose and stopped her.

"Wars, famines, droughts, all had a Queen to aid in keeping us in existence. Without humans, we cannot survive." My focus trained on another clipping, my voice gaining confidence as I spoke. "In 1590, the colony of Roanoke vanished into thin air. But the truth is something mortals will never understand or believe. Death came for them, and a Queen raised them all as vampires in retaliation."

"How did she do that?"

"Her blood. She brought them back, complete with their souls and all the powers of born vampires. Queens are hidden because of all they represent—not just because they're the means of our salvation, but because they're a threat to the Council's leadership."

"Come again?"

"They're our saving grace, but their considerable gifts mean they also have the ability to undo all our hierarchical framework in one fell swoop." Which was why the Council worked so hard to bury all information about them. I never would have learned all I had if not for Asher's tinkering. I owed that hacker more than he could ever know.

Roslyn hummed and inspected each article closely. "So what you're saying is, the Council doesn't like that I can make anyone I like into a born vampire?"

"Among other things. As a Queen, you single-handedly prove the attention paid to bloodlines is pointless. That the power the Council clings to is tenuous. Your power alone is stronger than all of them combined."

"I don't feel particularly strong."

"Darling, you're terrifyingly strong. And I don't believe your abilities have even begun to fully manifest themselves. Though, now that you've feasted, I wouldn't be surprised if that was about to change," I mused, the 'murder board,' as Roslyn called it, blurring as my attention turned inward.

"All right, I'm powerful, have five men who love me and bring me pleasure whenever I require, and I can stop the end of the world. So what's the downside to being a Queen? There has to be one."

"Other than the fact they've all died to save us?"

She visibly deflated. "Well, yes. That does put a damper on things."

"They burn bright and fast. Like a candle with too long a wick. Your perfect body was not made to contain this much power. That's where we come in."

"I assume you're referring to my mates and not using the royal we."

"Roslyn, be serious."

"Sorry, I'm just nervous. This is quite a lot to take in. I must have adopted Remi's habit of deflecting with jokes."

"Fair enough." I put my arm around her and reeled her into me, brushing a kiss to her forehead. "Yes, your mates. Together, we see to you. Refuel you. Keep you whole and hale. Though, I've never seen a Queen mated to any creature besides other vampires. Especially demons of Pestilence's line. Or *any* horsewoman's line." I blew out a breath, the answers I needed continuing to elude me. "This is a unique situation."

"You sound frustrated by that."

I pulled my eyes away from the riddle in front of me so I could meet her gaze. "Yes, but only because your uniqueness means there's absolutely no way to predict the outcome."

"And you don't like things being out of your control."

A bitter laugh escaped. "Who does?"

"Very true."

I smelled the shifter before he darkened the closet's doorway. Our time alone was over for now.

"Y-you're awake," Bentley said, leaning against the doorframe and grinning at Roslyn.

"She is."

Roslyn moved away from my side and into his arms. "Thank you for taking care of me after we . . ." Her cheeks went pink as she flicked her gaze away from him.

"Feasted?" I asked, loving her embarrassment after the things she let us do to her.

"Yes. That."

"Sugar, you sh-should know by now, I'll a-always take care of you."

"You did promise."

"I d-did."

"Is there a reason you're looming in my rooms, Mercer?" I tried for irritated but landed on vaguely inconvenienced. "We were busy."

His eyes roamed over my notes. "I can s-see that."

Something about the wolf seeing my board made me feel oddly exposed. This time, there was a definite edge to my voice as I snapped, "Again, why are you here?"

Bentley tightened his hold on her waist. "I w-was just checking on her. Do I n-need a reason to s-see my mate?"

Roslyn's thoughts were a buzz of anxiety as everything we'd discussed began tumbling through her head. Perhaps Bentley had been right to check on her.

"She's right as rain. Don't you trust me with her?"

I sensed the tiniest bit of apprehension, followed immediately by confusion from the shifter. His face didn't betray his conflicted emotions, but this new connection Roslyn had forged between us gave him away. He trusted me, and he wasn't sure how to feel about the revelation.

To be fair, neither was I. Somewhere along the line I'd stopped loathing the rest of my wife's mates and moved from barely tolerating them to, dare I say, actively relying on them. Who would have seen that coming?

I wasn't used to having . . . friends. If that's even what we were. In fact, I do believe this may just be the first time in my entire life I had a group of people I trusted—not just with my secrets, but with my most precious possession. It was a novel and not wholly comfortable experience.

"H-her heart is r-racing. She's anxious."

Fucking mate bonds.

"Gavin has unearthed a great deal about what it is to be a Queen. It was a lot of information. I need to process it all."

There she went, solidifying exactly what I'd been worried about. But I wouldn't be the man she feared I was. Hiding vital details from her. Keeping her in the dark about her safety. She was power personified, and I needed to help her be her strongest self.

We all did, if there was any hope of making it out of this alive.

"S-sounds like you n-need a distraction."

"What did you have in mind?" Roslyn grinned up at him. I caught the heady scent of her arousal. From the flare of his nostrils, so did Bentley. But he and I were of the same mind it would seem, because instead of taking her up on the obvious invitation, he gave her a lopsided grin.

"L-let's take a w-walk, sugar. Get s-some fresh night air."

"Night? Isn't it the afternoon? Is the clock wrong?"

He and I tensed. She'd slept through the moment we all realized the sun had never risen. "It's been night since before Remi was healed."

Roslyn's sharp gasp had guilt worming its way into my mind again. But no. She needed to know everything.

"Are you serious?"

"W-we're sure it's got s-something to d-do with Pestilence."

"Of bloody course it does," she muttered. "We have to stop her. I have to."

"And we w-will. But n-not this s-second, sugar. So come on. A w-walk will clear y-your head."

She nodded, and I frowned, not keen on the thought of her being out of sight. "Keep her at your side at all times, Bentley."

The big shifter looked over his shoulder as he ushered our mate out of the room. "You have my w-word."

Even a week ago, that might not have been enough to reassure me, but after all we'd been through together and seeing the depth of his dedication to our mate tonight, it was. He'd battled his inner-most demons to be with her. If there was anyone who would protect her as fiercely as I, it was Bentley Mercer.

Which was a relief, honestly, because it gave me much-needed time. Time to continue my research and, hopefully, time to find a solution that didn't involve the death of the woman who'd taught me how to love.

CHAPTER TWENTY-FIVE

PAN

The deep growl of hellhounds hidden in the shadowed corners of the chamber I found myself in reverberated deep in my bones. Oh no, not this again.

"I'm here, Mother. You can stop the theatrics. *You* summoned *me*, remember? Call off your dogs."

"Jenner, Iggy, Marie, Hopkins, come."

I rolled my eyes as the beasts stalked toward their mistress, wondering not for the first time why my mother bothered to name the creatures she so clearly loved after her biggest mortal nemeses.

Light bloomed, filling the space and revealing her curiously cozy living room. For someone who brought disease and rot everywhere she went, she really leaned into the classic mid-century modern decor. I took in the pea-soup green, shit-stain brown, and asparagus-pee yellow . . . Come to think of it, perhaps it was the color palette that drew her in. Suddenly her infatuation made a lot more sense. The sixties just might be her spirit era. Was that a thing?

I half expected the one true love of her life, Captain Tony Nelson, to stroll through the door and rub her lamp. Excuse me while I go vomit.

Yes. This was all one big plot to get her guests to sick themselves. I was sure of it.

She really was an evil genius.

Mum strolled to the tufted brown velvet couch and gracefully sat down, her black caftan flowing around her as the hellhounds joined her, not leaving any room for me. Not that you could pay me to sit on that vile thing. Knowing her, the bad taste might be contagious.

"You look . . . different, Pandemic. What's wrong with you?"

Oh, nothing. I think I'm in love with the woman I was supposed to be using, and I don't know what to fucking do with myself. But of course, I didn't tell her that. If she knew I was in love, she'd . . . Well, I wasn't sure what she'd do, but it wouldn't be good.

"I'm trapped on Earth and have to share my existence with my stupid half brother because of you."

"So nothing new, then."

I sighed and glared at her. "Why did you summon me, Mother? I'm wallowing in my circumstances."

Her gaze was filled with malice as she stared me down, petting those damned beasts of hers in such a calm manner you'd think she wasn't bothered in the least by the Apocalypse she was trying to bring about.

"I need you to kill her."

My stomach cramped so severely I'd have sworn she gave me something for a second. Then I recognized it for what it was. Fear.

My mother wanted me to kill my mate. How in the Lucifer-forsaken world was I going to get out of this? Then I remembered the terms of our new deal.

My knees were nearly weak with relief as I blurted, "I, uh, can't."

"What do you mean, you can't?" Her voice was so deceptively soft, I knew I was seconds away from finding myself on the receiving end of her wrath.

"I made a deal with her. They had me trapped in a circle, and I couldn't do anything to . . . to serve you like that. So, when she offered me a bargain, I took it. But I can't harm her."

She stared at me for a second before bursting into a fit of giggles. A trickle of sweat rolled down my nape. She was decidedly *more* terrifying in her merriment than she was in her anger.

"You stupid, simple fool," she laughed, wiping tears from her eyes. As quickly as it had come on, her amusement fled, and she leveled me with a dark glare. "*You* cannot be beholden to a deal with a *vampire*. Only demons, or the occasional fae, strike binding deals. Surely even you remember that most basic tenet of our kind. It's demon 101. Honestly, did I teach you nothing?"

"I . . ." My words dried up as I tried to come up with a valid argument on the spot.

"If you haven't harmed her or her ridiculous menagerie of men, it's because you didn't want to. Not because she's got some magical hold on your actions." She gave me a pitying look, but that was quickly replaced by suspicion. "Pan, what aren't you telling me?"

I shook my head.

It was the absolute worst thing I could have done. Now my mother was like a fucking dog with a bone. She was on me so fast, I hadn't realized she'd left her perch until she was already gripping my horn. Roughly, she yanked my head to the side and bared my neck to her.

No, not my neck.

My mark.

My *mating* mark.

Fuck.

"What is this?" she hissed. "What has she done to you?"

Well, there was no hiding it now. She already knew the answer to her questions, at least part of it, but if I didn't respond before she said it, I'd be giving her all the power. "I wasn't lying when I said I can't kill her. At least not now. She's my mate."

"That might be the most ridiculous load of crap you've ever said to me."

I blinked at her. "It's not crap. You're literally staring at the proof."

She shoved me. "Demons cannot be truly mated outside their species. It's a genetic impossibility."

"And yet, here we are."

She shook her head, her eyes narrowed with suspicion. "There's something else you aren't telling me. Something that makes this absolute farce possible."

Bugger. I'd really stepped in it. She couldn't find out Rosie was a Queen. Nothing was more dangerous than my mother getting her grubby little paws on that bit of information. It would be the end of my little monster.

Look at that; I was protective. Was this growth? Was I evolving? I'd better be careful; the next thing I knew, I'd be stammering and wearing plaid.

"She's mine. Face it, Mum, you fucked up when you sent me to her. Perhaps she has some demon blood we don't know about? Witches were always spreading their legs for our kind in exchange for power. It's entirely plausible there's some Blackthorne half-breed in her family tree."

Technically, the ancestor would have been on her mother's side, but fuck if I knew her maiden name. And honestly, no one fucking cared.

"I don't make mistakes. And her blood doesn't contain a single drop of anything demonic. Don't you think I'd know that?"

"You didn't know she was my fated mate."

Her jaw clenched as she closed her eyes and took a long breath. Lifting her face to the ceiling, she growled, "If you fucking angels are meddling, so help me, you'll be the first one I pluck and mount to my wall, Gabriel."

Oh good. Now her ire's directed at someone else. Talk about a silver lining.

Then she reeled back to me.

Spoke too soon.

"It's an unfortunate turn of events for you, Pan."

"I'm sure you see it that way."

"I hate to see you suffer, but perhaps you'll survive."

"What are you on about?"

"If you're her mate, you'll languish and wither away until you eventually die once she's gone." She sounded nearly gleeful at the thought, though I wasn't sure it was my death in particular or just the thought of a creature in general withering away. That was sort of her kink, so to speak. Decimation of any kind really got her going.

I frowned, dread pooling in my stomach. "I'm not going to kill her."

A wicked smirk twisted her face. "No. You've made that clear. You're useless to me now. I should take your horns, but you've already set yourself up for a punishment far more fitting than anything I could come up with."

"Mother," I warned.

"Enough. You've disappointed me at every single turn." She took her seat once more, resting both hands on her hellhounds and looking for all the world like an empress on her throne. "If you can't kill her, I'm just going to have to do it myself."

CHAPTER TWENTY-SIX

ROSIE

"W-what's she d-doing?" I heard Ben whisper from down the hall.

"Shh, don't ruin it. She's cooking and I think she's got it this time." Remi's hushed voice had my hackles up. I knew precisely why he was warning Ben. I didn't have a stellar track record in the kitchen, and I got a little jumpy when I knew they were hovering around watching me.

"Is th-there an occasion I d-don't know about?"

"Stress," Asher answered, his voice pitched low like the others.

The lull in conversation made me picture the concerned expressions *that* explanation caused.

"Hey, Siri!" I called. "Play the 'Just the Tip' playlist."

"Okay, playing Sexy Beast's 'Just the Tip' playlist." That robot was bloody brilliant. Music filled the kitchen and drowned out the sound of my mates and their uneasy conversation surrounding my cooking.

Determined to get it right this time, I'd started prepping early this morning, although with the sky trapped in a perpetual night, who knew what time of day it really was anymore? All we had was the clock to tell us when we should rise. My gut churned, but I pushed my trepidation aside in favor of the distraction in front of me. While my pot roast . . . roasted, I'd taken it upon myself to tackle freshly baked bread as well. Ambitious, I know.

No matter how many times I tried, I just couldn't seem to find my groove in the kitchen. I'd yet to manage more than toast successfully, but today was the day that changed. I could feel it in my bones. Today I *would* conquer my own personal Everest. Roslyn Blackthorne-Donoghue would no longer be defeated by some meat and veg. I could do this, dash it.

*"Blackthorne-Donoghue-*Mercer, *baby girl."* Remi's voice echoed through my head.

I grinned as I kneaded the bread dough on the freshly floured counter.

"And what am I, a ham sandwich?" Asher was all indignation and bluster.

"I like a sandwich."

"Is that even a question? You're a Mercer as well. Obviously," Remi answered without reservation.

"Was there a proposal I missed?"

"I, uh . . . No. It's . . . fuck. It's a . . ." Remi stumbled over his words.

Ben stepped in and rescued his brother. *"Pack thing. You're pack now, and we're the Alphas, so you take our name."*

"Huh. Interesting. I didn't realize that involved a name change, but I guess I'll go with it. Gavin's going to love that."

"Not happening."

I laughed out loud at Gavin's terse rebuttal while wondering about Pan's silence. He did so love to butt in, but I figured since he had no last name to speak of, perhaps he wasn't particularly interested in the conversation.

"Okay, boys. I'm turning off the group chat so I can focus on my task. I'll let you know when dinner's ready."

My men pushed to be let back into my thoughts. Gentle, probing, asking without words. But I sent them a soft request for privacy. The truth was, I had a lot more racing through my mind than whether I'd let my dough rise for long enough before popping it in the oven. The knowledge I'd likely have to die in order to thwart the horsewoman weighed on me like a boulder. My fear wasn't just for myself, though. It was for the misery and anguish my mates would endure until they eventually followed me to the hereafter. I'd already experienced a shred of Ben's torment when he thought I'd died last time. I couldn't stand the thought of any of the men I loved having to live with that all-consuming grief.

Panic crept up my chest as my thoughts began to spiral, but I took a steadying breath, closing my eyes and counting to four as I worked to get ahead of the attack. Pestilence was a battle I didn't know how to win, which is why I was focusing on one I could. I may not be able to beat a horsewoman—yet—but I was going to make a lovely Sunday roast for my mates. And perhaps afterward, they might enjoy my cookie for dessert. That would be the best distraction.

As the bread baked, filling the kitchen with the delicious scent of yeast and the comforts of a hot meal, I mourned the loss of my ability to eat human food. I could technically partake, but I wouldn't enjoy it. Not yet. Give me a few years into my life as a vampire, and I'd be able to sit down for a meal just like my brothers and father. Human food may never appeal to them as it once did, but they could still enjoy old favorites if they chose to. Right now, all I craved was blood.

The music changed to an angsty rock ballad from the eighties, and I couldn't help but sing along. When I got to the chorus, Remi skidded into the room, snatching the wooden spoon off the counter and holding it up like a microphone as he belted out the chorus. I laughed as he wrapped his arm around my waist and tugged me close.

"I'll be alone with you any time you want, baby girl. Just say the word."

"That would be your takeaway," I murmured with a smile.

"You were literally just asking how to get me alone. Was there another takeaway?"

"I was not. Heart was."

"Same difference."

"Oh, really?"

"Yeah. The words came out of your mouth, with a full-on eyes closed, right from the chest performance, might I add. So, clearly, you meant it. Ipso facto, *you* said it."

"Is this like when you make up a word and use it in a sentence?"

"Oh come on, you totally agree with me. If the other person knows what I mean when I use it in a sentence—"

My timer cut off the rest of his indignant response.

"Hold that thought!" I pulled open the silverware drawer and grabbed a soup spoon before opening the lid of the slow cooker and inhaling the delectable scent of the roast. Dipping the spoon into the broth, I brought a sample to my lips and tasted what would eventually be gravy.

"What's that face?"

I let the flavors coat my tongue. It was off. Something was wrong. "I ruined it." *Just like I always do.*

He sniffed. "Doesn't smell ruined to me. My stomach's been growling for hours."

Frustration crawled up my throat, my shoulders knotting with shame and defeat as I lifted the entire slow cooker—still plugged in, by the way—and spun toward the rubbish bin.

"Whoa, hang on! What are you doing? That's my dinner!" Remi lunged for me, eyes wild.

"No, it's going to poison you. I'm telling you something's off. It's rotten."

"No. It. Is. Not." He grabbed the handles, tugging the piece of cookery toward him.

"Yes. It. Is."

"Rosie. I swear to God, if you toss out this whole pot roast before I even get to try it, I'm going to . . ."

"Spank me? You should know by now that's only an incentive."

"I'll keep pirate Remi locked up and never let him out to visit again."

"What? That's mean."

He tugged on the slow cooker, and I tightened my grip, holding fast. It was Ben and the spaghetti all over again.

"Remi, let go. You'll get yourself hurt."

"Not gonna happen, baby girl. You made me dinner. I intend to eat it."

"Poison yourself, you mean."

"Hey, if Pesty couldn't do it, I'm sure whatever's in there isn't going to finish the job. Besides, I have my secret weapon. We'll just keep Asher on standby."

I released my hold on the roast, letting Remi have his way, and the handsome bastard simply smirked before placing the container on the counter at his side. Sighing, he dragged a hand through his hair before he locked eyes with me. His entire demeanor changed from one moment to the next. He went from playful to smoldering as he stalked toward me.

I guess he was hungry for something else now.

"No. Bad dog. You'll spoil your appetite," I teased, reaching for the first thing I could find to brandish in front of me. Instead of the spoon I was hoping for, I'd nicked a carrot.

Remi chuckled. "What are you going to do with that, baby girl? Stuff me?"

"I mean . . . Asher seemed to enjoy the experience."

He continued forward, gaze never leaving mine. "You know who else likes carrots?"

"I'm sure you're going to enlighten me."

"I am." Close enough for me to see the pulse fluttering in his neck and notice the way his pupils were blown with the excitement racing through his veins, he dipped his head and bit off the end of the carrot. "Bunnies."

"Yes, they do," I said breathlessly.

"You wanna be my bunny, Rosie?"

I licked my lips. "Yes?"

"Then you better run."

My heart was already racing when I spun and ran pell-mell out of the room. I zoomed past a perplexed Asher and a curious Ben as I made for the hallway. I didn't tap into my vampire abilities, because it wasn't like I was actually trying to get away. This was one bunny who definitely wanted to get caught.

I took the stairs two at a time, hoping to get a bit of a lead on Remi, but quickly realized he wasn't anywhere in sight. The man was working me into a trap. I was sure of it. But I still had to make an effort. This was about the thrill of the chase.

"Y-you don't look l-like you're r-running, sugar." Ben's voice was colored with a hint of his wolf as he stepped out of the hall and closed in on the staircase. "You want us to catch you." That last was all wolf, and I bloody loved it.

"Maybe."

"Good."

He lunged for me, but I sprung forward, just making it to the top of the stairs ahead of him. A quick glance showed the door on the left was already open, so I shot through it, slamming it behind me. A closed door wouldn't stop my alpha wolves, but it might buy me a couple of seconds.

Gavin looked up from his desk, taking in my heaving chest, disheveled state, and the carrot dangling from my hand.

"My, my, petal. You are in quite a state," he murmured.

"Hide me. They're chasing me."

He pushed his chair back and gestured under his desk. "Well then, you'd better get over here."

I dropped the carrot and then darted across the room, the knowledge of how close I'd be to his . . . everything only adding to my arousal.

"Fuck, I can smell how much this excites you. If I was the one chasing you, I'd already have you up against a wall."

Remi burst through the door, eyes laser-focused on me attempting to hide myself fully. “The anticipation is half of the appeal.”

Gavin pushed himself away before rising to his feet, and for a second I thought he was going to step in between Remi and me. No such luck. He moved so they both loomed over me. I stared up at them, quivering with the excitement of the moment. Now that they found me, what would they do?

But before either of them touched me, strong hands wrapped around my ribs, pulling me back with a strangled cry. He’d caught me by surprise, but it wasn’t fear I was feeling right now. Not even close.

Ben’s lips were at my ear, his voice a rough whisper. “Gotcha. You’re m-mine now.”

“Hey! No fair. I found her first,” Remi protested.

“I t-touched her first. She’s m-mine.”

“Technically, gentlemen, I touched her first.”

“Sharing is caring,” I breathed, tongue darting out to wet my lips as the three of them closed ranks on me.

“Uh, sorry to break up this moment, but the mayor is blowing up your phone,” Asher said, appearing in the doorway, munching on the carrot I’d dropped.

Ben helped me to my feet, and we all turned our attention to Asher.

“W-what does sh-she want?”

My fingers went to the amulet hanging from my neck. “Vampire insurance.”

“Sometimes I forget my bunny’s a deadly predator now.” Remi ran a hand over my back, then leaned in and kissed my shoulder. “We can pick this back up after dinner.”

Dinner.

I’d gotten so caught up in our game I’d forgotten about my meal.

“Oh, fork! My bread!” The loaf would be ruined. Charred. Nothing but a bit of carbon. A terrible bake.

"Already t-taken care of, sugar. It's c-cooling on the r-rack."

I reached for his shirt and tugged him close for a kiss. "Always coming to my rescue."

Ben slapped me on the arse. "A-any time you n-need me."

CHAPTER TWENTY-SEVEN

ROSIE

"Why am I nervous about seeing her again?" I murmured as Gavin and I stood on the mayor's front porch waiting to be let in.

By all rights, the woman shouldn't scare me. She was powerful, certainly, but no more than Gavin. He could literally tear her apart without the amulet. I doubt he'd even break a sweat. A dark smile crossed my lips at the thought of my Gothic hero facing off against the Southern beauty queen. It widened when my mental image of Gavin was replaced by Pan. How would Ms. Dubois react to my wicked demon?

I felt Gavin's curiosity brush against my mind, my expression clearly not matching my initial question.

As soon as I let him in, he chuckled in understanding. "I just might pay to see that."

"Me too. He'd have the woman running screaming from the room in seconds, I'm sure of it. Actually, one flick of his forked tongue and she'd be so scandalized she'd faint dead away."

"I seem to remember you enjoying the forked tongue. Quite loudly."

My cheeks burned. It was strange to be able to openly discuss Pan with him. No one was a fan of my demon. In fact, all of my men still wanted to kill him for what he'd done to us individually and as a group, but they wouldn't dare try. And it wasn't just because we were officially mated now. That alone would be enough of a deterrent. However, Gavin's research was quite clear on one point in particular. A Queen required *all* of her mates. Whether it was for the connection, the boost in power, or just to sustain herself was unknown, but the fact remained.

Fate had brought all five of them to me for a reason. I needed them, if only to stop the Apocalypse. But, if I'm being completely honest with myself, now that I loved them all, I wouldn't easily be separated from a single one of my mates.

Pan was part of me. Part of *us*. We were in this mess together, like it or not.

The front door swung open, revealing a smiling, perfectly coiffed Delta Dubois. Her lipstick, a tasteful shade of pink, made her appear soft and genteel, and her Chanel suit only drove the look home. Of course, it matched her lips. I'd look like a bottle of Pepto-Bismol if I wore anything of the sort. All she was missing was a silly hat.

"Rosie, Gavin, what a pleasure to see you again." Was it just me, or was her accent stronger?

I nearly swallowed my tongue trying not to laugh when Gavin's drawl sounded in my mind. *"Too bad we cannot say the same."*

"Thank you for the insistent invitation. We certainly couldn't decline." I pasted a smile on my face as I clutched Gavin's hand.

"Well, a deal *is* a deal, Rosie dear. But you'd know all about that, of course."

I stiffened. Had her eyes turned a sickly reptilian green for a second? And what the forking hell was that supposed to mean? She couldn't possibly know about my deals with Pan and Lilith . . . could she?

By the time I recovered enough to respond, she'd already turned her saccharine smile back to Gavin. "We must keep the good people of Aurora Springs safe. Especially with all these new visitors. Can't run the tourists off when they're bringing so much business to our fair town. And how would it look if a newcomer just dropped dead?" She snapped her finger to emphasize the point. "I might not be able to do anything about this . . . plague, but I can give them safe harbor from vampires."

"I don't think it's us this town needs protection from, Madam Mayor. Not long ago, I was attacked by an incubus."

Gavin's back stiffened. Oops. I might've forgotten to fill him in on that tidbit between reuniting with Ben and, well, everything else that had happened since.

My eyes darted to his, hoping he'd read the apology there, but given the way his gaze promised retribution, I knew we'd be speaking about my unintentional omission later. Likely while his palm pinkened my arse. When his lips curled ever so slightly, I also knew he'd caught the little shiver of anticipation that raced down my spine.

"An incubus? My, we haven't had one of those in town in . . . at least twenty-five years. But you're a vampire. Surely an incubus was no true threat."

"Perhaps not to one in possession of all their faculties. But due to your amulet, I wasn't able to do much to defend myself. I only got away because Ben intercepted us."

I was in for it when we got home. Gavin's grip on my hand was nearly crushing.

Delta's frown was as false as the sympathy in her eyes. "I suppose that means you shouldn't spend much time in town alone, then."

Swing and a miss. I tried to reason with her. It was worth a shot.

"She's always protected."

Delta raised one brow. "Not by you, though. You can't do much against"—she flicked the amulet hanging from his neck—"well, anyone, now can you?"

Gavin sucked in a sharp breath. "I can do enough."

Her pursed lips told me she didn't believe him. "That remains to be seen. Come in, won't you? We don't need to be standing out in the elements, especially when the two of you are so helpless."

She was lucky we had these bloody talismans around our necks, or she wouldn't have a head after the way she was poking at Gavin.

We followed her inside, her pretentious feline winding itself through her feet as she walked, purring incessantly. "Sassy, be a good girl and go sit on the couch now, would you? Mama's working."

Surprisingly, the cat did as it was told, chin held high, tail even taller as it pranced away.

"Remind me again why we don't want to kill this witch? The name she gave that poor creature alone deserves some form of restitution. Perhaps the feline would ally itself with us? We could stage a coup. You could take her place . . ."

I elbowed my duke in the ribs. *"Don't make me laugh. I won't make it through this without offending her. Besides, you and I both know Ben would make a much better mayor than me. The people of this town adore him, and he's a born leader."*

Gavin hummed softly but didn't respond further.

Sitting in the same positions we'd been in during our first visit, we waited while Delta did whatever witchy things she needed to do. When she finally turned back toward us, a dagger was in one of her hands. "Let's get the unpleasantries out of the way first, shall we?"

"Which one of us is going to tell her that every second in her presence is an unpleasantry?"

"Not it."

"And you call yourself a masochist."

"There's no pleasure in that pain, and you know it."

"Touché."

Delta snagged me by the wrist, not giving me a chance to react as she dragged the blade across my palm. Pain burned up my arm, and I cried out, the reaction causing Gavin to snarl in her direction.

"Hush now. It's just a little blood. This is basically foreplay for your kind, isn't it? Besides, this is the price you pay to remain here. Don't you think that's worth a bit of pain?" Delta held my hand over a bowl and let drop after drop of crimson fall.

She didn't release me as she stared down at the blood, transfixed. "I heard Remington made a miraculous recovery. Doctor Hatchet made it seem like things were dire for him. And we have quite a few townsfolk who seem to be getting worse rather than better. How on earth did y'all find a cure?"

I was very careful to keep my expression intact, not wanting to give away the jolt of fear her seemingly innocent question sent straight through me. The truth was, we still didn't know exactly how Asher had done the impossible. But even if we had, something told me I didn't want the word to spread. People would be lining up, begging for him to heal them, and if he couldn't—I shuddered. Desperation made people do terrible things. I refused to put Asher's life in danger. Well, more than it already was.

"It was a miracle," I said baldly, since in so many ways, that's precisely what it had been.

She narrowed her eyes, squeezing my wrist until one final drop of blood fell into the bowl. By the time she released me, my skin had knitted itself back together. One fingertip dipped into the bowl before she brought it to the amulet at my sternum. The scent of magic permeated the air as the stone heated against my skin, even through the fabric of my shirt. Then everything was back to normal once more, as though nothing had happened.

"A miracle. Of course," she murmured. "Well, here's hoping the good Lord sees fit to pass a few more of those around." She coughed, a delicate fluttery little thing, and for the first time, her perfect veneer cracked. "Aurora Springs could certainly use it."

"Delta . . . are you sick?" I asked, less worried about her health and more worried about ours. Maybe that made me a terrible person, but we'd only just gotten Remi back. I couldn't bear it if Gavin were to fall ill next.

"Just a tickle in my throat. Nothing to worry about." The unspoken 'yet' was very heavily implied as she made quick work of Gavin's amulet, spending far less time on him, then stood. "I'll see the both of you back in a month. Stay away from dark corners, Miss Blackthorne. We wouldn't want anything to happen to you."

"Donoghue," Gavin grumbled. "And it's Mrs. She's married."

I rolled my eyes. Possessive vampire.

"My apologies. Y'all don't be strangers now. If you'll excuse me, I have some work that needs doing. Those gargoyles are up to no good and causing a ruckus . . . again. If they keep this up, I'll have to reinstate Dallas as sheriff just to help wrangle them. Lord knows Scarlett can't handle them."

Gavin threaded our fingers and tugged until I was standing next to him, his jaw clenched, tension radiating from him, something akin to a live wire being touched to metal. That was when I saw the cat, her eyes focused on both of us, puffed up and ready for a fight. I understood now why everyone hated that feline. Familiars always gave me the willies, but this one was more unnerving than any I'd encountered.

"Thank you, Madam Mayor. It was . . . illuminating, as always."

Her smile was more a baring of teeth than anything else. "Yes. Illuminating. That's the word I'd use to describe our meetings as well."

And with that cryptic remark, she ushered us back to the front door. "Take good care." The door snapped shut behind us before either of us had a chance to respond.

"Well, that was abrupt."

"It couldn't have ended soon enough," Gavin muttered. "That woman is foul. She makes my fangs crawl up inside me."

"Like testicles in the cold?"

"Like you couldn't pay me to drink her blood if she was the last source on Earth."

"Let's hope it never comes to that."

He gave my hand a reassuring squeeze. “Come along, petal. We have a murder board to continue working on.”

“Ooh, I love it when you talk nerdy to me.”

“Asher’s the nerd. I’m an academic.”

“Potato, potato.”

CHAPTER TWENTY-EIGHT

BEN

The familiar strains of Blue Oyster Cult's classic "Don't Fear the Reaper" played on the sound system, and I knew almost down to the second how long it would take before Remi poked his head into my office to make his usual joke.

"Four . . . three . . . two—"

"I need more cowbell."

"One."

He grinned as he leaned against the doorframe. "Come on. That's hilarious. Walken is a legend."

I raised a brow. "Last I ch-checked, y-you went by Mercer."

"Shots fired, bro."

"W-will it make you f-feel better if I p-put a cowbell in your s-stocking this Christmas?"

Remi's eyes brightened as his expression morphed from disappointed to beaming. "Yes." Before I could open my mouth, Remi pulled out his phone. "Siri, add a cowbell to the Mercer list."

"Okay, Sexy Beast. Cowbell added to your shopping list."

"You're Santa's very best elf."

I debated reminding him that Christmas was more than half a

year away, but I didn't want to ruin his good mood. Anything that made him smile after the hell we'd been through the last couple of weeks was worth it. Besides, if he hadn't ordered it, I would have. A cowbell was a pretty small ask, all things considered.

"Isn't this weird?" Remi asked, walking over to me and sitting on the edge of the desk.

"W-weird how?"

"Being back at work. Pretending everything is normal. Having Rosie here and safe?" He dragged a hand through his hair. "I don't know. It just seems like I'm waiting for the other shoe to drop."

I got that. With the way things had been going lately, peace was definitely short-lived.

"I'm t-trying not to th-think about it."

"You? Bentley 'overthinks every-fucking-thing' Mercer is actively trying *not* to think? Shit, the world really is ending."

"What's the s-saying? D-don't borrow trouble?"

"I feel like it involves horses."

"That's a g-gift horse. It's different."

Remi cocked his head. "Is it, though?"

I shrugged, fighting the urge to follow his thoughts right down a panic spiral I'd never get free from. Already my chest was too tight, my skin prickling as anxiety tried to claw its way to the surface. Closing my eyes, I controlled my breathing and searched for the flicker of Rosie through our bond, needing the reminder that she was safe and whole. At least for the moment.

My phone buzzed in my pocket, causing my eyes to snap open as I came back to the present. I pulled it out, my face relaxing into a smile when I saw her name on the screen.

"I know that look."

I ignored my twin and opened the message she'd sent me. My eyes went wide, and lust punched me straight in the balls when I caught the naughty picture.

"Fuck," I whispered, tilting my head to better appreciate the pose her naked body was twisted in. "How d-did you even t-take th-this?"

"Excuse me? What now?" Remi leaned across the desk to snatch the phone from my hand, but I was faster. No way in hell was I letting anyone see this. She sent it to me.

"Mine."

"Now, Ben. We've talked about this. Ours. Sound it out with me. Ow-er-ssss."

I spared him a brief glance, my wolf taking control as I snarled, "MINE." That was all he got from me before my phone went off and my pulse leapt in anticipation.

SUGAR:

Just practicing my downward-facing dog so I'm ready to PRESENT for you.

ME:

Good girl.

"Ben, come oooooon. You're being mean," Remi unabashedly whined.

SUGAR:

Thank you, Daddy.

If I wasn't already aching for her, I would have been after that. Remi's phone dinged almost exactly after mine, and his smug smirk told me everything I needed to know. She'd felt his jealousy and taken pity on him.

"Sweet baby on the cross."

"I-in a manger."

Remi shook his head and used his fingers to zoom in on the photo. "Huh? Sorry, all the blood rushed to my dick." He hummed in approval. "Glistening already, baby girl?"

"She c-can't hear you."

"That's what you think." He brought the phone to his ear, and I heard her voice faintly coming through the speaker. "What are you wearing right now? Tell me it's the same thing as in the picture . . . absolutely nothing."

I stood to snatch the phone from him, but he waved me off, heading out of the office and calling over his shoulder, "I'm gonna take a ten."

"Asshole." A growl rumbled deep in my throat. There was no real heat to it, though. I couldn't blame the guy. I'd have done the same were our positions reversed and I didn't have a business to run. "Guess one of us should be responsible," I sighed, my gait more prowl than walk as I made my way down the hall.

The sound of coughing set my nerves on edge all over again as I entered the bar. We were busy tonight, but the energy was low, like everyone was drained. Well, everyone except the gargoyles. They were the same rowdy motherfuckers they always were.

"Bentley!" Harry crowed. "It's about time you showed your ugly mug. I'm parched."

"It's r-raining. Go outside and p-practice being a s-statue or something."

"Oh, you cut me deep. How ever will I recover?" He reached over the bar in an attempt to grab a pint glass, but I stopped him with a hand on his wrist.

"I've g-got it."

"Might as well be a good lad and make that three," Tom said with a smirk.

Darla caught my eye and gave me a knowing smile from the other end of the bar, where she was waiting on our newest regulars. The pirates had been here every night since they docked in town. The one called Caspian leaned forward to tuck a piece of her hair behind her ear and made her blush and giggle like a teenage girl. Had to give it to him, the guy knew what he was doing. I made a mental note to keep him away from Rosie. Didn't need to get arrested for murder. Again.

After passing each gargoyle a pint, I grumbled, "On the h-house."

They were loyal customers, after all. I wouldn't be able to get away with being an asshole forever.

"Mighty kind of you, Mercer," Dick said, raising his glass.

"Especially since every last creature here seems to be a sad sack lately." Harry glanced around. "What the devil is wrong with everybody?"

Tom smacked the back of his head and sent his bowler hat askew. "It's the plague, ye dobber."

"Wot? Plague?" Harry looked like a bad actor as he cast overly wary eyes around the room.

"Jee-sus. Where have you been, living under a rock?"

"Under a pretty pair of tits, more like," Dick said with a smirk as he necked his pint.

"I thought that was done and dusted. Remi came through it fine. Are you telling me they're all sick?"

Tom rolled his eyes. "Do you not have ears in your head? They're coughing up their lungs."

"It's only a matter of time before we get sick too!" Harry pounded his beer and locked gazes with me. "Hurry, Ben. Give us a dram of whiskey to chase away the pestilence."

Your choice of words is more accurate than you know, buddy.

Not sure when I turned into such a bleeding heart, I took pity on the poor idiot and poured two fingers of my cheapest bottle.

He knocked it back, then made to stand. "We have to get out of here."

Dick groaned and grasped the other man's shoulder before shoving him back down onto his stool. "We don't, you numpty. We're gargoyles. We can't get sick."

"That's what they all said! Look at them now. The bears are falling over in their seats. The fae have lost their glow. Even the king of the damn jungle is no better than a soggy bottom."

I didn't pretend to understand the last bit, but I could easily agree that Dallas was the worse for wear. He sniffled, then let out a wet sneeze. He was much less King Richard the Lionheart and far more sniveling Prince John. I half expected him to tug on his ear and call out for his mommy before sucking his thumb.

As if he knew exactly what I was picturing, Dallas shot me a baleful glare and held up his empty glass, silently demanding another. The man needed tea, not more alcohol. Or maybe a bit of both. I pulled him a pint, but also started heating some water so I could bring him a hot toddy as well.

Darla's squeal of amusement had my attention shooting to the table of pirates. Caspian had her seated on his lap, his lips at her ear as he whispered something that made her cheeks flush a deep pink.

"F-fucking pirates," I said under my breath as I dropped a slice of lemon in the mug I'd prepared for Dallas.

"I can hear you over there, mate. You should try smiling once in a great while, like your twin does. It'll do wonders for that handsome visage of yours."

I ignored the pirate and instead focused on Darla, whose guilty expression already had me softening. She mouthed, "Sorry," before removing herself from Caspian's lap and approaching the bar.

"I can take that," she offered.

"I've g-got it. You h-handle the gargoyles."

"Right away, boss," she chirped, giving me a little salute.

I rolled my eyes but smiled at her overeager display despite myself. Darla was a lot of things, but obedient was rarely one of them. Not like my Rosie.

Fuck, now I was thinking about that picture she sent me again.

Out of the corner of my eye, I saw my twin striding to his post at the bar. I knew that look. He was sated. Relaxed. Too fucking relaxed, thanks to his call with our mate. Lucky bastard.

"W-wash your hands!" I called as I headed toward our former sheriff's table.

Remi smirked at me. "Already did."

"Do it a-again," I snapped.

"But I sang "Happy Birthday" twice and used hot water, Dad."

I clenched my jaw and swore to myself as patrons laughed at his antics. Frustrated now, in more ways than one, I set down Dallas's drinks with more force than necessary, sending hot tea sloshing over the side of his mug.

"You trying to earn yourself a lawsuit, Mercer?" Dallas groused, his voice rougher than normal as he grabbed a wad of napkins and swiped at the wet spot on his thigh.

"S-sorry. I th-thought you m-might want something h-hot too. You f-feeling okay?"

The big lion shifter tipped his head back and sighed. "I feel like three-day-old roadkill."

"M-maybe you should g-go home and get s-some sleep."

"I'll sleep when I'm dead."

Spiders made of ice crawled down my spine at the saying. It sounded much more sinister when you knew it was a solid probability.

"You c-could always shift. I'm sure y-your lion w-would appreciate some time in the s-sun."

"What fucking sun, Mercer?" Dallas threw his arm toward the window. "It's been night for nearly a damn week. Besides, I can't shift." This last bit was petulantly muttered under his breath. It was so pathetic that I almost wanted to pat his head and offer some comforting words.

"What d-do you m-mean you c-can't shift?" I wasn't gonna lie; losing our ability to transform into our animals was alarming. That was how we healed quickly, how we defended ourselves. Every shifter in this town was more vulnerable if they were sick and couldn't make the change.

"You should know. Remi was sick. It's all I can do to walk from one end of the room to the other." Dallas's frown grew, his eyes dropping from me to the drink he now cupped between his hands. It seemed like he was trying to gather strength for what he was about to say next because when he opened his mouth, the words came out with the same heavy weight as a desperate man in confession. "My lion won't even respond when I try to tap into his energy. If it wasn't for that little spark inside me, I'd think he was gone."

Fuck. This was bad. A whole town of defenseless shifters and a looming Apocalypse.

"Holy fuck! Where'd you come from?" Remi's strangled cry put a stop to my weird heart-to-heart with Dallas. "Nope, I did not sign up for a damn poltergeist. Look, sweetheart, despite recent jokes and some hot as fuck roleplay, I'm not a Ghostbuster, and spectral porn really isn't my thing—except for that one book—so if you could back the hell up and get on the other side of the bar, that'd be swell."

The mostly transparent woman grew more opaque as the seconds passed, and I recognized her features as soon as she turned her gaze on me. She looked like our Rosie, only smaller, if that was possible, more pixie-like.

"Where's my niece? I need to talk to her."

Remi's expression shifted from panic to understanding. "Oooh, you're the ghost aunt."

I pulled out my phone, hitting the call button. Rosie answered on the first ring, her words coming out in a breathless rush. "What is it?"

"You need to g-get your pretty ass d-down here."

"Oh? Can't wait to see me until you get home?" she teased, her worry evaporating in light of my somewhat flirtatious answer. Too bad I had to crush her hopes.

"Your aunt is here. The d-dead one."

CHAPTER TWENTY-NINE

ROSIE

When I arrived at The Tip, I found Aunt Callie happily chattering with Tom, Dick, and Harry. She was mostly corporeal as she floated above her barstool, which was a change from her usually wispy appearance. She must really have wanted to blend in out here in the world.

Remi sent me a panicked look as soon as he saw me, his eyes wide.

"Can she just pop in like that anywhere? Anytime?" he asked through our mate bond.

"More or less."

"Great, now I have to worry about a feral ghost falling for me too."

"You're not her type, Remington. Your bits aren't on her list of things to see."

"Why not? My bits are awesome."

"True. Which is why I want to see them later."

He loosened up after that exchange, striding toward me even as Ben closed the distance between us from the other side. I was enveloped by them both and let myself have a moment of happiness at being the center of a Mercer sandwich once again.

"Well, well, well, Rosie dear. Looks like you've done quite well for yourself."

The gargoyles exchanged bewildered glances. "Who's she callin' Rosie?" Dick asked, lifting his hat so he could scratch his head.

"She's talking to me. My real name's Rosie. Roslyn, if you want to get technical."

"What happened to Nadia?" Harry asked.

I extricated myself from my wolves and gave the lumpy little man a one-shouldered shrug. "She outlived her usefulness, I guess." My false name wasn't really necessary anymore. All the people I'd been hiding from had more or less found me. Well, besides the Donoghues, but Gavin wouldn't give me up. And now that I'd turned, I was more than capable of defending myself. Or I would have been, if not for Delta's stupid amulet. Good thing I have five strapping mates to protect me, should the occasion arise.

"I love a wee bit of intrigue. Our little barmaid has a secret identity. She's like a super spy." Tom stared at me with nothing short of adoration in his eyes.

"Aye, like Natasha Romanov. Do you have a lycra supersuit you can wear for us next time you come in?" Dick ventured, earning a low warning growl from Ben.

"Sorry to disappoint. I'm lycra-free. But honestly, it's time to let go of Nadia since the whole reason I changed my name caught up to me. So, pleased to meet you, chaps. I'm Rosie."

Tom shot me a beaming smile. "It suits."

Callie gave a haughty little sniff. "I should think so. I chose it for her. Your dad would have you believe he made the decision, but it was me. Rosie, for the rose oil that kept your mum safe before they were together." Then she turned her attention to me. "Well, come on then, give your Aunt Callie a hug."

Hugging Callie was a bit like hugging an imaginary friend. I wrapped my arms around her spectral form while she did the same to me, neither of us physically touching the other. It wasn't comforting in the usual sense, but I would have sworn I could feel the subtle buzz of her energy pressing against me. And that was comfort enough.

"I kept waiting for you, you know?" Callie said after releasing me.

"What?"

"On the other side, after you died. But when you never showed, I knew something was up."

"Thanks for not ratting me out to anyone."

She smiled. "The last thing you needed was Cashel Blackthorne razing entire cities to the ground in search of you. I figured you'd come back when you could, and if you made the choice to leave, it had to be for a damn good reason."

"Well, Gavin would disagree with you."

When I'd left the protection of our safe house, I'd promised to keep my mental barriers down for him, just in case, so he heard my tart response as clearly as if he'd been standing beside me.

"And I would be right. Running away from me was the stupidest thing you've ever done, petal."

"Don't count on it. I'm sure there were worse things."

"So," I began, desperate to change the subject lest I put my foot in it again and end up on the wrong side of Gavin's ire. "Honestly, when I told Noah I needed help, I didn't expect you to show up. I thought perhaps you'd relay a message or have him ring me so we could speak that way."

Her brows lifted. "Oh, would you like me to leave? I only traveled across realms to be here, but I can crawl back to my lab like the family secret I've become."

"I like this chick. She's really good at the whole deadpan sarcasm thing," Remi whispered to Ben.

Callie's gaze flickered to him. "It comes with the territory. Sort of in the name, you know? *Dead*pan."

"Speaking of Pan . . ." Remi's smirk was wicked, but I didn't want to discuss the finer points of my demon with my aunt. At least not here. I cast a wary glance at all the potential eavesdroppers. Some secrets were still worth keeping. My ties to a bloody demon seemed top of that list.

"Nope, we aren't speaking of him."

"Aw, but why not, ma petite monstre? *I'm everybody's favorite subject."*

"Because you're still on time out for possessing Asher."

"When are you going to get over that? I'm a demon. It's what we do. You wouldn't yell at a fish for swimming or a bird for flying."

"That's hardly the same."

"It's exactly the same. Besides, it wasn't personal—"

"It was pretty fucking personal to me," Asher interjected.

"—nor was it my fault, honestly."

"Pan, so help me, if you say your mother made you do it . . ." I threatened.

"But she did."

"Mama's boy," Asher added.

Pan's response was a pulse of annoyance. *"Castoff. At least she kept me."*

"You're over a thousand years old. Grow a forking backbone."

"That's it, princess. Put him in his place. Might I suggest a dungeon?"

"The sexy dungeon's taken," Gavin chimed in, making me laugh.

"What is she doing?" Callie asked Remi, confusion flickering in her eyes.

"Talking to one of them."

"One of whom?"

"Her mates. It's either Gavin, Asher, or Pan. Ben and I are right here."

"My m-money's on P-pan. He hates b-being left o-out."

"It was all of them, actually."

Callie counted on her fingers and flashed me a saucy wink. "Five. Well done, Rosie. You one-upped Sunday, I see."

"It's not a competition," I grumbled.

"True, and I suppose none of it matters if everyone dies of this plague anyway." She clapped her hands together and leaned in. "So, tell me all about the symptoms."

I deferred to Remi, letting him fill her in on his experience, wincing as he gave her details I didn't want to know.

"And you recovered fully? How?" Callie reached out and ran a ghostly finger over Remi's neck, perhaps attempting to check his pulse.

To his credit, Remi didn't flinch. He wanted to, I could see it in his eyes, but he held fast. "Asher."

"What do you mean?"

"He healed me. He took all the sickness out of me, and I was just . . . better."

She hummed. "That's very interesting."

"Can't he just do his magic touchy thing to everyone who is sick?" Remi asked.

Callie shook her head. "It would take too long. There are far too many of them. I can see that nearly every single patron in this establishment is already infected. What you need is a vaccine. And fast."

"Great, so can you whip one of those up for us, or . . ."

Remi trailed off under Callie's indignant glare. "No, I cannot just 'whip one up'. What do you think I am? A magician? Do you see a top hat? A sweet little bunny? I am a scientist. These sorts of things require specific procedures. Time. A lab. Samples. Equipment. Test subjects. Lucky for us, I don't require sleep, so I can work round the clock. But even still . . ."

She continued her rant, but Remi had already tuned her out. His eyes heated when they met mine. *"She lost me at bunny. Wiggle that cute nose for me, baby girl."*

"Behave," I admonished, though I could feel the blush warming my cheeks.

"What was it Pan always says? No. Shan't."

"What kind of s-samples do you need?" Ben asked, his question bringing us back to the matter at hand.

Callie didn't even hesitate as she listed them off. "I'll want blood from Asher since he cured you, Remi. It wouldn't hurt to have some of yours as well. You'll have antibodies we can try to isolate. I'll also need some from an infected person—a few, if possible. And then there are those who seem immune. Rosie, Ben. Both of you are healthy, as far as I can tell. I'd love to run labs on your blood and see why that is."

"You sure she's a witch and not a vampire? She's got a thing for blood."

"Remi, she *is* a vampire. No witchy blood runs through her veins. That's my mum's side of the family."

"Ah, that makes a lot more sense."

Dallas staggered over to us, his arm raised above his head. "I hear you need a guinea pig. I volunteer as tribute."

The man was so desperate to serve and protect this community. Even though the mayor had stripped him of his title, he was offering himself up. My heart went out to him, which surprised me, given how he'd treated Ben. But there was just something about Dallas that told me his heart was always in the right place.

Callie balked as Dallas shoved his arm in her face. "Hold on there, cowboy. I can't just take your blood right now. There's a process to these things. Rosie, take them all to the doctor who worked with Remi. He'll make sure the samples aren't contaminated. Gather what we need and send it to me at the manor. As soon as I have a conclusion, I'll call. I promise."

"Can ghosts even use phones?" Remi asked.

"Stop thinking so literally, wolf. It's limiting."

"I thought you were a scientist. Isn't that what they do?"

"Potato, potato," she said before she winked at me and vanished into thin air.

Remi's eyes widened. "So *that's* where you get it."

Without so much as a warning, the floor jolted hard, sending me teetering into Ben's firm chest.

Dallas's arms shot out, the move making him look like a would-be surfer as he swayed on the hardwood. "What the fuck was that? I think I've had about enough for ton—"

Before he could finish his sentence, the earth began to shake with a force strong enough to bring down the bar.

"The sky is falling!" Harry screamed as bottles began toppling off their shelves.

"No, it isn't, knobhead. It's a bloody earthquake," Dick corrected, jumping off his stool.

Ben pulled me into a crouch, shielding me with his body as Remi called, "Take cover!" Patrons scrambled to get under tables as he squatted down next to us. "A hellmouth, a plague, and now earthquakes. What's next?"

"The end of the w-world."

Resolve swept through me, strengthening me even as I clutched Ben tighter. "Not on my watch."

CHAPTER THIRTY

REMI

Alaska wasn't a stranger to earthquakes. We were situated in the ring of fire, after all, but we'd never experienced one like this. The ground rolled as I watched, and instead of stopping after thirty seconds or so, this kept going. Shattering glass, breaking wood, and the terrified screams of our patrons filled the air.

My gut told me this was no normal earthquake. I seriously wouldn't be surprised if I looked outside and saw that fucking horse-woman riding down Main Street on her spotted steed. Or whatever it looked like. Not exactly like I'd ever seen one before. Horsewoman, that is, not a horse. I've seen plenty of those. *Focus, Remi. The world is coming down around your ears and you're thinking about horses?*

Just when it felt like it would go on forever, the shaking finally ceased.

"Everyone all right?" Ben called as he unwrapped himself from Rosie like she was a piece of candy. His voice was stutter-free, his wolf's need to ensure the safety of the people it considered pack pushing it front and center.

Grunts and groans came in response as our customers climbed

out of the rubble surrounding them. Bits of broken glass and shattered dinnerware covered the floor. The bar was a disaster; the mirrored shelves that once held all our top-shelf liquors were now a ruined spiderweb of cracks. My nose wrinkled at the overwhelming scent of all kinds of alcohol that filled the air from the destroyed bottles on the floor.

"The hits just keep coming," I muttered. First our cabin. Then Asher's hideaway. Now the bar. We were never going to get back on our feet. This would ruin us. We'd become kept men; Rosie would have to take care of us. Which, seeing as how we employed her, meant Asher was going to have to plan some sort of Ocean's Eleven-style cyber heist. Or worse, Gavin would have to provide for all of us. Oh God. Gavin didn't seem like the sugar daddy type. I could already picture us lining up like a bunch of Oliver Twists. *'Please, sir, we want some more.'*

Nope. No fucking way would I beg that guy for anything. *Heist it is.*

"Ben, I'm okay. You don't have to inspect every inch of me. Vampire, remember? I'm more impervious than you at the moment." Rosie took my brother's hands off her body so she could get him to look into her eyes. "Are *you* okay?"

The panic radiating off Ben only fed my own. In fact, everyone seemed to be feeding off it. Tension was high, and what started off as fear quickly morphed into anger.

"Get off me, Dwayne. You pathetic rat." Ivan Romanov shoved at the rodent shifter even though the man wasn't touching him. His voice was filled with unreasonable rage.

"Fuck you. You don't own this place. I'll stand where I want."

"Unless I break every bone in your body."

"I'd like to see you try."

Ivan's second, Yuri, snagged the last beer bottle standing and broke it on the edge of a table. "Go ahead, punk. I've killed men three times your size with nothing more than my fists. Try to come for Ivan and see what happens."

Fuck, this wasn't good. The bears were dangerous on a good day. Today was decidedly *not* good. But they weren't the only ones acting up. The pirates had risen to their feet and were all shoving at each other while Caspian tried to get them in line, to little avail.

"Oi, you lot. Save it for the sea. I'll not have a mutiny on my hands in a bloody dive bar."

I wasn't aware of the growl ripping from me at the insult to my bar until it happened. "I'm sorry, is our establishment not good enough for you? There's the fucking door, Peg-legged Pete."

"More like three-legged," Caspian shot back with a wink.

"Stop looking at him like he's a five-course meal," Scarlett screeched, grabbing a fistful of Darla's hair and giving it a tug. "I saw him first."

"It doesn't matter who saw him. It matters who he wants." Darla lashed out, scratching her nails across Scarlett's cheek.

"What the fuck is happening right now?" I muttered, not sure where to look as multiple fights broke out across the room.

Darla's attention shot to me as soon as I spoke, her eyes filled with malice and contempt. "This is your fault."

"Me? What did I do?"

"All of you. She showed up here and ruined everything." Darla grabbed a broken piece of glass and wielded it like a shiv. "If we take her out, this ends."

Fur broke out across Ben's arms as he started to shift, his warning growl low and dangerous. "Touch her and die."

"Fine, we'll start with you," Dallas said, lunging at him.

"Everybody just stop!" Rosie boomed, shocking me with the intensity of her command. I made to turn toward her, but my body was literally frozen in place. A quick check confirmed the same was true for everybody else.

Was this her doing?

She took a couple steps forward, coming into my view. Her hands were cast out, palms forward, expression fierce. "Just take a deep breath and calm down."

Even before the words finished leaving her lips, I was inhaling like my life depended on it. The weight of her suggestion covered me like a thick blanket, a sense of comfort and ease overtaking me. This wasn't a choice. It was an order. I had to obey because Rosie's will demanded it.

Thrall, my brain belatedly supplied. She was thralling us. All of us. I'd never heard of a vampire able to cast their net on this many people at once.

"Let Ben and I go, baby girl. We can help."

Rosie blinked, looking surprised to learn that she had us under her spell as well.

"I don't know how."

Gavin's voice broke through. *"What's happened? Why are you so distressed?"*

"Did you miss the giant earthquake?" I asked.

"What earthquake? There wasn't a bloody earthquake."

"Uh, yeah, there was."

"That doesn't matter right now. Rosie's keeping a mob from tearing us apart. She's compelling the whole fucking bar." Ben's words were filled with awe for the woman we loved.

Gavin immediately shifted back into his role as vampire tutor, his voice both hypnotic and soothing. *"Petal, this is just like choosing what to hear. Think of your thrall as a net. Pull it back to release the ones you don't want caught in it."*

Her brow furrowed in concentration as she attempted it. Within a few seconds, I could feel her hold on me slipping.

"That's it, sugar. Keep it up. You've got this," Ben praised.

As soon as she let us free, I went to her, taking her hand and giving it a squeeze. "How are we getting out of this with them all staying safe? You can't hold them forever."

"No, but I can send them to their homes with a trigger to break my compulsion. I've seen it done by my family. We've seen Gavin do it."

One by one, the patrons stumbled away, leaving the bar and heading home. They didn't even spare us a second glance until Darla. Rosie stopped her with a soft utterance of her name.

Our most trusted employee turned dazed eyes on Rosie.

"When you return home, draw yourself a bath and pour a glass of wine. When you have your first sip, Gavin's hold on you will break, and you will never be able to be compelled by him again."

"Petal . . ."

"Quiet, you. We'll be chatting about what you did when I get home."

"Uh-oh. Dukeykins is in trouble." I snickered. *"Does he get the spanking this time?"*

Asher's voice sent tingles of heat through me as he replied, *"I'd pay to see that."*

"So would a lot of people. That's what Iniquity *is for. But Roslyn and I will deal with this in private."*

"Come on, you two, there's nothing we can do about this place right now. We need to get home and check on the others," Rosie said, her concern for the rest of her mates flooding through our bond. Despite Gavin's assurance the earthquake hadn't reached them, I knew she wouldn't relax until she ensured their safety with her own eyes.

Ben's hand slipped to his favorite place, the small of her back, while I threaded our fingers tighter, and the three of us stepped over the debris of our livelihoods. As soon as the ever-constant night air hit me, I knew this was more than an act of God. The air stunk of sulfur; the sky was pitch-black with not even a single star visible except for the sickly green moon, and in the distance, a figure loomed. I could make out the long hair blowing in the breeze and the flicking tail of the horse she sat astride. As I watched, her steed slowly turned and walked out of sight.

Sonofabitch, I was right. A horsewoman actually *was* riding her damn horse through town.

Too bad I couldn't remotely enjoy it.

Pan must have still been paying attention to what was going on through his connection to Rosie, because his response was immediate.

"Looks like Mother has come for a visit."

CHAPTER

THIRTY-ONE

ASHER

I really missed my bat cave. My gaming chair with extra lumbar support. The multiple wide-screen monitors that spanned the width of my desk. The ambient mood lighting created by the fireplace glowing softly on my AIO LCD CPU cooler display and the reactive RGBIC backlights surrounding my monitors and mimicking my main screen. But mostly I missed my rainbow LED keyboard—don't judge me, my keyboard is an extension of myself, my version of a pen, really. Everybody has a favorite pen. What I was working with now was basically a mechanical pencil by comparison. My eye twitched. If we were going to be stuck here much longer, I might need to make an emergency supply order. A guy could only slum it for so long.

"Christ, even with my enhanced sight, I can barely keep up with what you're doing," Gavin muttered, creeping up behind me. "That infernal tapping of yours is so loud and rapid I can't hear my own thoughts."

I barely spared him a glance as I continued cross-referencing my data so I could add in last-minute notes and shortcuts to the PKM—

personal knowledge management system—I coded. "I'm compiling this for all of us. Stop talking. I'm doing smart guy shit."

"I thought you were just creating an electronic database built on my findings. That's basic data entry. Surely you must be done now."

Irritation skittered across my skin, pinpricks building strength every time he spoke. "Uh, buddy. That took me maybe thirty minutes. I was done with it days ago. And for the record, there's nothing basic about what I do. I'm so far ahead of you, I may as well be on a different planet right now."

"That'd be nice."

"I'm sure we can send you on a vacation. I hear Mars is accepting visitors. I can book you a trip. One-way."

"Ha, ha," he deadpanned. "I doubt you have the connections required for such a trip."

"I am a hacker. I don't need connections." I blew out a breath, finished typing out my thought, and then turned in my chair to face him. "Look, I can try and explain this to you, but I doubt your puny vampire brain is going to understand, so how about I just show you what all my 'infernal tapping' has created, and then you can go fuck off to your coffin and leave me to my work."

"I don't have a coffin. That's a myth."

"I could special order you one. Silver lined. With a lock. And maybe a muzzle."

"Show me what you've done, then. I highly doubt it's as well put together as my own research. There aren't even any red strings."

Rolling my eyes, I clicked back to the main screen, and an intricate database appeared, complete with red lines connecting events and dates. "You can organize it by date, or by location, or basically anything else you can think of." I clicked a few times, and the images on the screen rearranged themselves. At this point, it looked like a spiderweb. "What you had was a great start, but we needed more. We need it at our fingertips, something we can access with a few keystrokes. Computers were made to help mere mortals find connections we hadn't considered. By giving the system access to more information, we might be able to find those answers that have continued to elude you."

"Isn't that what the internet does?"

Jesus fucking Christ. I squeezed the bridge of my nose. "No, that's not what the internet does. We needed a specialized system that only pulls from relevant data. The internet is all porn and white noise bogging down your search results and distracting you. This is like . . ." I struggled to think of a way to explain the brilliance of what I'd created in terms he might understand. "The ad-free version. No celebrity gossip. No political drama. No fucking cat videos. Just curated and relevant search results. What the internet was supposed to be before capitalism ruined everything."

Gavin heaved a sigh at my rant, making me realize I might have gotten a bit carried away. I cleared my throat. "Anyway, like I said, what you had was a good start. This is better."

He grumbled and crossed his arms over his chest. "I thought it was fine. Nothing wrong with good old-fashioned paper and ink."

"Says the vampire. Go on. Give it a try. Type in something you want to cross-reference."

He leaned over me, typing F-L-O-O-D with the speed of a fucking sloth. God, I thought I might die right here waiting for him to finish.

As soon as he stepped back, I clicked the search button, impatience getting the better of me. Instantly my program filtered all relevant information about Queens and the flood, removing anything unrelated. Gavin took the mouse and shoved in close to me again, shouldering me until I got up and let him appreciate my genius.

"This is . . . you did all of this?"

Pride washed over me. Yeah, I fucking did. I wasn't just some useless human/demon/whatever. I had skills. Rosie's other mates could be the muscle; I was clearly the brains.

Gavin cleared the search and continued typing as he looked for record after record. It was excruciating watching him press the keys so slowly.

"You know, we should really set you up with a typing program or something. This is offensive. Things have come a long way since the Dark Ages. We have gamification now, and I'm sure we can find an app you like that will bring your typing speed to . . ." *Let's not get our hopes up and set the bar too high, Asher.* "Tolerable standards."

"I don't insult your dick size. Don't critique my typing."

My brow furrowed. "Those are two very different things."

"Are you offended?"

"Fuck yeah, I'm offended."

"Then it's the same thing."

A rush of apprehension that had nothing to do with Gavin went along my spine, like a bucket of ice had been dropped down the back of my shirt. I shivered, goosebumps breaking out on my arms.

"What the fuck was that?" I murmured.

Gavin had stiffened as well, his shoulders going tense, body frozen in anticipation. "Roslyn. Something's wrong."

Remi's voice hit me first, welcome but only serving to amp up my anxiety at the measured tone. This was someone trying to de-escalate a situation. Hostage negotiation 101. Keep them calm, make them think before they act.

"Let Ben and I go, baby girl. We can help."

"I don't know how." Rosie's voice ripped through my mind, carrying a heavier weight than normal. Almost like it was infused with something. Power, maybe? I wasn't sure what caused the change, but all the hair on my body stood on end.

Gavin stood, eyes closed as he spoke to her. *"What's happened? Why are you so distressed?"*

"Did you miss the giant earthquake?" Remi snapped.

Gavin and I exchanged confused glances before he responded. *"What earthquake? There wasn't a bloody earthquake."*

"Uh, yeah, there was."

"That doesn't matter right now. Rosie's keeping a mob from tearing us apart. She's compelling the whole fucking bar." Fuck, the way Ben said that made my chest tighten uncomfortably.

But instead of the news stressing Gavin out further, he seemed to relax. As if this was something he'd been waiting for. He must have sensed my growing confusion because he murmured, "Queen power." That was all the explanation he gave me before he addressed the group again, his voice radiating soothing confidence through our connection. *"Petal, this is just like choosing what to hear. Think of your thrall as a net. Pull it back to release the ones you don't want caught in it."*

I hoped Rosie knew I was there, that I was standing by in support when I had nothing I could really add to the conversation. Now was hardly the time to clog up the mental phone lines with anything that might be a distraction. I was treating this like Rosie was the bomb and Gavin was the bomb squad. Sometimes you needed to recognize when it was time to step back and let the experts do their job.

Dammit. He *was* useful.

I heaved an internal sigh. Fuck, were we going to have to be friends now? Ugh. I'd gone from zero friends to more than I could count on one hand. That was five too many.

"Don't forget about me, brother mine."

"Fuck off, Pan. We're not friends. We're barely even brothers."

"Sure we are. You literally can't exist without me. We're basically conjoined twins."

I shuddered at the mental image that conjured, my hands instinctively going to my hairline to check and make sure the small horns hadn't made a reappearance, while my tongue ran along my teeth to check for fangs.

Nope. All human.

For now, anyway.

I released a heavy breath, unable to find any relief. Who knew when those might pop back up? As far as I could tell, they were like my version of a demon boner. I'd been worried they were permanent, but the morning after the feast, they were gone. Thank fuck. One less thing to worry about. My give-a-shit list was too long these days already. One might even say my fuck-it bucket was full.

Gavin continued to work his magic on Rosie, helping her through this newfound skill, while I detached myself simply so I could function and not spiral. It was a skill I'd cultivated after years spent in hiding. A therapist would call it dissociation. Some might say it was unhealthy. Me? I liked to think of it as survival. Especially since it's kept me alive and mostly sane all these years. Though I used the trick less and less now that I had Rosie, Remi, and my good buddies, the puffins.

Amusement sparked inside me as soon as I knew the two most important people in my life (and Ben) were safe, because Rosie had uncovered one of Gavin's big secrets. He was in so much trouble. And I couldn't wait to see how that played out.

"Thralling another woman. Shame on you," I teased as soon as we knew they were on their way back to us.

Gavin glared at me. "Don't speak on things you don't understand." Then he deflated a bit and ran a hand through his hair. "It was a means to an end. Nothing more."

The fact that he gave me an explanation at all showed just how far we'd come since that night he tried to kill me and then I almost killed him with my fancy beam of light. Our time as prisoner and jailer had brought us closer together. Fuck. We really were friends now. I mean, I've even touched the guy's sac. But I guess that was bound to happen when we were both in love with the same woman. If you can't kill 'em, join 'em just took on a whole new meaning.

"Wipe that stupid arse smirk off your face. You'd have done it too if you were in my situation."

"Huh? Oh, the Darla thing? I've already moved on from that topic. You didn't fuck her, did you?"

"God, no. I haven't been with anyone since Roslyn and I were married. And I never will. She's my one and only. Unlike some of us." His pointed glare had me chuckling.

"Rosie encourages Remi and me to love each other. We don't have to justify our arrangement. Besides, I seem to remember you liking it plenty when I gave your—what do you call them? Bollocks? —a tug."

"Controlling a scene and letting you touch my balls is a far cry from my fucking you, trust me. I doubt you'd survive the experience."

I had to give it to the guy. No matter the situation, he could always be counted on to be an uppity pain in the ass. Was that a vampire thing or a British aristocrat thing? Or was it just a Gavin thing? A combination of all of the above?

Deciding it didn't matter, I gave him an uninterested shrug. "Then I guess it's a good thing you'll never get the chance. Remi and I share with Rosie, but you're not part of that triad. Now, I need to enter this earthquake into the database. I'm sure it had something to do with Pestilence, who—unlike your dick—will definitely find a way to fuck all of us."

"That seems to be a given. As soon as they arrive, we need to make sure we all sit down and discuss this. Roslyn's thoughts were frantic as she tried to keep her mates safe. The people in her thrall were all sick."

"All of them?"

Gavin nodded, his expression grave. "The mayor as well, though she tried to downplay it. It's clear the infection has spread to their brains and is affecting their impulse control as well as their anger."

"Oh my God, are you telling me this is a"—I swallowed before I whispered—"*zombie apocalypse*?" My mind raced with everything I'd learned from the movies. Shit, we were going to need supplies. Weapons for sure. Were these going to be fast zombies or slow zombies? Did we have a chainsaw handy? It was fucking Alaska. Of course we had a chainsaw. What about a flame thrower? Ben has plenty of axes. I wondered if I could get my hands on a machete . . .

I didn't realize I'd kept speaking out loud until Gavin shot me a pitying look, opened his mouth as if he was going to argue, then simply sighed. "Things are just going to get worse. We have to figure out how to use your healing ability on a mass scale, hacker. Before you have a chance to find out just what kind of zombies the people of this town will devolve into."

There weren't too many people in Aurora Springs I cared about, outside of our group, but the idea of anyone turning into a brain-eating zombie had my stomach twisting. Oh shit. I needed to check on Toderick and the pufflings. Could pufflings turn into zombies? I fucking hoped not. I shuddered at the thought of little puffins chowing down on brains.

"Count me in. The woman might have brought me into the world, but I want to bring her down just as much as the rest of you. More even. I just found my forever, and there's no way in hell I'll let it go."

"Given who our mother is, that might be more apt than you know."

Fuck.

CHAPTER THIRTY-TWO

LILITH

"What is that noise, Lilypad? I'm trying to recover from our session. I thought we agreed silent reflection was the best type of aftercare for me?"

For you, or for me? I cut my gaze across the room to where Drystan lay across the bed, bare arse on display, taunting me with something I craved. Him.

When had I become so attached?

Me? The original succubus. Nay. The original demon.

I was losing my edge. This fae prince had me questioning everything. Perhaps I needed to get rid of him. Banish him and send him back to the Fae Wildes where he belonged.

Just the thought had my stomach twisting painfully. I couldn't do it.

Nothing but death waited for my petulant princeling there. And while I might flirt with the idea of goodbye, I'd never want something permanent. I was too addicted to the things he made me feel. I mean, made my body feel.

Fuck.

My computer dinged again, a series of repeated notes alerting me to the notifications I'd specifically set after my visit to a certain sleepy little town in Alaska. Or not so sleepy, as the case may be.

"Something's happening in Aurora Springs," I murmured as I settled behind my desk.

"That dreadful place again? You seem rather fixated on it."

I hummed noncommittally as my eyes scanned the screen.

"Anything I should be worried about?"

Drystan may have everyone else fooled, but the man missed nothing. In our line of work, ignorance was a death sentence. Still, I couldn't resist teasing him. "Why are you suddenly so interested? Afraid I'll abandon you here while I reel in a burly fisherman?"

He rolled over and speared me with a look so heated, it reminded me of just how dominant Drystan Abercrombie Nightshade could be. A shiver ran through me at the possibilities. We'd played many games in our time together, but never that one. It was the carrot I dangled at the end of the proverbial stick. He thought it was to keep him in line. Truth was, it was to protect myself. Something told me I might not survive the experience. Not unchanged anyway. I wasn't sure I was ready for anyone to have that much power over me again.

Not after how things shook out with Lucifer.

But that was enough of that. I pushed the arousal away and ignored him, returning to my computer screen. The quaint hamlet was a fascinating place, and perhaps the ideal locale of a future investment, after all. Especially given the influx of supernaturals recently. One must do their due diligence when considering one's business. Diversification and all that. Something to consider anyway, assuming Rosie managed to put an end to this dreary Apocalypse.

Something that a certain horsewoman didn't want to chance, given what I was looking at. Bright red dots bloomed on the satellite map of Aurora Springs. Every single hotspot lit up like a bloody Christmas tree, the report of an isolated earthquake flashing on the screen.

"My, my, Pestilence. You're breaking out the big guns already? Someone is running scared."

"What?" Drystan got to his feet, walking over to me completely nude. For some, the act would be demeaning. Make them seem diminished somehow. Not for him. For my not-so-sweet pet, it was all barely coiled primal power as he prowled to my side.

I swallowed and recrossed my legs, body primed once more simply at his nearness. His dark hair was still damp with sweat, his silver eyes trailing over me before landing on the screen I'd been looking at.

"I know that wicked smirk. What's happened?"

I gestured to the computer. "Dollars to donuts, she's let the horse out of the barn. She's panicking. Blowing her wad prematurely. Things are about to get ugly."

"Aren't they already? There's nothing pretty about a plague."

I shrugged. "Uglier, then."

"She might actually win this one."

"Hmm. Perhaps."

Not if I have something to say about it. But of course I could never admit that out loud. Walls had ears. Yes, even mine. You never could be too sure who was listening. And we all had our parts to play, even in private.

I picked up my phone from the desk and dialed.

"You're making a phone call now? Really? Who are you calling?"

I stared at him pointedly, holding the phone up to my ear.

"Lilypad. You promised."

The worry in his voice almost stopped me.

Almost.

But the stakes this time were too high. And it wasn't just the mortals who stood to lose everything. My eyes lingered on Drystan's face, that punch of *something* I didn't want to acknowledge hitting me again. If Pestilence won, I would lose.

I never lost.

Besides, he needn't worry. I'd been playing this game longer than he'd been alive. I knew exactly how far I could stray over the line without truly breaking my promises. We demons did so love our loopholes, and I'd long mastered that art.

It was time for the master to get to work.

He must have read the intention in my face because he tensed, his voice low and thick with concern. "Lilith, you cannot intervene. They'll destroy you."

"Oh, pet, I'm not interfering." My lips curled up in my trademark smirk as I stretched out my leg to tap him gently with the tip of my stiletto.

He reached for my ankle out of reflex, my Drystan well and truly trained these days, his thumbs already pressing into my muscles as he massaged my calf. "Oh? What would you call it then?"

"I'm simply calling in my marker."

CHAPTER THIRTY-THREE

GAVIN

"Say it again, baby girl," Remington's voice hit my ears as they stumbled into the house. "'*We'll be chatting about what you did when I get home.*'" He impersonated her quite well, actually, but I gritted my teeth at the smugness in his delivery.

"I'm not saying it again. And for the record, *we* meant Gavin and Rosie. Not Gavin, Rosie, and Remi."

"Bullshit. We're a pack." His soft chuckle, followed by her hum of approval, immediately had me on my feet heading toward the stairs, Asher hot on my heels. "We means all of us."

"I'll r-remind you of that the n-next time you t-try to sn-sneak off with her alone."

"I wasn't the one who chased her through the woods and railed her under the moonlight BY HIMSELF, Bentley."

"Th-that was d-different," Bentley muttered.

As I rounded the corner, I caught sight of the three of them, bedraggled and dirty, but smiling through their obvious fatigue. "You lot are a sight."

"Yeah, that sort of comes with the territory when a fucking building threatens to come down on your head." Remington's dry delivery would have rankled any other time, but the picture they painted said things were more dire than they'd let on.

"Jesus," Asher whispered, catching up to me. "You three look like you took the scenic route but got smacked in the face by every tree on the way here."

Remington sighed.

"So he can comment on your appearance without issue, but I can't?"

"I love him, so yeah, pretty much," the shifter snapped.

"I need a shower, and perhaps a lie-down. But, Gavin, thank you for talking me through that. I was terrified I'd never be able to let them go." Roslyn stepped away from the twins and approached me where I'd stopped at the base of the stairs, waiting patiently for her to come to me. She wrapped her arms around me and snuggled close, settling something that always came unmoored within me whenever we were apart.

"I never had any doubt," I murmured against the crown of her head.

"You should have seen her. She was such a fucking badass." Remington shot a steely stare at Asher. "'*Everybody just stop!*' They all just froze. God, it was hot." The idiot pantomimed freezing in place.

"Sounds like it. Wish I could have been there," Asher said, jogging down the stairs to press a kiss to Roslyn's cheek before moving over to do the same to Remington.

"I had no idea I was doing it. Literally none. I just knew they were going to hurt my mates, and I had to do something."

"It was your instinct. You, my Queen, are coming into your own." I stroked her hair and inhaled her scent.

"Fat lot of good that does us when I can't figure out what I'm doing."

Asher laughed. "Welcome to the club."

"What happens next time when I don't have one of you there to talk me down?"

My arms tightened, and my voice came out with a bit more growl than I'd intended. "We will always be there."

"Hey, look at that. Gavin knows *we* refers to *all* of us. Proud of you and your personal growth, Daddy G." Remington winked at me, and I had to fight the urge to punch him.

Instead of taking the bait and reminding him, once again, not to fucking call me Daddy bloody anything, I kept my focus on Roslyn. "It'll get easier, petal. Just like being a vampire has. No one said you had to master this in a day. It will take time and practice, like anything else."

"We don't have time, Gavin. Today was proof enough of that. We *saw* her."

"And you're certain it was her?"

"Who else could it have been? She's the one orchestrating all of this," Roslyn insisted.

Bentley's affirmation came at the same time as hers, certainty bleeding through his words. "It w-was P-Pestilence. Sh-she was on her h-horse in the d-distance as we l-left the b-bar."

"We need to add that to the list," Asher muttered, eyes drifting up the stairs to his computer and the research it contained. He made to go up the stairs, but grunted and staggered as he transformed from human to purple demon before our eyes.

Pan turned to face us, his expression shockingly somber. "And if you won't take their word for it, take mine. I am perfectly capable of recognizing my own mother."

"I fucking hate when you do that," Remington grumbled.

"Get used to it. I plan on soaking up every minute I have before Asher gets control again." Pan shook out his long hair and crowded Roslyn and me. "Mmm, *ma petite monstre*, how I've missed you." In one quick move, Roslyn was in his hold rather than mine, pressed tight against his chest. He gazed at her as though she was the most perfect treasure, and that was possibly the most disturbing thing of all. "Don't worry, I won't let Mummy get you."

"You p-probably l-led her straight to us, d-demon." Bentley's hands were clenched tightly, the muscles of his forearms bunched and trembling.

Pan arched one brow and leaned close to Roslyn's ear. "I think your shifter has a bit of a toxic masculinity problem, darling."

"You th-think *I'm* the o-one with a problem?"

The demon lifted his head and tossed Bentley a wicked smirk. "What? Did I stutter?"

Bentley growled and took a step forward, but Remington stopped him with a palm to the chest. "You're giving him exactly what he wants."

"And th-that's a bad thing?"

I was so focused on the twins, I didn't see what happened beside me, but based on Pan's startled *oof* and doubled-over form, I could guess easily enough.

He winced and cupped his balls. "What the bloody hell was that for?"

"Do not make fun of Ben," Rosie hissed. "If you want to be part of this arrangement, you bloody well better stop setting yourself up to be pummeled. They are mine, the same as you."

"I had you first."

"So what? That doesn't excuse your poor behavior, Pan."

Pan looked truly baffled. "But I'm a demon. All my behavior is bad."

"And I repeat. That's not an excuse."

The demon sulked. "When are you going to stop judging me based on pathetic human morality?"

"Maybe when you accept that you are mated to a woman who used to be human and still subscribes to said morality."

"*Used to* being the operative words."

She huffed and shook her head. "Asher, am I wrong, or do things seem to be getting worse?"

"He's not here, *mon ange*."

Asher's voice came loud and clear in all our minds. *"You can't keep me away anymore, asshole. Remember? To answer your question, Rosie, yes. It's a lot worse, and it doesn't look good for us. All my data suggests things are going to get dicey, fast."*

"What are we going to do? I can barely control my gifts, Pan's no help, and so far, all being a Queen has done for me is make me insatiably horny and hungry. It's not like I can fork Pestilence away."

"I mean . . ." Remington started.

Bentley punched him in the shoulder. "No."

Roslyn wrinkled her nose. "Are you actually saying you *want* to try forking a horsewoman to save the world?"

"Want is a strong word, but it could be worth a shot. Make love, not war, right?"

Pan shuddered. "Please never mention *forking* and my mother in the same sentence ever again. Besides, you're not her type."

"I'm everyone's type."

Pan rolled his eyes. "You're too . . . rugged."

Remington pointed to himself. "Me? Rugged?" He laughed. "That's a first."

The way Pan looked at me with confusion, then back to Remington, then to me again, had me fighting a rare outburst of laughter.

"He knows what he looks like, right? Surely he understands the science of identical twins?"

"There's no telling with that one," I answered under my breath.

Oh God . . . we were having a moment. Camaraderie with a demon? I'd never thought I'd see the day. Even Lilith and I tiptoed the line between hatred and tolerance. Whatever was the world coming to? Bloody hell, it really must be the end.

My phone rang in my trouser pocket, and Roslyn winced at the shrill tone. I reached down to silence the infernal device. Anyone I might need to talk to was already here. But something stopped me from dismissing the call entirely, a niggling worm of apprehension.

Speak of the fucking demon.

As I stared down at Lilith's name on the screen, I knew this was one call I couldn't ignore.

Knowing I wouldn't be able to hide any details of this conversation now that they all had access to my thoughts, I answered, putting the phone on speaker.

"Lilith. To what do I owe the pleasure?"

"Aw, dukeykins. That would have sounded more believable if there was any hint of a smile in your voice."

"I'm sort of in the middle of things . . ."

"Yes, yes, I know. Terrible earthquake. How inconvenient."

"How do you know about that?"

"Darling, I know everything. But that's not why I called."

"It isn't?"

"No. What do I care about a natural disaster on the other side of the world? Not like I have any investments to protect."

Roslyn and I exchanged suspicious glances. *We* were her investments, thanks to the various deals we'd made. Just what was the succubus playing at?

"Then why did you call?"

She released a heavy, affected sigh. "You see, I'm in need of some . . . entertainment, and I'm afraid I'm fresh out. My favorite Novasgardian prince has found himself on the wrong side of a witch, and the patrons are getting restless."

"And that's my problem because . . ."

"Because you made a promise, Gavin. One I hope you intend to keep."

"You said I could choose when to pay my debt."

"Well, yes. As always, it is up to you whether you will uphold your end of the bargain. But I should warn you, duke, there are consequences for every choice. It would behoove you to make the right one."

"Is that a threat?"

Her laughter tinkled through the phone. "What need do I have to make threats?"

"Is it just me, or did that sound like a bigger threat?" Remington whispered loudly.

"Ooh, speakerphone with no warning. Gavin Donoghue, you

truly have become a little bitch. Rosie, darling, remember whose mark you wear and what I did for you. It's time for you both to repay me."

"I knew it was you!" Pan spat.

"Pandemic? Are you there as well? My, it *is* a party. No wonder your hands are full, Gavin dear. How about this? I will leave the choice up to you. Come now. Come in a day or so when things calm down. You still have your card on you, yes?"

"Of course," I grumbled, the heavy card she mentioned practically burning a hole in my pocket.

"Good. I'll see you soon. Bring the whole gang if you like. I'm sure they'd enjoy the show as well. I know I'm looking forward to it."

She hung up without warning, and Roslyn sighed as I pocketed my phone. "Great, I'll just pencil in 'trip to the sex club' in my diary, shall I? Right between bar brawl and Apocalypse."

"Better than the alternative," Pan offered.

"And what's that?"

"Lilith reaping your soul."

"She can d-do that?" Bentley asked, his worried gaze flicking between Pan and Roslyn.

"She keeps them in jars in her basement," Pan informed us rather sagely, then trained his focus on my wife. "Didn't I tell you to always read the fine print when making a deal?"

"It's not exactly like she presented me with a contract."

"That's exactly what she did. It's your fault for not checking the specifics."

"Sh-she took advantage."

Asher's voice broke through. *"Of course she fucking did."*

Pan gave Bentley a rather incredulous look. "Obviously. That is the cornerstone of what we do. Only the truly desperate make deals with demons. Rather is the point of the whole affair. How else are we supposed to fill our soul quotas?"

Remington snorted. "You have quotas? That sucks. Next you'll be telling me there's a demonic DMV. Or worse . . . post office."

"Who do you think gave humans the idea?"

"Fuck. You are truly evil."

"Thank you. Someone who gets it," Pan said with the air of a man who finally felt seen.

"That wasn't a compliment."

"Of course it was."

"Maybe you haven't realized it yet, buddy. But you changed teams when you joined our pack. You play for the good guys now."

Pan grimaced. "How positively revolting."

"Does that mean Pan's last name is Mercer now too?"

Remington instantly shot back a loud, "No. Hell no. Abso-fucking-lutely not."

Bentley's response was shorter but no less vehement. "Never."

"One of us. One of us," Asher softly chanted in our heads.

"You did say he was pack," Roslyn reminded him with a teasing smile.

The shifter looked shocked by the news, clearly thinking back over his earlier words. "Fuck. I did. But that's not what I meant. This is different." Realizing he wasn't getting anywhere with his flustered rambling, he pointed a finger at me. "Besides, Gavin is keeping his name—"

"Oh no, leave me out of this."

"Come on, you lot. Don't fight it. We're meant to be." Roslyn reached for me, but a loud crash echoed through the house.

"What the hell was that?" I asked.

Bentley raced toward the sound, returning in moments with undisguised fear on his face. "F-fire. We h-have to g-get out."

I snatched Roslyn's hand and tugged her toward the exit, but before we had a chance to escape, the window in the entryway shattered as a fiery bottle hurtled through it. In the blink of an eye, glass exploded onto the carpet, blocking our path as everything burst into flames.

CHAPTER THIRTY-FOUR

ROSIE

Terror ran through my veins, chilling and nearly heartstopping as fire ate its way up the walls and across the floor. Thick black smoke curled into the air, the heat singeing my eyelashes and making my skin tight and uncomfortable.

We'd gone from normal, or at least what constituted our version of normal, to finding ourselves in the very center of an inferno within the blink of an eye. But while my body had an instantaneous reaction, my brain was scrambling to process this sudden change of events.

"We have to get out. Now!" Gavin roared, his own fear telegraphing to me as if we shared the emotion.

Fire was one of the few things that could truly kill our kind. It was a frequent weapon used against us because of the devastation it could cause in such a short span of time. And it was usually quiet. Not now. Whoever had thrown the bottles through our windows wanted us to know they were here.

"Upstairs. Go!" Remi took my hand and tried to tug me with him.

I say tried because Gavin held me fast. "No, you fool, up is the absolute last place you're supposed to go during a house fire."

Remi speared him with an impatient look, his eyes watering from the smoke. "Do you see a better exit? The house could literally not be any more on fire."

"R-Remi is r-right. They're w-waiting outside. Even if w-we could get o-out down here, they'd b-be right th-there." Ben's irises glowed blue neon as he tried to reason with my husband. "Th-the roof is our b-best bet. W-we will survive the j-jump."

"Don't be so sure about that," Pan said, his eyes cast upward a split second before he was throwing himself on top of me.

"Pan—"

That was all I had time to get out before an ear-splitting *crack* drowned out my protest. The demon winced as a fiery beam landed on his shoulders, but he shook the heavy wood off like a duck shaking off water.

"Are you all right?" he asked, his eyes raking over me intently. "It didn't hit you, did it?"

I was momentarily stunned by his protective display, but even that paradigm shift was eclipsed by a much more pressing surprise. "Pan, you're on fire!"

"No, I'm not. I'm fireproof."

"You might be, but your hair isn't."

"What?" He glanced over his shoulder to see the flames licking across the ends of his purple locks. Instead of panic, annoyance flashed across his handsome features. He let go of me to extinguish the bits of flame with his fingers, as if it was a candle and not something attached to his body. "Oh, blast it all. That will take ages to grow back."

"Dude was literally on fire, and he's worried about his hair growing back?" Remi muttered.

"You h-heard him. F-fireproof."

"If you're impervious to fire, can you make yourself useful and get us out of here?" Gavin asked, scrambling away from the encroaching flames.

"There's nothing I can do for the rest of you. I can get myself out, but the blaze surrounding us is still impassable for anyone else. If we try, all of you will die. I can't control the flames. I'm not a bloody fae or freaking Moses. They won't just part for me because I will it. Not like our Roslyn's thighs."

"Not the time," I grumbled, the warmth in my face not wholly due to the fire. We needed to get out while there was still more than an inch of space between us and the wall of terrible heat creeping ever closer.

"So what are you still doing here, then? It seems more on brand for you to save yourself."

Remi had a point. Pan was consummately self-serving, but now hardly seemed like the moment to press for an explanation.

Glass from the windows shattered as the intensity of the heat built, heavy smoke making it hard to breathe and causing us all to cough as we fought to draw breath. My eyes flicked to Ben, hoping my Alpha wolf had a plan. As usual, he didn't let me down.

A muscle in his jaw ticked as he made his decision. "W-we don't have t-time for this. S-stairs, right fucking n-now." Ben grabbed my hand, tugging me toward the only safety we had left, but stopped short when he caught sight of the tunnel of fire that had once been a hallway. "Fuck." We spun around, intending to run back the other way, but more beams fell, blocking our escape. "We're t-trapped."

"Shit. We can't go out like this. I'm too fucking pretty to become a pillar of ash," Remi said, using humor to deflect from his obvious fear.

"We won't," Gavin said, pulling a card from his pocket. "Looks like we're taking that trip to *Iniquity* sooner than anticipated. Everyone grab onto each other."

None of us argued, not even Pan. I reached for Gavin as Ben pulled me close, Remi and Pan both placing their hands on my outstretched arm at the same time.

A hazy portal opened in front of Gavin, the smoke obscuring our view, but the promise of safety within our grasp. Without warning, the lot of us were sucked into the tear in reality, but no one balked. In fact, we welcomed the fresh, clean air of Lilith's club as we fell in a heap of tangled limbs onto the cold floor, all of us heaving great gasps of oxygen.

Lilith's laughter preceded her as she stood above us, her hands resting on leather-clad hips. "Well, that's one way to make an entrance."

"Sweet baby Jesus in a wicker basket, baby girl, you look . . ." Remi's gaze raked my form as he took in the outfit Lilith had provided me. She'd sent the five of us to her personal suite with explicit instructions to clean up and prepare ourselves for a night of 'devilish delights.' Her words. Apparently, tear-stained, soot-smudged, and stinking of smoke wasn't appropriate for what she had in mind. Or at least not the last two. As she'd rushed us through the club, I'd spotted more than a few patrons shedding tears.

"You like this?" I trailed my fingertips over the swell of cleavage offered up like a bounty by the shiny vinyl corset.

I felt like Christine from *Phantom of the Opera* in this getup. The tight bodice nipped in my waist while the fabric of the skirt flowed to my ankles. But it was the hip-high slits that changed the ensemble from sexy to carnal. Every time I took a step, my legs were visible, and so was my lack of knickers.

"Yes. I like it so much."

My focus drifted to the tight leather trousers he wore, the laces loose at the waistband, exposing the trail of coarse hairs that traveled down from his belly button. The pants were snug and low enough that his hipbones and that glorious V of muscle I loved to lick were on display as well. But the best part? Lilith had opted to give him a studded black leather harness to wear rather than a shirt. I curled my index finger beneath the supple strap crossing his pecs and tugged him an inch closer.

"Same." I ran my lips over his freshly shaven jaw and let out a soft moan.

"Starting w-without us?" Ben's voice was filled with amusement as he came into the room, sadly more clothed than his brother. Although, I didn't mind seeing him in a white button-down with a subtle gray pinstripe and the sleeves rolled up to his elbows. The trousers Lilith had given him to wear weren't skin tight like Remi's. These were tailored as though made for him in a charcoal gray that beautifully hugged his thickly muscled thighs.

"You look . . ." I had to swallow before I could finish my thought because my gaze caught on the glossy black leather belt around his waist. What could he do with that? What *would* he do? "Really hot."

The lazy smirk that tipped up Ben's lips had my heart fluttering. His smiles, while they used to be rare, seemed more frequent lately. Well, until the most recent disasters that plagued us. Oof, poor choice of words there.

Still holding my gaze, he scrubbed a hand across his stubbled jaw in a move that turned my insides molten. "You t-too, sugar."

Before I could act on my growing hunger, Asher's voice had me spinning around.

"I don't really have to wear the top hat, do I?" My handsome hacker glanced up from the tall black hat in his hands to take in the rest of us. He scowled. "Why the fuck do I look like I'm about to ask a crowd 'is this your card' while you three look like you're about to walk in a fetish fashion show? Is the succubus punishing me? Because I can't help who my relatives are. Tails? Really? Is that a joke? It feels like a joke."

Asher's hair was slicked back, parted neatly on one side and gleaming under the light. He looked so dashing, like an old Hollywood star at the Oscars. Pan had been annoyed at Lilith's insistence he give Asher control but had acquiesced begrudgingly when she reminded him how distinctive his appearance was and then cooed, "House rules, honey. I'm the only demon in residence, remember?

Can't have you stealing my thunder. Or word getting back to your mum that you're here. Something tells me she's looking for you."

The memory of Lilith's warning was enough to dampen my growing excitement. We might be safely tucked away in *Iniquity,* but it was only a momentary reprieve. We couldn't stay here forever. Eventually we'd have to go back. Pestilence wasn't going to simply give up on her Apocalypse because we'd vanished. If anything, she'd probably redouble her efforts now that we were out of the way. All those people were going to die at her hand, and we'd left them at her mercy. Their deaths might as well be our fault.

Gavin strode into the room with that devastating furrow between his brows and a scolding on his lips. "Don't let your thoughts run away with you, petal. We will return, but right now you are safe here with us, and that's all that matters. The town turned on us. We had to get out."

"I a-agree with him, sugar. You kn-know how I f-feel about Aurora Springs, but *you* are th-the m-most important p-person in my l-life. W-without you, I'm n-nothing."

Remi scoffed. "Gee, thanks."

Ben shot his brother a look. "You kn-know what I m-mean."

A soft smile spread across Remi's lips as he glanced at me, then at Asher. "Yeah, I do."

Their gentle admonishments were enough to cement me firmly back in the present. Well, that and the sight of Gavin when he turned around to pick up the suit jacket he'd draped across the back of a chair.

He took my breath away in his black-on-black ensemble, the fitted trousers all but molded to his legs and arse. The black silk shirt clung to his muscled arms. But my eyes were locked on the corseted vest. My husband was fit, but the *things* that vest was doing for his figure were absolutely sinful. I wanted to unlace the back of it with my teeth right here and now.

It hit me all at once as my attention bounced from man to man. They were, each and every one of them, my innermost fantasies come to life. The dashing duke, the brooding businessman, the sexy rockstar with a penchant for kink, and the movie star. These had been the players on rotation in my dreams since I was a teenager. How had Lilith known?

"I can hear you." Gavin's voice was a silky whisper that trailed across my skin like ghostly fingers.

I shivered. *"Maybe I want you to."*

"She's giving you your fantasies. It's what she does. How she feeds."

"I thought sex did that?" The mention of the act had my thighs clenching. I had them all right here at my fingertips. We had privacy. Why waste it?

"I thought you wanted to go down and explore the club. This is your first time here, isn't it?"

Bollocks.

Remi and Asher chuckled, making me realize everyone had been privy to my internal war. Even Pan's laughter twined with theirs.

"It never ceases to amaze me how you maintain your innocence despite being such a filthy little whore."

My core throbbed at his seductive rasp.

"You can have both, baby girl," Remi reminded me. "Some time downstairs before we come back up here and . . ."

"Make those fantasies of yours come to life?" Asher offered, smoothly finishing Remi's sentence.

"I suppose the wait will only make it that much better. Besides, I haven't ever been to a sex club. Maybe I'll pick up some new fantasies for us to try out."

"Edging is p-part of the fun." Ben's lips ghosted over the nape of my neck from where he'd placed himself behind me as I'd ogled Gavin. Then he ran his teeth across my mark, sending a shiver of pure lust through me.

"You're mean."

"Am I? Now be a good girl and p-put on your m-mask."

Gavin handed the intricate, glittering lace to me before affixing a black leather mask over his eyes. With gentle hands, Ben helped me with the silk ties as I secured mine.

"How did that make you hotter? Does mine make me hotter?" Remi asked, turning to Asher for confirmation.

Asher rolled his eyes, unwilling to give Remi the compliment he was so clearly fishing for. "Maybe if it was a ball gag. You're hottest when your mouth's full."

Remi licked his lips. "That can be arranged."

"Ready, princess?" Asher asked, turning his gaze to me. His eyes glittered from behind the purple leather covering the top of his face, the startling blue of his irises seeming almost violet tonight. How could an exposed jawline and lips turn me on so easily?

I ran my palms down the thin fabric of my skirt and nodded. "Take me to the sex club, gentleman. I'm ready to be debauched."

"Too late. I already did that."

Pan must have sent the thought to me alone, because none of the others had anything to say about his possessive remark.

All I could do was shake my head and laugh as Gavin took my hand and threaded it through his arm. "Well then, let's see if we can find ourselves a garden so I can properly ruin you."

Oh yes. My husband understood the assignment. But then, he always did.

The night might have started off rocky, but things were definitely looking up. And while I'd have to be an absolute fool to believe the reprieve would last, I was going to enjoy every second while I could.

I had to.

After all, the world might end tomorrow.

CHAPTER THIRTY-FIVE

ROSIE

If I could see myself, I was sure my eyes would be the size of saucers. I was the equivalent of Alice in Wonderland as the group of us sat nestled into a circular booth in the lower level of *Iniquity*. Everywhere I looked, I saw couples and groups locked in sensual embraces, undulating with the steady thrum of the music that pulsed through the room. That part wasn't actually all that surprising, to be honest. But it was still affecting to be surrounded by so much . . . lust.

However, the things that made my thighs clench were the little displays in various places throughout the room. These weren't performances, just patrons making use of the safety *Iniquity* provided while they gave into their most secret urges. A community finding a home free of judgment and rules other than those they established with their lovers. All under the watchful eye of Lilith, of course.

I didn't know where to focus my attention. In one corner, a fae woman was suspended from a series of hooks in her back. She was naked other than a collar at her throat and splayed above a table where her Dom conversed with several other businessmen. Every now and then, he'd reach up and touch her, alternating between light caresses and more punishing slaps. She could never tell what was coming next, and the anticipation had her—and me—trembling.

Further back, a man stood bound to a post, fully nude with nothing but a metal cage over his . . . member. He whimpered every time his partner trailed a fingernail over his chest. She never once touched him below the waist, but drips of precum escaped him nonetheless.

"Orgasm denial," Remi whispered in my ear. "Hot, right?"

"Some people like it. I'm not into it." Asher nuzzled Remi's neck. "I like the sounds you both make when you come too much to make you wait for long."

"That's the difference between you and a Dom. For us, it's about their pleasure, not ours. Anticipation only makes it all the more enjoyable, Asher. The longer you make your partner wait, the harder they come."

"That true, sugar?" The question just for me as Ben's voice whispered through my mind. I met his heated gaze as Gavin finished speaking, gave a small nod. His eyes burned as a sexy grin curled his lips. *"Hmm, I'll keep that in mind."*

The conversation at the table continued around us, freeing me from the sensual promise Ben's words wrapped me in.

"Aren't you a sadist?" Remi asked.

"Yes."

"You're all about pain, right? So why would you care how hard she comes?"

"When I control it, why wouldn't I want her climax to be so pleasurable it's pure, exquisite agony?"

Concern for the state of the seat under me grew as wetness flooded between my thighs. Suddenly all I wanted was to experience exactly that.

"How do we reserve a spot . . . up there?" I pointed to one of the raised platforms, my voice breathless.

Gavin's eyes were so dark they were nearly black. "I thought you wanted to watch tonight, petal. Have you changed your mind?"

I licked my lips. "Maybe? We do have a promise to keep."

"Yes or no, petal. There's no maybe."

"Moonlight," I whispered.

Without a word, Gavin rose to his feet and walked out of view. Excitement built in my belly because I knew exactly what he was doing. He was setting us up with our very own stage. I was finally going to know the kiss of his whip.

"I'm n-not gonna l-lie, sugar. The idea of y-you up th-there—"

"Shut up, Ben. Don't ruin this for me," Remi interrupted.

Ben shot his twin a glare. "If y-you'd let me f-finish, I was g-gonna say, it m-makes me fucking hard."

"You really don't mind all these people watching?" I asked, my voice hitching a little due to my inability to get enough air into my lungs.

His gaze was hungry as it bore into mine. "No, because I'm th-the one who gets to t-take care of you after."

"Of course you are. I wouldn't have it any other way."

Ben ran his palm over the top of my head, leaning closer to brush a kiss to my forehead. "Th-then go, sugar. Have f-fun with your duke. Just r-remember who else you belong to."

"Don't worry about us. We'll just be here . . . watching." Asher's voice was filled with heat. "You'd better put on a good show."

"We might be doing more than watching. No promises I can keep my hands to myself." Remi ran a palm up Asher's thigh, the contact making my hacker bite his lower lip as he swallowed a groan.

Gavin returned as if on cue, silently holding a hand out to me. Ben moved so I could slide out of the booth and place my hand in Gavin's.

As soon as I was in his hold, a spotlight illuminated a circular black stage, complete with a pole in the center. This wasn't simply one of the platforms scattered about the room. We were on the main stage. The focus of the entire club.

Any nerves I felt at the realization were purely excitement.

Gavin leaned in close, overwhelming me with his leather and vanilla scent. "What's your safeword, petal?"

"Blackthorne."

"Use it if you need it."

"But Lilith—"

"Isn't responsible for you. I am. Use your safeword if you need it," he repeated, leaving no room for argument.

He climbed the steps to the stage and turned to face me, his expression now cold and dominant as he held out a hand. "Come, my duchess. Show them what it means to be mine."

Anticipation sang in my veins as I traced his steps.With every roll of my hips, my skirt swished over my skin. I could feel every eye in the room on me, but in this moment, I only had eyes for my duke. Until Remi whistled, then grunted as either Asher or Ben must've elbowed him.

When I reached Gavin once more, he lifted my hand and pressed his lips to my knuckles. The tender act drew several shocked gasps from the crowd. The Duke of Tears had a reputation, and it did not involve tenderness. If we didn't have the room's attention before, we certainly had it now.

"Turn around for me," he murmured, one finger tracing the corset's top, tickling the rise of my breasts. "Pick one of them to stare at while I bare you to the crowd."

It was on the tip of my tongue to ask one of who, but of course he was talking about my mates. I'd barely found Ben's eyes when Gavin's fingers slipped over my shoulder blades to take the top of the corset in each of his hands. In one swift move, he tore the laced-up leather in two. He made short work of the skirt as well, cutting the thin fabric to ribbons that fluttered to the floor at my feet.

My sudden nudity was startling, my body reacting instantly in the pebbling of my nipples and slickness between my legs.

"Beautiful," Ben mouthed as his eyes devoured me. *"I love you,"* he added along our bond.

I didn't get a chance to respond before Gavin's hand was on my shoulder, shoving me to my knees. Ben's jaw clenched, but he stayed put, familiar enough with this dance.

"Crawl for me, petal. Over to the pole. I want everyone here to see how you're already dripping for me. And I do so love to watch your perfect arse sway before I redden it."

"Yes, my lord," I whispered. The hush that fell over the room was deafening. Even the music had been turned off. All eyes were locked on the Duke of Tears and his duchess.

Every drag of my knees across the wood, each sway of my breasts, seemed to move in slow motion as I made my way to the pole like he instructed.

"Lick it," he ordered when I reached the shiny metal structure. "Show them how you lick my cock."

There wasn't an ounce of embarrassment in me as I rushed to obey. All that existed was Gavin. His pleasure. His commands.

Remi groaned, and even though his words were whispered, I still caught them as if he'd spoken directly in my ear. "She's so fucking sexy."

"I do not disagree," Asher added.

I loved this. Putting on a show for them, giving Gavin exactly what he needed, knowing, in the end, Ben would get what he wanted most. I might be on my knees for Gavin, but I was serving them all. Even Pan, who I knew was watching and waiting his turn to be free. It was a heady experience, one that ratcheted up my arousal to new heights.

"On your feet, petal. Hands grasping the pole above your head."

I did as he said, a shock traveling through me as heated skin met cold metal.

"Keep your eyes open. Don't make a noise." His voice was right there, breath brushing my ear. Vampiric speed was useful in many ways, but this might be my favorite. "It's time to warm you up."

Warm me up? I was already burning.

But I quickly realized that wasn't what he meant as his palm cracked hard on my arse. I flinched but didn't let out a peep. He followed with blow after blow, slick beginning to drip down my thighs as pain turned to pleasure, the anticipation of the impact causing me to arch back toward him.

"Whatever you do, don't come. Your orgasms belong to your mates. No one else gets those but us."

I hadn't been on the precipice, but as soon as he told me I couldn't let myself fall over, it was all I was thinking about. And the bastard knew it too.

His lips feathered over my shoulder before he nipped my skin. "Are you ready for the whip?"

My heart fluttered. God, yes. I wanted it so much, but I couldn't guarantee I'd hold off my climax if he used it on me.

"I can't hear you, petal."

"Yes."

"Yes, what?"

"Yes, my lord."

"Good girl. Then go retrieve it."

My mind was cloudy with pleasure, but after a couple of blinks, a table I hadn't noticed appeared just off to the right of the stage. I would have sworn that hadn't been there when we started, but with Lilith as the owner, I was sure those little gifts were all too common.

I released the pole and took a step toward the table.

Gavin tsked. "On your knees, petal. You know better."

Recalling the library, my entire body lit up. And I knew, without being told, exactly what he meant by 'retrieve.' I made sure to keep my neck arched up, my strides sure and as sensuous as I could make them. I wanted to do my lord proud.

Some people might hate the idea of crawling. For them, it was a demeaning act, one that spoke of subjugation, humiliation, and disrespect.

But that's not what I found in the act. For me, it was empowerment. A way for Gavin to show off his prize and lord it over everybody else. I belonged to *him,* not them. I was the single most important thing in his world, and he wanted everyone here to know it.

So I retrieved the whip using only my teeth and crawled back to him, eyes locked on his burning stare the whole way. I didn't need to use our connection to feel the approval radiating off him.

He reached down and took the leather from my mouth before nodding, a silent confirmation I should rise and resume my original position.

"Hold on tight. Remember your safeword."

I nodded.

"Since this is your first time, we'll do one test lash first so you can get used to it. I want you to count."

"Yes, my lord."

Gavin trailed his fingertips down my spine before he moved away from me. I had a feeling if we were alone, he'd have used his lips, and the thought made me smile.

The crack of the whip took me by surprise, making me flinch. I thought it would hurt, but instead, a sort of heat striped across my back. No sooner had that idea flickered to life in my head than an intense burn bloomed over my skin.

"Petal . . ."

"Yes, my lord?"

"I told you to count."

"O-one," I gasped as he cracked the whip once more. This time I was ready for the blossoming heat that landed a bit lower. "Two."

"Good girl. Let's go to twenty and see how you do."

Twenty seemed like nothing. Or so I thought until the lashes came closer together. Gavin made sure the whip never landed in the same place twice, but he was incredibly skilled. It felt like the whip landed just to the side of where the last had been, until he was literally painting my back with his marks.

What started as a warm heat turned to absolute fire, and I'd only made it to 'seven' before I was squirming.

Try as I might, I couldn't keep my moans at bay, nor could I stop the flow of tears down my cheeks. My nipples were tight and painful buds, my center soaked and desperate for attention. I needed to come.

I must have been sending my need to the rest of my mates because, one by one, their voices sounded in my mind. Praising me and promising relief.

"You're doing so good, sugar. You should see his face. He's so in love with you. I'm proud of you."

"I can't wait to fuck you and give you the orgasm you deserve, baby girl. God, I can smell your sweet cunt from here, and it's driving me crazy."

"Almost there. You look like my wet dream come to life standing there like that. I'm so fucking hard right now."

"I wish it was me you were crying for, mon petit chou. *I wonder how my tail would feel when used as a whip?"*

Gavin moved just close enough I could feel his body heat, but not close enough to touch me. "Think you can take a little more, petal?"

"Yes, my lord. I can take whatever you want to give me."

He sucked in a breath. "You were made for me. My perfect submissive."

He may as well have just said he loved me for the way I preened. Pride made my heart swell as his words wrapped around my heart. I forgot about the audience, forgot we were on a stage. In my mind, this was me and my mates. No one else. We could have still been in Lilith's room upstairs for all the difference it made to me.

"Five more," he decided. *"Then I'll find somewhere we can take care of you properly."*

Three lashes in quick succession had me trembling, my knees nearly buckling, and Gavin blurred behind me in response. I thought he was going to hold me up. Instead his hand reached between my legs and cupped my sex, applying pressure to my swollen folds.

"Roll your hips, grind that needy little clit of yours on my palm, and leave me smelling of you. Remind me what I get to taste when we're through here."

I panted, sweat beading on my forehead as I shook my head. "I-I can't, my lord."

"You can. You will."

"You told me not to come. I'm so close already."

"You can do this, Roslyn. You will do this. I demand it."

The need to obey both commands warred inside me. I didn't want to let him down. Biting hard on the inside of my cheek, I rolled my hips back, swallowing a tortured moan at the delicious friction. My orgasm was so close. Little sparks danced in my periphery, and my toes curled from the effort not to come.

He released me, and I risked a glance back at him, core clenching at the sight of the man as he licked my arousal off his palm.

There was a beat when we just stood there, staring at one another, before he was moving again, the last two lashes curling up under each of my arse cheeks, the tip of the whip almost kissing my dripping center. The incredible burn, along with that much-needed pain, had me flying. I was lost in a sea of conflicting sensations.

It was then my knees finally gave out, but Ben was there, catching me up in his hold. "I-I've got you, sugar. You w-were perfect. My good girl. Let me t-take care of you now."

Gavin gave him a curt nod, but it was Lilith who spoke from the shadows. "Take her down the hall. You'll know which room is yours. The door will open for you."

As Ben strode away from the crowd, Lilith appeared at my side, one finger gently stroking a lock of hair away from my face as she whispered, "You did so well, darling. Enjoy the reward. You've earned it."

CHAPTER THIRTY-SIX

ASHER

"Where's he taking her?" I asked as Ben strode out of the room, Rosie in his arms.

Fuck, I was so keyed up I thought even a little bit of friction might send me over the edge. Watching her like that, seeing the arousal in every one of her microexpressions, had the same effect as that pink stuff Lilith had given us. Maybe it was because of our bond and how connected we were with her, but I felt her pleasure like it was my own. If I had to guess, I'd say she did that on purpose, shielding us from the pain and giving us everything else.

An impatient gesture from Gavin pulled me from my musings. "Well, are you two fools coming, or are you going to sit there with your dicks in your hands?"

Remi and I scrambled out of the booth, not needing to be asked twice. Where we were going didn't matter, so long as it was somewhere private where I could take care of the *situation* in my pants. Hell, right now, even the private part was negotiable.

The way Remi's cock pressed against the tight leather of his pants drew my gaze as soon as I had a chance to give him a once-over. He was in the same state as me.

"Let's go get our girl," Remi murmured in my ear just before he bit down on my earlobe.

It seemed counterproductive to mention that Rosie would probably be out of commission for the immediate future, too wrapped up in Ben to pay much attention to anyone else. Either way, we were there for her. Whatever she wanted, we'd give it to her.

I followed behind Gavin, weaving through the pairings of creatures in various stages of fucking as we went. A woman slipped her fingers up my arm, stopping Remi and me in our tracks as she purred, "You're not marked. Are you looking for someone to show you the ropes?"

I hadn't thought of that. Typically in establishments like these, there was a wristband, token, or some other indicator that told other patrons what you were into and what you were here for. Namely, if you were just watching, taken, or open to finding a partner for the night.

Remi threw his arm around my shoulders and tugged me close. "He's marked by me. Find someone else, siren."

Six months ago, I'd have been annoyed to hear him claim me like that, but now, I didn't hate the possessive growl in his voice. Rosie had brought us together in so many ways. She and Remi had shown me what it meant to belong. I *was* his, and there was no shame in telling the world he'd marked me.

The siren gave him a playful pout, tapping the illuminated sigil on the side of her neck indicating she was a Domme looking for a partner interested in ropes and punishment play. "Funny, I don't see one. Not the kind that matters here, anyway."

Remi growled again, his lips peeling back to reveal his fangs.

Christ, that was hot. I was used to the twins wolfing out over Rosie, but not Remi doing it for me. I must have bigger abandonment issues than I realized because this macho display of possession was doing it for me in a big fucking way.

Wrapping my arm around Remi's waist, I leveled the woman with my coldest go fuck yourself glare. "Maybe not to you, but it matters to me. I'm not interested, lady. I've got everything I want right here."

The siren backed away, eyes flashing like lightning over the ocean as she melted into the crowd, prowling for a willing partner.

"Well, well, Mr. Henry. Look at you staking your claim."

I rolled my eyes at Remi's teasing, but smiled despite myself. "Yeah, well, what can I say? You getting all growly over me turns me on."

"I can live with that." He brushed his lips over my ear and growled, "Mine."

Butterflies exploded in my stomach, and I swear my fucking heart started doing backflips. Remington Mercer flirting with me turned me into a damn teenager. Would he think less of me if I came in my pants?

"As long as you're ready to go again when the time comes, you can do whatever you need."

The group chat was a blessing and a curse. I hadn't quite mastered the mental barriers like the rest of them.

"Did everyone hear that?"

"Yes," they all answered in unison. Even fucking Pan, whose smirk rang out loud and clear.

Cool.

It took a lot to make me blush, but that right there? That was a contender for the top spot. We're talking boner in the front of the class levels of embarrassment. Or like that time I got caught jerking off by one of the nuns, using the Sears catalog, of all things. What? I liked the underwear ads, and it wasn't like there were any other options lying around. The nuns started cutting out those pages and burning them after that.

Remi snorted. "Sears? Really, Asher?"

"Fuck you, get out of my head."

"But it's so fun in there. I'm learning so many new things."

It was my turn to growl. It lacked the danger of Ben and Remi's, but it seemed to do the trick because Remi was back in my ear. "Okay, I see what you mean. Growly Asher is super fucking hot."

Gavin led us to a plain, nondescript hallway. It reminded me of a warehouse or clinic. Something unassuming and boring. It was blank gray walls, door after door, and it seemed never-ending.

"What the fuck is this?" I asked.

Gavin turned his head, and a wicked grin twisted his lips. "This is where Lilith gives you everything you've ever wanted. For a price."

"I didn't think this place had a cover since it's assumed everyone under this roof consents to letting her feed from their pleasure."

"Exactly," Remi replied before Gavin could.

"How does that answer my question?"

"You didn't ask a question, if you want to get technical about it, but let's just say, when you walk into one of Lilith's rooms, she feeds more deeply. Each one is a blank slate until you step through the door and give her access to your darkest desires. She takes from you, but she also gives. It's a beautiful symbiotic relationship."

Jealousy burned a hole through my lust. "How do you know so much about these special rooms, Remi?"

"Aw, jealous baby?"

I shoved my elbow into his stomach. "Answer the question."

Remi shrugged. "Everyone knows about Lilith's special rooms. They're invitation only, though, so I've never actually been down here before."

"You can thank Roslyn and I for the experience you're about to have," Gavin said, stopping at the only open door in the corridor. "Here we are, gentlemen."

We filed inside. The room was a sharp contrast to the den of sin we'd left behind. In fact, its warm and cozy setting reminded me a lot of the Mercer cabin. Of course Rosie would pick that place. It was probably the first time she felt truly safe.

My thoughts must still be bleeding through because Gavin murmured, "She didn't pick. The room did. It gives its occupants the thing they most desire. Nothing here was a conscious choice."

As I watched, the bed Ben had settled Rosie on grew larger, until it could accommodate all of us.

"Neat trick," I muttered.

"Do they make beds that big?" Remi asked. "Because if they do, we need to invest in one."

"I already have one on custom order. Once we select a permanent residence, we'll have it shipped," Gavin answered matter-of-factly, though his attention was still locked on Rosie.

Ben had her splayed on her belly, the bare skin of her back exposed as he gently ran his fingers through her hair. Eyes closed, she smiled serenely as he reached for a container of some kind of balm and began rubbing it into the welts the whip had left on her skin.

"So do we just stand here, or . . ."

Before I could finish the thought, a long stretch of plush couch lined the wall behind me.

"Uh, thanks?" I said to the room fairy, or whatever the fuck it was responsible for fulfilling the half-spoken need.

Remi threaded our fingers and dragged me to sit beside him as Ben continued caring for Rosie. Every time she moaned, I had to adjust myself. This fucking penguin suit was uncomfortable as hell. I wanted to be in jeans and a t-shirt, or better yet, nothing at all.

"Oh, that's better," Remi whispered. "Asher, is that a banana in your pocket, or are you just swinging around a big old dick?"

I glanced down. My clothes were completely different now. Gray sweats, no shirt, bare feet. And, of course, a raging hard-on.

How fucking great would it be if I reached in my pocket and . . . I pulled out a banana, and Remi and I laughed in surprise. "Looks like both."

The wolf snatched the fruit from me, peeled it, and licked a line up the length before biting down. "Mmm. I was starving."

"Guess the room knew you needed a snack."

Remi's eyes flared neon as they raked up my body. "I do love a snack, but you, Asher Henry, are a whole damn meal. Too bad the bed's taken. Otherwise I could lay you out and enjoy you properly."

Rosie's sleepy murmur floated over to us. "Don't hold back on my account, boys. If you want each other, you should do something about it. You watched me, after all."

"Shh, sugar. All you're s-supposed to be focused on is f-feeling good right n-now."

"Watching them love each other does make me feel good."

The flood of affection that accompanied her words had me smiling. I knew exactly what she meant.

Gavin strolled across the room and to the bar cart set up in one corner, where he poured himself what I could only assume was a blood cocktail of some kind. He leaned against the wall and drank in the sight of Rosie being cared for. The hunger in his eyes said it all. He loved watching the marks fade from her skin and couldn't wait to replace them with new ones.

Snagging the remnants of the banana out of Remi's hand, I tossed it behind me before launching myself on him. Rosie said go. I wasn't going to deny her.

"He's eager, huh?" Remi teased as I pushed him back until he was lying on the couch and my hips were between his legs.

"You complaining, Mercer?"

"No, baby. I want everything you'll give me."

"Are you sure?" I asked, letting a little growl slip into my voice as my hands went to the laces of his leather pants.

Remi slid his fingers through my hair and tugged my head down so his lips could crash into mine. "I'll give you everything. Anything. I'm all yours, Asher."

The words were potent, hitting me hard after that run-in we had with the siren. My mind filled with images of Remi bearing my mark right alongside Rosie's so there could never be any mistake about who he belonged to.

"Yes, Asher. Do it. He should have your mark," Rosie whispered, her focus trained on us as she sat up, Ben kissing along her shoulder and throat from where he cradled her against him.

"God, yes. I want it." Remi's voice was a desperate plea while I rocked my hips into him, the ridge of my erection brushing his.

"But how, I don't . . ." I probably should have known better by now. As I ran my tongue along the edge of my previously blunted teeth, I felt the little pricks of my demon fangs. There was no discomfort this time, no pressure or tingling to indicate I'd changed, but I knew without checking I probably had my little demi horns again too. "It's a goddamn room of requirement," I muttered with a soft, appreciative chuckle.

Remi reached up and confirmed that theory, making my whole body light up when he stroked the raised bumps on my forehead. "Horny, Asher?"

"Fuck yes. But you need new material. You've already used that joke before."

"Comedians reuse their jokes all the time."

I slipped my hand between us and freed his straining dick from his pants, making him whimper as I stroked the velvet shaft. "Okay, funny boy."

"It's fuckboi, remember?"

I stopped and peered down at him. "How did you find out about that?"

"Do you really need to ask?"

Pan. I sighed. "Well, if the dick fits, *fuckboi.*"

I squeezed him, rolling my wrist as I moved up and down.

"Jesus, Asher, you're going to make me come if you don't stop."

My gaze flitted to Rosie at the soft sound she made. Her eyes were bright and full of anticipation as she continued observing us. Ben's large palms cupped her breasts, his face buried in her neck. She moaned when I locked eyes with her.

"Enjoying the show, princess?"

She nodded, her teeth biting into her lower lip. *"I love the way you love each other. Make him come for me, Asher."*

Hot and cold tingles raced along my spine at her command. As much as this was about Remi and me, it was about her too. She rolled her hips backward into Ben, the shifter groaning as she did. No one was going unsatisfied tonight, that was for damn sure.

Retraining my focus on the man under me, I released his length and backed away, making him whine.

"Where are you going? Don't stop."

I moved backward on the couch until my shoulders were bracketed by his thighs. "Oh, I have no intention of stopping. Our girl asked me to make you come. You know I'd never deny her anything."

"Fuck," Remi moaned, his eyes rolling back as he lifted his hips closer to my mouth. Then he reached for my head so he could pull me where he wanted me.

"Hands up, Remi. Take what I give you."

"Jesus, I love it when you're bossy."

"Then do what I fucking say. Hands. Up. Now."

He raised them and threaded his fingers behind his head as I tugged his pants open wider so I had full access to every single inch.

"Swallow him down, Asher. He tastes so good."

Her voice, combined with the promise of Remi, had me rocking into the sofa as I took Remi's cock deep enough that I had to fight the urge to gag around him. Curious about something, I scraped my new fangs gently up his length as I pulled back, and Remi's entire body shook from the onslaught of sensation.

"Fuck!" Remi shouted.

"Like that, Mercer?"

"So fucking much. Do it again."

"Now who's bossy?"

"Swallow my cock, Asher. Right fucking now."

I grinned at the urgency in his voice. He was so close, and I loved it. Suddenly Gavin's earlier remark made a lot more sense. *'For us, it's about their pleasure, not ours. Anticipation only makes it all the more enjoyable, Asher. The longer you make your partner wait, the harder they come.'*

"Don't you fucking dare," Remi protested, either reading my thoughts or the intention in my smirk.

My lips went to his dick again, all the way to the base, and I hummed my approval when he writhed under my attention.

"Don't worry, baby. *I already told you I like the sounds you make too much to deny you."*

"You caught that, did you?"

"Pretty hard to miss."

"Is it . . . okay?"

"You can call me whatever you want, Remi. As long as you call me yours."

Those hands I'd ordered to stay put? They were in my hair and holding me to him as I let him move in my mouth. His cock throbbed, the orgasm I'd teased him with right on the cusp of spilling over. With one hand, I reached up and cupped his heavy balls, giving them a tug and tasting the salty burst of precum on my tongue.

"Come for me, Remi. Give it to me."

"God, please come for him," Rosie murmured on a moan.

That was all the permission he needed to topple off the cliff. The sharp bark that left him was one long unintelligible cry as jet after jet of his release pulsed down my throat.

I pulled back, wiping his cum off my lips before sucking my fingers clean.

Remi's irises burned bright as he watched me lap up the last bits of his release. A deep, possessive growl came from his chest before he reached for me.

"If I'm yours, come fucking claim me, Asher."

~

REMI

You know how they call the orgasm *the little death*? Could it ever end up as the big death? Like the end. Finito. Au revoir. Because it felt like Asher was trying to suck my soul out of my dick, and I loved it.

I loved *him*.

I loved this man beyond reason. Both of them, really. I wouldn't have believed it was possible to feel this way about two people if I wasn't currently experiencing it.

Rosie and Asher made me feel complete in some indefinable way. I'd never felt like I was missing anything, but how could you know you were incomplete until you finally knew what it was to be whole?

Okay, so apparently I wasn't just dying; I'd also turned into Nietzsche. Cool. Nothing like a post-orgasm existential episode to bring you back down.

"If I'm yours, come fucking claim me, Asher."

I was still trembling with the aftershocks of coming like a fountain, but my spent dick was already thickening with interest at the idea of his fangs in my throat.

"With pleasure. Where do you want it?"

There wasn't a question. The only place his mark belonged was on my throat, where every-fucking-one could see it. I turned my head, baring the unmarked side of my neck.

Asher crawled up my body, not needing further explanation. Wolves were always marked on their necks, and this way, his bite would mirror Rosie's.

"As it should. Leave your minds open for me, boys. I want to feel it with you."

I don't think either of us had ever closed our minds to her since she'd established our group connection, but I knew what she was saying. The three of us were in this together. This moment was ours to share.

My wolf was there too, just under the surface, prancing like an excited puppy. He wanted the three of us joined as much as I did. "Please, Asher. Don't make me wait for this too."

His soft chuckle made me ready to pull his head down and force his mouth on my neck, but I didn't have to. He took pity on me and placed the tenderest of kisses to the spot before his fangs sank into my flesh.

As the bond locked into place, a rush of pleasure hit me hard and fast, but it wasn't only mine. Rosie moaned as she came without assistance, bringing me along with her. Or maybe it was the other way around. Above me, Asher's body went stiff, his hips jerking as jets of his hot cum spilled across my stomach.

He released me and rested his forehead on my shoulder, panting and shaking. Then, Asher Henry, the man I never thought I could have, lifted his head and stared straight into my soul as he growled one word.

"Mine."

CHAPTER
THIRTY-SEVEN
PAN

So much was still unknown about the one vessel, two demon souls thing I had going on with my brother. It was no longer your run-of-the-mill possession, in that I wasn't in full control. Ever. Not even in the moments I was allowed to break free and take center stage. My autonomy could be snatched away from me again at any time.

It was absolute bullshit, if I was being honest. I'd never felt more out of my depths in my very long life.

I blame that constant ebb and flow of uncertainty for not realizing I wasn't just floating around in his mind watching 'Rosie-TV' while he and Remi took care of business. Say what you want about me, but I honor my deals. Privacy for Asher when he was *in flagrante delicto*, so to speak, was something we'd agreed upon. But this thing between them was so intense, I'd had to practically astral project my sexy arse so far out of his mind I found myself standing on the other side of the room.

I did so love playing the fly on the wall. Again.

I do not, in fact, love this, dear reader.

Quite the opposite. I loathe it. But then, does that really come as a surprise? Call me what you will—vain, self-absorbed, narcissistic. Satan knows every vile name you'd hurl at me is more than earned. But it doesn't change the fact that a demon such as me was used to being the main event. I was not born to simply sit on the sidelines and watch everyone else enjoy what's supposed to be mine. I wasn't cut out for it.

I wasn't made to *share*.

Oh yes, the irony of my current predicament is not lost on me.

Rosie's breathing picked up, drawing my attention back to her as a series of moans escaped that I knew signaled an approaching climax.

At least there was something fun to focus on this time. Even though I'd much rather be the cause of said moans. That stuttering shifter held her tight, his face buried in her hair, palms caressing the body I wished I were touching. Then she came, a pink flush creeping across her skin, her ragged cry filling the air mixed with the groans of the two men on the sofa.

"Yes, yes, you're all very good at orgasming. Bravo," I muttered sullenly.

Ben's head snapped up, eyes blazing as they focused straight on me. A low, rumbled growl escaped his throat before he put Rosie behind him and stood, that great hulking form of his tensed and ready for a fight. "Who the fuck are you?"

Look at that, no stammer!

But then I realized he was talking to me. Directly to me. I must be more skilled at astral projection than I'd thought. Perhaps I should send that witch a gift basket. It would seem she'd taught me a new party trick. "Don't play dumb, wolf. You can try to pretend I don't exist, but you'd be fooling yourself."

Rosie's head popped up from behind Ben, but he kept his arm locked on her waist, holding her to him. "C-careful, sugar."

"Pan?"

Why the devil did she look confused? Her brows were pinched as though she was trying to puzzle this moment together.

"*Ma petite,*" I drawled.

"Is that really you?"

Surely my presence couldn't be that much of a surprise. I glanced down, wondering if perhaps Lilith's magic room had conjured up some sort of ridiculous costume for me, and found myself rendered speechless.

I tore my gaze away from what had to be an impossibility and glanced over at Asher, ensuring he was still on the sofa. He was, he and Remi both dressed once more and looking equally bewildered by my presence.

Which meant . . .

This body didn't belong to him.

It belonged to me.

That was alarming on a number of levels. For starters, it wasn't actually *my* body. It wasn't purple. A quick spin in a circle proved that there was no tail. And a frantic rake of my hands through my hair confirmed that it lacked horns as well.

What the actual fuck?

A mirror shimmered into being on the wall across from me, and I audibly gasped. For staring back at me, miming every move I made was not Pandemic, Demon of the First Order, Firstborn and rightful heir of Pestilence.

It was Pan. The human.

Full fucking stop.

"Oh, Eve's withered leaf. I'm a monster. A hideous monster."

Rosie got off the bed and wrapped herself in a sheet, which promptly turned into a simple dress thanks to the room's magic—more's the pity—before padding over to me. With the gentlest of touches, she cupped my face, angling my head down so she could stare into my eyes. The physical contact sent another jolt through me. So apparently I was not astral projecting.

I had the sudden urge to vomit. This was really happening. I was really standing here, horribly misshapen. Deformed. Ruined.

The wonder in Rosie's gaze put a stop to my pity spiral. "It *is* you. Pan, you're beautiful."

"I'm human! This is a tragedy. Who did this to me?"

Gavin snorted. "Lilith's room. I'd think that was obvious."

"That crusty old hag. When I have my powers back—"

"It's not actually her. It's the magic of these rooms. Remember, it gives you—"

I stopped the vampire with a raised hand. "If you think what I most desire is to be a disgusting, thoroughly useless human who doesn't even have a tail, you have another think coming."

He shrugged. "I just call them as I see them, Pan. You're the one who manifested yourself as a pretty boy human with lavender hair."

"He's too pretty to be human. With those cheekbones and that mane, he looks more like a pixie or a fae," Rosie offered, sliding her fingers through my hair and making me shiver.

"Oh my God, he's Peter fucking Pan!" Asher stood, joining in.

"Yes! That's who he reminds me of. Can we call him Peter now?" Remi leaned against the back of the sofa, amusement making his eyes sparkle.

"No, you bloody well cannot."

"Pete?"

"No."

"Petey?"

"No."

"Pierre?"

"Absolutely not."

"Peta, Pearce?"

"Now you're reaching," Asher murmured.

"Come on. We can be lost boys, and Rosie can be Wendy."

Asher snickered and shook his head. "You and your roleplay. Leave the guy alone. Look at him, he's shook."

"No. *Shan't.* He deserves every second of discomfort." Remi looked at me, and despite the smile curling his lips, his eyes were hard. He still hadn't forgiven me for my hijinks. Not that I blamed him. The things I said and did to him while pretending to be his lover had cut deep. He may never forgive me.

I could live with that.

Probably.

"I mean, can you think of anything more poetic than the demon who possessed you without hesitation having an identity crisis? This is karma, my friends."

Was the wolf right? Was I being punished for the role I'd played?

Or did the vampire have the right of it, and this was *my* doing? Some subconscious wish the room had fulfilled. I wasn't a masochist. But deep down, did I want to make myself more palatable to Rosie?

Remi's version was easier to swallow. I could wrap my head around punishment, but *wanting* to be human? To willingly give up that which made me *me*? That would never make sense.

"How are you here, though?" Rosie asked, her fingers trailing across the sensitive skin of my neck as she drank me in.

"Perhaps I'm *your* deepest desire, *mon ange*."

"I wouldn't have changed one thing about you, though."

My shoulders slumped in mourning for my missing tail. See? She liked it too. Perhaps I'd let her suck on it when I got my demonic form back. But before I could make the suggestion, an icy stab of fear penetrated my purple little heart.

"Oh, Lucifer in the cradle of creation, this isn't permanent, is it?"

The men stared at me wide-eyed and shocked before Remi burst into a fit of laughter, followed by Asher and even the ever-stoic Ben.

"Look at him. I love this fucking room. Pan is getting everything he deserves for once."

Remi was on thin ice with me. Perhaps it was a mistake to help Asher save his life. I should have let him drown in his congealing lungs.

"Remi, not helpful at the moment," Rosie chastised.

Gavin offered me a hard stare. "It's unlikely this is permanent,

Pan. Lilith's rooms are special, but I doubt they're powerful enough for permanent body modifications."

Rosie bit down on her lower lip like she wanted to debate the point with him.

"You think differently, petal?" Gavin asked, not missing her expression.

"Hmm? No. It's not that. I just feel like my brother mentioned something about these rooms to me, but I can't quite recall it at the moment." She shrugged. "Must not be important."

"Brilliant. So the answer is, we don't know, and I might be stuck like this until the end of time. Maybe I won't help you lot stop the Apocalypse after all. The sooner the world ends, the better."

"Here he is, the true Pan. A whiny baby."

I snarled at Remi, but Rosie stopped me with a hand on my chest, right over my heart. "Let's cool down and just take this for what it is, an opportunity for all of us to be here together. For you to mend things between us. You have a lot to answer for, Pan."

My mouth dropped open. "I saved him, didn't I? How many more fucking miracles do you want from me?"

Remi's eyes narrowed. "What's he talking about? Asher saved me."

"With Pan's help," Asher admitted, seeming content to let things play out.

"Well, don't downplay it."

"I said you helped, didn't I?"

"Helped?" I scoffed, my indignation rising with each breath. "I saved the bloody day. If it weren't for me, you would have just sat there sobbing over your dead boyfriend. I told you what to do. I handed you the cure and said, this is how you save him, Asher. I didn't have to do that. In fact, I shouldn't have. If I'd let him die, this would be over, and my mum would have won. Instead, I'm stuck here in a human body I don't want, trying to defend myself to a bunch of ungrateful—"

"Watch it," Ben snarled.

"—creatures."

Remi's defensive stance softened a touch as he let my words sink in. "Well, shit. Thank you?" He rubbed a hand over the back of his neck and gave me a sheepish smirk. "I didn't know that."

"Of course Asher took all the credit. Just like a little brother. I never asked for this, you know. I had a mission. I wasn't even supposed to be here. I can't help it I—" I broke off, chest heaving.

Fell in love.

That's what I'd just been about to say.

Fuck. That.

I was entirely too vulnerable right now. They didn't need any more ammunition to lob at me like a grenade. I was hoping they'd simply forgotten the first time I blurted it out.

I sank to the floor, my hands cradling my head. "All I ever wanted was to help my mother. I never counted on . . . this."

"So what changed?" Rosie asked, her voice gentle but still making me flinch as she knelt beside me.

"You." I lifted my head up and held her gaze. "You and your damn deal changed everything."

"So what is it you want now, if it's not to help your mother?"

I didn't have an answer for that. Not one I could give voice to.

"I think th-the real question is, wh-whose side are y-you on?" Ben stood directly in front of me, blue eyes burning.

"Haven't I made it obvious?"

"N-no."

I sighed before turning toward Rosie. "Hers."

The suspicion that still clouded everyone else's gaze was lacking in hers. She was the only one who didn't doubt me. I wasn't sure I deserved her trust, but I was grateful for it.

I hadn't counted on how lonely it could be, being a demon in the mortal world. Rosie was my tether. My lifeline. My . . .

Oh bloody hell, there I went again. In a human body for barely fifteen minutes, and I already had feelings again.

I groaned and knocked my head back against the wall.

I hate it here.

"Sorry, Pete, that's not good enough. *Hers* could mean either of them."

"I've already given her my word I won't do anything to harm you."

"So? Demons lie all the time."

"We do not. Not when a deal is struck." Or a blood vow given.

It really bothered me I couldn't kill Remi. I wondered if Rosie'd forgive me for sewing his lips shut, though? Just for a century or so. Maybe two.

Remi still looked unconvinced. As did the rest of them.

"Oh, all right. Fine. If you insist." Heaving a sigh, I got to my feet. "I, Pandemic, son of Pestilence, pledge my loyalty to Roslyn Calliope Blackthorne—"

Gavin coughed, and I rolled my eyes.

"Blackthorne-Donoghue—"

Remi gave a far less discreet cough. "Mercer."

"We will never get through this if you make me list all your family names."

"Just one more, to make sure this oath of yours sticks," Remi said, his eyes glittering. He was enjoying this *far* too much.

"D-do it," Ben said, piling on.

"Roslyn Calliope Blackthorne-Donoghue-*Mercer*—"

"Th-thank you," Ben said, proving that while grumpy, he was still the politer of the two twins.

"No other shall sway me or cause me to break my vow. I am hers. Forevermore." I held out my hand and waited for Rosie.

Her eyes widened. "What?"

"Cut me."

"Are you serious?"

"Yes. Cut. Me. I can't make this vow with all these numbskulls standing around without bleeding for you. Use your vampire claws and take my blood."

She did, slicing a neat little line into my palm and watching as the blood welled to the surface.

"Now do you," I ordered.

She repeated the action on her own palm. The moment I pressed our wounds together, heat blossomed and raced through my arm. So, I was still a demon then. Bully for me.

"Done. There, are you all happy?"

Remi was the first to react. "Actually, yeah. That makes me feel a lot better."

"It's a s-start," his twin said on his heels.

"Infinitely," Gavin added.

"No." Everyone's heads snapped to Asher. "What? He lives in my head, I wasn't that worried to begin with."

Glad that was behind us, I looked back to Rosie and waggled my brows. "Well, now that we're all here and assured of our loyalties to one another, should we celebrate our alliance by taking this new body for a test drive?"

The door to our room blasted open. A very unwelcome guest stood in the doorway.

"Oh, come on. You couldn't give me twenty more minutes?"

The angel Gabriel peered down his nose at me. "No. Definitely not."

Well, this was bloody fantastic.

CHAPTER THIRTY-EIGHT

ASHER

"Okay, who the hell is this guy? I can't keep up. These rooms are supposed to be private, aren't they?" I really needed to have a talk with Lilith about her security if this was how things worked here.

"Gabriel," Pan sneered.

"Angel," Gavin supplied.

"Messenger of God," Remi added.

The blond man in the doorway seemed to wilt. Which was funny, given his choice of motorcycle leathers. It was endearing. Sort of like seeing a Navy SEAL throw on a Disney princess costume for a tea party.

"That's my line," Gabriel grumbled.

"He's a bit of a showboat." Remi squeezed my shoulder as he leaned in to whisper, "But don't let him hear you say that."

"You did that backwards, Remington. If you didn't want me to hear it, you should have whispered the first part. Or better yet, not said it at all."

"He's also got zero sense of humor."

"Though I'm told he's a hopeless romantic," Rosie said, taking a couple of steps closer to him. "I don't believe we've met, but you helped my brother. I'm—"

"Roslyn Blackthorne," Gabriel finished for her.

"Donoghue."

"Mercer," Remi singsonged.

"Hells bells, here we go again," Pan groused.

"You g-get used t-to it."

"Do you really?"

"No," Ben said with a heavy sigh, answering Pan but keeping his eyes locked on the heavenly interloper as if he wasn't sure yet whether he trusted the guy. "But it's over f-faster if you j-just let it h-happen."

Gabriel ignored all of them as he stepped the rest of the way into the room and took Rosie's hand. The door, what was left of it, closed behind him.

"You need no introduction, dear. Your reputation quite precedes you."

"Wh-what are you d-doing here?" Ben's question question brought me right back to the situation, and I really let myself sit in the fuckedupness of an angel in a succubus's sex club.

"Yeah, this doesn't seem like the kind of place for heavenly bodies or whatever you are." I strode toward him, needing a better look at the man. He had a strange sort of magnetic energy that pulled me in. He was almost familiar.

He let out a considering hum as I got close. "Father above, you look just like your sire."

I blinked. "Excuse me?"

Gabriel blinked back, seeming to realize he'd said that out loud.

"You know my father?" I prodded when he didn't seem inclined to follow up his observation with anything else.

"Once upon a time."

"Th-this just gets w-weirder by the day," Ben said beneath his breath.

No fucking kidding.

I looked the angel up and down. "I didn't realize you guys rubbed elbows with us mere mortals so often."

"We don't, as a rule. But your father isn't a mortal. Or a human, for that matter. He's one of the fallen, obviously, since you're a Nephilim. Well, half, anyway." He said it so damn matter-of-factly. As if he was chatting about the weather, not delivering life-altering news.

Blood rushed through my ears. "Obviously."

Gabriel tilted his head, studying me and my reaction. "You didn't know."

"I spent my whole life being punted from foster home to orphanage over and over, so no, angel, I didn't know."

"If it's any consolation, I had no clue you existed either."

"Nope. Not really."

Gabriel shrugged, entirely nonplussed, though I was starting to think that was just how he always looked.

"So, let me just make sure I have all the facts. Things seem to be changing on a day-to-day basis around here lately. You're telling me my mom's a horsewoman and my dad's a fallen angel?"

"And she gave me grief over angel porn. What a hypocrite," Pan scoffed behind me.

Gabriel gave him a half-interested once-over before returning his attention to me. "Yes."

"Cool. Sounds like I'm the ultimate outcast."

Rosie took my hand, linking our fingers. "Not an outcast. You're mine, remember?"

"Not to sound like a broken record, but what she said," Remi added, taking my other hand.

Gabriel closed in on me, his eyes narrowed as he peered into mine. "You've barely tapped into your grace. Someone hid it away long ago, but it's been unlocked. The more you use it, the stronger you'll become."

"My grace?"

"Your celestial light."

"The purple beam thing?"

"Yes. You're not strong enough to smite, but you can do some damage. Only those of us who are full-blooded angels have the strength to reduce our foes to so much ash with only our hands."

"Grace. Fascinating." Gavin's voice was awed. "I'm lucky to be standing right now after you hit me with that blast."

I didn't share his awe. More like apprehension. I was still trying to wrap my head around the part where I was apparently half angel.

"So, let me get this straight. I'm not a demon?"

"Technically you're both angel and demon."

"I h-have a question," Ben said.

Me too, Benny-bear. So many fucking questions.

Rosie's lips twitched, and I realized she'd overheard my thought.

Gabriel turned his attention toward the shifter, who'd stood as he did up the last few buttons on his shirt. "Yes, Bentley?"

"If h-he's Nephilim, wh-why haven't you k-killed him y-yet?"

"I'm sorry, what?" I couldn't hide my alarm.

"Th-the story g-goes that angels wh-who fell m-mated with human w-women and made n-Nephilim. But th-they w-weren't supposed to b-be allowed t-to live. They w-were too dangerous."

"So the archangels hunted them down and took them out," Remi finished grimly.

"I do so love when people know their history," Gabriel said. "Grace really doesn't belong on this plane. It's dangerously unpredictable when merged with mortal weakness."

"Weakness," Gavin repeated. "You mean sin."

"What else is sin but weakness?"

"A damn good time," Pan answered.

I shook my head, bitterness creeping up my throat. "That fucking light is why I was sent away in the first place. They said I was a monster, and I believed them. This confirms it."

When the angel turned back to me, I tensed and, for some reason, slid into my best ninja pose. The angel wrinkled his nose. "What's this? What are you doing?"

"Protecting myself. I can't let you kill me, man."

"I have no intention of killing you."

"I should hope not," Rosie said, her voice murderous. "He's mine, angel. You can't have him."

Remi growled his agreement.

"Why is it you are so quick to believe the worst people say of you, Asher?"

Uh, maybe because my entire life that's all anybody seemed to agree on when it came to me? The fact that no one ever wanted me? That no matter what I did, I only made everyone around me miserable, including myself.

Rosie squeezed my hand, still having a front row seat to my crisis. *"Not everybody."*

Unaware of my internal meltdown, Gabriel continued, "You aren't a monster." He reached out, and I flinched away as Remi growled in warning again.

"Calm down, wolf. I don't want him," Gabriel insisted, looking around for help. "We seem to have gotten off topic."

"Well this is incredibly entertaining. Do go on. I love seeing God's own Messenger flustered." Pan was leaning against the wall, legs crossed at the ankles, hands in his pockets.

"Don't cast stones, Pandemic. It's not becoming," Gabriel snapped, much to Pan's amusement.

"If you're not here to kill me, what do you want?"

"To send you five . . . erm, six on your way. You can't stay here forever. Lilith's intentions were pure, shockingly, but there's no protecting you from your destiny. You have to go back."

"So that's why she suddenly called us in. I'd wondered at her timing," Gavin murmured.

"But she didn't. Call us in, I mean. She gave us a choice, remember?" Rosie reminded him.

Gabriel's lips curled up. "Ahh . . . free will. She's been paying attention."

"Excuse me?" I asked, feeling so fucking lost not even a map could help me.

"It doesn't matter. The point is, you need to return to Aurora Springs and face Pestilence."

"Why would we go if we're just going to die?" I asked. "Seems stupid."

"We're not going to d-die."

"You don't know that. Gabriel? Are we walking to our deaths?" I shot at the angel.

"I can't say. I don't know the future, just that you are destined to fight this fight. And that help always comes to those who ask. Though perhaps not always in the way they'd expect."

"Useless, just like an angel," Pan grunted.

"I'm going to ignore that because you are part of this, Pan."

"For better or worse, it would seem."

"At least you seem to have found yourself on the right side." Pan's expression twisted at that, but Gabriel turned back to me. "Hold out your hands."

"What?"

He rolled his eyes. "I know you aren't hard of hearing, so please do not make me repeat myself. It's a bit of a pet peeve of mine. Messenger and all."

I held out my hands, giving Rosie a 'what the fuck is happening now' look.

Something heavy and, dare I say, ancient settled in my outstretched palms. A big as shit broadsword was there in my grasp. I was so startled at its sudden presence that I almost dropped it.

"Careful!" Gabriel hissed. "That's not a toy, Nephilim. Nor can it be replaced."

"Uh . . . thank you?" I offered, before asking the telepathic group chat, *"What the fuck am I supposed to do with this?"*

Remi was the first to answer me. *"Sword fight?"*

"If you tell anyone you got this from me, I will deny it, but I couldn't send you into the fray unarmed, nephew."

Nephew. Did that make God my grandpa? That was fucking weird. My family tree—which I'd once in a moment of absolute self-pity compared to Charlie Brown's Christmas tree—was growing new branches every time I blinked. It was a goddamn Sequoia. I winced. Was I allowed to say goddamned now? Gran-damned?

Rosie rubbed my back soothingly. *"You can say whatever you want. I recommend fork if you're looking for an alternative. It's surprisingly adaptable."*

Between Remi's joke and hers, I did the impossible and smiled. All of this was a lot less terrifying, knowing I didn't have to face it alone.

Gabriel scanned us with his quicksilver gaze before his expression hardened, and with a solemn tip of his head, he said, "Grab hold of each other. This part isn't pleasant."

"Was any of this supposed to be pleasant?" Pan asked conversationally as he joined our ragtag group and reached for Rosie. The rest of us did the same, until we were all connected in one way or another, Rosie's hand still on my back while Remi wrapped his arm around my waist. Ben's hand on his shoulder, Gavin's hand circling the back of Rosie's neck.

"Close your eyes. It's easier that way." Gabriel placed his palm on my shoulder, and the world began spinning, unimaginable pressure in my ears forcing my eyes closed before I could follow his command. "Go with God, Asher. Good luck. I'll see you soon."

CHAPTER THIRTY-NINE

GAVIN

Remington retched as the six of us materialized in the living room of the small apartment above The Tipsy Moose. Apparently his delicate sensibilities couldn't handle angelic travel, though I supposed it had only been a week or so since he'd last knocked on Death's door, so perhaps I was being a mite hard on the shifter.

Remington reached over and grabbed the first thing he could get his hands on. Namely my suit jacket.

On second thought . . .

"Unhand me. If you're sick all over this jacket, I will defang you myself, wolf."

"You say that, but we both know you love me, Daddy G."

I growled at him. "I *tolerate* you. There's a difference."

"Potato, potato," Roslyn chirped, making the others laugh and bringing a very begrudging tilt to my own lips.

My smile vanished as quickly as it appeared. She'd made all six of us laugh. Six. Not five. Pan and Asher were still separated as they'd been in Lilith's special room. I guess I hadn't given her enough credit. Though greater than I'd initially assumed, the magic of

Lilith's rooms must not have extended to Pan's true form since he was a towering wall of purple demon once more. Before I could comment on their separation, Bentley groaned.

"Th-this place is a f-fucking mess," his words were laced with frustration and disappointment.

Roslyn tightened her hold on him and deposited a kiss on his neck. "It's nothing we can't clean up. Once this is over, we'll set it all right again. I promise."

"We've just been sent in to fight a war for the existence of all life on this planet, and you're complaining about a little mess? Someone send me to hell, please?" Pan's tail flicked back and forth, reminiscent of an irritated cat.

"I wish I could," Remington grunted. "Hey! You're you again."

"Pan? Holy Gramps, it's you." Asher said, his eyes wide.

"Gramps?" Remington asked under his breath.

Asher shook his head, not bothering to elaborate, his attention locked on the demon. "But . . . it's *you*."

She might love them, but they weren't the brightest bulbs. It took them minutes to catch up to what I'd already noticed. Simpletons. That's when I realized that while the two had shared a head and a body, Asher had never come face-to-face with Pan before. I assumed it could also be true the other way but given his dicey history one couldn't really be certain what Pan did or did not know. I crossed my arms, settling in for what was sure to be an illuminating meet cute.

"Yes, we've established that. I am, indeed . . . me." Pan rolled his eyes.

"I drew pictures of you when I was a kid. I had dreams too, but they made me forget. Did we know each other?"

"No. But it would seem we were more connected than I thought. Portraits? Really, Asher."

"Weird," Remington said.

"Is th-this the f-first time you've s-seen his face, Asher?" Bentley asked.

See. Simpletons. It was bloody exhausting being the smartest person in the room. Everyone else was always playing catch-up.

"Yeah. He was in my head, but that was it. I never saw him. And until recently, I didn't remember anything about my connection to him. The priest took my memories and bound my magic when I was little."

"Caleb?" Roslyn asked.

"No. Father Tate. But I guess he wasn't really a priest anymore by the time he got to me."

"Yes, that man was possessed long before you were born. He worked for Auntie War. Poor sod is probably hanging over a pit of hellfire by his toenails about now." Pan stretched and flexed, examining his hands and the claw-tipped fingers at the end. "It's good to be the real me again. I've missed this. It looks like Auntie Lilith gave me my freedom from Mummy's prison. I'll have to write her a thank you note. Perhaps send her a fruit basket."

Remington raised a brow. "You'd send a succubus a fruit basket?"

Pan shrugged. "I suppose we could swap out the banana for a dildo, but really, aren't they the same thing?"

"No."

"Speaking from experience?"

Remington's cheeks went pink. "No comment."

Roslyn shot him a look. "Remi . . . you're blushing."

"I was fifteen, okay? I was curious, and it was all we—"

"But they're s-soft . . ." Bentley said, shooting him a look.

"Not when they're still in their wrapper."

"Wrapper? You mean peel?" I asked, inwardly loving the way he squirmed at our questioning.

"Wouldn't th-that still hurt?"

"Not when it's safely tucked in a condom."

"Is that why condoms are referred to as banana wrappers?" Roslyn asked, her eyes twinkling with amusement.

"Listen, we really don't have to talk about this. Who among us hasn't experimented with the odd vegetable or popsicle in our time?" Remington asked with an embarrassed chuckle.

"Popsicle?" Asher asked, both his brows lifting.

"Hey, look, the sky is falling," Remington said dramatically, pointing to the window.

"Is not," Pan teased. "Though it does seem as though the moon has taken a vacation."

Unease twisted my gut as I blurred to the window and stared out at the pitch-black sky. No moon. Not even a sliver of light.

"That can't be good." Asher's words were ominous. "It looks like the moon is completely gone."

"It is," Pan said calmly, as if this wasn't major fucking news.

"I've heard of one being lost to the moon, generally in reference to shifters going mad during a mating frenzy, but never the moon itself being lost. Sounds like a fae tragedy, or knowing them, a romance." I worried at the cigarette case in my trouser pocket, thankful for the gift Roslyn had given me. It was my touchstone. A comfort as I worked through my racing thoughts.

"No, it's not. It can't be. We would feel a difference, wouldn't we? The earth needs the moon, just like the sun."

Remington shoved his way to the window. "It's fucking snowing, Asher. Look at it out there. Not just little flurries. Big fat flakes."

"So? It's Alaska. Of course there's snow."

"It's the summer. We might be in Alaska, but it doesn't snow like this in the fucking summer. This is clearly February snow."

"February snow?" Asher repeated, but upon seeing how put-out Remington was, he held up his hands. "Never mind. Doesn't matter."

"'*Immediately after the tribulation of those days shall the sun be darkened, and the moon shall not give her light, and the stars shall fall from heaven, and the powers of the heavens shall be shaken,*'" Pan murmured, no trace of amusement in his tone. "She's going to do it. She's honestly going to succeed."

"Not if I have anything to say about it," Roslyn growled. "Where is she?"

Pan's eyes widened. "How should I know?"

"You're her minion. Don't you have some kind of connection to her? Some weird mother/son bond?"

"No," he sneered, reminding me of a petulant child. But then his expression cleared, and he rubbed a hand over his chest. "At least, I don't think so. Last I saw her, she was riding off into the figurative sunset. Or maybe it wasn't so figurative after all, seeing how it's yet to return."

"So we're just meant to wait here until she shows up? That's ridiculous. We have to find her and stop her. What was Gabriel's game if not for us to be ready to fight? He gave you that bloody great sword. He sent us into the lion's den. I can't believe we're simply supposed to be sitting ducks."

Roslyn was wound up tight enough that I worried she'd snap. "Petal, calm down. We need time to strategize, make a solid plan of attack."

"We don't even know who she is! For all we know, she's one of the bleeding gargoyles!"

Pan coughed under his breath. "I can assure you, she's not."

There was a weight to his tone, as if he knew something about the gargoyles the rest of us weren't privy to. I narrowed my gaze on him, about to dive into his mind and suss out his secrets when the scrape of wood over the floor came from below.

I stiffened, going on high alert. "Someone's downstairs."

"L-looters?" Bentley asked, his body tensing beside mine.

"Maybe. Or are they here to finish the job they started at the cabin?" Remington asked. "Make sure we're truly out of options for a place to stay?"

I shook my head. "They couldn't know we're back already."

"Who cares why they're here? Let's go give them a proper welcome."

I was impressed with the violence bleeding through Asher's words. Didn't realize the hacker had it in him.

A loud crash echoed from downstairs, causing us all to tense, but Bentley sprang into action, heading for the door.

"S-stay behind me. Be r-ready to fight."

We followed him down the single flight of stairs until we found ourselves in the short corridor that led to the main bar.

Based on the way everyone was already stood facing the stairs when we arrived on the main floor, our visitors heard us coming and decided to stay and wait.

Sudden foreboding prickled along the back of my neck as a familiar aroma hit my nose. It was subtle, masked by the scent of wood and the crisp air coming in through the broken windows, but I'd recognize it anywhere.

Ignoring Bentley's order to let him remain front and center, I shoved Roslyn and her shifters behind me. "Mother."

"Oh, look! I'm not the only one with mummy issues here. Brilliant." Pan's voice grated on my last nerve, but I was focused on the woman standing flanked by every single member of the Council.

My mother was a cold and calculating beauty. She was also a power-hungry, self-serving bitch. Until Roslyn, I'd been in line to follow in her footsteps and hadn't wanted much else for myself. Things were different now.

"What are you doing here, Mother?"

An icy smile twisted her lips. "Is that any way to greet the woman who brought you into this world?"

"I'm still not entirely sure you did."

"Stork theory, huh?" Remington asked behind me. "Yeah, I can see why you'd buy into that. Your mom seems like a right cunt, Donoghue."

"Oh, she is. The cuntiest."

Roslyn snickered at my confirmation, which I supposed was a bit out of character for me. I'd been spending too much time with the riff-raff.

"You've yet to answer my question. Why. Are. You. Here?"

"Imagine my surprise when a nobody mayor from a nothing

town rang me to inform me what my darling son and his presumed-to-be-dead wife were up to. It didn't take long to realize that you two have become somewhat of the vampire equivalent of Bonnie and Clyde. What with the murder sprees and deception you've rained down on this poor, insignificant town."

"What the fuck?" Remington said, not even attempting to disguise his incredulity.

"I th-thought I was the o-one who got a-accused of m-murder." Instead of sounding upset, Bentley sounded amused. He didn't see the group in front of us as a threat, not like he had the first time they'd met. Something had changed, and it didn't take our newfound connection to realize it was all because of the woman standing between us.

The High Chancellor stepped forward, his paper-thin skin so pale it was nearly translucent. But I knew better than to take him for a frail old man. The Council could tear all of us to ribbons. We should have been more careful. Roslyn was my responsibility to protect, and in the chaos of Pestilence's war, I'd lost sight of the very real threat they presented. "Gavin Donoghue, Duke of Canterbury, you stand charged with the murder of your father, the late Duke of Canterbury. As well as aiding and abetting a criminal in her escape from punishment for the attempted murder of Cashel Blackthorne."

"That's preposterous," Roslyn cried out.

"Wait your turn, Mrs. Donoghue. You'll be answering to your own crimes soon enough."

"Mercer. Oh, wait, are we not doing that this time? My bad."

Growls erupted around the room, though surprisingly, it was Pan who stalked forward and gripped the High Chancellor by his throat. "Rosie, love, want me to make it fast or draw it out a bit? I promise you, either way, his death will hurt."

"Put. Me. Down."

Pan looked stunned when he obeyed the High Chancellor's order. "Your thrall's not supposed to work on me," he murmured.

The ancient vampire grinned. "Surprise." Then he whipped his arm to the side, sending Pan flying through the air across the room. The demon crashed through the wall and crumpled beneath a storm of dust, debris, and bits of broken furniture.

"Pan!" Roslyn screamed.

The only way we were going to escape this was if we did exactly that. Escape. We didn't stand a chance against them. Not with how many extremely powerful vampires stood in our way.

"Okay, Ben, you take lefty, and I'll go for lazy eye over there. Asher, you can use that sword and take down Ginger Spice while Gavin faces off with his momager. Rosie, you use your queenie mind power mojo and keep these fuckers out of our heads, okay?"

Remington's voice broke through my whirling thoughts, and for once, I was thankful for him.

Roslyn silently nodded, and I felt it as she cast a mental barrier over us.

"The fact that you honestly think you could go toe-to-toe with any of them is laughable, Remington."

"Eh, how bad could it be? That angel thinks we can stop an Apocalypse, so surely the walking dead fall somewhere below that on the shit-we-can-handle meter."

"They will kill you. All of you. Then they'll take Roslyn and me and make an example of us for all of vampirekind to see. They know she's a Queen. That's the only reason they're here."

"I'd rather go down fighting than run scared." This came from Asher, who'd already brandished the sword, though it was obvious from the way he held it that he had absolutely no idea how to use the weapon.

Pan was nowhere to be found in the rubble of the wall he'd gone through, but we heard him clear as day. *"Aren't you forgetting me? I'm not letting that fossil take me down."*

"Then get out here and do something. No matter what, we need to protect Rosie. She's all that matters."

"Ben, I can fight."

"No, Roslyn, he's right. You are the most important part of this, and

you know as well as I that the Council doesn't take prisoners unless they mean to publicly kill them. You are a threat they cannot allow to remain, and they will stop at nothing to destroy you. Let us do what we were born to do. Stay behind us and keep your wits about you."

Pan pushed up out of the rubble, covered in dust. *"Great speech. I'm going to start killing people now. Are you coming?"*

"Okay, everyone. All for one and one for—"

I cut Remington off, bolting forward as I sent the order in my thoughts. *"Now!"*

CHAPTER
FORTY
ROSIE

My mates rushed forward, Remi and Ben shifting into their wolf forms between one breath and the next as they lunged at two of the nine Council members. Gavin headed for his mother while Asher held up the sword Gabriel had given him, thought better of it, and let it clatter to the floor, holding a palm out toward his target instead.

A few of the remaining vampires moved into place in front of the High Chancellor, using their bodies to shield him. The coward.

That left one odd man out who grinned as he came at me, his irises the color of pitch, empty and soulless. I'd seen that fathomless void before, in sharks. He assumed I'd be easy pickings. A weak bit of prey he didn't even have to hunt. He was wrong.

My fingers twitched, anticipation racing through my veins. I needed a weapon, preferably my bow and a full quiver, so I could make quick work of these arseholes. But, alas, there wasn't an arrow to be found here at The Tip. The councilman closed in, and all I could do was ready myself in a defensive pose. I supposed I could go for his throat? Tear it out before he got to my heart?

The shark-eyed bastard leapt at me before I'd settled on my plan of attack. I knew he was using his vampiric speed, it was one of our kind's greatest assets, but I watched everything play out as if it was happening in normal time. This was the problem with vampire against vampire fights. We were too evenly matched unless we had other skills or abilities to tap into. Noah had bemoaned this very thing every time he and Westley sparred together. No one had the high ground.

I was sure to any bystanders, our fight appeared a well-choreographed dance. He moved, I moved. He lashed out, I dodged smoothly. Every time I escaped his reach, that dullness in his eyes disappeared a little more, replaced by fury that burned brightly.

"You have to be faster than that," I taunted.

"Do I? You have nowhere to go."

I didn't look away from him, but as my surroundings registered, I couldn't disguise my mounting fear. I'd been backed into a corner. A classic move and I fell for it.

"You stupid girl. I'll be sure to send my condolences to your parents after I kill you. Of course, they won't understand why, since you've been dead for months."

Sharp-tipped claws raked across my throat, barely scratching my skin, but it was enough. I caught the metallic hint of my blood as it hit the air before my mind registered the pain.

I ducked under his still outstretched arm, popping up to find him unmoved, still facing the corner where I'd been standing, with one noticeable difference. An entire table leg was lodged through his chest. As far as stakes went, it was a bit overkill, but in fights such as this, what better kind was there?

He stumbled forward, a wet gurgle escaping him as he dropped to his knees, then crumpled into a withering pile of limbs. My gaze raked the room, finding each of my mates engaged in combat with one or more Council members, except for Pan. The demon stood in the opening created by his trip through the wall, breathing heavily, covered in dust and a spot or two of blood.

His stare pinned me to the spot before he said, "You're welcome.

You can thank me properly later." Then my demon strode forward, his cocky smirk in place as he taunted them. "So, which one of you motherfuckers is next?"

Enraged snarls met his inquiry as two of the High Chancellor's guards peeled away.

"Oh, lookie. Two on one, my favorite."

"If you think you're doing this without me, you'd be wrong," I growled. I would not be left to swoon like some Victorian ingenue.

"Then stop standing there and help me."

I'd show him. I blurred to the corpse, already turning to ashes, and pulled Pan's makeshift stake free of the remnants of the body. I gripped it so tightly the wood splintered into sharp shards. They might not be arrows, but they were the next best thing.

Pan held one of the vampires' heads between his hands, but the second jumped at him, forcing him to scoot backward out of reach. "Well? What the hell are you waiting for?"

I grinned. "An opening." With three of the shards balanced between my fingers, I flicked my wrist, slowly releasing them one by one. Well, slow for a vampire. To the human eye, it probably appeared as though I'd released my makeshift weapons randomly and all at once instead of with the deadly aim I'd intended. Years of archery had made my accuracy impeccable, and my newly acquired vampire speed only made my timing more so.

When the three projectiles sank through their individual targets, I beamed. "Bullseye."

The one going for Asher gasped before falling to the floor, my stake hitting the mark perfectly and shredding her heart. But the other two must've been older. They staggered, releasing Pan and moving toward me like the walking dead. Pan grabbed one by the hair and snapped his neck while I spun around and landed a kick to the end of the wood embedded into the other's chest, sinking it into his heart.

My mates turned toward me, nothing short of awe mirrored in their expressions.

"What? Like it was hard?" I teased, pretending to dust off my hands.

"Don't celebrate too soon, petal. Five more remain, and they're all ancient. Can't you feel Chancellor Macleod pressing against and testing your barrier?"

My smile dropped immediately at his gentle chastisement. I hadn't noticed, not until he mentioned something. I still wasn't used to thinking of my telepathic abilities, not just as weapons, but at all. They'd grown by leaps and bounds since discovering I was a Queen, but they were still uncharted territory for me.

As if he knew we were talking about him, Macleod let out a low laugh, the sound akin to the rustle of paper. "To think I was there the night you were married. If I'd only seen your true nature, all of this could've been avoided."

"I could say the same for you," I shot back, my answering smile brittle. "I should have known you were no good when you didn't stop them from blindsiding me with the wedding."

I felt a flicker of pain from Gavin at my words, but couldn't spare more than a wave of assurance through our bond. *"A wedding is not a marriage, my lord. I chose you then, and I will always choose you."*

His relief and love flooded me, but his expression was as stoic as ever as he stepped close to me, blocking my left side, protecting my heart so seamlessly a less observant person wouldn't have even noticed. "That wasn't even the worst of it, petal. Are you forgetting my parents' plans to blackmail you into becoming nothing more than a broodmare to give the Donoghues more power than even the Blackthornes have? Don't be shy. Tell the High Chancellor why you really ran. It certainly wasn't because you're a spoiled princess. The things they planned for you were crimes the Council would have made them answer for if they'd been caught."

The dowager duchess let out a nervous titter. "I can't believe you let this little fool warp your mind, Gavin. Cast her off and come with us. I'm certain the Council will show you mercy." Felicity Donoghue reached for her son, but there was a gleam of something nefarious in her eyes.

A snarl ripped through the air, Ben's dark wolf flashing in my vision as he rushed her. Two things happened at the same time. She screamed, and her arm gushed bright red blood. Though it wasn't an arm any longer, it was a gory stump. Ben had the rest of it in his mouth.

"Stand back," he warned us as he gave the amputated limb a shake, sending drops of blood spraying and forcing the now unconnected muscles to release.

I didn't understand his intent until something small fell to the floor. The item broke, a silvery liquid spilling onto the hardwood. Then Ben dropped the arm in the puddle, the flesh sizzling and rotting away as we watched.

"Mother," Gavin mock gasped. "Were you really going to murder me? Your own son? And in the same manner you murdered my father."

"Don't be precious. You're no shrinking violet, and you never cared for that wretched man to begin with. You'd have done the same if given the chance. Everyone thought it was you. Besides, you had every intention of killing me as well."

"Have. I *have* every intention. And I don't need to resort to common parlor tricks to do it." His arm shot out, his fingers curled into wicked claws as his nails shredded through cloth, flesh, and muscle before ripping out her still-beating heart. He let the spewing organ drop to the floor, his mother's mouth opening and closing like a fish. "What a fitting end for our tragic story. You gave me a terrible life, and I gave you a terrible death."

Pan chuckled. "I didn't think you had it in you." Then he kicked the now silent body part until it rolled into the same puddle where her smoldering arm was.

I had to swallow back the bile climbing my throat as her heart began bubbling.

"That's never going to come out of the floor." Remi's thought had me fighting a hysterical giggle.

The High Chancellor glanced around, his voice rolling through the room like soft thunder. "Stop."

His minions immediately ceased their fighting, falling back into formation around him.

"Okay, princess. I need to know what we're doing. I'm charged and ready to blast some vampires into dust." Asher wasn't lying. His arms were aglow from fingertips to elbows.

"It looks like little brother has finally grown into his birthright. Lovely. At the very last second too. How appropriate."

Asher shot him an annoyed look. "Oh, good. I was worried I was just starting to like you. Thanks for setting me back on the righteous path."

Remi shifted back to his human form, remaining crouched on the floor. "You can put the glow sticks away, Asher. Rave's over."

"I've got a glow stick for you." Asher's flirty retort came to us through our bond as his eyes traveled over Remi's nude form.

Remi's brows lifted in undisguised interest. *"Oh, do you now?"*

"Save the fuck me eyes for later. We're not finished here," Ben growled at them. He'd been quiet and concentrated, just like always when there was a threat to my safety. Bentley Mercer in protector mode was resolutely focused. I appreciated that about him. And I'd make sure to show him exactly how much later.

Unaware of our mental conversation, the High Chancellor cleared his throat. "It would seem we were operating under false information, Your Grace," Macleod said, dropping his gaze to the floor. "My deepest apologies."

Gavin's back stiffened, but it was only a heartbeat before he composed himself once more. "I assume the charges are dropped, then?"

"Of course."

"And my wife?"

"Pardoned, with an understanding she remain loyal to the

Council no matter how strong she may become." Macleod shot a pointed look at me over Gavin's shoulder.

"She'll do whatever she damn well—"

I interrupted my husband's retort by stepping out from behind him and putting myself right in front of the High Chancellor. Ben came up to my side, leaning his warm wolf body into my leg as he emitted a near-constant low growl. I threaded my fingers through the soft fur between his ears as I leveled a steely glare at the vampire before me. "Glad we've managed to clear things up. There's just one more thing before you go."

"What's that?" he asked.

"We let you leave this time. You'd do well to remember that. Because if you ever come back here and threaten one of my mates again, there will be *no* survivors."

The vampires exchanged nervous glances before he finally gave me a slow nod. "Understood."

Asher took his place on my other side, fingers twining with mine, while Gavin and Remi stood behind me. Pan whispered in my mind, reminding me he was always with me, *"Don't flinch until they're gone,* ma petite. *They are looking for any show of weakness. They're snakes. I should know."*

So I watched Macleod and his ilk leave the bar, standing my ground until the moment they were gone.

Remi looked down at his brother, still in his wolf form. "What's with the fur coat, bro? You afraid someone's going to see something they haven't already, 'cause newsflash, we're identical." Remi chose that moment to start wildly wriggling his hips, effectively helicoptering his . . . you know.

"Jesus," Asher said around a laugh.

"For fuck's sake. I hope you pull something, asshole."

Ben's grumpy retort had me giggling. "Please don't hurt yourself, Remi."

Tears sprung to my eyes as he continued, putting his hands behind his head and saying, "Look, no hands!"

"Anyone else suddenly in the mood to play ring toss?" Pan asked.

Gavin burst out laughing, causing all of us to stare in shock.

"Oh God. Is he okay?" Remi asked.

"He'll be fine," I murmured, reaching out and cupping Remi's jaw. "Now go on, put on some clothes so we can strategize. We still have to figure out how we're going to stop the Apocalypse."

The sound of slow, measured clapping filled the room, as well as the tinkle of a bell. Both grew closer, accompanied by footsteps from down the hall.

"Oh, Grandpa, what now?" Asher groaned.

CHAPTER FORTY-ONE

REMI

That fucking cat pranced around the corner, tail swishing, sour face still looking like she'd sucked on a lemon.

"Madam Mayor?" I asked, instantly covering my dangling bits. Listen, I was all for casual nudity, but not around her. Something about her and that cat gave me the creeps.

"Head's up." Asher unzipped his hoodie and tossed it my way. I caught it with one hand and wrapped the fabric around my waist apron style.

"Remington, don't cover up on my account. You're looking mighty . . . healthy." The way her eyes twinkled had my balls attempting to climb back into my body.

Before I could come up with any sort of response to that—shocking, I know, I'm usually totally on top of those things—Pan stepped forward. I'm not sure what I was expecting, but it certainly wasn't the big-ass purple demon defending us all from the Southern beauty queen as though she'd pulled a gun on us.

"Stay back. Don't let her get close to you," he said, real fear in his voice as he put himself right in front of Rosie.

"What are you on about, Pan?" Gavin asked, derision in his voice.

"Yes, Pan, is it? What are you on about?"

Lady Godiva Sassafras puffed up and hissed at him.

"Not much of a pussy whisperer, are you, buddy? That's okay. I can teach you," I murmured.

"I've been whispering to pussies since before you were born, boy. I get by just fine on my own, thanks."

The fact that Pan could sound so coldly offended by my words without acknowledging me—not even so much as a twitch of his tail—was pretty impressive. He must have known or sensed something about the mayor that we didn't because he hadn't taken his eyes off her once. In fact, I'd say the demon was on high alert. He stood there with intense stillness, muscles coiled, like a cobra ready to strike.

"So this is it, then? The end of it all? I would have expected a bit more panache from you, *Mother*."

"Mother? Did he say Mother?" I glanced from Ben's wolfy eyes to Asher's, then Gavin's. Rosie's hand clutched tight to mine as she sucked in a little gasp.

"That's what I heard," Ben confirmed.

Asher was the next to use our mental bond. *"We sure this is Pestilence? Doesn't she look a little bit too, I dunno, normal to the rest of you?"*

"What were you hoping for? A gorgon?" Gavin asked incredulously.

"Not in so many words, but can you blame me? I found out my egg donor was a horsewoman of the Apocalypse and I sort of expected something...scarier. But this bitch looks like she could be a weather girl—person."

"Don't let the Southern belle act fool you. She's vicious. She'll have you drowning in your own fluids quicker than you can spell your own name. Although, for you Mercer, that might take a while."

"Wow, demons must not get very good educations. How hard do you think it is to spell Remi? R-E—"

"Not the point," Ben growled in my head.

Delta's smile stretched. "Fine, how's this for panache? Surprise," she said, Southern accent gone as she tossed up some jazz hands.

I'd heard that voice before. In my fever dreams.

"She's no Fosse, but I guess it's something," I joked as a way to ignore the growing unease in my stomach.

I stared at the woman point blank, and like only a trauma response could, I was hit with an echo of the plague I'd narrowly survived. I blamed my showdown with the vampires for the extra time it took for all the dots to connect. Pan's mom being here. Her wearing Delta like a disguise . . . or was she Delta? I was a little confused on that point.

A tickle in the back of my throat had me letting out a dry cough as she smirked.

"It was you."

Her eyes widened. "You'll need to be a bit more specific."

"You infected me. You touched me at the bar, and then I got sick. You tried to KILL ME."

"Oh yes, that does sound like me. Germs are my specialty, after all." She winked. That bitch fucking winked. I lurched forward, ready to rip her head off her body.

I didn't get far, though, because Gavin slammed a hand to my chest. "Allow me."

The vampire rushed her, fangs extended, murderous intent vibrating from his entire body. Maybe this would be over before it could really start. Wouldn't that be great?

Before Gavin reached her, he was blown back by a burst of white light, his large frame skidding along the dusty hardwood floor until he nearly collided with Pan.

"What the fuck was that?" I asked.

"The forking amulets," Rosie muttered.

Gavin and Rosie each reached for the crystals around their necks, trying in vain to remove them. All they got for their efforts were trickles of blood where the chain sawed through their necks and seared skin where the crystal burned into their palms.

Rosie snarled. "She us proofed herself. Tricky bitch."

I didn't comment on her using a curse word. There wasn't

anything more appropriate to describe this cunty-mccuntface. Well . . . I stand corrected.

The deep growl Ben was nearly constantly emitting clued me in on his frustration. He wanted us out of here, away from the threat, so we could regroup and make a plan.

"Stand down, all of you," Pan insisted. "The last thing you want to do is touch her. She's a literal contagion, remember?"

Asher's hand began to glow. "Good thing I don't need to touch her to take her out."

Delta's lips twisted in the mockery of a frown. "Aw, but Asher. You would never hurt your own mother. Don't you remember the little deal we made?"

Pan groaned. "You didn't. Please tell me you didn't."

"Deal? What deal is she talking about, Asher?" Rosie asked, her panic flooding our bond.

But there was no answer. I turned to look at him, knowing there had to be a good explanation for this, but his expression was wiped clean, eyes vacant.

Asher wasn't home right now.

Asher

The sick taste of dread filled my mouth at the sound of her voice. Her true voice. This was the woman who'd been in my head. The one I'd all but written off as a dream. But as soon as she looked at me, the vault was broken, and I was thrown back into the memory she'd locked away.

It played through my mind on a reel, but this time, the missing pieces of our conversation returned to me, and I wanted nothing more than to punch myself in the face for the stupidity and desperation that led me to make this choice.

"Put me back."

"That isn't the magic word. You must agree to our deal first. Like I said, we're sticklers for the rules."

"What do you want from me?"

"Nothing much, just your help to ensure all the pieces are in place when the time comes."

"So you want me to set up your little party?"

"Exactly. We're going to celebrate the end of the world together, you and I."

"Celebrate seems like a big ask."

"Okay, fine, you'll be there while *I* celebrate."

"Anyone ever tell you you're not a very good salesperson? What's in this for me?"

"Why your life, of course. And your mates. I'll need to borrow them for a while, but when I'm done and my victory assured, I'll return them to you."

"Whole?"

"Of course. Who do you think I am?"

"A fucking horsewoman of the Apocalypse."

"Sure, but I'm not a monster."

"Debatable."

"When I summon you, Asher, you'll bring me Roslyn and all her pathetic mates. You won't fight it, and you won't try to stop me."

"I don't really like being told what to do, you know. I'm kind of a rogue agent."

"Seems to me you don't have a choice if you want your body back. Is it really such a big ask in the grand scheme of things, considering how you'll profit from the deal?"

"That's really it? You just want me to bring them to you?"

"Like a shepherd herding his flock."

"It sounds sinister when you say it."

"I am a horsewoman, darling. Sort of comes with the territory."

"And then I get to have them again? I get to be me again?"

"For the most part. It's this or die. Make your choice."

"Fine. I'll do it. Now get me back in my body."

"Good boy. I always liked you best. Oh, one more thing, dear heart. You won't remember the terms of our bargain."

"I won't?"

"No. I can't have you blabbing to your little mate or letting her in your mind. When the time is right, your memory will return to you. I'll see you soon, darling."

~

BEN

THERE WERE VERY few times I didn't like being a wolf, but this was one of them. My teeth and claws were sharp, but Pan was right. Touching her meant contracting whatever disease she decided to afflict us with. I wouldn't be any use to Rosie if I was dead.

Which meant I was useless. Not fit to face off with this bitch as a man or as a wolf.

My frustration slipped out of me as a low growl.

"It's all right. We will figure something out."

Rosie's assurance was welcome, even if it was naively optimistic. There wasn't time for us to figure anything out. It would be too dangerous to split our attention and try to come up with some sort of plan while she was standing right here in front of us. And it wasn't like she was about to let us walk out the front door and take a rain check on this little meeting either.

Asher's palm still glowed, but he seemed off, like he was uncertain. That wasn't like him. The hacker was always over-confident—cocky, even—when it came to his intelligence and ability to strategize on the fly. This was not good. He'd made some kind of arrangement with her, and now she had him over a barrel.

"Are you going to tell them, Asher, or should I?" Delta asked, an evil smile curling her lips.

"No."

"Enough with the dramatics, Mother. The costume and

posturing are ridiculous. You're no better than Auntie War with her French accent. I really thought better of you. I guess my expectations were too high."

"Wait . . . she's not Delta? I'm confused," Remi asked, his voice bewildered.

Pestilence laughed. "That trumped-up Miss America wannabe would be so lucky. My borrowing her body was the damn highlight of her insignificant life."

"And by borrow, you mean . . ." Remi trailed off.

"Possess. She means possess, you absolute imbecile."

"Ah, so like mother like son."

"Except I can easily walk in any body I choose for as long as I desire. Unlike poor Pandemic here. He kills them so quickly. No finesse. Until you, Asher. You were the perfect vessel for him, strong and beautiful. Made to withstand any illness he threw at you due to his less than stellar control."

"I assume you're going to take credit for that too. It couldn't have anything to do with the fact that my dad's an angel?" Asher spat.

One brow arched as she let his words sink in. "Someone's been telling tales, I see. Technically, your father was fallen. That makes him as close to demonic as angels get. What a night that was. You should have seen his face when he realized I wasn't his human mate. Absinthe. Such a powerful drink. She didn't even realize I was killing her until I was wearing her skin."

"It says a lot about you that you have to wear another's skin to get someone to fuck you," Rosie said, not stumbling at all over the curse word as she glared at the horsewoman. She was fury incarnate, the insults thrown at her mates amping up every one of her protective instincts.

Hatred burned in Pestilence's eyes. "Hold your tongue, you insolent little whore."

"Hang on a minute. That's only okay when I say it," Pan interjected.

But before she could respond, what used to be Mayor Delta

Dubois tipped her head back and screamed, her jaw open so wide I heard her bones break. Smoke trickled out of her mouth, a vile acidic green that twisted faster and faster until it wasn't a trickle but a whole-ass tornado. Wind whipped around the room, sending bits of paper and dust scattering.

The storm was over as quickly as it began, the smoke turning into a column that soon settled into the shape of a woman. Meanwhile, Delta's body fell to the ground, her skin peeling away from her bones as she rotted from the inside out. I had absolutely no idea what Pestilence had infected the woman with, but I didn't feel like I was completely out of line assuming it was literally everything.

The stench was overwhelming, my wolf's sensitive nose wrinkling in disgust the instant the odor hit me.

"I . . . um . . . gross." Remi gagged, bending over as he heaved. "Was that really necessary?"

"It would seem so. She's given us an example of exactly what she can do to us, Remington. I would suggest we all keep our distance." Gavin wrapped an arm around Rosie and tugged her tight against him, as if the act might protect her from the sickly looking viscous goo seeping out of Delta's corpse.

"There's still only one of her and six of us. I don't care what she can do. Those are my kind of odds."

"Oh, Asher . . . whatever gave you the impression I was alone?"

The door at the entrance of The Tip creaked as it opened and snarls heralded the arrival of a horde of demons. Not all of them pestilence demons by the smell of things. I stood, ears back, fur ruffled, teeth bared.

Finally, something I could kill.

CHAPTER FORTY-TWO

PAN

This town wasn't big enough for more than one demon. But currently there were at least a dozen flooding the bar. I stopped counting when three of my hellions came through the door. Ah, my minions were here to offer me aid. *Take that, Mother.*

"Hattie! Well met!"

"Oh, go sit on your tail."

I stiffened at the wholly unexpected and undeserved insult. "I beg your pardon?"

To my left, Ben pounced on a rushing imp, making short work of the little thing and leaving it bleeding out and twitching on the floor.

"You heard me," Hattie snarled as she approached, not stopping until she kicked me hard in the shin.

"Ouch! Bloody hell, Hermione! What was that for? You'll pay for your insolence."

My mother's laughter grated on my nerves as the pointy-eared creature seethed and continued assaulting me.

"My. Name. Is. Hannah!"

All around me, the demons were engaged in hand-to-hand fights with Rosie and her mates. I, on the other hand, was now surrounded by three of my most unloyal minions, all of them screeching obscenities and using both fists and feet to attack me. One bit me on the tail. The *tail!*

I jerked my second most prized appendage aside, but her hold was such that she lifted off with it. After a few quick shakes, I was finally free of her.

"Juniper, no!" Hannah wailed as the nameless hellion sailed through the window.

Ah, right, Titmouse. She'd be a hard one to replace.

Remi's laughter ghosted through my mind as he raced for his next opponent. I had to admit, he was a striking wolf, all sleek and gray with a liberal amount of blood staining his muzzle. But I'd never tell him that. *"Nice moves, demon boy. You should try mine next time. Although if you want to stick with your tail, I guess it's more a propeller than a helicopter, huh?"*

"Oh, go bite a corpse."

Hannah rounded on me once more, looking positively fierce as she scowled up at me—well, as fierce as a three-foot imp with bugged-out eyes and wobbly ears could. "You will die for that!"

I snorted. "I'd genuinely like to see you try."

She ran for me, head down, ears back, a high-pitched battle cry filling the air. I stopped her with a palm to the forehead, holding her as she ran in place. "This is bloody ridiculous. What the hell has gotten into you?"

"You treated us like dogs. Worse than dogs. Well, guess what? Dogs bite back, but hellions kill."

Before I had a chance to summon any sort of response, a stabbing pain ripped through my back. I glanced down to see the business end of an enormous cleaver embedded into my side so deep the blade wasn't even visible anymore.

Catherine grinned maniacally. "How does it feel to be the pincushion now?"

I grunted, blood running down my hip and soaking my pants. Well, these were ruined. Brilliant. "I don't know, you tell me."

I raked my claws across her face, taking her eyes with me. She screamed as I shook my fingers free of the mess she'd left on them, one of the lantern-like orbs stubbornly clinging to my nail. I grimaced as I plucked it off as one might a grape and then flicked it away.

From the corner of my eye, I caught sight of my mother. She'd perched herself on one of the few remaining tables, chin propped on her fist, an amused smile on her face. She was loving the chaos she'd unleashed, already assured of her victory. I hated her.

"Asher, a little help, please?" I called as my brother used his glowing magic hand and blasted a stinking pestilence demon away from him and Rosie.

He pulled her tight against him, but the light guttered and died. "I'm tapped out. I can't do much more than fight." The same demon he'd knocked back came stumbling toward them.

"Don't let it touch her!" Genuine fear tightened my chest as the creature charged at my mate.

Asher slammed his fist into the demon's jaw, and as soon as it hit the hardwood, he brought his heel down hard, crushing its skull into a pulpy mess. *Well done, little brother.*

"Can we please wrap this up? I have places to be," Mum whined as she inspected her nails.

"Kill her, Asher. She's your target." Gavin's voice echoed in my head. He was engaged in a tussle with an enormous cyclops. Well, technically it was a relative of the cyclops, but I wasn't in the mood for details.

Honestly, I was impressed at the number of bodies that littered the floor. For a ragtag group, we were far more formidable than I expected.

An enraged shriek was my only warning before pain shot through my arm. It was so overwhelming I couldn't even pinpoint the source until I glanced down to find Hannah hanging from a second knife that she'd just run through my chest. Well, closer to my shoulder if we were being technical.

The crazy bitch had taken a go at my heart. Oh, they were serious? That was cute.

"You missed," I sneered.

Her weight on the knife pulled it down, helping it sever what was left of the tendon and muscles there and dragging out an unintentional moan from me.

"Did I?" she panted, eyes wild. "Or do I have you exactly where I want you? Skewered and bleeding out at the end of my—"

Two things happened in close succession. Agony tore through my side, then Hannah's head fell clean off her shoulders, interrupting whatever else she'd been about to say. I turned to my right, finding Rosie holding the cleaver she'd ripped out of my side, her face twisted with the promise of further violence.

"No one gets to take your blood but me."

My brows lifted. This was *so* not the time to get hard, but damn if her possessive display didn't have me sporting a semi.

"You do love me."

"Don't push your luck, Pan," Asher interrupted before she could agree and put all of them to shame.

"There are three left, but they're all pestilence demons. None of us can touch them," Gavin growled as he joined us. The man was covered in black blood, eyes blazing, chest heaving. "We have to make a run for it."

Ben and Remi joined us, fur matted with all sorts of ichor I didn't want to question.

"Use your compulsion on them, sugar. We just need them to stay put while we go out the front."

"I can't." Rosie's frustration leaked through both her words and our bond. *"I've been trying, but I must have used up my reserves with the vampires."*

"Aw, this is always my favorite part," my mother said, her voice deceptively sweet as she clapped her hands together gleefully.

"The part before you die?" Gavin sneered.

"The part where the heroes finally realize they have no hope of winning. You can't defeat me. You know it. I know it. Hell, even those pesky angels know it, or they wouldn't have tried so hard to interfere. You're surrounded. You're weaponless. You don't have a snowball's chance in hell. Trust me, I live there. I would know." She stood and began a slow glide toward us. "I thought perhaps you'd put up a better fight, especially after you bested the Council. Those fools weren't as determined to kill you as I'd hoped when I called them. But you disappoint me. It's almost too easy."

But we weren't weaponless, were we?

Asher and I had the same thought, Gabriel's sword flashing in our minds simultaneously. He ran for it, scooping it up from where he'd so carelessly discarded it earlier. The second he held it aloft, it blazed bright with holy fire, ready to smite anyone in its path.

I took two steps back. *"Keep that thing away from me."*

A sick sense of glee took hold as I watched my mother's expression morph into horror. "Where did you get that?"

"This old thing?" Asher asked, giving it a careful swing. "It's a family heirloom."

He tightened his grip and clenched his teeth as he spun, slashing through the bodies of the three remaining demons in one clean blow. They fell, turning to ashes before hitting the floor.

"That was so fucking cool." Remi's awe was unmistakable in his hushed words.

Asher's wide eyes met mine, then flicked to Rosie. "Holy fuck. I've always wanted to do that."

Remi shifted back into his human form, his body still coated in goo. His gaze was trained on the empty space where Mummy dearest had been standing only moments before. "Yeah, you'd better run. My boyfriend will smite you so hard."

"Is it over?" Rosie asked.

"For now," Gavin murmured, pulling her into his body and brushing a kiss on her forehead.

The vampire was right. There was no way this was over. Asher's grace was clearly something she hadn't counted on, but she was too close to everything she'd ever wanted to simply quit now. She was going to regroup. Plot and strategize before striking. And now she knew about the ace up our sleeve, so she wouldn't just return—she'd come back bigger and better than before. Where do you think I got my flair for the dramatic?

"If I know my mother, this is only an intermission before the final act."

"W-we should head somewhere s-safe. Rest up. Eat. W-we n-need to be r-ready wh-when she c-comes back."

Ben was right. We should make the most of this reprieve. She sure as hell would. Before I could tell the others that, my head swam, my body suddenly off-kilter. What was this? Weakness? I wasn't weak. I was a fucking demon.

But when I glanced down my glorious body, I saw the thick coating of my own blood covering me and the growing pool of it at my feet. For the first time, I realized those damned hellions might have done a better job assassinating me than I thought. "Et tu, Hattie?"

"P-Pan, you don't l-look so good," Ben said, brows pulled together.

"Funny thing. I think I'm dying."

My knees buckled, and a naked werewolf caught me before I hit the ground. The world went black, and like the romantic hero I was, my last thought was of Rosie.

CHAPTER FORTY-THREE

ASHER

"Where do you want me to put this arsehole?" Gavin asked, annoyance coloring each word.

We looked around the Mercer cabin, still in a state of disrepair after the raven attack. It was obvious someone had been back and attempted to start setting this place to rights, but they hadn't made it far. Piles of glass littered the floor, what was left of the furniture was upended, and windows were missing their panes, a cool breeze sending the curtains fluttering. What a mess.

"Uh, the table?" Remi offered, setting down the bags of groceries he'd pilfered from The Tip's kitchen.

"The t-table?" Ben's expression reeked of disapproval.

"I don't want him bleeding out in my fucking bed, do you?"

"N-no. The t-table it is. P-put a t-towel down or s-something."

Rosie darted down the hall, returning so fast if I hadn't been watching her like a hawk, I wouldn't have known she'd been gone. Three large towels were draped over the old wood table before Gavin laid Pan out on the now protected surface.

She was trying to hide it from us, but she was worried about the bastard. I'd be lying if I said I wasn't too. Somewhere along the way we'd gone from bitter rivals, if not outright enemies, to something resembling a relationship. Not quite friends, frenemies? Estranged brothers?

Oh shit, I was living out my *Vampire Dairies* fantasy. I was the Damon to his Stefan. I sighed. No, I wasn't. He was clearly the Damon. Cocky asshole. That was fine. Stefan got more time with Elena. Right?

I glanced over at Rosie, thinking she even sort of looked like her.

"Who do I look like?"

Her voice caught me off guard, and I flinched. "The most beautiful woman I've ever seen."

Remi gagged. "God, you need to work on your pickup lines. You've gotten lazy."

"You're just jealous you weren't the one getting complimented."

"True," Remi agreed easily, making us laugh.

"Now's not the time for your ridiculous and incessant banter."

"Agree to disagree, Daddy G. It's always time for incessant banter. It's my thing. My calling card, if you will. Everybody's gotta be known for something."

"Th-that's what y-you want to b-be known for?"

"It's that or my dick, big bro."

Gavin snarled, clearly fed up with Remi's BS. "Pan's losing too much blood. If we leave him untreated much longer, he's going to die."

Rosie swallowed, her eyes taking in Pan's supine form. "I've already tried giving him my blood, but it didn't work. What else can we do?"

All eyes turned toward me, but it was Rosie's silent plea that hit me right in the heart.

"I don't know if it'll work."

"Try?" she asked softly. "Please?"

"Hold on a sec, baby girl. Are we sure that's what we want to do? I mean, the guy possessed Asher. Manipulated you into a deal. Lied to all of us. Repeatedly. Almost killed Darla, definitely killed some other people. And let's not forget his alliance with his mother, who's currently trying to end the world. Is losing him really the worst that could happen?"

"Wouldn't this conversation have been more appropriate before I carried the bastard here? We could have just left him to die at the pub if that was the end goal." Gavin's words were mostly for his own benefit, but I could understand his annoyance.

"He saved your life, Remi. Fought with us when he didn't have to. Protected me *when he didn't have to.*" Rosie's words were fierce as she emphasized her points. "Pan chose a side when he made his blood vow, and it wasn't her. And if you want to get technical, the deal was my idea. Both times."

"Ookay, just making sure we were all on the same page." He gestured for me to go ahead and do my thing.

But this time it was Ben who spoke up. "Th-that doesn't undo all the d-damage he's done. It's not going to bring those people back."

"No," Rosie agreed, "but it's a start. There's not one person in this room without blood on their hands. He's making amends in the ways he knows how. Don't forget, I was a monster once, and you forgave me."

"You were the one who f-forgave me."

"And I'm choosing to forgive him. He's my mate, Ben, just like the rest of you. Each one of you holds a piece of my soul. He just so happens to have the darkest part. It doesn't make him any less mine. Fate brought him into our lives for a reason. We cannot leave him to die. Not if there's something we can do to save him."

Gavin sighed. "Not to mention, if he dies, she may potentially go with him, *and* she may no longer be powerful enough to stop Pestilence. You know, if you needed more motivation."

With a curt nod, I approached the dying demon. The bleeding seemed to have slowed, now just a light trickle every once in a while. If I didn't know better, I'd say he was healing. But I could sense the truth. His purple heart was barely pumping, most of his supply now on the floor of The Tip or soaking these towels.

My head swam as I tapped into his physical state. Every move I made felt like swimming against a current. Fuck, I didn't have much time at all.

Letting instinct guide me, I placed both palms over his wounds. I really didn't know what to do, but it stood to reason that this is where a doctor would start. Stitch him up. With Remi, I had the love between us to latch onto. That had been the thread I'd used to heal him. I didn't have that with Pan. All I had was tolerance. I didn't think that would work. At least not in the way we wanted it to.

Think, Asher. She's counting on you.

Almost as if I'd summoned the memory, that old stray Cupid floated through my mind. Pan said it was my love for the orange tabby that did it. But that wasn't quite true. I hadn't been in love with the cat either. My compassion for the unloved creature had been enough. I just wanted to make him feel better. To take the pain away and stop his suffering.

It was hardly a science, but it seemed like enough to go off. I mean, if five-year-old Asher can accidentally do it, surely grown-up Asher could.

I pushed every other thought from my mind and focused only on Pan's pain. My hands grew warm, the light causing a glow where skin met skin. It was working. I could feel the edges of his wounds knitting together, see the color return to his face. Superhero Asher to the rescue.

I stumbled back as Pan sucked in a breath, Remi right there to catch me. "Easy."

I nodded my thanks, still a little too light-headed to manage more than that, as Pan's eyes fluttered open.

"How very dare you."

"What?" I asked.

The demon sat up and stared straight at me. "It took you that long to decide to save me? You really had to debate the point and waste precious seconds of my life? I could have *died*."

Rosie leaned down and kissed his cheek. "To be fair, I did try to save you straight away, but it didn't work. We decided to bring you here in case anyone else thought to storm the metaphorical castle. Give us some credit."

Pan wove his fingers through her hair and brought her mouth to his for a more thorough kiss. "I give you more than you know."

"Well, now that the purple people eater is okay, we need to get everyone fed and then rest. Who knows when the next round is going to begin."

"For the record, Remi, I don't eat people. Too fatty."

"What do you . . . you know what, never mind. I don't want to know. Can we at least keep him in a different room or something?"

"Hang on, you're all so quick to judge the demon in the room, but what about the Trojan horse standing right there, huh? He's the one you should all be worried about. Or did you all conveniently forget that he made a deal with our mother because he's got a pretty face and some angel blood? He's going to sell us all out."

I winced. With everything that had happened, I sort of forgot about that part. Or maybe I was intentionally blocking it out. Either way, I definitely had some explaining to do. The problem was, I doubted I'd be able to say much of anything. She'd seen to that. So how could I warn them when I wasn't allowed to talk about the terms of our arrangement?

"If I could tell you, I would," I argued. "Pan, don't try and twist this to make yourself look like a rose. You know better than anyone how these kinds of bargains work."

Pan narrowed his eyes before he rushed me in a blur of purple. Large clawed hands gripped my face as he pressed our foreheads together, and he stared into my mind with an intensity bordering on painful.

"What are you doing? Pan! Let him go," Rosie cried.

"See, told you we should have let him bleed out," Remi grumbled.

"Simply looking for a loophole, darling. Let Daddy work."

Ben muttered behind me, something that sounded a lot like, "I'm her Daddy."

"Ah, there it is," Pan whispered. "He can't tell you the terms. She's made that very clear. But it's your lucky day because I certainly can. Relax, Asher. This will be less painful if you do."

The sensation of Pan rifling through my mind was not unlike when we'd shared a body. It was the first time I truly understood what it meant to be soulbound. We may have been physically separated, but part of us would always be linked, and not just because of our mother's DNA. Pan had access to me in a way not even Rosie did.

"What are the terms?" Gavin asked.

Pan took a deep breath and, with annoyingly dramatic flair, launched into his monologue. "In exchange for his soul returning to his body during that very ill-advised exorcism you idiots decided to hold, she also made him promise to bring us all to her at the moment of her choosing."

A murmur of protest left my lips. It sounded terrible when he put it like that, like I was leading them straight to the slaughter, but Pan was leaving out the most important condition.

"Hold on to your knickers. I'm getting to it, angel boy. She also vowed that she would return you all to him once she was through with you."

"That doesn't sound so bad," Remi said. "We always knew we were going to have to face off with her."

"Oh, it's bad. She never said she'd return any of you alive and kicking. The devil, as they say, is in the details. Mortals are so shortsighted. It's how we've claimed so many souls."

"H-how do we g-get out of it?"

"We don't. The ink is dry, the deal struck. Unless Asher wants to forfeit his soul, he must see the terms through."

"I'll do it. Lock me up and throw away the key. I won't take you all to die."

"Are you fucking kidding me?" Remi rounded on me. "No. No

way. Not an option." He turned his gaze on Rosie. "Tell him, baby girl. He can't leave us again. I can't keep losing you two."

"No one is forfeiting their soul," Rosie said, leaving no room for argument. "Fate made me a Queen for a reason. *This* reason. I was born for this. Or reborn, I suppose. We will go to her when she summons us, thereby fulfilling Asher's side of the deal. Pestilence will assume she has the upper hand, but thanks to Pan, we know far more than she ever intended us to. We will not walk into this trap blindly. We need to use this time to recharge, both our power and our physical strength. I'm not going to lose. It's not in my nature. I'm a forking Blackthorne vampire. We never lose."

"But d-didn't Gavin say—"

"Gavin is right here and can speak for himself."

"—Queens always d-die," Ben finished, speaking over him.

"Not this Queen. Not this time. I don't know how, but I will not let that bitch take anything else from me. She stole my blood. She tried to steal my mates. I am done letting her win. I will not lose anyone else I love."

"Is it just me, or is this the sexiest game of Pandemic I've ever played?" Remi murmured.

"Love that game," Pan said.

"N-not the time, you t-two."

"She's fucking hot when she's all badass and determined," I said, agreeing with Remi.

"Sh-she's always h-hot."

Gavin rolled his eyes. "If you're all finished ogling our mate, I'm going to see to her hunger. You all should eat something. You'll need your strength."

Remi ran a hand through his hair and sighed before he nodded. "On it."

"So just to be clear, we aren't angry at Asher for betraying us all and selling us out to the big baddie? It's fine? He's off the bloody hook?" Pan asked.

Rosie walked right up to him and pressed her palm to his chest.

"I'm the last person who should judge someone for making a deal out of desperation, don't you think? It's not a betrayal. It was the only way he could come back to us. I would have done the same thing."

"What she said," Remi murmured, coming over to drop a kiss on my forehead on his way to the kitchen.

Jesus, that hit me right in the heart, which at the moment was basically a raw nerve. Tears pricked my eyes, and I had to look away to keep from letting the overwhelming flood of relief and gratitude spill down my cheeks. I couldn't fucking cry right now. Then again, maybe I could. They wouldn't judge me. Pan might, but fuck him.

Ben clapped a hand on my shoulder. "Asher, y-you look b-beat. G-go lie d-down. I'll have h-him save you s-some f-food."

I mumbled something incoherent and stumbled after the vampires who'd headed off toward the bedrooms, a bit surprised at how drained I felt. It hadn't been this way with Remi, but then that had been more miracle than anything, so maybe this was how it normally was after bringing someone back from the brink of death. Maybe the type of injury or illness mattered? It was hard to know for sure. I was far from an expert on these things.

I found myself in Remi's room and fell facedown on the bed, the rumpled sheets still smelling faintly of him. A happy sound escaped as I snagged a pillow, pulling it to my chest so I could pretend it was him. If things were different, this would be my happily ever after.

I hadn't realized I was asleep until the voice startled me into consciousness. I sat up in the dark, heart racing, Remi curled up beside me.

"What is it?" he mumbled.

But I couldn't answer. I couldn't do anything as her words raced through my head.

"Duty calls, Asher."

CHAPTER FORTY-FOUR

BEN

Devil's Lake had always unsettled me, but this time I approached with a heavy sense of dread on my shoulders. It wasn't anything special, just a lake surrounded by trees, the odd picnic table chained to a trunk here and there. By all accounts, it shouldn't be a scary place.

I realized now that my instinct had been trying to warn me about the secret lurking beneath the water. A truth that was now revealed in its full, terrifying glory.

The lake itself was gone. In the absence of the once pristine water, there was only a rancid smell, spongy dirt, and the corpses of all the dead and rotting fish who used to call it home. In the center, there was a tear I instantly recognized as the hellmouth. It was a gaping maw in the earth, a sinister red glow emanating from the bowels of hell that pulsed with purely evil energy. Whispers curled in my ears, carried on the wind. Promises of my deepest desires being fulfilled if only I'd step to the edge and peer down into that hole.

"Don't listen to them," Pan warned. "They're worse than sirens.

You step anywhere near the edge of the hellmouth and you'll become part of it."

"Why is it the portal to hell always looks like a fucked up vagina?" Remi asked.

"Remi," Asher said, shaking his head.

"What? We were all thinking it. That thing is a vag. You know it. I know it. I bet it even gives birth and the monsters will crawl right out of that fucker. It's the scariest pussy I've ever seen, but it's true. And I love a pussy. This is an injustice."

"What would you prefer it look like? An arsehole?" Gavin asked, his neck still discolored from his earlier attempt to remove his amulet. I bit back a curse, wondering if Delta's magic would prevent him and Rosie from vamping out during the upcoming fight.

"Like those too," Remi murmured thoughtfully. "I don't know, maybe an onion. Onions taste weird and make people cry. Pretty rude for a vegetable, if you ask me. And the hellmouth would for sure make people cry. Seems like a match made in hell."

"Remi, this isn't the best—" Rosie started, hitching her quiver higher on her shoulder as she clutched the bow she recovered from our house, but Pan interrupted her.

"Let him finish. This is wildly amusing. I think I see why you like him."

"I'm done."

"So is the trick to shutting you up actually being interested in what you're saying? Hmm, I'll have to remember that."

Remi frowned, but I had to admit the little bit of levity helped ease my nerves. That was, until the earth trembled under our feet and the glow from the hellmouth intensified to a nearly blinding brightness. As we all watched, Pestilence rose from the depths, a smile on her face and her fucking cat in her arms.

"See . . . I told you. Vagina," Remi whispered loudly.

"W-we should rename this p-place Devil's Cunt."

My twin held up his palm, silently asking for a high five. I didn't even need to glance his way as I returned the gesture.

Gavin looked at us both, but Remi simply shrugged and said, "Ben gets me."

"I see you got my invitation," Pestilence called, gently setting her cat down beside her.

"Is it an invitation when you can't refuse?" Asher spat.

"Hasn't anyone ever told you not to poke the bear? We don't even know if Gavin and I can attack her, thanks to the mayor's spell."

"I don't see why you couldn't," Asher countered.

"Have you already forgotten what happened last time we tried?"

"But she isn't wearing Mayor Dubois like a coat anymore. And she's *not a local."*

"As much as I'm loath to admit it, petal, Asher's right. Delta protected the townspeople from us. Pestilence is not a member of this town."

Meaning the amulet's protection no longer applied to Pestilence. Just like they hadn't worked against the Vampire Council members. A little hope sparked to life inside me at that. I grinned despite myself.

Unaware of our mental conversation, the horsewoman arched a brow but didn't respond to Asher's dig as she stretched back up to her full height. I had to say, I didn't know what I'd expected to find once we got here, but a beautiful woman in an emerald green gown with an uppity Persian cat wasn't it. She hardly looked like a threat, with her flowing blood-red hair and lithe form, minus the part where she'd just climbed out of the ground like it was the most natural thing in the world.

"I must say, I had hoped you'd all show up, weapons drawn, ready to fight."

"Not like you gave us much of a choice," Asher muttered.

Pestilence ignored him and kept on talking. "It makes this so much more fun for me. I can claim all your souls for the price of one."

"You and what army?" Remi taunted.

"I don't need an army." She snapped her fingers, and her cat was swept up into a bright green mist. It swirled and grew like a cyclone, the air making her dress and hair ripple in the sudden breeze. She never once looked away from us, not even when the smoke disappeared and a horse stood in its place. It was unlike any horse I'd ever seen. Its coat was a startling white and its eyes a glowing eerie green, bits of mist in the same color floating off its hooves. It stood unnaturally still, but there was a sense of coiled energy about it. Like it could spring into action at any moment.

"I fucking knew something was wrong with that cat," Gavin growled.

I could feel Rosie's apprehension along our mate bond. She'd been quiet, but from the way she held her bow and the slight twitch in the fingers of her free hand, she was looking for the right moment to strike. If Gavin was right, she'd be able to hurt the bitch. For the first time in a long fucking time, I said a little prayer.

"Nothing to say, Rosie? My, my, I hadn't taken you for a quitter."

"I don't waste my breath speaking to people who are about to die. I prefer to focus my energy on the ones who matter."

Remi snorted. "Shots fired."

"It seems Pan was wrong about you and your willingness to obey. Of course he was. Never in my entire existence did I think my son would betray me for . . . love."

Rosie stiffened and flicked her gaze to Pan, who stared straight ahead, the irritated flick of his tail giving him away. Pan's silence since his mother's arrival was almost as unnerving as the horsewoman herself. It didn't bode well for any of us that he was taking this confrontation so seriously. Or was he reconsidering his allegiance again?

Maybe he needed a reminder of what he was fighting for.

"Love seems l-like the b-best reason to m-me."

Pestilence's shrewd gaze landed on me. "You would. You're pathetically predictable in that regard, shifter. Demons should know better."

"I didn't come here for a chat," Rosie said, notching an arrow.

"I'm sorry, did you have somewhere better to be? Something

more important to do? Is the Apocalypse really such an insignificant event to you?"

"No, but you are." Rosie let her arrow fly.

It should have landed straight through the horsewoman's heart. Dropped her instantly. Instead, the woman grinned wickedly and knocked the arrow away as easily as if it were made of paper. Disappointment flickered along my mate bond, but I sent Rosie reassurance.

"This is good, sugar. You were able to shoot at her and nothing happened to you."

"For all the good that did me."

"You aren't fighting her alone, baby girl. Six on one are my kind of odds."

As if she could sense our confidence, Pestilence let out a patronizing laugh. "Nice try." Her focus drifted, no longer on us, as she turned her head to the side. "Now that she's had her shot, are you three ready to play?"

What? Who the fuck was she talking to? My gaze darted to the treeline, frantic, as I searched for our unknown adversaries.

"We certainly are." The Scouse accent was so unexpected my heart dropped to my feet.

"Harry?" I asked in disbelief as three familiar figures came into view.

"Heya, Benny boy. Surprised to see us?"

"What are you doing here?" Rosie asked, her brows furrowed in confusion. "Are you in her thrall or something? Does she have thrall?"

The last was directed at Pan. "They aren't who you think they are. From the looks of it, they haven't been for a while."

Without another word, the three gargoyles, lovable creatures who'd practically become mascots of The Tipsy Moose, if not Aurora Springs as a whole, disappeared. In much the same way as the cat, the visage fell away, revealing the truth of their identities.

"Ugh, I thought I'd never be free of that mischievous oaf," the blonde one said. She was dressed all in black but had the appearance of a schoolteacher who seemed far too sweet to be intimidating.

"What happened to not needing an army?" Remi called.

The one on the far left took a step forward, her sword and red armor leaving no doubt that she was an absolute threat. "She is the army, sweetheart. We're simply the cheerleaders."

"Pregame warm-up, if you'd rather," the third one said, her pale, milky eyes unsettling as they focused on us one by one. Of the four women, she looked the least human. Her black horns and fanged teeth clearly marked her as a demon.

"Sisters," Pestilence crooned, "pick your poison. As for me . . ." She let the words hang, her grin sinister as more of that green smoke swirled at her feet. "I prefer to be airborne."

"Is she making jokes, or does she mean that—"

"Literally," Pan confirmed, not bothering to look at Asher directly.

We watched as the horsewoman and her trusty steed transformed into one terrifying bird. No, bird was the wrong way to describe it. Pestilence was an enormous amalgamation of inky black raven and iridescent dragon, with glowing green eyes and that same sickly smoke pouring from the nostrils above her razor-sharp beak. She flapped her oil slick-hued wings, the gust of air sending us all backward a step.

"Sh-shit. I h-hate birds."

As Pestilence took to the sky, the three other horsewomen darted toward us.

"Protect her, no matter what," I shouted down the group bond.

"With my life," Gavin vowed.

"And mine," Asher swore.

"No matter the cost," Remi agreed.

Pan stayed uncharacteristically silent, his expression carefully blank, but not due to disinterest. He looked like he was weighing every option at once. Something told me if push came to shove, he would be right there alongside us, doing everything he could to ensure Rosie remained safe. Or maybe that was just hope.

"She's coming! Get ready," Rosie cried, tensing for an attack.

Confident her mates had her back, I made the shift from man to wolf, my twin right beside me as we prepared for the fight of our lives.

CHAPTER FORTY-FIVE

REMI

The instant my paws hit the ground, I readied myself to pounce on the nearest threat. Everything smelled wrong, and I was immediately disoriented because of it. My wolf was screaming at me to get out of here. He wanted nothing more than to put Rosie on his back and run as far away as possible because it wasn't safe. Newsflash, no fucking duh.

I sneezed, the scents overwhelming my wolfy senses. Unfortunately, that was the only opening my horsewoman needed. While I'd been busy trying to orient myself, the three women had peeled away from the giant fucking Pesty bird and selected their targets. It would seem the one with milky eyes and hair had chosen me.

Cool cool cool.

Shaking off the weight of her gaze, I crouched and let out a deep growl of warning. I was going to fuck her up.

"Is that supposed to scare me, dog?" Her voice reminded me of someone else. Strangely sensual and seductive, but with an undercurrent of danger. It would have been hot if she wasn't such a raging bitch.

Ah, there it was. She was a poor man's American Lilith. Kind of like when the US took a British show and tried to re-make it. The version we got was always watered down and never as good.

I am so not a dog, lady. Look at these fangs. These babies look like something your buddy Fido would have? I'm the Wolfman, not Old Yeller.

I knew she couldn't hear me, but it made me feel better. Sometimes you had to be your own hype man.

I sprang forward, intent on tearing her throat out, but she caught me midair, her eyes swirling like a galaxy as she held my gaze.

"You don't want to do that, Remington," she purred, her voice rolling over my body like a warm summer breeze.

"Yeah, I do, Pamela." Wait, why was I talking? I was a wolf. Except no . . . I was a man again, naked and swinging for all to see as this creature held me. Fuck. She'd turned me back with her eyes alone.

A shiver crawled across my skin. I'd underestimated her power.

"Pamela?" she asked, her brows drawing together, eyes going milky again.

My voice was tight as she continued squeezing. "Yeah. You know, PMAL. Poor Man's American Lilith. Sort of sounds like . . . You know what, just go with it."

She canted her head, studying me like some kind of science experiment. "You're an odd duck."

"And you're a crusty old bitch."

She didn't look much older than me, but no woman liked to be called out on her age. Given the way her fingers tightened around my throat, seemed like the horsewoman was no exception.

"Which one are you, anyway? Are you the cool one or the one responsible for the potatoes?"

"The cool one?" she sneered. "You mean Death?"

"Well, yeah. I mean, the chick with the sword is obviously War. And Pesty is pretty much the Queen of Dramatic Entrances, so there's no confusing her flapping around in the sky. Which means you're either Death, which would make you the cool one, or you're

Famine." My heart was pounding in my chest, but I forced myself to shrug. "And I'll be honest, Pamela, no one is scared of Famine."

"You should be."

Without another word, she brought her lips to mine and didn't so much kiss me as suck the air from my lungs. Every muscle in my body tightened as pain ripped through me. I hurt everywhere, soul deep. Oh God, she was reaping my motherfucking life force.

She released me from her kiss of death and smiled wickedly at me before crooning, "Feast or famine? I choose to feast."

"Remi, what just happened?" Rosie asked, her voice frantic.

"Don't worry, baby girl. She just wanted to kiss me a little."

"That didn't feel like a kiss."

"I think she might have also sucked out some of my soul. No big deal."

"Jesus, Remi," Asher started, but I couldn't let them get distracted by my battle. They had their own to worry about. Not that I could really see what was happening. But if I was good at anything, it was causing a distraction. So I'd be the best fucking distraction this bitch had ever seen.

"Scary Spice," I choked out.

"I'm sorry?"

"You're Scary Spice."

"I thought you said no one is scared of me."

"Still true, but the horns and the eyes, that's the only possibility. You're not sexy enough to be Posh. None of you are. Offense absolutely intended. Pesty has the red hair, which makes her Ginger by default. War has to be Sporty because she's the one with the weapon, and the blonde is Baby. Ergo, you're the Scary Spice of the horse girls."

"What the fuck are you doing?" Asher's voice echoed in my mind.

"It's annoy her to death or let her eat me."

"That's . . . kind of genius."

"I mean, it seems to work on everyone else. I figure eventually she'll give up."

"Who has eyes on the bird?" Asher asked.

"She's circling. Why hasn't she made a move yet?" Ben's voice was all wolf.

"First rule of the high ground, assess your surroundings. Don't you know that?"

"No, Hellboy, I didn't."

"It shows."

"Boys," Rosie snapped, *"fight them, not each other."*

Asher and Pan were immediately contrite.

"Habit," Asher said by way of apology.

With the way Pamela had me gripped, I couldn't see what the others were up to, but from the sounds of it, everyone was engaged in some sort of battle.

"Heads up, I'm about to force the issue. This could go terribly for the rest of you." That was Pan's only warning before he shouted up at his mother. "I thought this was supposed to be your Apocalypse. So why are you hiding up there and letting these bitches do your fighting for you?"

"Oh, we aren't, nephew," the sweet blonde—Death, I realized with a shudder—informed him. "We're always the opening act, but there's no doubt this is her show."

"I want a refund. I didn't pay to see a second-rate Spice Girls tribute band," I croaked, really wishing I could get out of Pamela's grip. She was stronger than she looked, and that little soul-sucking trick of hers had packed a punch. I didn't think I'd be able to stand on my own if she released me.

Oh God. Did she just suck away years of my life like that one dude from *The Princess Bride*? Why couldn't I at least have a cool moniker like The Dread Pirate Roberts? Or maybe a mask? Everyone loved a dude in a mask.

The air around us exploded with an eardrum-shattering screech as Pestilence dive-bombed us, green fire erupting from her beak. The trees were covered in it, dripping with what I now realized was slime rather than flames. The viscous liquid bubbled and smoked as it ate away at branches and plopped onto the leaf-strewn ground.

Note to self: avoid the green goo.

"You guys ever play the floor is lava?" I asked the others. *"Cause now would be a great time to put those skills to use."*

"She spits acid. Unfair advantage. Thanks for the heads up, Pan," Asher complained.

"I didn't know she could do that. I've never seen her take this form." Was it just me, or did he sound a little envious?

"What else can they do? Disease, lava breath, obviously wars, and soul sucking. What's next?" The way Asher asked the question only added to our group's apprehension.

"Zombies." The one word whispered through Rosie's thoughts unbidden.

"Don't say that, princess. I left my flamethrower in my other pants."

"We are so not prepared for a Walking Dead *LARP session,"* I added.

I could sense her clear and present terror, though, and knew, even though I couldn't see them, she wasn't suggesting zombies were a possibility. She saw them. Fuck.

"I'm sorry, am I boring you?" Pamela taunted, giving me a little shake.

I blinked, realizing I'd gotten distracted by our mental conversation. "Yup. You're not very interesting, to be honest. Your sisters can spew acid, raise the dead, and turn into the ultimate warrior. But all you can do is kiss people without their consent. Color me unimpressed." I yawned.

I didn't even see the backhand coming. One minute I was being strangled, the next, the entire left side of my face was ablaze with agony as I flew through the air. I slammed into a tree, the bark scraping my bare back to shit as I slid to the forest floor.

"Remi?" Ben called, too busy dodging whatever War threw at him to look my way, but likely feeling the blow through our twin bond.

"I'm okay." Fuck, even my mental voice was winded.

It took me a hell of a long time to get to my feet, but I did it. Jesus, the bitch broke my cheekbone. Staring across the battlefield, I spat out a mouthful of blood as I got my bearings. Pamela's lips were turned up in a self-satisfied smirk, like she had a secret she wasn't going to share. What had she done to me?

Casting a frantic glance around me, I let out a relieved sigh when I saw the absence of death goo in the nearby trees. But she looked far too pleased with herself as she stalked toward me.

"Oh, Remington, I wanted nothing more than to steal your soul and feed on it, but I suppose it's more poetic if you die this way instead."

I gulped, fear turning my stomach to liquid. I'd totally underestimated this bitch.

And now I was going to pay for it.

CHAPTER FORTY-SIX

GAVIN

As soon as Pestilence took to the air, Roslyn and Asher trained their attention skyward, trying to keep her in their sights. As the only two among us with any sort of ranged attacks, that made sense, and left the rest of us to deal with the threats on the ground.

With Remington focused on Famine, I faced off with the small, gentle looking horsewoman, her doe eyes and sweet face a mockery of innocence. I saw death reflected in her irises and immediately knew who she was.

“Oh goody, I get the broody vampire. My favorite.” She grinned at me, her teeth blindingly white and perfectly straight. “You know, your brother-in-law was delicious, but you . . . my, my, you are a snack.”

Roslyn stiffened at the mention of Noah but I sent her a warning not to listen to the woman’s taunts. She was trying to weaken us, break our focus, and help her sister. We couldn’t allow it.

“I wonder. What happens when Death herself dies?” I spoke with the calm, disinterested air of an aristocrat addressing their servant, even though apprehension was charging through my veins with every beat of my heart.

"Is that any way to talk to the one who marked you?"

I went still at that.

"Oh yes, Gavin Donoghue. I know you well. You're one of mine. You sent me such a pretty gift. Danika, was that her name? Gorgeous girl. So young. So sweet. My favorite shade of purple ringing her neck. What a perfect tribute." She sucked in a breath as if recalling a delicious meal.

"I do not belong to you."

"Don't you?" She cocked her head. "A sadist and a vampire. You never stood a chance. You belonged to me the day you were born, and I turned you into an excellent weapon indeed. I always knew you had potential. That's why I picked you for her, you know." Death slowly pointed at each of Roslyn's men, skipping over Pan. "One of you, to represent each of us. That's how it always goes. It's why we call it the Mate Games, you know." She winked. "Aren't we clever?"

My stomach churned. "The only one I belong to is my mate."

"You truly believe that, don't you? I can see it in your eyes. You were simply a means to an end. A way to get her here. You all think you're so special. This was always the end of the line. First, you make her strong enough to think she can win. Then, one by one, you die and take a piece of her with you. All you really are is an albatross. I do love a good dose of irony."

"Enough of this," I snarled, fangs extended as I lunged for her.

She giggled—fucking giggled—as she spun out of my grasp.

"No, no, that's not how this game goes. But if you're that desperate for a fight, vampire, my friends should keep you occupied."

Remington's voice broke through my thoughts, his frantic energy clueing me into the dire straits around us. *"You guys ever play the floor is lava? Cause now would be a great time to put those skills to use."*

A quick look to my right showed me what he was talking about. I didn't have time to do more than acknowledge it before my eyes shot back to the woman grinning as she wriggled her fingers.

The conversation continued in my mind, but I was only half paying attention to Asher's complaint, still trying to work out what Death was up to.

"She spits acid. Unfair advantage. Thanks for the heads up, Pan."

"I didn't know she could do that. I've never seen her take this form."

"What else can they do? Disease, lava breath, obviously wars, and soul sucking. What's next?"

I didn't want to tell him what I saw coming through the woods. But Roslyn did it for me.

"Zombies."

Dozens of what were once furry and harmless woodland creatures began shambling out of the forest, their eyes no longer bright but cloudy and swollen with rot. Many of them had stringy muscles and tendons peeking through matted fur. A couple had body parts missing, others skin hanging off bones or blackened entrails dragging from slashed open bellies. One particularly sad-looking bunny had a blood-red eye dangling from its socket.

It was every child's nightmare come to light. The Velveteen Rabbit brought to life, but not so he could be loved.

In my periphery, Remington flew past, his body crashing into a tree hard enough the trunk audibly cracked. We all turned toward him, Bentley the first to call out.

"Remi?"

The cocky shifter gingerly got to his feet, a weak, *"I'm okay,"* coming down our mental chat line.

Relief flooded us all, but when I heard the rustling behind me, my heart sank. Things were about to get worse.

I swallowed, afraid to turn around, but it was my only choice. When the rack of antlers came into view a couple feet above me, I knew I was in trouble.

"Is that . . . a moose?"

"It used to be. Bright side, it's not a bear," Asher offered from my left.

"That doesn't feel like much of a bright side at the moment.

Roslyn, stay behind me." I tugged her out of the animal's path and shielded her as much as I could with my body.

"I'll take care of the small beasties," she offered, notching her bow.

"No. Save your arrows, sugar. You're going to need them for Pestilence."

Bentley made an excellent point.

"He's right, petal," I said down the bond, not wanting to risk being overheard by the horsewomen. *"She's your only target."*

Death had a serene smile on her face as she watched the scene unfold, her attention on me as she soaked up her victory.

"Make him your bitch, Daddy G. Ride him into submission."

I was pretty sure Remington meant the moose, but a rasping scream caught my ear a second before a disgusting little squirrel carcass launched itself at me from where it had been hiding in the moose's antlers. Teeth sank into my neck as it clutched my shoulder.

"You dirty little fucker," I snarled, tearing the thing off me and pulling its head from its still flailing body. It went limp as soon as I crushed its skull under my heel. "They can die. At least we know that."

"They can also eat our faces if they gang up on us at the same time."

And that was exactly what these creatures were doing, tightening the circle around us, backing us into a metaphorical corner where there was no escaping them.

"We can't kill them all with our bare hands," Pan muttered. "Our wolfy pal is busy with War. And Remi apparently decided to get naked with Famine."

"Wasn't a choice," he rasped, trying to back away from the white-haired horsewoman currently stalking him.

"We're never going to make it to the grand finale at this rate," Pan said, lifting up what had once been a wolf and ripping it in two before flinging both pieces into the forest and abandoning us as he ran through the break in the horde. His attention flicked skyward, no doubt clocking the dragon-like creature his mother had become.

I was busy destroying my own foe, my hands coated in guts and ichor, my head swimming. But there wasn't time to stop, let alone breathe. There were too many of them, and Death could easily replace any we killed. Not to mention use our lifeless bodies against us to take down Roslyn. We couldn't let her win.

Asher attempted to use his light on the zombies encroaching his space, but aside from blasting them back a few feet, nothing seemed to affect them. They were impervious to everything aside from total destruction of the connection between brain and body.

"It's no use," he panted down our bond. *"Everyone knows the only way to kill zombies is a shot to the head. I'm useless against these fuckers. Where's my shotgun when I need it? Fuck."*

"Asher. The sword. Use the sword. Cut off their heads and buy us some time." Roslyn's panicked tone called us all inward even as the corpse of a grizzly stumbled out of the woods, snarling and snapping as it closed in. *"Gabriel gave it to you for a reason. I'm sure this is it."*

"Good thinking. She can't bring back what's been turned to ash. Hey, do you think that's part of my namesake? Is this destiny?"

No one answered him as Roslyn put her foot through the head of a fox after it tried to take a bite out of her, the sickening crunch of brittle bone making her grimace.

Asher reached into the bag on his shoulder and pulled out the sword, flames immediately bursting to life along the blade.

The creatures froze in place.

"That's right, you assholes. You don't like daddy's big sword, do you?" Asher taunted.

He swung hard, taking out five at once, turning them to ash just like he did at the bar with the demons.

I continued ripping undead creatures apart as Asher made quick work of the majority, but something was wrong. I felt . . . off.

When Asher was done, the flames extinguished. "And . . . stay . . .

fucking . . . dead," he said through heaving gasps as he stabbed the moose straight through its skull, adding its ashes to the pile.

"Remi? You good?" he called.

But there was no answer.

I blinked, and it felt like my eyelids carried seven-ton weights. I couldn't seem to reopen them.

"Roslyn," I gasped, staggering forward.

If she responded, I couldn't hear it.

I couldn't hear anything beyond the chasm of darkness that had claimed me.

CHAPTER FORTY-SEVEN

ROSIE

With every beat of my heart, my mates seemed farther from my reach and closer to death's icy grip. Nothing in my life had prepared me for this. I didn't know what to expect when facing off with a horsewoman of the Apocalypse, and I certainly didn't feel capable of handling all forking four of them. It wasn't exactly a topic they covered at Ms. Esther's School for Young Ladies.

That was the true source of my fear. That Gavin was wrong, and I wasn't really a Queen. That my newfound power was ultimately useless. I wanted to protect my mates, but blast it all, I didn't know *how*. The only thing I was remotely good at was compulsion, and even then, I was a bit dodgy on the details.

The zombie animals closed in, all snarls and feral growls. Every single time I ripped one apart, another took its place, and those that kept their brains intact simply reanimated and dragged their broken bodies toward us all over again. I reached out with my mind, attempting to compel the monsters, but their brains were barely sparks, with nothing for me to hold on to. We couldn't win. Not with Pestilence in the sky and the undead on the ground.

Ben wasn't fairing much better. I could hardly spare more than a half-second to glance his way, but War must have had a similar trick to her sister because he seemed to be fighting a forking tree, of all things. And was that Pan helping him? I only caught a glimpse of purple as he tried to tackle the lumbering mass before I had to refocus on the fight happening in front of me. If I gave myself the chance, I'd be frozen in terror for my mates. I couldn't lose any of them. I wouldn't.

"Don't lose heart, petal. Don't give her that power over you." Gavin's words were a command in my mind, just for me. Exactly what I needed as Ben flew through the air and landed in a heap at the empty lake's edge.

Instinct had me wanting to step toward him, but a sudden wave of intense exhaustion hit me. My body suddenly felt a thousand pounds heavier, and my energy nearly drained. No one had touched me, so I couldn't blame it on one of our attackers, but there was no denying that *something* was happening to me.

A prickling in the back of my mind had me rethinking that statement. *Happening to me? Or to one of my mates?*

Sending my awareness down the threads that connected us, I instantly found the source. Remi. He was fighting it, but there was no hiding he'd been hurt. Badly. Another wave of stomach-churning *wrongness* hit me, this time not coming from my normally playful shifter.

Gavin.

Cutting a glance at him, I gasped at the sheen of clammy sweat on his brow and the dark circles under his eyes. The wound at his throat had blackened around the edges, and dark lines extended beyond the already necrotic margins. Was he going to turn into one of those . . . things?

No. I wouldn't let Death claim him. He was *mine.* They all were.

I had to do something.

Asher's voice pulled me back to the battle. *"It's no use. Everyone knows the only way to kill zombies is a shot to the head. I'm useless against these fuckers. Where's my shotgun when I need it? Fuck."*

That's when I remembered the angel's parting gift. *"Asher. The sword. Use the sword. Cut off their heads and buy us some time. Gabriel gave it to you for a reason. I'm sure this is it."*

"Good thinking. She can't bring back what's been turned to ash. Hey, do you think that's part of my namesake? Is this destiny?"

A mostly decomposed fox snapped at my leg, but there was no way I'd let any of them get their teeth on me. I put my foot straight through its brittle skull, fighting a shudder at the feel of it caving in on itself.

So focused on the fray surrounding us, I didn't see Asher brandish his sword, not until the bright light of angel fire illuminated our little group.

Asher was too busy taunting the creatures to notice, but I still caught Death's hiss before she called out, "Sisters, that's our cue. Odette, you're on your own. Good luck ending the world. Can't wait to see how this plays out."

Overhead, Pestilence let out an unhappy shriek, the shadow of her wings ghosting over us.

Remi snickered weakly. "Odie. Figures you'd have a stupid—" His words were cut off with a pained whimper, but I couldn't risk a glance back at him, not until these zombies were all nothing more than fertilizer. As Asher razed them to the ground, we continued fighting.

The sense of unease coming from Remi and Gavin built into a raging tempest I couldn't ignore any longer. I needed to go to them. To fix them.

Asher stared down the last remaining creature, his blade poised to strike as he said, "And . . . stay . . . fucking . . . dead."

The moose fell, turning to ashes while Pestilence's sisters vanished from sight, leaving us streaked with dirt, blood, and more entrails than I'd ever care to see again.

"Remi? You good?" Asher called.

But I knew he wouldn't answer, just as I knew Gavin had reached the end of his reserves. Two of my cherished mates fell, barely clinging to life as they fought for me.

I wanted to go to them both more than anything, but even with the horsewomen fleeing and taking their magic with them, this fight was far from over. Pestilence was still airborne, still our biggest adversary, and we were in a bad way.

The enormous tree that had Ben in its grasp broke apart, dropping him from a height that would have killed a human. Thankfully, Pan was there, catching my wolf before he could hit the ground.

"Ben!" I screamed, lurching toward him on instinct. I had to save one of them.

But Asher stopped me with an arm about my waist. "No, princess. He's okay. Look, he's awake and human again already. We have bigger birds to pluck. Pestilence is coming, and she's pissed."

I glanced skyward, my gaze catching on the monstrous black and green dragonesque bird intent on running us down. She hadn't been in range before, cowardly allowing her sisters to try and take us out for her, but now she was. And I was a perfect shot. This was my time. With my senses so enhanced as a Queen, I could make out the weak spot in her chest, the place where her scales turned to feathers. That was my target.

No words were spoken as I took aim and let loose four arrows in succession. Praying all the while one would find its mark. Every one of them did. Unfortunately, it didn't make a bit of difference.

I let out a furious scream. I couldn't kill the bitch from here. My supposed gifts were utterly useless.

"Here, use my fire," Asher offered, holding his sword out to me. "You saw them. They ran as soon as the sword lit up, just like she did at the bar. The horsewomen are clearly afraid of it. If you hit her . . ." He trailed off as I shook my head.

"No, Gabriel gave it to you. It's your weapon, Asher. Not mine."

"You're my mate. What's mine is yours. Just try it. Light her up, Rosie."

He gripped my forearm, and I felt it, the heat of his grace flowing through him and into the sword. I moved to put the end of my only weapon in the brilliant fire, but before I could, the arrow burst into flames.

"Wicked," Asher murmured.

But there wasn't time to be astonished. Pestilence had circled back and opened her beak, more of that gurgling sputum aimed straight at us.

"Now, Rosie!"

I called on my power, filtering all my focus on the goal. Then I let my flaming arrow fly, and my breath caught in my throat as I watched it light up the night. It might have been beautiful if not for the details it revealed of the flying nightmare looming over us as the projectile made contact.

"Bullseye," I whispered as my arrow sank through its target and the bird began to plummet.

There wasn't time to appreciate the achievement, though. Her shriek of outrage was so shrill I could feel the warmth of blood trickle from my ears along with the unhappy roll of the earth beneath my feet.

"You did it." Asher's words were reverent beside me.

Pan and Ben joined us, watching as she hit the ground so hard the trees shook. "Don't get too comfortable, brother. She's down, but far from out. Mummy dearest isn't so easily defeated."

CHAPTER FORTY-EIGHT

BEN

The fingers—or were they still considered twigs?—of the diseased treant squeezed tighter around my ribs, stealing the air from my lungs. I had to dig deep to come up with a term for the animated tree, going back to Remi's and my video game days to land on anything close. There were a solid few years where the two of us were deep into World of Warcraft. I know, shocking. Trees weren't exactly a creature I faced in the real world very often unless I was chopping one in half. I was fucking amazing with an ax. Unfortunately, I couldn't carry one with me in wolf form.

When War set her sights on me, I'd been sure she'd want to do the job herself. Swing that big blade of hers around and make a show out of taking me out. I'd been caught completely off guard when the fucking forest came to life and started attacking me instead. Luckily, trees were about as agile as you'd expect. As in, not at all. So, for the most part, I'd been able to dodge the branches attempting to turn me into wolf putty and run circles around the trunk.

I loved a good game of chase, or even fetch. But not when I was trying to take down an enemy. All this bunch of splinters was doing was distracting me from my real goal, the goddamn horsewoman helping her bitch of a sister.

I'd been doing pretty well at holding my own, all things considered. At least until Remi's pained whimper distracted me. That had been the only advantage the treant needed to make its move.

The tree wrapped its gnarled limbs around me, squeezing hard enough my ribs creaked and groaned, the air escaping me in a harsh burst.

"What exactly do you think you're doing up there? Having a nap?" Pan asked. "Do you need a hammock?"

I bared my fangs at him. *"A little help would be nice."*

The demon shrugged, assessing the nearly fifty-foot ancient cedar. "What do you want from me? I could rub two sticks together and try to light it on fire. That's all I've got. Unless you'd rather I try to tickle it with my claws a bit. Carve a love heart with R + P forever inside? See if I can rustle its leaves a little until it drops you?"

"Why are you even here if you're not going to fight?"

Pan's jaw clenched, and I wheezed as the tree began to shake me.

"I'm not the one who ran headlong toward an unwinnable battle. What did you think you were going to accomplish going up against her? She's War."

A bright light from below had me closing my eyes on instinct. Pan's apprehension chased down our link with Rosie, forcing me to cast one last look at my mate. Asher was using the sword. Good. At least she'd make it through this fight. I might not. But we'd all agreed Rosie was the only thing that mattered.

My vision grayed, my head swimming from the crushing weight on my chest. I knew my death would be painful, but I hadn't realized how hard it would be to leave her. Unable to draw breath, I lost my battle with consciousness, wishing more than anything I'd been strong enough to protect Rosie.

My mind blanked, and the next thing I knew, I was blinking up at Pan. "Wh-what . . ."

"You're welcome," he sneered.

I blinked again, needing time to process my surroundings. The tree was . . . well a tree, once more, the magic animating it gone. The horsewomen were gone. I was human again and, apparently snuggled up against a demon.

"P-put me down."

Pan dropped me. "See if I ever come to your rescue again, you ungrateful beastie."

"Th-they're running," I murmured, hope filling me.

"They're cowards. She's not." Pan rolled his gaze skyward, and a chill ran down my spine as the shadow of the winged monster closed in on us.

A streak of light swept across the night sky. "Is th-that—"

I was going to ask if it was a falling star and could only blame the lack of oxygen for my sluggish thoughts. It couldn't be. It was arching up, not down.

"Clever girl," Pan murmured. "That's holy fire. She might take Mum down after all."

I held my breath despite the burning in my lungs as we watched the arrow hit its target. My ribs were knitting together, but still not fully healed. I needed a minute or so longer before I was back to, if not full strength, at least being functional.

We were already running toward Rosie and Asher by the time Pestilence started to fall.

"You did it," Asher whispered.

"Don't get too comfortable, brother. She's down, but far from out. Mummy dearest isn't so easily defeated."

"Ben!" Rosie wrapped an arm around me, squeezing me tight. "I thought I lost you too. I'm so glad you're all right."

"I'm fine, thanks for asking," Pan muttered.

I squeezed her back, breathing her in before her words registered.

I thought I lost you too.

"Remi?" I asked, brows furrowing as I cast my gaze around in search of my twin.

Pan shook his head and gripped my forearm, stopping me from

rushing toward Remi's collapsed form. "Nothing you can do for him now. We live through this, angel boy will take care of it. Right now, all that matters is how we're going to deal with her." He tipped his head toward the giant bird slowly pushing back up to her feet.

"A-anyone have s-suggestions?"

We wouldn't stand a chance against this beast. Not with the shape we were in. Asher's skin was clammy and pale, Rosie had blood leaking from her ears, and her limbs trembled. Gavin was barely alive and nothing more than a heap in the dirt, and Remi . . . I couldn't think about him.

Pan's gaze turned considering, his luminous eyes landing on the sword still blazing in Asher's hand. "I might. But it's going to require a distraction."

"Wh-what kind of d-distraction? W-we're tapped out."

He gave me a knowing look, but I wasn't strong enough to be any kind of foe against her right now. I'd barely survived the fucking tree. If Remi were conscious, he wouldn't have shut up about it.

"I might be able to help with that," Rosie offered, switching to our mental link as Pestilence took her first lumbering step in our direction. She was hurt, but not as bad as we were. *"Asher was able to share his grace with me via our bond. I think I can do the same with my gifts."*

"Wait. What? What do you mean, share?"

"I'm going to give them to you, Ben. Everything I have left. You're the strongest of us at the moment. And I think with a little push, your wolf might be a match to her bird."

"Won't that weaken you? You're already hurting, sugar. I can't."

Not giving me a chance to argue further, she gripped my wrist and held me tightly. "You can. For the sake of all of us."

"Y-you'll die if you're n-not careful."

She gave me a sad look. "Don't you remember? The Queen always dies."

"Rosie, n-no." I was shaking my head, terror turning my insides to ice. I'd already lost this woman once. I couldn't handle the idea of losing her again. "D-don't do this. P-please. Use me in-instead. I'm d-disposable. Y-you're n-not." With each frantic word, my throat grew tighter, fighting me every step of the way. "T-take m-my e-e-energy so y-you can f-fight."

"You're the best fighter of us, Ben," Asher said. "We all know it."

"Y-you're just g-going to l-let her d-drain h-herself? Sh-she'll be a s-sitting d-duck."

"Not if you win," Rosie offered, locking eyes with me. I knew I couldn't argue the point with her anymore. She was firm in her decision, and we were out of time.

"Y-you're the only r-reason w-we're f-f-fucking alive, baby. I c-can't let anything h-happen to y-you."

"Which is exactly why you have to take my power. Do what you do best, Bentley Mercer. Protect your mate."

Refusal sat heavy on my tongue, but there was a new emotion rising up to join it. Something that felt a lot like pride. My wolf surged to the surface, ready to do exactly that. She was our mate. It was our duty, our sole purpose, to protect her. So we would.

Or we'd die trying.

"Okay."

This time it was my wolf who spoke.

Rosie dipped her head in a nod, holding my gaze as she tapped into her power and began to send it into me.

Shove might be a more accurate word. My muscles went taut as wave after wave of power unlike anything I'd ever known crashed into my body. It was as close to being electrocuted as I could imagine without experiencing the sensation. Power that felt like lightning crackled through my veins. I was swollen with it. Not just swollen, stretching to accommodate everything pumping through me.

As Rosie continued to siphon her power, I shifted without conscious thought, my form quadruple its normal size. Not a wolf, but a monster. Usually the transformation was a choice, a decision to give over control to my beast. This time, I was all Ben, but my body was lupine once again. Whatever Rosie had done to me, my animal instinct wasn't ruling my decisions, which was exactly what I needed to take down this enemy. One cunning monster against another.

Rosie finally released me, the trickle of blood at her nose much worse than before she'd started. She took a step back and staggered, but Asher was right there.

"I've got you, princess."

Through all of this, she held my gaze. "You can do this, Ben. You have to." Her voice was so weak it shot fear through me. She was barely hanging on.

A growl was the only response I could give her before I turned my back on them and stared down my prey. I couldn't kill Pestilence, not before she took me out, but I sure as shit could do some damage and weaken her. Pan had something up his sleeve, and I was going to do whatever I could to ensure he got his chance.

Thanks to Rosie's sacrifice, I was stronger, faster, an apex predator ready to attack. I couldn't focus on the fact that this was her gift, her power, surging through me. The only thing that mattered was winning this fight, even if I wasn't the one to land the killing blow.

Everything else we'd deal with after. Or we'd all be dead so it wouldn't matter. The Apocalypse had a way of putting things into very clear perspective.

Asher could heal them all if we stopped Pestilence. Even if I didn't make it, Rosie would have the rest of her mates by her side. Four out of five wasn't bad.

Pestilence screeched a warning as I rushed her, muscles coiled, ready to strike. I moved faster than I ever had before, realizing distantly that this must be vampire speed. Just before I took my shot, I sent a thought to my Rosie. One last thing for her to hold on to. Something to remind her she needed to fight for us, to stay alive.

"Tell Remi I'm so fucking proud of him. When this is over, and the moon is back where she belongs, promise me you'll look up at her and think of me. And know that I'll be right there, looking back down at you. I love you, sugar. Always."

CHAPTER FORTY-NINE

PAN

"*One of you, to represent each of us.*"

That damned phrase had played through my mind on a loop ever since Auntie Death shared that little nugget. One mate meant four total. Four. Not five.

Not. Five.

I was never supposed to end up with her.

Fate wasn't at work here. I'd simply stolen something that didn't belong to me.

Of bloody course I had. Even when I was doing something as unbelievably out of character as falling in love, I had to do it in a dastardly manner. But for some reason that didn't give me the warm and fuzzies it usually would. I didn't want to be her stolen mate. I didn't want to be *less than* the rest of them. A spare part that could easily be replaced or ignored. Or worse, removed.

I wanted her to look at me and love me with the same 'you are the air within my lungs' intensity she did the others. Lucifer's cunt, I was ruined.

"If you've got a plan, now would be a really good time for you to share it, Pan. As impressive as he is at the moment, Ben's not going to last. You and I both know that." Asher cradled Rosie against his chest, rocking her back and forth as he brushed his fingers over her forehead. "It's going to be okay, princess. I've got you. Just hold on for me, all right? I need you to fight to stay with us."

My fiendish heart tripped over itself at the sight of her unconscious form. She'd put her trust in us to see this through. I couldn't fail her now. Not after everything else I'd already taken from her. She came to me because she wanted a fresh start. I'd been selfish then, taking everything I wanted and giving very little in return. It had been a game, and she a means to an end. I'd been such a fool. One look at her and I'd been done in. What started as obsession turned into something far deeper, something I never could have anticipated. I'd been hers the second she teased me about my name.

This time I would take a page out of her book. I'd be selfless. I would fulfill the original terms of our bargain and give her that second chance she'd wanted so dearly.

Better late than never, right?

At least this time, she'd have everything she wanted. Without me.

The urge to gag was suspiciously lacking.

Bloody hell, I meant it.

I really did want to do this. For her. Because stolen or not, my love for her was real. While I may not be one of her intended mates, she was still mine. The only one capable of teaching this demonic heart how to love. The only creature on any plane I cared about more than myself.

If that wasn't true love, well, it's as close as one such as I could ever get.

My mother's scream of agony pulled my focus from Rosie. Ben was latched onto her throat, blood pouring down her dark feathers as he shook her like a rag doll. She knocked him off her, tossing him aside hard enough he yelped in pain, but as I watched, she staggered and changed from bird to demon. One hand covered the gaping wound in her neck as her diseased blood ran down her front. But she was still standing. That meant she'd heal. It meant this wasn't over.

Ben growled and tried to get up, failing twice before he regained some strength. His fur was matted, coated in her blood and dirt from the forest floor. The wolf coughed, a deep, wet sound that spoke of death. His breaths were numbered. The second her tainted essence came into contact with him, it was over. And the shifter knew it as well as I. But he charged her again, and he would continue doing so until his heart stopped.

I'd asked for a distraction, and he'd more than fulfilled the role.

I had to clear my throat before I managed to speak through the gravity of the choice I was about to make. "Asher. I need to borrow your sword."

My brother looked up at me, his eyes wide. "I don't think it will work for you."

"Well then, I need you to help me."

He swallowed and gently lowered Rosie to the ground beside Gavin.

My hands were shaking. My heart racing. I couldn't fucking believe I was really going to do this.

Asher returned to me, the sword in his hand once more. "What do you need me to do?"

I stared at him, wondering when the man I'd considered a ball and chain had truly become my flesh and blood. Or when he'd started to consider me the same.

Fuck. I'm not ready to do this.

"I'll be right with you. There's something I have to take care of first."

Call me sappy, but I couldn't go out without doing this one last thing.

I dropped down beside Rosie, taking her face in my hands and pressing my forehead to hers. My hair curtained us, giving us the illusion of privacy as I worked up the courage to tell her a fraction of my truth.

"Somehow you, *ma petite monstre,* etched yourself onto my very bones. Do you know that? You thought I stole your soul in our bargain, but you were the thief. And now, here I am, walking to my death because of you. I don't know why it happened or how, but I fell in love with you and I can't take it back. Now you'd better wake up when this is over so my valiant sacrifice is worth it. Someone needs to mourn me properly. Perhaps erect a statue in my honor in the town square. And you're the only one who could get my measurements right." I brushed a kiss over her lips, whispering this last part. "But save your tears. You've already given me more than enough of those. I prefer your smiles. Or your moans."

Then I swallowed and pushed myself back to my feet, blinking a few times to clear the dampness at my eyes. "Okay, I'm ready."

"For what? You haven't told me what I'm doing yet."

"I thought it obvious. I need you to cut off my horns so I can kill the bitch. What's a little matricide between brothers?"

"But won't that kill you too?"

I shrugged. "Eventually. But I mean, can you think of a more fitting swan song? I do love a dramatic exit."

"Pan . . ."

"I thought you would relish the opportunity to take me out."

"Maybe before, but—"

"There's no time, Asher. It's this or let the world burn. And trust me, the amount of fucks I give about this place are less than zero, but that woman there? It matters to her. And she matters to you. So do this. For her."

His eyes flicked over my shoulder to where Ben was rapidly running out of steam. We had seconds at best before her focus would return to us.

"Now, brother. It has to be now."

His eyes filled with apology as he raised Gabriel's sword. I flinched, expecting a wave of heat, but the glow was warm. Comforting, even. And then I knew nothing but agony as the archangel's blade sliced through my horns, severing them from my body. I dropped to my knees, my mouth filling with blood as I bit down on my tongue to swallow back my screams.

Already I could feel my body weakening. I would not last long without my magic. But I didn't need long. Just an opportunity.

"Keep her turned away from me," I managed through the blood filling my mouth.

Asher nodded grimly and held his weapon high as he ran toward the faltering wolf and joined the fight.

With shaking hands, I picked up my smoldering horns and used the continuing fray to my advantage as I positioned myself behind her. She was struggling, the blood loss causing her to sway and lurch rather than fight with the grace she usually possessed. Even so, Ben collapsed, foaming at the mouth and seizing as he shifted from beast to man. All that remained was Asher.

"Where's your pitiful brother?" she spat, breaths heavy, labored.

"He ran. He abandoned us the second it looked like you might actually win."

"Of course he did." Her laugh was more of a gurgling wheeze, voice a rasp. "I'll deal with him later. For now, I will celebrate my victory with my favorite son."

"What victory?" I snarled, ramming the pointed tip of my horn through her back and straight into her heart. She arched in surprise, her head falling onto my shoulder, allowing me to drop my lips to her ear. "You lose."

Her fingers reached up to the stumps on my forehead. "How could you . . ."

"Oh, easily. You see, Mother, I despise you. And it turns out, I'm a hero after all."

A sharp gasp escaped her as Asher ran her through with the flaming sword, the tip very nearly sinking into me as it poked out her back. "Fuck your Apocalypse," he grunted, twisting the blade for good measure.

She didn't turn to ash or burn to a cinder, but she was well and truly vanquished as she went limp against me. The horsewomen couldn't ever be truly killed. They were immortal, but she wouldn't be at full strength for a very long time. There'd be no more Apocalypse attempts from her any time soon, which was all that really mattered.

"Well done, brother," I murmured, releasing her and letting the twat fall as my knees buckled. I didn't have long.

Asher lurched forward, catching me before I could hit the ground. "I find it funny that she thought the two of us would be her secret weapons. Guess she never factored in the part where weapons can be used against you."

"Egomaniacs rarely see their own weaknesses. Trust me. It takes one to know one." I coughed, blood choking me as I worked to breathe.

"I'm not so sure about that, Pan. You seem pretty aware of your weakness."

My eyes drifted to Rosie, and a smile ghosted my lips. I was surprisingly at peace, considering I was knocking on Auntie Death's door. "Oh, I don't know. I'm starting to think she's my strength."

As we lay there, the sky was flooded by the silvery light of the moon. Stars winked into existence. The world righted itself. And I knew we'd done the impossible. We stopped the Apocalypse.

"What are you waiting for? Save them, Asher. You've earned your happily ever after."

"What about you?" he asked, seeming torn.

"Demons don't get happy endings. Now, save our girl. And make sure she misbehaves for me, yeah?"

He stood, carefully settling me on the ground before racing to Rosie. She would be okay. I knew it in my bones, and that was enough for me.

God's teeth, I hurt everywhere. My tail curled up on my chest, and I gripped it to me like a prized stuffy. "At least I still have you, old friend."

With a ragged breath, I closed my eyes, prepared to let the dark have me as one final thought ran through my mind. I'd once compared myself to a superhero. Perhaps that was what this felt like.

When the darkness swelled, there was a smile on my lips.

Captain Aubergine. Out.

CHAPTER FIFTY

ASHER

Pan was dying. Hell, he might already be dead for all I knew, same as Gavin and Remi. But I couldn't worry about them right now. Pan was right, and Rosie needed me. She was the one who would help me bring back the others. If I could heal her, maybe her blood would be enough for Gavin or the shifters.

It was a long shot, but all I knew for sure was that if I took the time to heal the others first and she somehow didn't make it, they would string me up and flay me alive. Deservedly so. Rosie was the one we agreed to save. She had to come first. She was our reason.

I cast a furtive glance at Remi, who was too still, too quiet, and deathly pale. My heart ached. I was losing everyone I loved. But dropping to my knees beside Rosie's barely breathing form, I did the one thing I could. My palms pressed to her chest, I sent every last drop of my power, my angelic grace, through her and willed her to heal.

"C'mon, princess. Come back. We need you. Fuck, I need you here so you can try to poison me with your god-awful cooking. Remi and I won't be right without you. Neither will Ben or Count Chocula. Don't leave us hanging. Please."

I'd been running off adrenaline for the better part of the last hour. Between the zombie bunnies, the abominable horsewoman, and the army of the goddamned trees, I was at my wits' end. All I wanted was for the people I loved to be safe and here with me. It wasn't fair that I was kneeling here alive and well while they'd all suffered.

Panic built inside me and tears clogged my throat, forcing me to swallow back the absolute terror of living without her and Remi.

"Please, Rosie. Please come back to me. I don't want to do this without you. My whole life has been spent running. Usually away, but sometimes toward things, like the family I always wanted to find. I'm finally ready to stop running. Because of you, I'm ready to stay. But you have to stay too. You and Remi are my family. So you can't leave me. You promised you wouldn't. Everything is pointless if you're not here. We stopped her, princess. We fucking did it. Now open your eyes and give me something to live for."

The glow at my hands dimmed, and I sucked in a shaky breath. She hadn't so much as twitched a finger yet, but I didn't have any more to give.

"Please, Rosie. I love you so fucking much."

"I love you too."

It was faint and only through the bond between us, but it was her voice. Her beautiful sweet voice. I leaned down and pressed my lips to hers, desperate for her to kiss me back, open her eyes, *something*.

She did better than that. Her fingers slipped into my hair, and my girl deepened our kiss before pulling back and staring straight into my soul.

"Hi," she whispered.

"Hi," I whispered back.

"Sounds like you're a hero."

"Of course he's a hero."

I stiffened and then snapped my head in Remi's direction. "You're alive!"

Remi blinked his gorgeous blue eyes at me. "Like Frankenstein's monster?"

My laugh was part sob. I couldn't fucking help myself. I'd hoped we could heal him, but wasn't sure we'd make it in time. I had no idea who or what to thank for this miracle, but I wasn't about to question it.

"Go to him," Rosie whispered.

I helped her sit up as both Ben and Gavin came to, each of them groggy and bleary-eyed, but alive.

"What'd I miss?" Gavin asked, scooping Rosie up into his arms.

"Asher's a monster slayer."

Gavin aimed one of his rare smiles in my direction. "Well done, you."

"It wasn't all me," I said, feeling suddenly bashful.

Remi ruffled my hair. "Aw look, he's shy." He kissed me, just a soft brush of his lips on mine, but I really fucking needed that.

"I h-happen to r-recall helping," Ben protested as Rosie held out an arm for him. Gavin didn't release her; instead he and Ben sandwiched her between them.

We were all here. Safe. Whole. Alive.

Everyone except . . .

"Pan," I murmured, my gaze trailing to the demon's body. There was no way he was alive, not with how he lay so still.

Rosie's expression faltered, then fell as she looked to him. "Put me down. Please. I need to go to him."

Ben and Gavin gave in to her request, but from the way they both tensed, it was the last thing they wanted to do.

"What happened?" Rosie asked, racing to him and falling to her knees. I stood behind her, looking down at my brother.

She reached out tentative fingers and let them hover over the bloody stumps where his horns had once been. From her shocked inhale, she'd figured out what he'd done, but I could feel the others' confusion buzzing through our connection.

"He sacrificed himself."

"How? He's not hurt, not that badly," Remi asked, coming up beside me.

"A demon's power lies in their horns," Rosie explained. "Removing them is one of the few true ways to kill a demon."

"Sonofabitch. He *did* end up being a good guy. Are we sure he's dead? Rosie, you can heal him right? Even if there's just a spark of life. Isn't that how it works?" It surprised me to hear Remi advocating for Pan, but they seemed to have worked through their differences for the most part. Not to mention, anyone who stood alongside us in a fight like this deserved another chance.

Rosie shook her head, a tear slipping down her cheek. "My blood doesn't work on him, remember? Otherwise it would have saved him last time."

"Asher?" Remi asked, looking at me.

"I don't have anything left. I used it all on Rosie."

"We can't just let him die. He's one of us."

"Remi, h-he's already g-gone."

"That's not fucking fair. He gave up everything and now he just . . . what? Goes to hell? Or is it heaven when you're punishing a demon?"

"Actually, he's not going anywhere."

We spun around, finding Gabriel casually leaning on a tree behind us. A tree that looked a whole lot healthier than it had a few minutes ago. That's when I allowed myself to look around and realized the entire clearing looked better. The gaping vagina that was the hellmouth was still there, but the sense of rot and decay was fading. The land was healing, just like my family had.

"Way to show up at the eleventh hour. We're already done," I shot at him.

"Yes, I know. That's why I'm here." The angel strolled over to the spot where Pestilence had been. Now all that remained was a black scorch mark on the earth and the sword stabbed through halfway to the hilt. It reminded me of the sword in the stone. "I'll just take this back for safekeeping." He yanked the blade free, and it disappeared in his hand.

"Did you know this would happen?" Rosie asked.

"Know?" Gabriel made a considering sound. "Not the word I'd use. *Hoped* would be more accurate. You see, it always comes down to choices. When free will is involved, you can never know anything for certain."

"Is it over?" Gavin asked, placing a hand on the nape of Rosie's neck as he assessed the angel.

"Again, not the word I'd use. But this game is finished. The board reset. You have played your parts and saved the world. Huzzah! Well done, all of you."

"And so we're supposed to what? Just go back to the way things were like none of this ever happened?"

Gabriel shot Remi a disappointed look. "That's entirely up to you, but it would be such a shame if you learned nothing from your adventure."

"Wh-what were we s-supposed to l-learn?" Ben asked.

The angel's eyes slid his way. "Well now, if I tell you that does defeat the purpose, doesn't it?"

"Haven't you learned anything from this, Ben?"

Ben crossed his arms and stared down his twin. "I d-don't know, Remi. D-did you?"

"Yeah, that the greatest gift is to love and be loved in return. You know, just like in *Moulin Rouge*. Only the best tragic love story ever made. AND she had the pestilence! I always admired how she could still sing her butt off even when dying of consumption. Not to mention it has another hottie with an accent. Ewan McGregor . . ." Remi sort of trailed off with a dreamy look in his eyes.

"Pretty sure he didn't learn anything," I murmured.

Gavin nodded his agreement.

"Have you quite finished?" Gabriel asked on a long-suffering sigh.

"No. Hey, Siri. Add the soundtrack to *Moulin Rouge* to my playlist."

"Okay, Fuckboi, adding *Moulin Rouge, The Original Motion Picture Soundtrack,* to your sex machine playlist."

"Asher," Remi growled.

I snickered. "Man, talk about the long game. I've been waiting for you to do that."

"Well, now that I experienced . . . whatever that was, I think it's time I leave you. Good luck with that one, Roslyn. He seems a bit dodgy." Gabriel turned away, but Rosie stopped him.

"Wait!"

"Yes?"

"What about Pan?"

"What about him?"

"Are you seriously telling me that all he gets is death? He is the reason this is over. He sacrificed himself for the literal world."

"I seem to recall several sacrifices that were made today. Bentley sacrificed himself so Asher had the opportunity to use the sword. You sacrificed yourself when you gave him your power. Smart move, by the way."

She waved him off. "But we are all still standing. He's not. Please. Help him. He deserves a second chance."

Gabriel studied her with interest. "Does he? He deceived you, Roslyn. He was his mother's puppet. The instrument she used to set all of this into motion. He was never supposed to be yours, you know. Four mates. That's the amount the horsewomen agreed on."

"Yes, but a Queen traditionally has five. Maybe the entire reason I became a Queen in the first place is that he snuck his way in and made himself my mate."

Gabriel winked at her. "That is the beauty of free will, is it not? We can give a little nudge, but at the end of the day, it's up to you to jump or not. The outcome cannot be predicted. Not by a Seer, nor a prophecy."

"Wait, I'm confused," Remi said.

"What else is new?" Gavin asked.

Remi side-eyed him, but kept talking. "So was Pan supposed to be her mate or not?"

"Not. But his manipulation of events to become one is—as Roslyn so brilliantly surmised—the reason she became a Queen, and in turn, the reason the six of you were able to work together to defeat Pestilence. One could not exist without the other. Every piece had a purpose they must fulfill. We just didn't know exactly what that would be until everything unfolded. That is the mystery of my Father's plan."

Rosie's eyes swam with tears. "Still, the fact of the matter remains. He saved us. Now save him."

"Please," I added.

This time I was the one to receive Gabriel's intense stare. "Oh, all right. Shove over." He knelt next to Rosie, grumbling the entire time about being on his knees for a bloody demon. But he placed his palm on Pan's forehead, right between his ruined horns, took a deep breath, and then went silent for what seemed like an eternity but was really only a few minutes.

"I'd stand back if I were you," he warned.

Blinding light, very similar to the kind that shot out of my hands, surrounded Pan, lifting his body off the ground.

"Holy shit, it's a Beauty and the Beast moment."

"Remi," Ben said, but it lacked any heat.

Remi waved a hand. "But it is. Look at him. He's totally turning into a prince."

"Not a prince," Rosie corrected, "a human."

"He's going to be pissed," I said, already picturing him lamenting the loss of his tail. Again.

"You might be surprised," Gavin said. "Remember Lilith's room. It fulfills a person's deepest wish."

"He *wanted* to be human?" Remi asked. "That doesn't seem like him."

"No, you fucking donut. He wanted to be able to keep Rosie."

By the time the light faded, Gabriel was nowhere to be found, and Pan's demon body was replaced by the human form he'd worn at *Iniquity*.

"He really is a pretty bastard, isn't he?" Remi asked.

Pan's eyes fluttered open. "You're only just realizing that? I always thought you were a bit dim."

"Pretty on the outside. A giant dick everywhere else."

"Sounds like your version of a wet dream."

"Pan," Rosie chided, laughter in her voice.

He glanced down at himself, holding out his hands for inspection, then sitting up and running his palms over his forehead. "Human. The featherless arse really did it."

But he didn't sound disappointed. He sounded . . . relieved.

"You're beautiful." Rosie ran her fingers through his long purple locks, then held out a hand to help him rise.

"I had to have something going for me. Gabriel offered purgatory or a life on Earth with you if I'd let him take my demonic power from me. I said, make me the hottest human possible, and we have a deal." Pan grinned and flashed a dimple. "And you know what, I still think I got the better end of the arrangement. Must be those centuries of practice. I'd have come back as a damn kitten if it meant I could be yours a little while longer."

He stood to his full height, which, while not as towering as his demonic form, was still over six feet. In fact, his build was still the same when it came to proportions, he was just human sized now. He reminded me of a purple-haired Viking. Or maybe an elf without the pointy ears. Even his eyes were the same striking shade of lavender.

Rosie was going to have her hands full keeping the girls away from him. With that accent and those looks? He was for sure going to get his fair share of attention.

"So, what's next on the agenda, gents? Anyone up for an orgy? I've got some new parts I need to test out."

"Let's start with picking up the pieces of this town, huh? We need to check in with Aunt Callie, see about the cure she's been working on. So many people are sick," Rosie said, her brow furrowing.

"No, they're not." Pan cocked his head as he assessed her.

"What?"

"Look around. Everything is healing. Ben, Remi, Gavin, they're all recovered."

"Pestilence is gone," she murmured as the truth hit her.

"Yes. Without her here, anyone who was infected with her plague will be recovered or well on their way now that their supernatural healing and immunity can kick back in. Her power was the only thing that kept the infection going."

"So it really is over," she breathed.

"Does that mean it's orgy time?" Remi asked, rubbing his hands together.

"I enthusiastically vote yes," Pan said, raising a hand in the air as if this was an actual vote.

"Th-there's still a lot of w-work to d-do. The b-bar alone—"

Remi made a face. "Yeah, yeah, yeah, but that'll still be true tomorrow. Come on. We earned it. We just saved the whole fucking world."

"Celebratory orgy, huh? What happened to Disneyland?" I asked.

"Forget Mickey Mouse. Inside Rosie is the happiest place on Earth."

"Her body is my favorite ride," I agreed, loving the way she blushed as I gave her a slow, intentional once-over.

Remi pouted. "I thought I was your favorite."

"Jealous, big boy?" I teased.

He grinned, and it reminded me of sunshine bursting through the clouds. "Nah. But only 'cause she's my favorite too. Why choose, right?"

"Why choose indeed. I'll advocate for excess all day long," Pan murmured, nuzzling into Rosie's neck. "Just consider me the demon on your shoulder."

"Does that make me the angel on her other?" I asked.

"If you two are playing Jiminy Cricket, we're all going to hell," Remi said with a laugh.

"I happen to know all the best people. Our afterlife will be anything but dull," Pan promised. "Whips. Chains. Screams. The unholy trifecta."

Gavin groaned and looked to Ben. "You realize with Pan we're outnumbered now. Two Doms against three cocky bellends. I foresee many punishments in our future, just to keep our girl in line."

"That's my kind of maths." Rosie's words were colored with laughter.

"Can I volunteer to help with some of those sessions, Daddy G? You know what a good boy I can be."

"Jesus on a b-bike, Mary on the h-handlebars, and Moses in the b-basket," Ben muttered.

"It loses something without the accent," Remi said.

Ben flipped him off.

Meanwhile, Rosie stood between them with the most beautiful smile on her face.

"What are you thinking, princess?"

"That I finally got everything I wanted. A home filled with love."

"And debauchery. Let's not forget the debauchery," Pan said, tugging her against him. "I reckon you didn't count on being stuck with me for eternity when you drunk summoned me that night, did you, *ma petite monstre?*"

"Maybe not, but a part of me hoped for it."

Something like wonder filled Pan's eyes, making him look far more boyish than I'd expected.

"It's because I'm so good in bed, right?"

"And that's the tender moment ruined," I said with a laugh. "Come on, you guys. Let's go home."

"Where exactly is that?" Remi asked.

"Wherever Rosie is." Ben's words were clear and strong. "That's my home."

"Mine too," Gavin agreed.

"I mean, when you put it that way, it's pretty obvious," Remi said.

"Fine," Pan groused. "I'll jump off the feelings bridge alongside the rest of you. I am human now, and if I learned anything during my imprisonment inside Asher—"

"Too soon," I groaned.

"—talking about our feelings seems to be the way of things."

Rosie giggled. "Might as well join us, Pan. The water's fine. And I promise I'll be here beside you while you learn how to wade through the feelings pool."

"I'd expect nothing less, *mon ange*." Pan's expression was adoring as he pressed his lips against hers. I had to admit, happy looked good on him.

"And while we're talking about our feelings, I love you too, Pan."

Pan stiffened and then melted against her. "You heard that?"

"Every word."

"I meant it, you know."

"I know," she promised, feathering her lips over his. "I would have known without the words. I feel it through our bond everytime you look at me. But it was a damn good speech."

Remi leaned over, his lips at my ear. "I'm gonna assume I missed some grand gesture while I was out."

"You missed a lot of things, but I'll get you caught up." Threading my fingers with his, I looked at Rosie as I said, "As for our home, at the risk of sounding like a greeting card, home is wherever we make it, as long as we're together."

Rosie beamed at us, sending pure love and happiness through our bond. "Then lead the way, boys. I do have one request, though."

"Wh-what is it, sugar?"

"Yes, do tell, petal."

"Can we have a sexy dungeon?"

It was on the tip of my tongue to tell her that abso-fucking-lutely we could, but Pan beat me to it.

"A sexy dungeon, you say? Well, this is an unexpected treat."

Rosie grinned at him. "That's what you said the first time you saw me."

"And it's still true, *ma petite.* I'll show you exactly how good I am in the dungeon. You'll have three Doms by the time I'm through with you."

"Is that a challenge?" Gavin asked, cocking a brow.

"More like a wager. If I prove it, she calls me Daddy too."

"You m-mean another deal?" Ben asked.

"Exactly. But this time I don't want your soul, Roslyn Blackthorne," Pan said, gazing at Rosie.

"Donoghue," Gavin corrected with a smug grin.

My eyes moved to Remi, waiting for him to chime in, but it was Ben who coughed, "Mercer," making us all laugh.

Rosie's cheeks were pink as she looked at Pan. "So what do you want?"

"Just your heart."

She rolled her bottom lip between her teeth, eyes bright with excitement. Then, a little breathlessly, she said, "It's a deal."

EPILOGUE

ROSIE

Four months later

I added a couple more drops to the bubbling pot, giving it a few good stirs with my spoon.

"That smells good, princess," Asher said, his eyes closing as he paused in the doorway. "Pine?"

"Cedar. *Sexy* cedar actually."

He took a deep breath, pure relaxation causing his shoulders to drop and face to slacken. "God, I just want to roll around in it. Maybe take a bath in it. Did you make bubble bath too?"

"I haven't, but I certainly could. Are you telling me you want to be covered in Remi all the time? Is that what I'm hearing?"

His eyes snapped open. "That's what it is. Nice."

"He said the same thing about the scent I made for you, you know."

"Guess that means he likes me." Asher moved to stand behind

me, his fingers fiddling with the ties of my frilly purple apron. "How can you stand to sell these to people? Doesn't it bother you?"

"What?"

"All these customers buying our scents, surrounding themselves with something that should only be yours."

I pondered that for a moment, letting it sit with me. "No."

"Why not?"

"Because they don't have you. Not really. Just something they can smell any time they're near you anyway. It makes them happy, and we make a little money out of it. But at the end of the day, I'm the only one who gets to truly have you."

It was the God's honest truth. When we rebuilt Aurora Springs, plenty of shops were left without owners. People ran after the almost-Apocalypse, but we were determined to salvage the town. It was our home. The place where all six of us could put down roots and start over.

For Ben and Remi, it had always been home, but even then it had been shrouded in the grief of their past. Not anymore. When we'd fought against Pestilence to save this place, we'd reclaimed this town. It wasn't just somewhere to hide, as it had been for so many. Now it was *ours*. Which was why we were the first to step up and fill in the gaps the missing townspeople had left behind.

Ben had unanimously been voted in as the new mayor, much to his chagrin. Which came with perks none of us anticipated, namely that fancy house in the middle of town. Gavin hated it and insisted on funding a full remodel so he wouldn't be forced to 'live in Southern belle squalor' as he'd called it. And then Asher installed a security system so elaborate I was sure NASA would be jealous. On the bright side, we now had a home that reflected all six of us with more than enough room to spare. And I got that dungeon I'd asked for. It was, indeed, very sexy.

Remi had taken over The Tip, which the town had come together to help rebuild first—even Ivan and the rest of the bears chipped in —citing it as the single most important business in Aurora Springs.

Then they'd pitched in to buy a sweet plaque that dubbed it a historical landmark. Ben teared up when they hung it outside. He also surprised us all by hanging a photo of his parents, a dark-haired baby held by each one of them, next to the bar. That one had made Remi cry. None of us knew he had that picture.

Gavin was less interested in public service, but I couldn't help but notice the number of charitable donations he'd made, even if he adamantly refused to talk about any of them. He seemed most interested in helping families who couldn't afford it as they picked up the pieces and rebuilt their lives. He also created and funded the Mercer Foundation run by Dallas and Darla, so that any children whose parents didn't survive the Death Rattle—the name they'd given Pestilence's plague—had a safe place to grow up. That had made Asher cry.

So, everyone cried, except for Gavin. And of course Pan. That was fine. They could make me cry later.

"You're thinking about us, aren't you, princess?" Asher asked, brushing a tendril of hair that had escaped my bun out of my face.

"Of course I am. I just get . . . overcome when I think about all we've done since banishing Pestilence." He cupped my cheek and stared deeply into my eyes as I continued, "We've all found our places. We've settled in and have somewhere we belong. It just makes me so happy."

My hacker was back at it, but instead of taking jobs for shady characters, he was helping people find freedom and safety. He'd also retired his fake beards and false identities. Well . . . for the most part. Henry made an appearance in the sexy dungeon every now and then.

He glanced at the pot of melted wax I'd been stirring, then looked over at the molds set out on the counter, one brow raised. "Replicas this time?"

I giggled. "No. That's reserved for Captain Aubergine. I'm not making a sexy variety today. This one goes into jars and tins. Want to help?"

"I can't believe you named a dick candle after him," Asher said with a laugh as he took the pot off the stove and carried it over to the jars waiting to be filled.

"Did you see how happy it made him?"

"He hasn't shut up about it since. Which is impressive, considering the only other thing he talks about these days is *Pan's Box*."

Pan was incredibly pleased with himself for coming up with that name for his brand new supernatural sex club. No one dared to remind him it was actually Lilith who hired him to run and manage it for her. He struggled to find his purpose in our world for the first month or so, unmoored as he was. But then Lilith and Crombie dropped in for a visit at The Tip one night with news that changed everything for him. She'd purchased one of the abandoned buildings and had plans to expand *Iniquity*. Apparently she'd been serious about doing this since her first visit to Aurora Springs. No one had thought she'd actually follow through.

Pan jumped at the chance to run the club, and I had to admit, he was the perfect choice. I also enjoyed the perks of being mated to the manager. Especially since I convinced him to test out my new line of sensual candles and oils.

Wax Play, my sweet little candle and essential oils shop, was the main supplier for *Pan's Box*, which garnered me many new patrons. Business, as they say, was booming. And I'd finally found a way to combine my urge to be in the kitchen with creating products that were actually usable. As soon as the requirement to be edible was out of the picture, it was like everything clicked. And, my nose was the best in town, which made me a natural perfumer.

My phone vibrated from its little perch on the counter, Noah's name and photo flashing on the screen.

"And that's my cue," Asher said after he finished filling the last tin. "Tell you brother hi from me. I've gotta stop by and see the new pufflings before I meet Remi for lunch."

"Kiss him for me, and take pictures so I can see the babies."

He kissed my temple and dashed away as I accepted the video call from my brother.

"Noah, this is a surprise. Is everything all right?"

"It's a sad state of affairs that we immediately assume the worst when one of our siblings rings us up. Can't I just call you to say hello?"

"Are you?"

He grinned. "No. I have news."

"Is the world ending again, or . . ."

He laughed. "Probably, but at least it's not our problem this time. I was actually calling to let you know that she did it."

There was only one *she* he could be referring to. Callie.

"She finalized the vaccine?"

"She did. Next time Pestilence tries anything, we'll be ready for her."

"I forking love science."

"Me too."

A loud crash followed by a bellow filtered to my ears from somewhere in Noah's home. He stiffened, then sighed.

"What in God's name was that?" I asked.

"Alek."

That sounded bad. The berserker was usually so cheerful and easygoing, despite his bloodthirsty inner monster. "Did something happen?"

"It's his twin, Tor. He's refusing contact with anyone. Not his family, not his friends. He's as good as vanished."

"Why?"

"We don't know. Not really. If it wasn't for Lilith, we wouldn't have any clue he was even alive."

"If she knows where he is, why isn't she telling you?"

"All she's said is that magic prevents her from speaking of it, but that he isn't safe."

Another loud crash came from the depths of the house, and this time, Kingston hurried in with Eden strapped to his chest.

"Can you use your weird vampy mind magic to reach Sunshine and get her to come home? She's not answering my calls. Moira can shop for crystals or whatever on her own. Alek's going to bring down the house if she isn't here to help him calm his berserker."

Noah frowned. "Sorry, Rosie. I gotta go."

"It's okay. Go take care of your family."

"Ring me more often so we stop assuming the worst. And plan a visit home soon. Your niece is going to be a year old at this rate before you see her. She deserves to meet her aunt."

Nervous butterflies filled my belly. "I've been meaning to tell you, I'm taking everyone to meet Mum and Dad next month."

"Should we plan on being there? Or would you rather have them to yourself?"

The thought of not seeing him when we were all going to be together made my heart ache. "Of course you should. All of you. It'll be a party."

"Brilliant. I'll get the details from Mum. Love you, Rosie."

Eden babbled happily before kicking her chubby legs furiously and nailing Kingston right in the crotch. "Mother of dragons, sunbeam. That really hurts Daddy. Don't you want siblings?"

She did it again, and he removed her from the contraption holding her in the danger zone. "That's it. No more baby wearing for this wolf. Take her, Thorne. I need to ice poor abused Jake."

I waved at Eden as we hung up, then went back to my task of candle making. I was just wrapping up when my phone buzzed again. This time it was my handsome stoic shifter calling. Probably in response to the wildly inappropriate for work text I'd sent while he was in a city council meeting.

I was in trouble. And I couldn't wait for the consequences.

"Hello, Mister Mayor."

"Sugar," he growled, his voice all wolf, eyes glowing even through the video call. "You have ten minutes to get home and get naked or I'm coming to find you."

My heart picked up. "Oh? And what happens if you have to come find me?"

He grinned. "Guess you'll f-find out."

I smirked wickedly and undid the top two buttons on my blouse and leaned forward, exposing the lace at the top of my bra. "Hurry, Daddy. I've been a bad girl."

GAVIN

"DID anyone ever tell you you'd make a hot professor?"

I looked over at my wife and grinned. "Once or twice."

She came over and sat her perfect arse on the corner of my desk as she looked at my research. "What's all this? A new murder board?"

"In a manner of speaking."

"What are you chasing now?"

"The next horsewoman. Obviously it will be either Death or Famine, but we need to be as prepared as possible for things to begin again."

"We've already played our round, Gavin. There's nothing any of us can do this time."

"Even so, we should be prepared. You're still a Queen."

She arched a brow. "Am I, though? My power never returned after the battle. I'm just an ordinary, run-of-the-mill vampire these days."

"You are many things, petal, but run of the mill is not one of them."

I couldn't resist running my palm over her denim-clad thigh as she released a heavy breath. "So you're telling me this is going to be our life? Waiting for the other apocalyptic shoe to drop? Never feeling safe?"

"No. I'm saying we have to be prepared because we'd be stupid not to. I'm working on finding a clear path to the next harbinger, so we can continue to be safe."

"Do you think my power will return?"

Since Queens had an alarming habit of dying in pursuit of their fate-blessed purpose, I really had nothing to go on besides my intuition. "One day, if needed, it very well might."

"And in the meantime?"

I gestured to the wall. "In the meantime, we pay attention and live our lives. We, more than anyone else, know just how quickly everything can be taken from us. So we live in the moment, petal, and we cherish the gifts we've been given."

She smiled at me. "You're starting to sound like Asher. When did you turn into a bright-eyed optimist?"

"When I lost my wife and then by some miracle, found her again." I didn't even try to disguise the tremor in my words as I pushed back my chair and stood, placing myself between her thighs. I reached for her, grabbing her nape and looming over her. "I may not be able to stop the next round of the Apocalypse, but this is the one thing I *can* control, petal. Knowledge is power, and the more I know, the more I can keep my thumb on. I need it."

I'd grown a lot in the time that I'd known Roslyn, as a man, as a lover, as a friend. But one thing hadn't changed. I still came apart at the seams when I felt too out of control of my surroundings. Since the only tears I craved these days were those of my wife, I needed other ways to spend my time. A new way to fill in the gap that my predilections had once filled. Books had been the answer. Research had become my touchstone when nothing else made sense. I had Asher to thank for that. Whenever it felt that I'd reached a dead end, he'd be right there, working his magic to help me discover a new path. The hacker and I had grown closer than I thought possible. Much to everyone's surprise, but none more so than my own.

My wife brought me back to the present, cradling my cheek in her palm. "Thank you for always keeping me safe."

"It's the first promise I made when we were wed. Whether you heard it or not, I vowed to protect you at all costs."

"I love you, Gavin Donoghue."

"And I you, Roslyn Blackthorne."

Her lips quirked. "Donoghue."

From somewhere in the house, Remi's voice echoed off the walls. "Mercer!"

I rolled my eyes, but then an idea flickered to life. I opened my desk drawer and pulled out the velvet box containing her collar before pulling the jewelry free of the container. "Shut the door, Duchess. I can think of another way to ensure I feel in control."

Heat flared in her gaze, and as I fastened the collar around her throat, she smiled. "Yes, my lord."

~

Pan

Business was booming. Apparently the residents of Aurora Springs were very kinky indeed. Of course, Auntie Lilith would have known that. There's only one reason she would have spent the time and money creating *Pan's Box*. Profit. Well, and the additional source of sexual sustenance. Say that five times fast.

Couldn't do it, could you? It's okay. Not all of us are professional wordsmiths.

Where was I? Oh, right, the latest feather in my cap. You see, I don't think any of us doubted our club would take off. What we hadn't expected was how *fast* it would happen. But with reality being what it was, and the day in day out drudgery of rebuilding an entire town, Lilith's investment was exactly the sort of escape the good folks of Aurora Springs needed. Everyone craved at least a little mischief now and again, and I was more than happy to provide a location to find it.

Unfortunately, I was running myself ragged doing so. I hadn't had a proper day off since we opened. My little monster was only able to get her Pan time in short bursts of degradation during stolen moments of quiet. No one told you being your own boss—a self-made man, if you will—was so demanding. Perhaps it was my new human body as well. Simply put, I had limits now. But I wouldn't give up my humanity for my tail. Not if it meant I'd have to live without Rosie. I was a changed de-man. Get it? Aren't you glad I retained my sharp wit? But as I was saying, these days I'm a paragon of love and devotion.

Inspired by my darkest fantasies, I did try to play the role of house husband. That wasn't successful, even though I quite enjoyed strolling around the house in nothing but my aubergine apron, waiting for Rosie to get home from her shop so I could help her make that special Captain Aubergine candle mold.

Sadly, I wasn't cut out for a life as a kept man. I was a doer. An ambition-driven creature filled with pride. Which is why I'm now bemoaning being run off my feet. *You can't have it both ways, Pan.*

I sighed gustily as I stared at the piles of paperwork I'd been ignoring. Setting up the performers and greeting patrons at the door? Easy. Paperwork . . . well. The devil is in the details, and while I excel at contracts, I hate the rest of this, especially bookkeeping. Remi was right. Math could kill anything. Spirits. Boners. Joy of any sort.

"Pan, darling, you work too hard."

Lilith's croon caught me off guard. I spun to face her, taking in her amethyst dress with surprise. "What's the occasion?"

"Didn't you check your email? My pet and I are hosting tonight. You, my dear one, have the night off."

A quick check confirmed that Crombie—or was it Drystan now?—was standing just behind her. He wore an expertly tailored black suit, his pocket square and cravat a perfect complement to her gown. His dark hair was slicked back, his silver eyes arresting even from the shadows. He looked like he belonged in one of Gavin's gentleman's clubs. I should ask him who his tailor was. I had to admit, it was quite sharp.

"Are you having me on? A real night off?" Was my voice the hopeful brightness of a child speaking to a department store Father Christmas? Yes. Did I give two figs? No, I did not.

"Oh, you poor soul, I should have come sooner. Apologies, Pan.

But I think once you see the present I left you, you'll find it in your heart to forgive my tardiness."

Prezzies? No one said anything about that. "What are you up to, Auntie?"

"Room five, darling. You can thank me later."

And with that, she and her willing captive walked away, the gold chain connecting them glittering in the absolutely perfect lighting.

I wasted only enough time to ensure my office was locked up before I beelined for my surprise. Unfortunately, the problem with being well, me, was that everyone and their mother tried to stop me on my way. First it was Scarlett, to complain about how rowdy the pirates were being. Then it was my newest entertainer, a sea witch with a gift for electricity. One might say she's . . . shocking. I narrowly dodged a confrontation with The Beast as he shoved his way to the bar, mostly grunting his displeasure with everyone he encountered. He'd become a regular since he arrived in Aurora Springs only a few weeks ago, mystery following in his wake. Although, as I tracked his path, I was surprised to see Lilith greeting him as one might an old friend. Interesting. But more on that later. I had a gift waiting for me.

Finally I reached the gray door marked with an elegant number five. Unsure of the protocol, I lifted my hand but hesitated before knocking. If doors could roll their eyes, I was certain that was the attitude I was sensing. Especially given the slightly irritated huff I heard as it swung open.

But I didn't have time to waste worrying about the possible sentience of inanimate objects because inside the room, wearing nothing but a cheeky grin and holding up a canister of salt, was my favorite monster. All she was missing was my ring through her nipple.

Before the thought fully formed, it was there. As if it had been all along.

She glanced down with a smirk. "Feeling possessive, Pan?"

"Remind me to do something more permanent about that when we're through here."

"It feels pretty permanent to me. Too bad you can't test it out."

Her eyes dipped meaningfully to the ground where she'd set herself a circle. I was reminded all too clearly of the night my world was turned on its end.

My feet traveled forward on their own accord, bringing me to her. "You know that doesn't work anymore, right?"

Her gaze raked across my body, lingering on my already throbbing cock. "Don't be so sure about that . . ."

Something about the way she said it had me looking down at myself. Elation raced through me as I found my body returned to its demon form. My tail—oh, my glorious tail—curled and swayed as though greeting me. "You're back. I've missed you, old friend."

Before I could bring my eyes back up to hers, I watched as she kicked her foot out and broke the circle. "Oops."

A devilish grin twisted my lips. "Oh, but you are very naughty, aren't you?"

She bit down on her bottom lip and nodded. "Terribly."

I reached out for her, my tail coiling around her slender throat as I yanked her to me. "You're going to pay for that, *ma petite monstre*."

"I've been counting on it."

"Because you're my filthy little slut."

"Yes," she agreed, licking her lips.

"Do you know what sluts are good for?"

Rosie shook her head.

Using my tail, I pulled her down to her knees. "Sucking cock."

She blinked up at me and opened her mouth without another word.

"Pace yourself, *mon coeur*. We've got all night. And I intend to make very good use of it."

~

Remi

I stretched up, returning the bottles to the top shelf and smirking to myself as Asher's hot gaze ran over me. I'd felt his eyes on me all night and had made a point to show off my assets as often as possible. But I had to work. What could I say? I was a responsible business owner now that Ben had handed me the reins. He had a town to do all his mayoring in. I had a bar to do my . . . bar ownering. Except the bookkeeping. I delegated that shit faster than you can say hot potato. Thankfully, I knew a guy who had a head for numbers and took payment in the form of enthusiastic blow jobs.

"One more for the road, Remi? What do you say? It's the least you can do for the three of us poor souls. We spent weeks trapped in our stone forms because of those bloody cows," Tom slurred as he leaned against the barstools I reserved for them nightly.

It had been an unexpected relief when the three gargoyles stumbled into town, covered in stone dust with no memory of the last month. Just to make sure, Gavin had infiltrated their minds and verified their story. Gargoyles never died, so when the horsewomen stole their forms, they reverted to statues until the bitches ran. And since none of us ever ventured to the old church, we hadn't thought to look for them there.

We'd memorialized them as soon as we started rebuilding. Their names were mounted on the bar at each of their regular seats. Instead of the solemn or emotional reaction a normal person might have had, they'd taken one look at their names and crowed, 'Finally!' and then proceeded to get absolutely shit-faced, as was their way.

I pretended to be annoyed and even told them I already missed the silence. Truth was, I had never been so happy to see those sloppy assholes in my whole life. They were family.

"Yeah, mate. One more pint for old time's sake," Harry added. "S'been a toll on my mind, that month of solitude."

"He said last fucking call thirty minutes ago! Bar's closed. Get out. We'll see you tomorrow."

"Someone's in a hurry," I teased through our bond. Rosie's power may not have returned after her showdown with Ol' Pesty, but that gift remained. It was useful as fuck. Faster and more private than a text, with none of the drawbacks. As far as I could tell, the only downside was you couldn't send dick pics. Wait . . . could I? How had I never tested this before?

I closed my eyes and pictured my dick, specifically my scheduled afternoon jerk session.

"I saw that."

"Nice."

"Tell me this is a private line."

"If it wasn't, you know Pan would have chimed in by now."

"True. Show me again."

"You wait a couple more minutes, I'll let you enjoy the real thing."

Asher's needy groan rolled down my spine and settled in my balls. Now I was the one in a hurry.

"I'll take some chips if you've got 'em too!" Dick called back into the kitchen, ruining the fucking mood.

Dante sauntered out, a smile on his face. "Sorry, fellas. Kitchen's closed. I've gotta get home. The wife's pregnant again, and she needs me in the worst way. Why don't I walk you three out? We can pick this up tomorrow night, and I'll make a special batch of fries just for you, okay?"

I mouthed, "Thank you," to Dante and flashed Asher a wink before jutting my chin toward the hall that led to my office.

"I'm heading out, boss. See you tomorrow."

"Night."

Asher had me up against the wall as soon as I walked through the door, his body pressing into mine, a hand fisted in my shirt.

"Well, hello to you too," I said, leaning in close and breathing him in. Fuck, I loved the way he smelled.

His lips hitched up in a sexy smirk. "I find it really amusing that we have a literal empty bed upstairs, and you still chose the office."

"I'm sentimental. Sue me."

"Is that your way of asking me to bend you over the desk, Remi?"

"I still have emergency lube in the top drawer. Just in case."

"That's good to know, but I'm already prepared. I've been waiting to get you under me all fucking day. Don't think I didn't notice all that bending and stretching you did."

"Gotta keep the patrons happy."

"Mmhmm. Right."

"I mean, Hook said he'd be back eventually."

Asher's eyes flashed a warning, his little demon horns appearing at his hairline.

"Oh, bad Asher is coming out to play. I love angel Asher, but the devilish version of you makes me hard as fuck. Maybe I should try to make you jealous more often."

His lips ghosted along my throat, teeth grazing the mark he gave me, and I shivered in anticipation of more. Would he bite down? Suck on the spot until my skin was bruised? Taste my blood? I'd begun to crave that particular sting since Rosie turned, and now that he occasionally had fangs too, they both gave it to me.

"Maybe I need to remind you whose mark you're wearing."

"Rosie's?" I teased, knowing this was only going to go better for me if I played the brat. Okay, played was a bit misleading. I was absolutely a brat. No acting needed there.

My palm skated down his chest as he teased me with little nips and then his teeth on my earlobe. He knew that was one of my spots. Damn him. Except I never wanted him to stop. So . . . undamn him?

"You're thinking too hard, Mercer," Asher growled, taking me by the throat and bringing my lips to his. "When my mouth's on you, the only thing I want you thinking about is me."

"I'm always thinking about you, baby. Even when I'm sleeping, you're running through my mind. Aren't you tired?"

Asher laughed, his warm breath fanning over my lips just before he claimed me with another heated kiss. This time, his tongue delved into my mouth, keeping me from talking and ruining the moment.

He kept one hand on my throat, controlling me and forcing me to accept whatever he was willing to give. The other slid the rest of the way down my belly and into my pants. A groan spilled free as his fingers brushed against my cock.

"This all for me?"

"Maybe."

"Wrong answer." But he was grinning as he gave me a soft shove, the hand curled around my cock, gripping me tight.

"Fuck, Asher. You're a fucking tease."

"This is what you get for teasing me all night."

His palm drifted up my shaft, curling over the aching crown and back down. It was torture. Perfect, beautiful torture. So I gave it back to him in kind. My hand crept under the waistband of his jeans, where I found him equally hard, hot, and ready for me. Moisture collected at the tip of his cock, just begging for my tongue.

For each slow, torturous stroke he gave me, I matched it, holding his gaze in the most sexual game of chicken I'd ever played. One of us was going to break. Sooner rather than later. I was really hoping it would be him. Asher fucked like a goddamn champion when he let go and gave in.

"Take off your shirt, Remi," he ordered.

"You take off yours first." I was mostly unintelligible moans and panting, but he got the drift. Doing that would mean we had to stop making each other feel good, even if only for a moment. No one wanted that. Not yet.

That said, I really wanted a look at his new tattoo. The man had inked up his entire left side, and the piece was a love letter to Rosie and me. I loved staring at it, and it was finally healed enough I could trace the lines with my tongue.

Asher's smile stretched, but he didn't call me out. He just reached behind him and gripped the back of his shirt, yanking it up and off. I did the same, my eyes devouring all that inked skin.

"You're so fucking beautiful."

"Funny, I was just going to say the same thing about you," he said, his eyes traveling down my body.

We were both breathing hard, taking each other in and drawing out this moment. Nothing was stopping us from being together anymore; we had all the opportunities to touch and taste we could want. And yet there was something about being in here, back in the place where we first began, that always made us appreciate what we'd found with each other.

"Am I interrupting? The door was partway open." Rosie's teasing voice pulled us from our lust-fueled staring contest. Her eyes were bright, cheeks pink, lips swollen as though she'd been biting them.

"What took you so long?" Asher asked, not taking his eyes off me.

"Got held up with a customer. I didn't miss anything, did I?"

My attention snapped back to him. "Wait. Did you plan this?"

Asher's smile was all smug satisfaction. "You always say an open door is an invitation. And I just so happen to think the same about an open line."

"An open line . . ."

Then it hit me. He'd been channeling everything he'd been feeling and doing with me to her through our bond.

"You sneaky fuck. I love it. I'm only pissed I didn't think about it first."

"There's always next time," Rosie offered, stepping into the room and shutting the door. "Don't let me stop the two of you. I'm perfectly happy to stand quietly in the corner and watch."

"Oh no, not this time, baby girl. Get that pretty ass over here and sit on the desk. Cunt bare, legs spread wide."

Asher's eyebrows lifted. "Oh, are you in charge now?"

"I'm always in charge. I just let you think you are."

Asher and Rosie laughed as they both started undressing.

"Is this like that time you said I only top because you let me? That's cute."

Rosie was faster than Asher and me. She had disrobed and splayed herself out like a dessert buffet on the desk before I even had my socks off. Yes, I took my socks off for sex. I'm not lazy with my lovemaking. Besides, I was going to be bent over said desk, and I needed non-slip footing, okay? Safety first.

"I want you to make her scream for me, Remi."

"Funny," Rosie said, the little hitch in her voice betraying how turned-on she was. "I was just going to tell you the same thing. Love him hard, Asher."

"Don't you mean 'fuck him hard'?" I asked, running my hands along her naked thighs, pushing them open just a bit more.

"Same thing," Asher said, his fingers skimming my spine and drifting down to tease my ass. "Especially when it's the three of us."

I shivered in pure anticipation of what he was about to do. "You got that right. It's the smartest thing you've said today."

"Remi, stop talking and get to work. She's dripping for us."

"Just enjoying the view. Such a pretty kitty. The only kind of cat I like."

Asher fisted my hair and shoved my face into Rosie's pussy. "Eat her. And don't fucking stop until she's coming on your face."

"Sir, yes, sir," I breathed, turning Rosie's soft laugh into a ragged moan as I ran my tongue along her seam.

The cool drizzle of lube down my crack had me tensing, but then his fingers were there, massaging my taint, my balls, teasing my opening slowly. I groaned against Rosie's clit, which made her buck into me and dig her hands into my hair.

"Yes, baby girl. Tug on it. Put my mouth where you need it while he gets me ready." With my mouth occupied, I'd never been more thankful for our bond. Well, except that one time we stopped the Apocalypse together, that was pretty big.

Taking a page out of Asher's book, I telegraphed everything I was feeling back to him. Testing out the 'open line,' as he called it, to let him know how good he was making me feel. He let out a soft 'fuck' and redoubled his efforts.

Hell. Yes.

Inspired, I tried the same with Rosie. I knew it had worked when her body writhed beneath me.

"I can feel it. His fingers in you. The shivers it sends along your skin. Oh my God, Asher. Don't stop. It feels so good."

"Remi, if you keep that line open, I'm not going to last. I can feel everything."

My mouth was still busy, so I sent him a retort. *"That's the point. I thought you were the smart one."*

"Two can play that game," Rosie said.

It was my only warning before a tidal wave of her pleasure crashed into me. My cock jerked, balls drawing tight at the overwhelming sensation. I didn't have words to explain what it was like experiencing two impending orgasms at the same time. Was I going to pass out? I seriously thought I might. Fuck, I'd flown too close to the sun.

Apparently Asher had reached his breaking point because he pulled his fingers out of my ass and replaced them with his dick, sinking in deep and drawing a garbled moan from me. Rosie's whole body trembled in response, and I nearly came all over the desk but managed to keep it together.

Barely.

"I need you to come for me, baby girl. I was given an order. I can't let this end until you come on my face."

Not to be outdone by the two of us, Asher shared his pleasure with us as well. That was all it took for Rosie to detonate like a fucking bomb. Annnnd, so did I. Dammit.

If I thought two building orgasms were intense, three was out of this fucking world. I'm pretty sure my soul left my body, and I was floating in the stars or some shit, because there was no way one person had been meant to experience something this perfect.

My release coated the desk, some of it painting her thigh from the force of my orgasm.

Asher followed right behind us, his cock thickening impossibly as it pulsed inside me. I'd be feeling him for days, and I fucking loved it.

He pulled me back, still seated firmly inside me, and caged me against him with one hand pressed to my chest. Then his lips were at my ear, and he whispered, "You made a mess, Remington. Clean it up and put it where it belongs."

Rosie propped herself up on her elbows and watched as I collected my cum and slipped my fingers inside her, ensuring as much of me as possible filled our mate.

"Fork, that's hot."

"It'd be hotter if there was a real risk we were playing with." I thought it before I remembered we were still connected mentally.

Rosie's eyes dipped down, and there was no missing the way her arousal dimmed at my totally unintentional slight.

"Fuck, I didn't mean it like that."

She smiled at me. "I know. It's okay."

Asher reached around me and held his shirt out to her in case she wanted to cover up or clean up.

I felt like such an asshole. Everything had been going so well, better than well, and I had to go and shove my foot in my mouth like an idiot.

"We love you, and our pack is perfect as it is. That was just my primal instinct, you know? The wolf in me will always want to breed you and link you to me as much as possible. I'm sorry. I don't want you to feel like you're less than exactly what we all want."

Rosie covered herself while Asher and I did the same, my heart aching with every second of silence from her. I cast him a pleading look that said, *'come on, help me out here.'*

But when he opened his mouth, I don't think any of us were prepared for the words that came out.

ASHER

REMI'S PUPPY dog eyes were impossible to ignore. I didn't need our connection to know he felt awful. And it was hard to be upset with the guy when he so clearly hadn't meant to hurt our mate. That was the danger with thoughts. We weren't always consciously choosing to think them. They just floated around like little asteroids in our minds. And shit, could they do some damage.

"Rosie . . . do you want children?"

Those stunning amber eyes met mine. "It doesn't matter what I want. It's not an option."

"But if it was," I insisted, not ready to make an offer that might take the fallout from Remi's accidental insensitivity from bad to worse.

She lifted her shoulders in a shrug as she glanced away. "Originally, when I'd made the deal with Pan, my circumstances were very different. I was being hunted by a family that wanted to breed me for my bloodline. They intended to use my body against me. And then Pestilence wanted my blood for her plague. Bringing children into a world like that, where the same could be done to them? It seemed cruel."

"And now?" I pressed, sensing that this was the first time she was really admitting how heavily this decision still weighed on her.

"Well, everything's changed, hasn't it?" She cast a wistful glance at Remi. "Until the Donoghues, I'd always pictured having a family at some point. I've never had a burning desire to hold a cherub-faced baby in my arms, but I didn't ever *not* want one either. I think . . . knowing I took that from you, not even just you, but all of us. I took that option from us willingly, and now, even if we decided to have a baby, we couldn't. So now it seems cruel that I'm the reason for that lack in our lives. Our future could go in so many different ways, but making children isn't one of them."

Remi took her hand in his, pulling her down onto his lap. The relief he felt when she willingly sank into him was impossible to miss. Even if we weren't bonded together, it was written all over his face. "There's no knowing whether children were ever in the cards for us. Deal or no deal. Please don't blame yourself for doing what you had to do to survive because I promise you, if the option was a life with Rosie or a life without, I'd choose you every fucking time. No matter what."

"All of us would," I agreed. "We just want you to be happy, princess. Whatever that looks like."

This time her smile didn't seem so forced. "I know. I guess sometimes I can't help but imagine what they would be like, you know? Our babies. Would they be quiet like Ben? Brilliant like you and Gavin?"

"Absolute fucking disasters like Remi?" I teased.

Remi opened his mouth to protest, but stopped. "That's fair."

"Oh shit, what if they ended up like Pan? Intent on world domination, but tiny and vicious."

Rosie really laughed then. "I can picture him now, chasing them down." Then her gaze dropped to Remi's fingers entwined with hers as she softly said, "I guess the answer to your question is, if the deal hadn't taken the choice from me, I'd want to leave it up to fate. Let the chips fall where they may and see what happens. Because children with any or all of you would be a gift I'd never deny."

That was all I needed to hear.

Gabriel had visited me a few more times since things calmed down. He told me about my father, Gadreel. Why he fell, what kind of man and angel he'd been before he lost his mate. About Nephilim and how, as a hybrid, my grace would always be a bit of an unknown, but that there was one miracle I could always count on. Healing.

The poetic justice of my gift, given who my mother was and that she'd intended for me to be a weapon, wasn't lost on me.

I may not be able to do the sorts of things a full-blooded angel could do, or a demon for that matter, but I could heal. Which meant I could return what had been taken from her.

Pan was no longer a demon. The deal, for all intents and purposes, had been honored by both parties until it had been voided. No one was going to come for any of us for breach of demonic contract. There was nothing stopping me from doing this for her.

Unless she didn't want it.

But from the sound of it, she did.

"Come here, Rosie." I was shaking and hoped she didn't notice as she did what I asked.

Then I simply pulled her into my arms and held her tight. This wasn't like healing a wound. She wasn't wounded. Nothing about her was broken. But she was missing a piece of herself. Something she'd willingly sacrificed. So I clutched her to me like she was in danger of coming apart and pressed my lips to her forehead. I sent all my grace through that kiss, giving her back the one thing she wanted to reclaim. Choice.

She shivered in my arms, her sweet face tipping up so she could look at me. "Asher? What did you just do?"

I offered her a smile. "Gave fate a fighting chance."

BEN

CITY COUNCIL MEETINGS might be my own personal hell. I wasn't sure I was cut out for this mayor thing. All I really wanted was to take care of Rosie, live out my days here in Aurora Springs, and make good memories with her to chase away the dark ones I'd held onto for too long.

"Rough day?"

I glanced up after tossing my keys in the dish alongside the others, Rosie's voice doing wonders for the tension building at the base of my skull.

"No m-more than usual."

She tilted her head, silently calling me out on my bullshit, but I was too busy appreciating the way she looked standing there in my shirt. I wondered if she was wearing panties under there. Maybe I could toss her over my shoulder and haul her upstairs so I could find out.

"I'm f-fine, sugar." Reaching out, I snagged her by the wrist and tugged her against me, needing her body close so I could breathe her in.

"Don't lie to me, Bentley Mercer."

I blew out a breath, knowing she wasn't going to let it go until I gave her the truth. I leaned away just enough to run a hand along the back of my neck and look down at her. "Wh-what if I l-let them all d-down? Am I d-doing a g-good job?"

Her brows furrowed. "Of course you are. Ben, you're a natural leader. You were literally born to lead a pack." She gripped the front of my shirt and gave me a little shake. "Aurora Springs *is* your pack. You couldn't fail these people unless you actively tried. How could you even doubt it?"

Her faith in me was a balm to my soul. One I hadn't realized I was craving until she gave it to me.

"Y-you always know the right th-thing to s-say. I l-love how much you b-believe in m-me."

Those big amber eyes of hers locked on mine, and for the first time all damn day, I finally felt right. Settled. Where I was supposed to be.

"You do a fine job of giving me every reason to. This town is lucky to have you. They know it, even if sometimes Dallas can be a bit of a wanker about city ordinances."

I laughed, realizing I'd telegraphed exactly why my mood was so sour. The sheriff was a real stickler for codes, rules, and regulations. Which was why he'd been reinstated so quickly. I just hadn't planned on how far up my ass he'd be after I gave him his job back. You'd think the guy would be grateful, especially after the way he treated me. But you sure as shit wouldn't know it with how he came at me during our weekly check-ins.

Rosie's fingers brushed across my brow, causing me to relax the scowl that had crept up on me. "Stop. He peppers you with questions because it's his job. You two will learn to work together soon, I promise. Not having all the answers doesn't make you an impostor."

I didn't even mind she was gleaning all of this from my internal thoughts. It helped me express what I couldn't put into words. Words would never be my thing.

"I think you need a bit of a distraction, Mister Mayor."

"Oh y-yeah?"

"Mmhmm," she nodded and started working the button at the base of my throat.

"You g-got one in m-mind, sugar?" My palms drifted down her back, over her hips, then cupped the globes of her round ass.

Instead of answering the question, she just kept working her way down the row of buttons, her voice deceptively casual as she said, "Oh, before I forget. Asher performed a little miracle today."

"He d-did?" I had to admit, my mind was barely on the conversation. I was much more interested in the feel of her beneath my hands.

"He did. So you have two options. Tonight you can either pull out, or . . ."

She let that 'or' hang long enough that I realized I was missing something. I replayed her words, my eyes narrowing. "Or w-what, sugar?"

Rosie gifted me with a smile that hit me right in the gut. "Or you don't, and we see what fate has in store."

Awe chased through my veins as everything solidified into this one moment. "Really?"

She shrugged like it was no big deal. "He wanted to give me back my choice."

"H-how do you f-feel about that?"

Her eyes were bright with hope and excitement. "Optimistic."

My brain buzzed with all the possibilities laid out before us now. If we wanted to, we could make our family bigger, and we could share all the love we have with a child we created together. I'd written that off so long ago, long before I ever met Rosie, and her deal with Pan had only solidified that for me. But now? My wolf pushed at me, telling me exactly what he wanted.

Knot her.

Breed her.

Give her our pups.

I picked her up, drawing a happy squeal from her as I took off toward the bedroom.

"I thought that might cheer you up."

Cheer me up? I was ready to punch a hole through my fucking pants.

I lifted her until she wrapped her legs around my waist. My hips rocked into her as I ground my steel-hard length along her—yup, bare—cunt. "Does that f-feel like I'm ch-cheered up?"

She made a happy sound as she ground into me. "I mean, someone is certainly excited about my news."

"Sugar, you h-have n-no idea." I hitched her a bit higher, holding her weight with one arm so I could throw the door open.

She brushed her lips over my brow. "I think I have *some* idea. Take me to bed, Daddy. Let's see if you put a baby inside me."

All I could do was groan at that. I think this is what my late night research calls a breeding kink. I really fucking liked it. And now that it might really happen . . . fuck. A shiver of need rolled down my spine as I walked us to the bed, trailing kisses down the side of her neck as I laid her on the comforter.

God, she was so fucking perfect. And she was mine.

A little growl of approval rumbled in my chest at the thought as I started pulling off my clothes. That handled, I rested a knee between her spread thighs, skimming the tips of my fingers along her leg.

"A-are you s-sure?"

"Yes. The odds are slim, though, especially between vampires and wolves, but it'll be fun to try."

Bracing my hands on either side of her head, I lowered my face until my lips brushed hers. "It will be f-fucking fantastic when I fill you f-full of me. Every. Single. Time." I punctuated my words with slow rolls of my hips, my aching dick rubbing across slick hot skin.

"Oh God, Ben," she whimpered as my length ran across her clit.

I wasn't going to last once I got inside her. Not with everything she'd told me, with how worked up I was. Add to that my wolf's primal need to knot her, and I was surprised I hadn't thrown her on her hands and knees and slammed deep into her from behind as soon as I got the go-ahead.

"Me too," she breathed with a laugh, letting me know she was right there in my head.

A huff of laughter blew a few strands of hair off her neck as I pressed my forehead to hers and then looked to the side. "I w-was trying to b-be a gentleman."

"When did I ask for a gentleman? The rule is, gentleman in the streets, beast in the sheets, Ben."

"In th-that case." I slammed into her then, driving deep and filling her in one hard thrust.

"That's more like it." She dragged her nails down my back. "Take me. Hard and rough, Daddy. Let your wolf have what he needs."

"You want the wolf?" I asked, pure anticipation burning in my veins as my beast spoke through me.

"Yes."

I pulled out, cock twitching, balls pulled tight, body pissed as fuck that I was denying us her slick heat. But the wolf took hold, knowing exactly why I'd done it. I stood next to the edge of the bed, staring down at my mate. She was on full display for me, swollen with arousal, glistening, needy. One slow stroke of my fist over my shaft had her writhing as she stared me down.

"Ben, please."

"Alpha."

She nodded. "Alpha. Please."

"Tell me. Where do you want my cum, mate?"

She reached down to play with her clit as she locked eyes with me. "Inside me."

I couldn't tease either of us any longer. Reaching for her, I grabbed her splayed legs and tugged hard, bringing her right up to the edge of the bed. Then I sank to the hilt, my body on fire for her.

I gave her exactly what she asked for. Thrusting hard, deep, and fast. Making those beautiful tits bounce as I ruthlessly fucked her.

"You're mine. Every fucking part of you." I was all wolf dressed like a man. She loved it.

"Yes," she gasped, unable to say more.

I gripped her legs so hard, I was sure she'd be wearing bruises by the time we were done. But her whimpers of approval just reaffirmed how much she loved the bite of pain along with her pleasure.

"Gonna knot you so full." I had to force the words out as my legs trembled from the effort to hold back.

"Yes, Alpha. I want it."

"Fuck." The word was long and drawn out as the base of my cock swelled and her walls clenched around me, flooding me with her release.

"Look at you, taking my knot like a good girl. Not letting a drop go to waste."

She was still breathing hard as she beamed at me, reaching for me with her hands. I didn't need words to know what she was asking for. My good girl wanted a cuddle. I cradled her back and lifted her into my arms as she wrapped her legs around my waist, both of us moaning softly as I shifted inside her.

"I love you, sugar. I could s-stay like this with y-you forever."

Carefully, I laid us on the bed, nestled together as we waited for my knot to release us. She sighed happily and smiled at me.

"I love you too. So much."

In the quiet darkness, we lay there, hearts beating in tandem, bodies joined. "D-do you th-think it worked?" I whispered, hope filling my words.

"I guess we'll find out," she said, her own wistfulness threading through our bond.

"We sh-should probably t-try again. Just in c-case."

"Not fair, dude. You already got the first shot. I'm next."

Rosie and I laughed. I'd wondered when my twin was going to

pipe up. He'd been uncharacteristically quiet all day. He must have known Rosie was going to surprise me and was giving us privacy.

"I made the miracle happen. I think I should get the next turn."

"I'm her bloody husband. If anyone is going to try and impregnate her, it should be me. I'm genetically superior to you all. She was made to breed with me."

"Hello . . . I'm half angel. My grace can shoot down your vampire swimmers."

"You're half demon too, you twat. You're about as special as a human."

"You mean like you, Pan? The weakest link. You shouldn't even try. Her body will probably reject you."

"Rosie, tell him that's not true."

She giggled at Pan's demand. *"I'm an equal opportunity lover, gents. I think there's only one fair way to settle this."*

I could practically feel each one of them perk up. My knot had only just started to go down, but even I was interested in finding out what she had in mind.

"Please say feast . . . please say feast . . ."

Remi's wishful chant matched my own. Rosie's laughing eyes told me she knew it, even if I hadn't given voice to it.

"Boys, I'm quite famished. I could really go for a feast right about now."

"Yesss."

I could already hear Remi running down the hall on his way to join us.

"Don't you dare start without me," Gavin warned.

"What are you gonna do, spank me, Daddy G? Maybe I want you to."

"Careful what you wish for, dog. One day I'll take you up on that, and trust me, you will cry."

"I'll grab the paddle. Just in case," Asher said, his voice tight and definitely interested in that prospect.

As far as I knew, Asher and Remi were the only ones really involved in anything outside of Rosie. There was the occasional wandering hand, but those two seemed to only have eyes for her and each other. But it was clear as day from her reaction, she wouldn't say no to a night of curious exploration between any of us who were willing.

"You like the s-sound of that, d-don't you, baby?"

Rosie squirmed in response, and I groaned as she shifted around me.

"You guys should see her right now. She wants to watch you play."

"Is that so?" Gavin asked, clearly intrigued. *"Then perhaps we should reconvene in the dungeon."*

"Of all the times to be without my tail. I suppose a whip will do."

"I'm the only one who gets to use a whip."

"Oh shit, I'll grab more lube," Remi said, his footsteps now going in the opposite direction.

"Remi, you know we keep it stocked," Asher said.

"Yeah, but not with the good kind."

"There's a g-good kind of lube?" I asked.

"He's a fan of the one Lilith gave us."

"We're all here waiting, princess. Should we start without you?"

"No. If you guys are going to play, I want to be there to watch."

"Then hurry up, ma petite monstre. *You asked for a feast, and your mates need to give it to you."*

I pulled out of her, both of us gasping at the sensation. "Let's g-go, sugar. Gavin and Pan w-want to m-mark your pretty skin and I n-need to take c-care of you after."

"Ben," she whispered.

"Just g-giving you wh-what you want."

She caressed the side of my face and kissed me. "You always do."

"And I always w-will."

BONUS EPILOGUE

GABRIEL

Four women, all unassuming by human standards, stood together on a misty English hillside. It could've been picturesque, as though these four were friends gathered for a picnic or a leisurely stroll. But I knew better.

It was why I was here, after all. To watch and to report.

"So I suppose condolences are in order," War said.

Pestilence glared at her sister. "You don't have to sound so smug about it."

"She's just glad she's not the only loser," Famine said.

"Sadly for you, sister, you'll never get a chance to fail. My plan is in motion, and I intend to win." Death toyed with a blonde curl and smiled when it bounced back into a perfect ringlet.

"What makes you so sure you'll win? I was closer than we've ever gotten, and I still lost." Pestilence crossed her arms over her chest, looking a little worse for wear.

"That's because you three continue to make the same fatal mistake."

"Oh please, do enlighten us," War said, sarcasm dripping from the words.

"You keep choosing men who want to be heroes. When push comes to shove, they can't help their need to play savior. Which is why I'm going with the much more obvious, and dare I say perfect, choice."

"We're waiting," Pestilence muttered.

"Men whose hearts are as black as their souls. Who won't shy away from walking the dark path or fear making enemies. Men like us."

Well, well, this was interesting.

"So you've already selected your players, then?" Famine asked, intrigued despite herself.

"Oh yes, they're being rounded up now." Death began listing them off on her fingers. "The Beast, The Pirate, The God, The Villain, and of course my leading lady, The Writer."

"So fucking dramatic. Spare me." War shook her head. "I had The Priest, and still they won."

I smiled, thinking of Caleb. He'd surprised us all.

"Uh, hello. I had *two* villains. The Duke and The Demon."

"That sounds like a romance novel," Famine muttered under her breath.

"No, sweetheart," Death chided. "They were anti-heroes at best. You're just biased because one was your son."

War rolled her eyes, unimpressed. "Don't forget the angel. He's her spawn too."

Pestilence hissed in annoyance. "Don't remind me. What a waste of fucking talent."

"You said you're rounding them up. Where, pray tell, are you sending them?" This from Famine, her voice almost bored.

"The only place the daughter of Death can tap into her power. Blackwood."

The hairs on the back of my neck stood on end. There was only one Blackwood she could be referring to. The asylum for dangerous creatures. A low-security prison designed to keep supernaturals with out-of-control powers contained. This place had nothing to do with the human connotation of what an asylum was. It served purely to protect the paranormal world from those with its most dark and dangerous powers.

And I was barred from crossing the barrier keeping it hidden. Even if I wanted to meddle, I couldn't. Death had clipped my wings, and as she looked up from her conversation, her eyes found mine from where I hid in the trees. A devious smile curled her lips.

The next round had just begun.

ACKNOWLEDGMENTS

It's always incredibly hard to write acknowledgements at the end of a long series because there were so many people who were instrumental to the process. But, here we go...

As soon as we knew we were going to have a Brit heroine we had to reach out to our Pickles. Thank you so much Hannah and Catherine for making sure our Britishisms were on point. We hope you enjoyed your shout outs. Sorry again for offing you, but it was an epic death scene.

To the ModGods, thank you for being the world's best cheering section and stans for all the boys (and Lilith). Tara and Khris, your Polyamory and LGBTQ+ sensitivity reads were invaluable. Kat, Gina, and Kenz your pep talks kept us going, and we live for all the GIFs and reaction videos. You are the secret sauce of this organization. (Who are we kidding, there's zero organization.)

Ravens, your constant support and activity in our FB group let us know we're not doing this alone. We love your love for this world and hope you'll stick with us on our next adventures too.

NespressMO we love you. Full Stop. Thanks for making our words shine (even if they are dirty). Caleb wanted us to tell you, you've been a very good girl.

BookTok, thank you for embracing The Mate Games. Your videos blow us away and we're so glad you found us.

To our narrators (though you will likely never see this ***Kim skids in to interrupt* They will when I send it to them. Let me love you, dammit.**) Your voices inspire our stories more than you know (fun fact, we actually build the characters around them...so like, thanks for that). And thank you for bringing these characters to life in the most awe-inspiring ways. There is no doubt in our minds you were the right people for this job. From the second we heard Pan's soft croon, and Gavin's seductive drawl we knew we'd found magic. It was only confirmed when we got to hear the gift that is Siri, Ben's heart-warming stutter, Asher's snarky swagger and... *insert heart eyes here* Remi. That crazy ass bitch. The tears, gasps, goosebumps, and giggles are innumerable. Thank you for making our dream a reality. Stella, Teddy, JF, James, John, Jacob (Jingleheimer-schmidt) we love you. Go team Pesty. (Yeah, she's the baddie, but let us have this one)

Arthur, thank you for giving us #teamjuniejohnson and nanner. You're too cute for your own good. Never read these books, but we hope you grow up to be just like your daddy. He's pretty special.

Tyler and Ashlee, aka the A-team. You two make our productions something to talk about (seriously, check out those reviews). Thank you for making magic with us.

Wade, Betty, Luke (and Henry too, I guess) thanks for the cuddles.

Until the next round begins, love and demon kisses,

Kim and Meg (AKA KimAnne)

...psst...Kim...thanks for being my person. Here's to the next round (or 7, let's keep this train going until the wheels fall off).

...pssssst...Meg...don't make me feel my feelings.

cackles

THE MATE GAMES UNIVERSE

BY K. LORAINE & MEG ANNE

War

Obsession

Rejection

Possession

Temptation

Pestilence

Promised to the Night (Prequel Novella)

Deal with the Demon

Claimed by the Shifters

Captive of the Night

Lost to the Moon

Death

Haunting Beauty

Hunted Beast

Hateful Prince

Heartless Villain

More by Meg & Kim

Twisted Cross Ranch

A dark contemporary cowboy reverse harem

Sinner's Secret

Corruptor's Claim

Deadly Debt

Also by Meg Anne

Brotherhood of the Guardians/Novasgard Vikings

Undercover Magic *(Nord & Lina)*

A Sexy & Suspenseful Fated Mates PNR

Hint of Danger

Face of Danger

World of Danger

Promise of Danger

Call of Danger

Bound by Danger (Quinn & Finley)

The Chosen Universe

The Chosen

A Fated Mates High Fantasy Romance

Mother Of Shadows

Reign Of Ash

Crown Of Embers

Queen Of Light

The Chosen Boxset #1

The Chosen Boxset #2

The Keepers

A Guardian/Ward High Fantasy Romance

The Dreamer (A Keeper's Prequel)

The Keepers Legacy

The Keepers Retribution

The Keepers Vow

The Keepers Boxset

The Forsaken

A Rejected Mates/Enemies-To-Lovers Romantasy

Prisoner of Steel & Shadow

Queen of Whispers & Mist

Court of Death & Dreams

Prince of Sea & Stars

A Standalone MMF Romantasy Adventure

Gypsy's Curse

A Psychic/Detective Star-Crossed Lovers UF Romance

Visions Of Death

Visions Of Vengeance

Visions Of Triumph

The Gypsy's Curse: The Complete Collection

ALSO BY K. LORAINE

The Blackthorne Vampires

THE BLOOD TRILOGY

(Cashel & Olivia)

Blood Captive

Blood Traitor

Blood Heir

BLACKTHORNE BLOODLINES

(Lucas & Briar)

Midnight Prince

Midnight Hunger

THE WATCHER SERIES

Waking the Watcher

Denying the Watcher

Releasing the Watcher

THE SIREN COVEN

Eternal Desire (Shifter reluctant mates)

Cursed Heart (Hate to Lovers)

Broken Sword (MMF menage Arthurian)

~

STANDALONES

Cursed (MFM Sleeping Beauty Retelling)

~

REVERSE HAREM STANDALONES

Their Vampire Princess (A Reverse Harem Romance)

All the Queen's Men (A Fae Reverse Harem Romance)

About Meg Anne

USA Today and international bestselling paranormal and fantasy romance author Meg Anne has always had stories running on a loop in her head. They started off as daydreams about how the evil queen (aka Mom) had her slaving away doing chores, and more recently shifted into creating backgrounds about the people stuck beside her during rush hour. The stories have always been there; they were just waiting for her to tell them.

Like any true SoCal native, Meg enjoys staying inside curled up with a good book and her fur babies . . . or maybe that's just her. You can convince Meg to buy just about anything if it's covered in glitter or rhinestones, or make her laugh by sharing your favorite bad joke. She also accepts bribes in the form of baked goods and Mexican food.

Meg is best known for her leading men #MenbyMeg, her inevitable cliffhangers, and making her readers laugh out loud, all of which started with the bestselling Chosen series.

ABOUT K. LORAINE

USA Today Bestselling author Kim Loraine writes steamy contemporary and sexy paranormal romance. **You'll find her paranormal romances written under the name K. Loraine and her contemporaries as Kim Loraine.** Don't worry, you'll get the same level of swoon-worthy heroes, sassy heroines, and an eventual HEA.

When not writing, she's busy herding cats (raising kids), trying to keep her house sort of clean, and dreaming up ways for fictional couples to meet.

www.ingramcontent.com/pod-product-compliance
Lightning Source LLC
Chambersburg PA
CBHW021625030826
48979CB00037B/2300/J
* 9 7 8 1 9 5 1 7 3 8 5 6 3 *